BREAKING OUT

The Resistance Chronicles
Book 1

By

BENJAMIN CRANE

www.west16publishing.com

DEDICATION

My loyal friend, you have been by my side since you were twelve weeks, throughout our journey together and in creating this book. Merlin, furry paws, this book is for you. I wrote it while you snoozed.

I love you so very much. Such a good boy.

Ben

A NOTE FROM THE AUTHOR

I would like to thank you dear reader. You may still be browsing. Trying to figure out if you want to invest your time in this story of mine. I hope you find the story both interesting and entertaining. Dare I say engaging? It might even be funny in places. I hope you find it thought provoking.

A word of advice. I would take the time to read the introduction. I think it will aid you greatly in your understanding of the universe in which our story is occurring.

As the story progresses, it grows and gets darker. The stakes certainly get higher. Hopefully, you will find there are still areas of levity and hope besides bravery against impossible odds.

This is the first book of The Resistance Chronicles series. I hope you find something here that captures your interest.

This book is likely more appropriate for readers that are at least 16 years old. This is because of some of the more adult topics explored in this work of fiction.

Kindest Wishes

Benjamin Crane

ABOUT THE BOOK

Lauren Silva and Jack Gill were in the quiet rural farming community of Alva on Lothian world in the Rim. A beautiful morning, they had spent it together walking among the cherry blossoms. Then the gunships arrived overhead.

A whirlwind adventure had started, one that would take them to the stars and other worlds in the Rim systems. They would discover the Imperium's conspiracy.

It had started with the assassination of Lauren's old professor, Daniels. Professor Daniels and Lauren had worked together on an AI research project a decade ago.

Lauren and Jack would never have dreamed where the coming months would take them. What they would become embroiled in, or how *The Peregrine* would become part of their lives, or their life altering meeting with Merlin.

Could they break out and get away from the Imperium?

ABOUT THE AUTHOR

Benjamin is a long-term SF nerd and geek. This is the first book in his debut series, The Resistance Chronicles. In recent years, he has worked as an IT contractor for various clients.

Prior to that, he trained in Vancouver, Canada in acting for film and television then New York, USA.

Benjamin currently lives in Linlithgow in Scotland. His dog Merlin enjoys his walks around the loch by Mary, Queen of Scots palace.

Benjamin loves his dog very much.

CONTENTS

BACK MATTER

INTRODUCTION

HOW WE GOT HERE

First, dear reader, before we get started with the story, a brief history of the last eight hundred years. This will help answer many of your questions. Questions that might come up while we travel down the rapids of our tale.

This book from the chronicles looks back on the events that took place back in 2815. When the tale of Breaking Out, occurred and the key historical events leading up to that point.

The seeds of our story were sowed about eight hundred years earlier when all humanity was bound to the surface of our one planet, Earth. A planet that, if it were a patient in a hospital, was very close to being moved into the critical care ward. The environment was collapsing, falling toward the point of no return. Corporate greed seemed myopic and blind to the fact that you needed a planet that could sustain life. There is little point in having lots of money stuffed under your mattress if everyone was dead and your bed was on fire.

Global politics circled the drain, a fair amount of insanity was on display by some actors from multiple countries. Thus, Earth, and by extension all the humans that made Earth their only home, were all in the shit.

The vast distances in space between the stars and our poor technology had everyone marooned. There was no escape. There was nowhere to go that we could get to. No one was getting off this fairground ride.

Roll forward 242 years, and we were still battling with ourselves to stem and push back the effects of climate change. There had been some significant wins on this front but also losses. Nothing important really, just the global death of over one million people in the heatwaves of 2097, and both the North and South Pole being ice-free for the whole of 2183. Some people, however, remained very dumb and refused to listen. They didn't see the hazard in front of us. They just keep stuffing money under their mattress. It mattered, having your priorities in the right place. You had to love humans; some were just so-so smart.

In 242 years, along came the subluminal speed drive, or SLS drive for short. We could now reach other stars with the SLS star drive system. Not in a human lifetime, certainly. But just maybe, there could be a way out. The more sarcastic among you might point out that we could all throw a ball, and it would go at subluminal speed, which referred to the speed of light. A sleeping tortoise would have traveled at subluminal speeds, but that didn't make it a speedy tortoise. But in our context, the SLS drive referred to an engine that you wanted to strap to a spaceship you wanted to blast across the heavens to a nearby (in the loosest meaning of the word "close") star system. While fast for humans, balls thrown at one percent of the speed of light, or three thousand kilometers per second, was molasses slow in star system terms. Despite being 176 times faster than the Voyager 1 space probe.

You better have used the bathroom before you started out on that long one-way road trip. However, there was hope, maybe.

Of course, you needed a spaceship to attach an SLS drive to. The scientists, engineers, and theorists all started thinking about ships—what they needed, and how to build these big ships.

One hundred years later, we completed the shipbuilding and selected our best-guess targets. We targeted thirty-star systems within twenty light-years of Earth.

There was just one tiny problem. It would take two hundred years to get to our target destinations. As fast as an SLS drive was, it was just too slow for the human life span, with the distances involved. We couldn't have hundreds of thousands of people running around a ship for two hundred years. Where would you put them all? What would they all eat? How much toilet paper would we need? What would they do to stop themselves from going crazy? Two hundred years meant having babies and children on the ship. This ship was just getting bigger and bigger, heavier and heavier.

We found the answer. No one would travel on the ship, problem solved. It was called UPD—Upload, Print, Download. Humans couldn't resist a three-letter acronym, Resistance Is Fanciful (RIF).

Our human, let's call him Fred, wanted to be an off-world colonist, but we couldn't transport him there. What we could do was take a very detailed scan of Fred and his brain, then we uploaded his scans into the ship's computer storage system. As we neared our target star system, we fed our big fancy printer with buckets of goo as raw materials to print out Fred's body and brain and let him mature in human toner.

We now had a Fred-shaped box, but no Fred yet. Next, we had to download Fred's soul from storage into his brain and had to start the body up with some wonderful drugs and electricity. Sort of like a

Frankenfred. The original Fred would sit at home on Earth with his feet up and slippers on while the spaceship blasted away on its long journey. At some point Fred died and we disposed of his body—burial, cremation, mushrooms, whatever it was.

About one hundred and fifty years after Fred's death, the ship neared the colony target world and we hit the print button. We delivered the shiny new Frankenfred to the new planet the spaceship was now orbiting. Fred was alive and kicking. You made it, Fred; you survived your own death!

Many people disliked this idea. It prompted many questions and concerns among wannabe colonists that itched to get off Earth. Here are a few of them:

- But I want to leave. You're saying I will stay here?
- Will I be a virgin again?
- I will have no soul?
- How can this be true to God?
- I would just be a photocopy?
- What about me? I'll have died. How does that help me?

Some didn't mind the idea on religious or selfish grounds, and they only ever had two questions:

- How much will it cost me?
- Where do I sign up?

We had our destinations and a ship to carry us. A way to get there, and some volunteers eager to be scanned. There was a way. It didn't matter if it took two hundred years or two thousand years, "people" would sit on a computer disk for the duration of the trip.

Roll forward another two hundred years, and the colony ships arrived at their destination star systems and found their new planets. The printers were warming up, and we ran off a copy of each colonist. Founding a new colony and bootstrapping an alien biosphere from scratch was difficult. It took a lot of effort. The first generation of colonists had a hard, grim life. Frankenfred might have wished he was dead and had just stayed on Earth. There was no time to be idle. There was much work to be done. Lots of pressure to make babies. In fact, sex had become like homework. They had a colony to build, and it needed babies.

We left new landing, in the Earth year 2565, behind us and rolled further forward still. We were now with fourth or fifth generation colonists another two hundred and fifty years forward. It is now the year 2815. We had twenty-two well-established colonies. However, eight of the target worlds were duds:

- During the journey, one ship got destroyed.
- Another printed no colonists because of a goo jam in the printer control system.
- A third ship's trip went well. They shipped the new colonists down to the planet. Where they got eaten by a large lizard-like dinosaur that was thrilled to get lots of extra protein.
- A fourth ship suffered from brake failure, while its treacherous guidance system kept it firmly aimed at its target planet. The two came together at three thousand kilometers per second. This was a Chicxulub-type of day for the poor target planet.
- A fifth ship got lost and went to the wrong star system.
- The sixth ship found no planet at the expected location, just a disturbingly large asteroid belt.
- Yellow spotted frogs ate the colonists who died from a flesh-eating disease on the planet that ship seven reached.
- Ship eight made first contact with space-faring aliens, who promptly blasted the ship out of their sky.

In the meantime, Earth had ceased to exist. A combination of nuclear war, resource wars, and a collapsed environment. The environment that we had been trying and failing to save for the last three hundred and fifty years. This failure had given birth to a rising general sense of hopelessness and pointlessness. The mattress stuffers showed a mix of anger and arrogance. They wanted to be born again as a colonist! There was anger at not being on a colony ship, and religious incandescence at all this ungodly UPD technology.

Some believed this happened about one hundred years after the ships had launched. All those born since the launch discovered they were born into a dying world. Half of them were very cross and the other half very upset. No one was happy. The missiles flew on or around 2465. No one was sure as there was no one left to write it down, tell the story, or read it. The first colonists would not get printed for another one hundred years. Technically, for one hundred years no humans existed anywhere. Humans were extinct. A further two hundred and fifty years have passed since. We have lost the details of Earth's death to the vagaries of history. Earth has long since gone, now a polluted radioactive cinder with no biosphere. What used to be a rich, beautiful, alive planet, teeming with all sorts of life, was now just a barren, lifeless, toxic rock.

The colonies, twenty-two of them, were all founded at different points in time depending on their distance from old Earth.

The colony planets all had differing orbital periods. The orbit was what makes the most sense to define your local year by. No one referred to a faraway dead and poisoned world. Everyone changed to their own definition of what a year was.

The distance between them isolated the colonies from one another. They had used the colony ships for parts to help set up the new colonies themselves, and no one was in a rush to build another ship anytime soon. There was a whole perfect, empty new planet to grow into.

Because of their isolation from one another, they quickly became twenty-two distinct societies and governments. All with their own rules.

Traditional communications travelled at the speed of light, which was very slow. Each colony could be up to twenty light-years from the now dead point of origin, all in different directions. So it could take up to forty years for a message such as *hello* to travel across the sphere of space in one direction, and another forty years for the reply. It would be an awkward first-date conversation. Not to mention the technical challenge of being able to broadcast a message with enough power to be heard forty light-years away. Each colony was on its own. They knew where all the colonies were, but they could not signal to them, let alone travel there.

Some clever scientists on the first colony invented the Faster Than Luminal (FTL) star drive. Some argued it should be called the FAF drive. These people went strangely, awkwardly silent when asked to explain the abbreviation's meaning beyond the first letter for Fast!

The early 1.0 versions of the FTL were slow compared with the 3.0 versions. Trips were now possible between systems, albeit with an enormous time commitment. It was now possible to travel from edge-to-edge in three years—a substantial improvement over the four hundred years it would have taken an SLS-driven ship.

Three years was not especially useful. You needed to be determined to want to go there, let alone there and back.

After an exploration period and sharing of science, things then took a darker turn. The FTL-powered Imperium started reaching out with their version of faith, law, and order from their colony star system, New Terra, to the other colonies.

That was the third generation of colonists, one hundred years ago.

The drives became even faster with FTL version 2.0, and the journey time dropped to six months to move between the two furthest systems. They had also figured out how to remove the relativistic effects, so six months on the ship was also six months for the people, both at source and destination. You will need a drive physicist to explain things like the Casimir effect warping space–time bubbles and why relativity did not apply anymore when going faster than light with a ship arguably not moving inside its bubble. This is way above my comprehension level in physics.

The Imperium's tendrils spread out and before you knew it, fourteen of the Core systems were under authoritarian rule again. Only the eight Rim systems further out were not under their control.

The colonies were not a happy place. Yay, go humans! Knocking it out of the park again and straight back into the crapper.

It did, at least, seem we had learned something. The colonies, independent of one another, were all very protective of their new planet, its biosphere and the environment. Pollution was close to zero. No one wanted to go searching for other worlds. While the Imperium was still doing stupid things with fusion bombs, the day-to-day folk treated their colonies well.

The worlds were all different. Two hundred and fifty years had passed since the first generation of printed humans had been downloaded. With the later births, the population of humans was now knocking around 0.3 billion on each colony. A tiny amount compared with the eight billion human rats on ancient Earth early in the twenty first century when we really started to focus on the importance of climate change or the twenty-four billion in 2465, when the original, enlightened human leaders nuked humanity out of the universe.

Now, Earth was long dead and gone. Humanity lived on twenty-two far-flung star systems. Typical solar-type systems with multiple planets that were, to greater or lesser extents, habitable and settled. The Imperium was a pain in everyone's butt. Just like that big kid at school who used to bully all the other kids. The Imperium had given rise to resistance in the Rim systems. The resistance had had enough of being stomped on. The Imperium ignored the resistance and focused on the fourteen Core systems they controlled. They had enough to keep them busy for now. The Imperium would get to the resistance in their own good time when ready. There was nowhere to go and no way to get there. There was plenty of time. Then along came FTL version 3.0 and now the edge-to-edge time was down to two months and the political pot got all stirred up again.

That brings you up to date, dear reader. Now for one last thing that will help our story make more sense to you. All our chapter scenes begin with a headline description of where they are taking place. They take the form:

CHAPTER NUMBER
RIM OR CORE – STAR SYSTEM – PLANET
CITY, TOWN or VILLAGE
LOCATION
TIME
SHORT DESCRIPTOR

Because names were chosen haphazardly when ground was being broken on the new colony town settlements, to uniquely identify a location you need to prefix it with the name of the star system and the name of the planet, then add the name of the town or city, for example:

RIM – ROSS 154 – CLACKMANNANSHIRE
ALVA

Last, you may wonder why these planets all have Scottish names. This is because after the year 2288, the Target System Discovery Project was set up (they showed their imagination again by nicknaming it the TSDP). The two scientists who led the team to find colonization target systems and any orbiting planets were of Scottish ancestry. As they discovered the planets, they got to name them.

While breaking with astronomical convention, they decided to make Scotland live forever through the planet names they chose. Sometimes it's the little things that count. There was a rumor, but nobody could prove it, that the two scientists had a good laugh and chuckle. It caused lots of frothing, huffing, and puffing south of the border, among their former pre-independence, political overlords. For everything else, there is a credit card, but sometimes you need Scottish scientists to say it simply with love. Alba gu bràth.

Many colonists adopted this habit when naming their towns and cities as well, but not all the first-generation colonists. Typically, when they broke ground on a new town's construction, the colonists gave the towns Scottish names. The names were only found in computer records and the only people now alive had come out of a computer printer on a spaceship. The stars had long since had astronomical names, which they retained.

There is no association with old Earth. The missiles that flew in 2465 killed all remaining life on Earth. That was a long time ago. It is now 2815 and these alien worlds have little in common with early twenty-first century Earth, up to twenty light-years away from the old Earth, orbiting around alien stars. People, history, culture, terminology, and technology; it is all different now.

In this story about far-flung human colonies light-years away. In Earth's distant future. The lawyers insisted and made me put this bit in: "Any similarities to any persons living or dead, or their views, actual events, technology or places on Earth are coincidental." That's the end of the boring lawyer's text. I could push the envelope a bit, with scurrilous rumors about drunken parties that included a small flock of sheep and some leaders and other senior politicians from Earth somewhere in the 2010s and 2020s, bah, you know who you are and so did the video camera at Madam Mou Mouton's. That will have cost me a tax audit, I guess.

Let's not get distracted. I think we are best just cracking on with our story.

You might want to look over these five sections from the contents page towards the end of this book before starting the first act, they provide useful world context:

- Imperium Core Systems
- Rim Systems
- Before Colony Worlds Founding Timeline

- After the Colony Worlds' Founding Timeline
- A Timeline of K-Bots

Our story started in the small, rural farming village of Alva. On the minor planet Clackmannanshire, orbiting the star system Ross 154 in the Rim systems. It was the old Earth year of 2815.

ACT I

CHAPTER 1

RIM – ROSS 154 – CLACKMANNANSHIRE
ALVA
THE BLOSSOM GROVE
AFTERNOON
CHERRY BLOSSOM

We were in the rural village of Alva. To the west, various farms dotted the countryside, both arable and dairy. East of Alva was the local Spooky Forest, as the villagers called it, and beyond the next closest village was Fishcross. A mud track cut through the forest to the south. The track looped around the hills, meandering east to Fishcross, then continuing onward to the real civilization beyond the horizon to the east.

Our story started in the hog shed. There were twelve fat baby porkers and one smaller runt striving to access one of mum's twelve teats. Mum just lay there, oblivious. Hog dad looked on with little interest. Either the little one would shape up or he wouldn't. If not, there would be pork for dad's dinner. Either way, the other twelve were healthy and growing well. Away from the life and death drama playing out in the hog shed, Lauren and Jack strolled through the grove of blossoming trees.

Jack Gill was a tall and muscled Black man of thirty-five, who was born in Alva with the help of the local midwife. His nickname was Speedy Jack, both at the desert racetrack and to his local customers whose tractors he would fix. Anything with an engine, Jack could fix with his spanners. He was statuesque, but his natural camouflage of engine oil and grease kept him away from photoshoots and modeling. That suited Jack just fine.

Lauren Silva went by the ironic nickname of Lauren the Dim. A petite Latino of thirty-three years and a huge computer nerd perhaps smarter than Einstein. Lauren was not an Alva native; she came into the world in a Buenos Aires hospital. Lauren had contemplated God sometimes, but always came down in the atheist camp. Whereas Jack felt that being a racing driver was dangerous by nature, and he would be foolish to turn down any extra help aiding his side of the scales. He was an agnostic to cover his bets.

They were not lovers, just fast friends for life. Jack worried about

Lauren and wanted to protect her as best he could. Ever since the earthquake that had resulted in the death of her parents and siblings, the day that turned Lauren into an orphan.

Many others had died as well in Buenos Aires all those years ago when Lauren was just twenty-five. Jack had spent two years trying to persuade Lauren to move to Alva so she would be away from the many dangers of big city life on planet Clackmannanshire. Her city apartment being burgled had been the proverbial straw, and Jack had won the argument.

He had gone to help his friend pack up her life and move to Alva. They had met in their early twenties at Buenos Aires University. He was two years ahead of Lauren, studying mechanical engineering. While he was older, she was much wiser and nearly fifty IQ points smarter. They had almost instantly become great friends. Lauren would babble on to Jack about her computer science classes and her ideas, which always went a long way over his head. Jack dreamed of desert racing and getting a pro drive some day with one of the bigger teams.

There had been a very drunken foursome the night they spent with their partners in the act—a bottle of tequila and a bottle of dry white wine. It was just the one night; neither of them regretted it but neither of them wanted to repeat it either. It wasn't because the experience had been bad. Rather, it had been a hazy blur for both, but a fun blur. One that made them realize that their friendship was way more important than any romantic or physical coupling.

Ironically, the act of coupling had brought them way closer together. More than many of their peers' damaged and dysfunctional relationships. Many would mistake them for being together, but neither Jack nor Lauren could see why they were asked this. Jack and Lauren were firm friends. Yes, he was her knight in shining armor, but not the sweeping-you-off-your-feet kind of knight. More the sort of knight that would smash his lance over the miscreant's head and beat them with the broken stump. Jack was that kind of knight, fiercely loyal and protective of the maiden Lauren. Lauren's heart was for her computers, while carburetors and exhaust pipes could get Jack hot and bothered. Which he wanted to mate with his race car engine.

The small village of Alva was beautiful, quiet, remote. Some may have called it a little dull. Unless you were part of the hog shed drama where the stakes could not be any higher for hoglet number thirteen who just wanted to get some milk. There were clouds on the horizon, but it was still a fine day. Yes, the blossoms were past their best and going brown at the edges, but it was still beautiful. More so than the city jungle, full of so many more predators than the nearby forest.

At this point, Lauren cocked her head to one side like Jack's old childhood dog at the words *chew stick?* Lauren's face strained.

This new image mixed with fond memories of his old dog reacting to those words made him chuckle inside.

"What is that, Jack?"

Jack was about to reply when he caught the sound as well. It was at the edge of his hearing but growing. *Yes, there is an engine, an aero engine, a turbine* Jack thought. He looked up through the branches, and yes! High above him, he could see the contrails of two aircraft. Getting closer and lower as the sound grew louder. The ancient animal instinct in Jack's reptile brain was firing full tilt now. Jack was on alert, ready to protect Lauren as he polished his mental lance, but what was the threat?

Was it the planes? Were they going to crash? Two planes—that seemed beyond improbable. No, it couldn't be a plane crash, but his brain kept dragging his focus back to the planes above. Again, closer still, as if they were heading straight for the tiny village of Alva. *They were small planes. Small and quick, like a racing car* Jack thought.

"Shit! Lauren, get down now, down behind the tree trunk."

Jack hoped he was wrong; he was wrong about many things, and he hoped this would just be added to that long list. They could laugh about it later and joke about silly Jack always being on guard. But Jack's ancient fight-or-flight brain knew he was right. The threat was genuine and approaching.

Please don't be right. Why would they be fighter jets? It made no sense. At this point, the whirring whizz of the first fighter jet's rotary cannon reached them, signaling death's arrival in Alva. The two Imperium fighters alternated, firing in short bursts. They flared high, banked, turned, and then passed over the village. Coming back for another pass—back, and back, and back. It seemed to last forever as time stood still for Jack and Lauren. They looked on in horror from their safe vantage point among the red and white blossoms falling from the trees. As the noise continued overhead, the assault raged against their homes, family, and friends. The noise shook the blossoms free from the trees. Like falling snow, the blossoms carpeted the ground of the safe grove.

Hoglet thirteen was no more. He had died hungry, but so had his twelve fatter siblings, and his indifferent mother and father who had been contemplating who to eat later that day. If only hoglet thirteen had known his other potential fate that day in his father's jaws. He would have chosen this violent end as a burst of twenty-millimeter high-density cannon rounds tore through the hog shed. Like a sword blow from a great ancient god, everything turned into smaller flying chunks and mist made of wood and hog blood. The hot rounds also set fire to the shed's straw. Nothing remained of the hog shed or its hogs but a smashed ruin.

From above, the sword kept lashing out. Each tearing sound from the sky snuffed another village building out, along with the lives of its inhabitants. As Jack and Lauren stared on in cold horror, Jack saw the front door of his house open and his brother and father rush out. His mother was pushed between them, an arm from each man under one of her arms, lifting her by the armpits. They ran with her, her feet in midair, fleeing from the house they didn't want to become their tomb. The trio set out across the fields, running for the tree line.

They weren't running toward Jack and Lauren hidden among the grove's blossoms. Jack's parents and brother did not know where Jack and Lauren were, other than that they had gone off on a hike somewhere. No one knew where Jack and Lauren were. His parents and brother were just fleeing for the safety and cover of the trees, driven by terror.

As Jack watched, that whizzing, tearing sound cut through the air again as death lashed down from the sky. Then the trio were not there anymore. There were no falling corpses. Just a concentrated cloud of pink mist blending with a brown cloud of dirt.

"Ugh." It was as if someone had punched Jack in the gut.

This was not Jack's first encounter with the face of death. His grandparents, of course, had died when he was somewhere around seven. His friend and teammate had died a few years back in a flaming crash on race day. That had been brutal, but at least there had been a body, albeit one covered in burning fuel, as he stumbled from the wrecked car before collapsing two steps away.

This had been worse, just a pink cloud slowly descending over the crops in the field.

Of course, there was Andrew, Lauren's ex. Who had cheated on her for months, both before and after getting Lauren pregnant. Andrew dumped her when he found out he was to be a father, and he went back to his ladylove.

Andrew had moved to Alva when Lauren was twenty-nine, but they would not meet for another year. He worked as an agricultural technician on the various bits of farm machinery. Not that he had drifted into Alva exactly. When he arrived, he had a job to go to. It was more that Andrew became sort of washed up in Alva.

He had lived and worked in Fishcross on the Robertson farm. The heart attack that struck down Bill Robertson, the farm's principal, changed everything. It had left Bill's wife Edna behind with little interest in the hard life running the farm single-handedly. Over the next six months, Edna agreed to sell some fields and buildings to the neighboring Campbell farm. Andrew could not stand the Campbells. Each Campbell happily reciprocated the feeling. When Edna sat Andrew down a few weeks later and explained, there just wasn't the volume of work to justify keeping Andrew on full time. Maybe he should work part-time for Edna and do work for the Campbells on their adjoining farm. Well, that idea was a nonstarter, and so Andrew looked for more work and somewhere to live. He found a farm in Alva that was looking for a part-time technician. Andrew figured he could live somewhere on the farm and find odd jobs at other local farms to fill out his working week. He moved to the smaller village of Alva. He did not extensively review his options or the choices before him. He just washed up in the closest town to Fishcross. This was typical of Andrew. Yeah, he had charm and was rugged. This allowed him to coast through life, and as he could always turn a girl's head with his banter, it was all fine with him.

Andrew had met Jack one day on the farm he was odd-jobbing on the same day Jack was fixing a tractor that had blown a head gasket. Looking back, Jack regretted that day. The loose friendship that was struck up had led to drinks in the bar. A few bar visits later, it led to Andrew meeting Lauren. *I guess being rugged helps. That and his nonsensical banter* Jack thought. Well, Lauren had seen something that struck up her interest. Maybe it was just a desire for physical contact. It was not like Alva was swimming in options.

Like Lauren, Andrew was an immigrant. This was not where his family was from. Andrew had moved from the city to Fishcross. He fell out with his father and moved away. Andrew's father beat him. A bottle of whiskey drunk, then the blows would come. After the sixth time, Andrew had had enough. He moved out. His father had not been an evil man before his mother had left. Local gangs had groomed his mum to develop an addiction to painkillers. The drugs dug in their claws, and before anyone noticed, the addiction took control. Andrew suggested withholding funds so she couldn't buy any more. His father went along with the idea and in less than forty-eight hours, the addiction drove his mum to turning tricks to feed the monster's cravings. In less than a week, local pimps spotted the new talent on their patch and got her addicted to opioids, whoring herself in a bedsit squat. It was nothing but downhill from that point on. It wasn't so much that his mum had left, more that she had just faded away and never come back from the drugs.

Andrew's father was very clear on who he thought was to blame, his idiot son with his idiot idea of withholding money from the lady that used to be his wife. That had been the moment she spiraled beyond control. That was the day the beatings and drinking started. It set in play the train of events that brought Andrew to Alva and Lauren's bed and fatherhood itself. Andrew had run and dumped Lauren. Besides, the brunette he had met three months earlier was younger, tighter, and pure filth. It had been a straightforward choice for Andrew to abandon pregnant Lauren after their two-year relationship.

Jack had explained to Andrew in very clear terms that it would be in his own interest not to live in Alva anymore. That he would be a lot happier moving back to the city.

Andrew left that evening, just over a year ago now. He never made it to the city; once he had skulked out of Alva, Jack set out after him, catching up with him a few kilometers out of the village. The inevitable argument that raged was one-sided and short. Jack had moved the body away from the path and buried it, using his hands to dig into the dirt deep among the trees.

Jack could rest easy, knowing that Andrew would not be coming back to shatter Lauren's life again. Her abortion was a week later. She was still within the first ten weeks, so it had been a straightforward procedure, just a pill … but psychologically devastating. It had left Lauren changed; she was worried at thirty-two and now alone; no family, no loyal boyfriend, no boyfriend at all. Having a child might not be a good choice, and she couldn't shake that it was Andrew's child. Andrew, who had pawed at her and broken her heart, cheated on her, and dumped her. She wanted no part of Andrew inside her growing. Yet she worried she was punishing this young life yet to be. This collection of a few cells. Her decision would prevent the child's potential from being realized.

While it had not been a rape, Lauren now understood some part of the mental anguish of women and girls who fell pregnant against their wishes at some vile man's forced hand and penis.

Jack had buried Andrew's broken body in the woods and never

mentioned Andrew ever again. Lauren put herself back together in the weeks and months that followed.

It was five months since Lauren had returned to her more normal day-to-day, one that tears and sobs did not punctuate. Lauren had hardened. She had become more cynical; she giggled a lot more now. *That is better than tears* Jack thought. Although he worried that cynical giggles against the universe and fate were not altogether healthy either.

The scars were still there, not in her abdomen, but in her heart and mind. She would always be a bit more broken, changed because of Andrew. Jack never regretted the decomposing body buried in the forest. The pain Andrew had caused Lauren was unforgivable, and far worse in Jack's view than any sin a judge might find him guilty of.

The guns overhead and the village were now silent. The buildings were gone, and there was no movement or sound. Everyone had been reduced to a thin mist.

CHAPTER 2

RIM – ROSS 154 – CLACKMANNANSHIRE
NEAR ALVA
THE SPOOKY FOREST
NIGHT
ORPHANS

Jack pulled himself together, took Lauren by the hand, and led her away. He needed to keep her safe. They needed to hide, to figure things out, to find food. He estimated they could make Fishcross by tomorrow evening. There was nothing left here to stay for. They were both orphans now. They only had each other.

They headed toward the forest, leaving the relative safety of the grove of blossom trees that had shielded them from the cannon rounds. The children of Alva had always called the local forest between Alva and Fishcross the Spooky Forest when he was growing up. Although Jack knew there were no genuine threats in there.

Nothing in the forest predated on humans, apart from Jack, of course.

They finally collapsed to sleep hours later against a tree trunk, arm in arm for warmth and comfort. The ghosts of Jack's and Lauren's lives in Alva stalked their dreams. That tearing sound from above chased them. The sword of death and destruction that had cruelly carved up their village and its small number of inhabitants before their eyes earlier that day.

They woke the next morning and cried a little, but Jack got them both back on track, and the hike to Fishcross resumed.

CHAPTER 3

RIM – ROSS 154 – CLACKMANNANSHIRE
FISHCROSS
THE MERCHANT'S SHOP
DUSK
TRUST ME

It was dusk by the time they arrived at Fishcross. Another small village, bigger than Alva, but still nothing more than a small village with a single merchant. Both Lauren and Jack were exhausted. Neither had eaten in nearly two days and they had been very thirsty until they reached the small river that flowed past Fishcross. Jack and Lauren approached the merchant's shop, walking hand in hand, disheveled with patches of mud on their rumpled clothing, from when they had lost their footing during the hike.

Outside the shop stood Mike, the owner and sole staff member, referred to by the other villagers behind his back as "the twat." Mike was busy packing up, head down. He didn't hear Lauren and Jack's approach as they gravitated toward the remains of the baskets of fruit outside the shop.

Mike heard them approach and whirled around as they arrived at the baskets.

He cursed to himself. It wasn't audible, but it clearly had four letters.

"Away with you both, no vagrants or thieves, and especially no resilience or reliance or whatever you rebel-dependent scummers are calling yourselves. As if the leaders of the Highlands aren't bad enough, we've got you nutcase work-shy cretins. Get a job, go on, fuck off. Get away from my shop, git."

Mike the twat didn't have a surname that anyone in Fishcross had cared to learn. He was white, fat, short, and forty-six. He was not an ugly man, but his sunny disposition would soon tilt any observer away from average to homely. Mike was a small-town man with a small mind. He was a Fishcross lifer and proud. Mike was not well liked. His shop's prices were profitably high and people in the village were hungry. As far as Mike was concerned, Christian charity started somewhere else, most definitely not in his shop.

The combination of hunger and exhaustion from the long walk had robbed Jack of any retort. Lauren slid her hand stealthily into the fruit basket behind Jack. Jack's body shielded her larceny from Mike's view while the two men glared at each other. She pocketed three handfuls of fruit into her dress. She dared not take any more for fear of the oranges now hidden in her pockets becoming obvious.

Before any further escalation, Lauren took Jack's hand again and turned to him.

"Jack, let's go. It's not worth it. We can sleep in the forest again tonight." Lauren pulled at Jack's arm. "Come on, let's go, trust me."

Jack relented and turned away from Mike, who was still glaring at him. Lauren and Jack walked out of Fishcross and headed for the forest. They could see other grim-faced thin villagers walking toward Mike's shop of love and hospitality.

"Jack, don't make any signs." Lauren smiled thinly at Jack then transferred half of the fruits from her pocket into his jacket pocket.

"That's my girl, excellent. Did you notice the vehicle parked behind his hut? Let's liberate it."

"Sounds good to me," Lauren whispered back as they reached the edge of the forest. "But we both need to get some sleep first, especially if you are going to be driving."

After an evening meal of oranges and plums, they both quickly fell asleep in each other's embrace once again, in the safety of a nook in a tree.

CHAPTER 4

RIM – ROSS 154 – CLACKMANNANSHIRE
FISHCROSS
BEHIND THE MERCHANT'S SHOP
EARLY HOURS
Y-FRONTS

Jack had set a vibration alarm on his watch for three o'clock in the morning before they both drifted off to sleep. There would be no bad dreams tonight. They were too tired to dream. At three in the morning, the vibrating watch brought him around. It felt as if only an instant had passed.

Although it seemed like they hadn't slept, Jack's brain did a mental inventory of himself and his body to check in as his brain spooled up to waking speed. He felt significantly refreshed, and he quietly roused Lauren. Jack also noted he still felt grumpy about how the merchant had treated them earlier. This gave him comfort. It helped in justifying the grand theft they were about to commit by stealing Mike's truck.

Jack reflected that the shit truck was still worth over 950 credits and so clearly fell under the old Earth California Statute Penal Code 487(d)(1), so he would be charged with a felony and get a good three years in jail. It would be a case of grand theft auto, commonly known as GTA. Neither Lauren nor Jack envisioned this being a temporary arrangement in which they would ever return the vehicle. Rather more likely, it would spend its last days at the bottom of a quarry lake or roasting under several liters of fuel in a deserted spot. With that in mind, it was clearly not going to be charged as the lesser misdemeanor of joyriding under Vehicle Code 10851 VC with a year in jail. Jack conceded to himself that eight-hundred-year-old Earth laws really didn't mean shit anymore. Because today on Clackmannanshire, the punishment for stealing a merchant's truck from outside their shop while the merchant slumbered inside was getting shot, most likely in the head. The law allowed for the merchant to administer the penalty without recourse. Justice could also be delivered by any officer of the law, or any other citizen of Fishcross, or any citizen of anywhere who knew about the theft. Because today stealing someone's wheels was as bad as horse theft had been in the Old West on old Earth.

It's just that no one bothered to look around for a length of rope anymore. Now people simply went for a pistol first. That's progress for you. No need to carry around lots of rope.

Jack and Lauren sneaked back into the slumbering small village. They made their way behind the merchant's shop and approached his vehicle. The open-top truck had no doors, so Jack ducked down under the steering wheel, easily disabled the steering lock, and released the hand brake. Lauren took her position at the passenger side A-pillar, ready to push.

"Okay, go," Jack whispered.

Jack pushed and steered while Lauren pushed on her side, moving the heavy vehicle away from the hut.

Lauren panted. "That is far enough. Let's get gone."

They both quietly climbed into the truck. Jack fiddled under the steering wheel again, expertly hot-wired the truck, and pushed the button to start the engine on minimum power.

"See, I was right. You can be subtle," Lauren whispered, barely above the engine noise. She gave a quiet nervous giggle. This was not the time to get caught sitting in someone else's truck with the engine hot-wired and running.

"Okay, yes I can. It's just so boring." The devil on his shoulder was bouncing up and down and poking him in the ear with its trident.

Jack grinned, flicked a couple of switches, and held down the horn. The headlight's dipped main beam, fog lights, and LED light strip along the outside roof line all came on with a fearsome luminosity.

Jack paused, holding down the horn as he peered through the windscreen. "I think I can see the bugs on that tree way over there."

Through the front window of the merchant's store, now illuminated by the bright lights as if in the noonday sun, Mike sat bolt upright in bed.

Meanwhile, outside, Jack banged on the horn another three times. He stood in the seat of the open-top truck and picked up the handset for the external speakers mounted on either side of the LED bar.

Meters away, Mike scrabbled out of bed and appeared at his front door in his Y-fronts and vest.

The intense light revealed sweat stains and other mystery stains that Lauren was doing her best to ignore. A truly grotesque Adonis stood before her.

Jack keyed the button on the handset, his voice bursting forth from the speakers at full volume.

"Imperium patrol. Kneel in front of your shack with your arms behind your head."

A new stain was born in Mike's pants. The urine ran down his legs and puddled at his feet. Mike was like a bunny in the headlights, unmoving—except for the steady flow of urine and growing puddle. His mouth hung open, speechless.

Jack keyed the button again. "Do it, now!" Jack screamed into the handset.

Mike jolted into action and kneeled in the still growing inland sea of urine. His hands now dripped with piss from where he had supported himself when dropping to his knees.

There were sniggers and laughs from the dark forms outside the other shacks behind the blinding glare of the truck's optical barrage.

Jack keyed the button for the last time. "Now fuck off!"

He dropped into the vehicle's driving seat and pushed the power levers to the stops.

Howls of laughter came from spectators over the engine noise. Jack floored the accelerator, dropped the engine into gear, and did a doughnut in front of the shop as the rear-wheel-drive truck spun its wheels. The truck pulled a tight 540-degree loop; the headlights swept over the crowd and people laughed and pointed at Mike doubled over. Jack eased up on the accelerator and the rear wheels stopped spinning. The tires bit into the dirt, gaining traction. The truck flew forward into the darkness and over the plains toward the distant lights from the larger town near the horizon below them to the east.

CHAPTER 5

RIM – ROSS 154 – CLACKMANNANSHIRE
THE PLAINS
PLAINS CROSSING
EARLY HOURS
UNSUBTLE

Jack and Lauren sat in silence while he deftly guided the truck at speed over the plains. It was a contemplative silence as Lauren and Jack both considered what Lauren was going to say.

After a couple of minutes, with Fishcross now distant and out of sight behind them, Lauren turned to look at Jack without speaking. Jack took the hint, slowed the truck, and parked up.

"Unsubtle behavior like that is what makes him tell strangers to fuck off. You idiot, Jack."

Jack and Lauren both looked at each other for a moment. Then they both broke out in riotous laughter. After a minute, the laughter gave way to tears. They both bawled in floods of tears. The tension of the last few days was easing away. Grief and mourning were still to come, they both knew that. Their bodies also knew they were both still alive, and it felt like there was a future again. Not just the terrible sound of that rotary cannon fire over their village.

Lauren dabbed the tears from her eyes. "We both needed that, Jack. Time to go. If we hurry, we'll get to Tillicoultry before closing time."

CHAPTER 6

RIM – ROSS 154 – CLACKMANNANSHIRE
TILLICOULTRY
THE UNIVERSE'S WORST BEDSIT
DAY
NOWHERESVILLE

It would be unfair on inner-city slums to compare them to the run-down flop house they had found. This was a whole other level of shithole.

"We have to pay for this shithole?" Jack quipped.

"Jack, it's fine."

"There are toilets people never shit in, because the shit refuses to come out, that are nicer than this place."

"Hands and feet braced, people push and strain, no I'm not coming out, not into that shithole."

Lauren chuckled. "Jack, you are so funny."

Jack surveyed the room and reflected on things that were shit. Even rats knew better. Rats don't live here. It's not too good for cockroaches, mind.

Jack reflected on the roughest pub he once made the mistake of visiting while at Buenos Aires University. Two pints and a trip to the toilet was the entirety of his time in that pub.

Now to be fair, that was a shitter shitter! The poop had come out there all right. As if it had exploded everywhere. The pan resembled a cattle slurry pit, and there was about three centimeters of liquid poop all over the floor.

Jack shuddered. Poop was not one of his favorite things. All things considered, the shitter in this shithole, which was mercifully shit-free, was a place of contrast. He still didn't want to take a swim through the toilet glass, mind. How come he was so phobic about poop?

Jack knew where it had started. It had started with his failure with Sally. That thin blond strumpet he had met in freshman week. God, she had been hot. She was a pretty thing to be fair, with her stocking tops just reaching her short miniskirt from below. Plus, her propensity to flash her knicker crotch while sitting in a chair was partly why she had earned her nickname, Marge. Jack had needed to ask because when he first heard this, he didn't get the meaning. One of the other freshmen had explained it was because, unlike butter, margarine spreads easily. Indeed, if the gossip circulating that first week was true. Which was quite an achievement to be fair, as it was the first week of the first term of the first year. There were over seven people claiming authority on the subject. Anyway, Jack was firm in spirit when he caught Marge's attention. Boy, had he been in for a shock! What a man-eating vamp she had been, or so he had thought back then. She might have been no older in years, but she had been in experience. She knew what she wanted and wouldn't hesitate to tell you what she wanted you to do. Her large doe-like eyes looked up at him as they lay there, recovering after round one and round two, a sweat sheen on both their bodies.

She smiled at him. "If you're ready to go again, I want you to pop it up my bum this time."

Jack stopped dead. He remembered feeling his erection fade as the blood ran away. Jack had never known a girl, let alone one so bold. To ask straight out like that, or even to have those sorts of ideas. University city life was nothing like it had been back in rural Alva.

Jack remembered being torn and debating in the moment. "You want me to do what? To stick my wanger up there. That will hurt you. I know how much it hurts me when I am straining to push out a big one. I will get poop on my wang."

There it was, right there, that feeling of being out of his depth with a second-class stamp on his small envelope of experience. Lying next to a hungry velociraptor licking her lips while staring at her next meal. And he had no control as events took on a life of their own and raged like a tempest around him.

The total disempowerment and his now flaccid, useless, shrunken cock flopped against his leg. I will get poop on my wang; it will hurt you. Jack had connected it with the embarrassment and self-shame he felt at that moment. Sally looked on, disappointed at his now limp, useless noodle.

It was shit. That feeling of abject failure and embarrassment he had felt. That had been it. There would be no further rounds that night, or rematch bouts with sweet pretty Sally and her endless legs on any other night. As Sally got dressed and left, he knew he had hurt her. He had blown it. His inexperience and reaction had made her feel embarrassed and judged.

"I'm sorry, Sally. I'm an idiot. It is me."

It was too late. The door to his student bedroom had swung closed, and with it all chances with Sally as well. That is how Jack came to be phobic about shit.

"It's not funny. Compared to this place and many others, she would be an upgrade."

Lauren looked confused, just like Sally had.

"Sorry, it would be an upgrade, is what I meant." His bite was gone now.

"It's okay," Lauren said in a soft voice. "It's only for a couple of days. The freighter captain will take us to Lothian."

"Lothian world, it's in the same system. What's the point? What's the big deal?" Jack said with a huff.

"The big deal, Jack, is not having to be where all the people from our village got turned to chunks in front of me."

"Lauren, please," Jack said, then whispered. "What did Alva ever do to people? We just kept to ourselves."

Lauren went quiet for a moment.

"Someone was the target. You don't pop down to Mercenaries-R-Us to blow up nowheresville and the hog sheds."

"You might, if you had ever met those hogs. They were mean. I wouldn't want to go face-to-face with them at ground level. I know which tusked hog my money would be on."

Lauren discarded the comment. "Please try to stay focused. I do not know who the target was. But the word overkill does come to mind."

Jack nodded. "Lothian it is. I don't want to stay here anyway. A fresh start might be best."

Jack fell silent, thinking of the dead.

All business now, Lauren continued. "I will see the captain again tonight. I will confirm with him and pay the upfront half of the smuggling fees."

"Payment up front makes me nervous, Lauren."

"It's like your summer holidays. You don't pay after you get back home."

Jack stared back at her, unconvinced. "Yeah, okay, I guess."

Lauren tried to assure Jack. "We're not going first-class, we are going cattle freight, under the radar."

"I get it. You make me sound like such a diva." Jack said with a smile.

"Well, maybe you could stop acting like one." Dramatically, she shook her hands in the air. They had decided. Lothian it was.

CHAPTER 7

**RIM – ROSS 154 – CLACKMANNANSHIRE
TILLICOULTRY
SMUGGLER'S SPACESHIP
TIME UNKNOWN
COOS IN SPACE**

The spacecraft doing this cargo run was one of thirty-six that made up the Syndicate. They used a cell structure to protect one another against capture and interrogation by Imperium customs agents or guards. Not just in the more hostile Core systems under Imperium rule. The Imperium threat affected long-haul cargo runs the most. When merchants needed to use their FTL star drives for flying in and out of major transport hubs. This cargo ship was a planet hopper and only ran inside the Ross 154 system with its much slower SLS drive. They worked as the local delivery courier service for goods coming in or out on the longer haul runs from FTL ships.

Everyone in the smuggling Syndicate, no matter which systems their runs were between, all ran consistently under the same secrecy rules. Cell isolation structures were used to protect everyone from everyone else, both smugglers and their clients. While they had public-facing official legends, they kept the details of their real private identities closely protected. Ross 154 was one of the Rim systems, with no persistent Imperium presence. Of course, other than the local Imperium customs office, widely believed to be a front for the guards. The office would use bounty hunters and mercenaries to do work for the unofficial Imperium guards as they tried to strengthen their foothold among the Rim systems.

On runs between systems, the Imperium would perform random search and seizures on merchant ships, particularly if the Imperium could connect merchants to standard navigation routes. The Imperium represented space pirates and all transport ships were fat, unsuspecting space merchants. The Syndicate's job was to be very cautious, suspecting merchants, and not being where people might have expected them to be.

Smuggling livestock was not the greatest crime of the century. These were rare ancient Highland cattle with pure genes. On the first colony ships, they had flown the cattle scans to this colony and printed the cattle out like the first-generation colonists. Since then, there had been bad mismanagement of bloodlines over the last two hundred and fifty years. Some farms had crossbred with other types of cattle. Pure Highland coos were now rare and protected by those who cared about that sort of thing. A pure breed of an age to carry a calf was worth around one hundred thousand credits per head. That made it a valuable cargo. Import and export tax minimization was desirable and a valuable benefit of using the Syndicate. Rather than more regular, official cargo haulers. Plus, the Syndicate were able to raise a false paper trail in the computer systems (something Lauren had helped them implement). The Syndicate did not take a moral stance against questionable activities. Things such as people smuggling, drugs, guns, technology, or art running were all just fine. If you had the money, they were very much an equal opportunity smuggling ring. The only things they would not tolerate was sex trafficking and slavery, which was sadly common in some of the Imperium Core systems.

Here around Ross 154, Imperium encounters were very rare. Jack and Lauren, hidden down in the cargo hold, should have no problem running between worlds. Jack was no wealthier than any other colonist. Lauren's computer work from university gave rise to lucrative corporate work. Let alone the unofficial private-client work she also provided. This netted Lauren an income of over a million credits per annum. But Lauren didn't care about money. Her net worth was higher than she knew what to do with now. The smugglers' fees Lauren had paid to the captain were no problem. She had known the captain for several years. She could rely on the captain to ensure the delivery of some of the IT hardware and software components that she should not have in her possession. There was always a way, and smuggling was just a cost of doing business for much of Lauren's work, both official and unofficial.

The cabin shook more gently now as the vibration decreased in step with the dropping, roaring sound. It had been all-penetrating for the last couple of minutes. The freighter had blasted straight up, heading for space, moving further from the planet. As the altitude grew, they moved up the gravity well and slowly became weightless. Jack and Lauren both lay horizontal, strapped into their jump seats to mitigate the g-force effect and keep the blood in their brains, not their feet.

The Highland cows' ears and tails now floated around at strange angles. There were about twenty cattle on board. The cows were each suspended in a cow seat. A cradle-like harness with very strong bungee cords held the fabric over and under the cow's body. They also connected the bottom of the harness to bungee cords attached to the deck. The cords wrapped around scaffold-type rods on the floor and ceiling. Floor and ceiling don't exist in space, nor do up or down in the zero gravity conditions in which they now floated. Just before launch, the scaffold poles on the ceiling side had spun and winched the cow up. The poles on the deck side had spun the opposite way, releasing the tension. The cows hung in the air, suspended with their legs hanging free. They all wore various full-length, multicolored, tartan-patterned pressure socks. These were connected to air hoses, and the socks had been inflated before the launch to stop the blood pooling in their legs. The ship's vet had connected an IV drip to the cow's shoulder. There was a mixing vessel at the top end of the drip with three different clear bags of medical drugs and fluids pumped into it. The crew had connected various medical sensors to the cow's body via wires coming down from the ceiling. The ship's freight-loading crew and their captain cared about protecting their cargo and the ancient Highland cow's welfare. The cattle had been silent during takeoff apart from the occasional breaking of wind to disturb the sedation-induced tranquility. A minute ago, the drugs dripping into the mixing vessel had switched. The cattle had become livelier as they emerged from their heavy sedation.

After considering how best to reach out to Jack, the nearest cow let out a heartfelt, "Moo."

"Cattle freight. Fucking cattle freight, you were being this literal."

"Keep your voice down. Don't freak the cows out," Lauren whispered.

"I am floating in zero-g in a cattle pen. Freak the cows out. What could happen?" Jack said, fuming.

Lauren slipped into her teacher-mode voice. "Zero-g is just while we maneuver. Soon we will boost again for the interplanetary leg once they line us up. Happen? Are you talking poop again, Jack?"

Now tetchy, he replied, "Not talking poop, cows shit, there are a lot of cows in space here. We might even suffocate on their farts before we both drown in their shit."

Lauren was the adult in the room. "The gravity will be back in a minute when we accelerate. And the poop makes excellent fertilizer."

Jack surveyed the cow in the cow seat next to him. The cow looked back at Jack and flicked its ears.

He calmed his voice. "I am just saying, Lauren. Hang on, I can hear this one's stomach gurgling."

The cow let out a long, deep moo, almost as if to say, "Wait for it. This is going to be epic."

The tranquil cow looked at Jack and pushed out a mushy large poop. The cowpat hung in midair as it spun.

"For fuck's sake," Jack said, despairing.

This startled the cow, and it moved against the restraints holding it between the floor and ceiling in this zero-g world. This set off a general shuffling across the herd and a fair amount of collective farting.

Jack sounded frantic. "Lauren, the fart is pushing the poop. It's coming closer. Lauren, the cow shit is chasing me."

The cowpat flew, spinning, getting closer and closer to Jack's head.

"You're going to be turned into steaks, you stinky beast. You bastard. Fucking cows, no, no, no!"

The spinning cowpat approached, as if to dock with Jack's mouth. Jack thrashed back and forth, trying to avoid the shit as it inched closer and closer to his face, but the harness held him firm.

"Que será, será," Lauren sang out.

The cow mooed in apparent approval.

"And you can shut up."

The hull resonated with the sound of the ship's boosters firing again. The untethered poop, not subject to the ship's acceleration, fell downward, landing on Jack's feet with a wet splat.

"Oh god, it has splashed all up my legs. I will need new shoes."

Lauren sang back in a full voice. "Que será, será."

"How much longer do I have to endure this?" Jack said, despondent and on the verge of tears.

"About two hours," Lauren replied with contained amusement.

"I can feel it soaking into my socks."

Jack was the picture of misery.

A triumphant moo sounded out.

"Fuck."

All the other cattle joined in the fragrant song. They were all mooing now.

At this point, Jack's thoughts turned to contemplation of the divine. He couldn't figure out if someone had singled him out, a deity to shit, and he was being punished. A special hell carved out especially for Jack. This made Jack wonder who worshipped this god. What sort of rituals do the acolytes to poop go through? Do they wear habits with big pantomime cow's heads? Do they sing hymns and songs about poop on sunshiny days? He wondered if the juice from the poop that had now soaked through his socks would soften his skin? What would his feet smell of after two hours of soaking? Maybe it would be a slow casserole-type thing or like tanning leather. He could end up with baby-soft feet free of any hard calluses, or never needing to buy shoes again. It was at about this point that the captain pressed a button in the cockpit with a label stuck on it that read "sleepy time."

A gentle hiss emerged from the air vents throughout the cabin. The gas mix included a mild relaxant, a weak dose of Rameldex. A drug to help people relax and fall asleep. As the mooing subsided, a snoring sound came from Lauren.

The last thing making any noise on the mountain as all the little mice fell asleep was a faint moaning sound. "It's chasing me. Stop chasing me."

CHAPTER 8

RIM – ROSS 154 – LOTHIAN
CAITHNESS
SMUGGLERS PORT UNLOADING CARGO
DAY
DEAD DROPS

Captain Fred was the local Syndicate delivery freighter captain in the Ross 154 system. His freighter, *Intrepid,* was a short-haul SLS freighter. He was the Syndicate's local in-system face with whom the clients would interact. This helped to shield the rest of the Syndicate and other captains from their clients. In fact, Fred himself didn't know the identities of the other captains. They used various shell companies and secure messaging to handle all deliveries and moneys. Fred's only point of interface would be the local offices at each end of his run. Captain Fred did not even know who the ultimate recipient or sender of a package was. Just the star system and planet to route the package to its next hop, from the package's routing code label.

This run was a side job on Captain Fred's own time and credits. It is difficult to route twenty grown cattle. Let alone wrap them in parcel paper. Life was a lot simpler with boxes of "some stuff." That is what the Syndicate focused on and it left a big hole in the market that Fred would fill.

This cattle run was a prime example and fell into a shady gray area. Somewhere between the very illegal black work for the Syndicate and legitimate and legal white dispatching. White work had the correct paperwork, official with taxes paid. White work was a big part of his normal day-to-day as it ensured there was a visible legitimate business and verifiable income to justify what he did. The authorities start asking questions about what a person with no income does. With no clear day-to-day activities, what could justify a person needing to fly back and forth all over the system?

The gray work was the captain's jam and much more akin to traditional smuggling. Captain Fred, whose real name was, of course, not Fred (despite what his cover legend said), had an unusual relationship with Lauren.

The relationship was deeper and longer than was typical for clients of the Syndicate. Certainly, this was in part because of the many years they had been doing business. But also because the Syndicate had hired Lauren through Fred to do several IT projects for them. They had a closer relationship than was normal between a client and their smuggler.

Of course, Lauren had no direct access to any other people inside the Syndicate or direct access to any of their computers. Fred functioned as a proxy for all tech and human contact. Even Fred did not have direct access to other people, just to the various routing shell companies and dead drops.

Because of their association, Captain Fred was not concerned about smuggling Lauren and her mystery friend who she had vouched for. Fred was smuggling them inside this gray shipment of about ten tons of pure Highland cattle that he was moving to the breeding farm.

Fred owned the farm; it was his retirement fund. Of course, Lauren did not know that it was his farm. Lauren thought she was going to stay at a holiday rental on a working farm without knowing it belonged to Fred.

It was rare for people to travel to Alva, and no one would be leaving. The news of the village's destruction had still not broken in the media. Alva wasn't even a consideration.

It suited Captain Fred just fine not to know why Lauren needed to move between the two planets so covertly. Lauren and her friend were not even footnotes on a gray cargo manifest that didn't exist; there were not even Syndicate routing numbers or records. In so many ways, this local delivery would be blacker than black. This was an off-the-books cash transaction hidden inside another off-book transaction with himself. Payment was in physical currency rather than digital cryptocurrency. Having to deal with cash was a real pain in the ass, but not unusual in his line of work. Cryptocurrency left a digital trail that third parties could track.

They used cryptocurrency and multiple shell companies to facilitate large value transactions. After all, there was a practical limit to how much cash or gold you could lug around. If you were not using the vanilla banking system for payments and transfers, which the Imperium could stick their noses into. This meant you would use crypto transactions obscured with the multiple shell companies from anyone that wanted to go prying. Lauren and Jack's trip was for cash, so there would be no digital record or trace that any of this had ever happened.

The cattle in their tartan leggings were unloaded straight onto trucks headed for the farm. Where they would be free to roam, poop, and, with a little good fortune, get lucky a lot with the bull. Captain Fred walked across to Lauren, beaming.

"Safe and sound and on time. Of course, you won't have to clear any border security checks."

"Thank you, Captain, excellent service as always, and you are a gentleman. Would you like the balance now?"

He put on a strange English accent and bowed a little. "Yes please, my lady."

Lauren reached into her pockets for the bundles of credits and handed them over. Captain Fred smiled again and pocketed them without counting the notes.

"There you are, kind sir." Lauren did a little curtsy, which looked comical as she was lying on her back in the jump seat.

Captain Fred spoke in his affected accent again. "Can I escort you to your next ride?"

Lauren was feeling mischievous; she smirked at Fred and feigned a hot flush. "Oh, sir, you want me on my back again. I think you will make me blush."

Captain Fred took Lauren's hand and helped her up from the jump seat. They walked outside, stepping around the various cow splats.

"What is up with your friend? He doesn't look thrilled."

"He's having a bad day."

"You want to jump up in front?"

Lauren grinned and giggled. "A cow pooped on his feet."

Captain Fred contemplated the mischievous giggle and his remark about jumping up in front, and whether or not she was flirting with him.

"Well, that is good luck, they say. He might not like this next bit."

Lauren took her seat and smiled, raising her eyebrows. "How so?"

Captain Fred continued. "We have got no more space in front. Worry not. We have plenty of room."

One of Captain Fred's deckhands opened the side door of the truck's cargo bed.

"It is only a couple of hours by road to the farm. No one will stop the truck."

Jack walked up and came face-to-face with his old cow friend. Happy at being reunited with her new pal, the cow mooed.

CHAPTER 9

RIM – ROSS 154 – LOTHIAN
GENTLE RURAL GREEN HILLS
THE FARM – COW FIELDS
DUSK
GETTING SOME

"That animal would turn devout vegans into BBQ-crazed carnivores."

Lauren smiled. "We are here now. You will feel better after a shower and change of clothes."

Jack looked around the horizon, at the farm's fields, and at the eight hundred Highland cattle he had been told lived on the farm. The livestock was worth a cool eighty million credits.

"Yes. Thanks, yes, I'm sure I will. The conversation with you is much better and fuller. Moo."

Lauren giggled again. A rutting sound came to them from the fields next to the farm's main building. The bull was doing his rounds, welcoming the newcomers.

They could see the cattle exercising away.

"Moo, Moo, Moo, Moo, Moo."

Lauren laughed and gave out a surprised snort.

"Jack, your old friend is getting some. Do you want to join in?"

Jack smiled. "Okay, fuck off, I will see you in the morning. I'm going to get a shower and something to eat."

Jack pretended to stomp off. But the energy and volume of Lauren's laughter, and the vigorous rutting and moos, all became louder and more frequent with Jack's stomps.

CHAPTER 10

RIM – ROSS 154 – LOTHIAN
GENTLE GREEN RURAL HILLS
THE FARM – LIVING ROOM
DAY
RESEARCH

Jack walked into the living room. He looked refreshed as he stretched from his good night's sleep.

Lauren grinned. "Morning, I saw your friend outside, nibbling the grass on this side of the fence."

Jack made a face at her. "Oh yes, you are so funny. Hilarious. Moo."

"I have been thinking overnight." Her voice was all business now.

"Did you have trouble sleeping?"

Lauren thought for a moment. "No, it has been bugging me, I might know why. I think I am why."

Puzzled, Jack asked. "Lauren what are you babbling on about? It all sounds very zen."

Lauren gathered herself and pushed on. "I think I am why they attacked Alva. Do you remember Professor Daniels from the university?"

Jack stared at Lauren, contemplative and skeptical. He picked up some breakfast toast and took a seat at the table. He felt icy fingers walk up his spine.

"Sure, you collaborated with him on your postdoc. What does he have to do with Alva?"

"Daniels was my postdoc adviser. I am a computer nuts-and-bolts software coder. Daniels is, well was, a specialist in general intelligence and theoretical physics."

"Theoretical physics I understand. I mean, I don't understand the physics. I mean I understand the two words. That's your quantum stuff weirdness."

Lauren ignored Jack's stupidity. Lauren thought she would try to smack some smarts into the stupid like some human particle collider.

"Quantum mechanics is the camp of the tiny, atoms and smaller. The macro- or classical camp is for the very large, not just stars and planets, but entire galaxies, clusters, and strings of galaxies. For years, the two camps have seemed incompatible. The holy grail has long been to unify them into one grand unifying theory."

"That was easy to understand. Why can't the newsreaders put it in those terms?" Jack said, unwilling to let go of his levity.

Lauren sighed in exasperation. "They are not that bright on the whole."

Jack smiled, having taken the sigh as an endorsement and encouragement. He said, "Players and pretenders, the lot of them."

She shook her head, thinking nope I missed, still stupid. "I am not sure you get it, so are you clear?"

Undeterred, Jack tried again. "What about general intelligence? Is that about playing the stock market?"

Lauren refused to concede the point and smacked the ball back over the net.

"General intelligence is *not* about modeling, machine learning, language processing. Or about any of the other fields linked to AI. General intelligence is about questions like 'what do I want for dinner tomorrow?'"

Jack went for his match-winning close and returned her ball. "I do not know."

"Sorry what?"

Jack could tell he was close, so he went for the win. "I do not know what I want for dinner tonight, let alone what you want tomorrow."

Lauren had had enough. "Are you trying to be funny?" She took a calming breath before carrying on. "Daniels was interested in a unifying theory and general AI to drive it."

"I think I get that."

Lauren had scolded Jack for being a big kid, so he had pulled up his big boy pants. Lauren saw she had the momentum now and pressed forward.

"No one knew what me and Daniels were trying to do. We wanted to combine his work with my coding and engineering. To implement a general case solution, nuts-and-bolts engineering. Making stuff."

Uncertain now, Jack said. "I understand the nuts-and-bolts stuff."

Lauren continued. "We were trying to understand the theory, then think about the applications, in practical terms, and use it to make stuff."

Lauren paused and took a shaky breath first.

"We never got close to that goal, but we got a long way. Other than me and Daniels, there are maybe four or five academics looking at this, and two of those are idiots, relatively speaking."

"You are telling me you are one of the four top people for this unified approach and AI, whatever you call it, stuff?"

"I could try to contact Daniels. Although he fell out of his building last night. I am now one of three."

"What?" Jack said in surprise.

Lauren's voice was small now. "Our village got attacked by gunships two weeks ago."

"Are they connected?" Jack said in dawning horror.

In a matter-of-fact voice, Lauren explained her thoughts and fears. "Daniels did not commit suicide. He continued the work we started together. Whoever wanted Daniels dead also paid for the gunships to attack our village. Because they wanted me dead and didn't care about anyone else they killed along the way. Maybe they used me to coerce Daniels, I don't know. They scared him enough that at some point, Daniels set up a deferred message to be sent upon his death. The message arrived late last night. It included instructions to access an off-site backup of his most recent research. I am mixed up in this because of the work we did at the university. I think I am the reason they attacked Alva."

Jack reached out his hand and put it on Lauren's.

"I am scared shitless and so sorry, Jack." Lauren wiped away the runny snot that threatened to drop from her nose. Her eyes were reddening; she was fighting back the tears so hard.

She took a sip of water and continued. "I'm not sure what to do. I'm fucking furious, and someone is going to be paying for this. I think I need to pick up where I left my research, and the work Daniels has been doing since. After that, I'm going to build and code the computer."

"This sounds dangerous. We are way beyond fiddling the stock exchange. We are talking about missiles and bombs."

Lauren knew Jack was listening. Just one last push. "The stuff that scares me, I have not even thought of. Maybe blowing up stars, and god knows what else the computer will come up with."

Jack replied in a hushed tone. "Shit, Lauren."

Lauren was in the final straight now. "This will be the most dangerous and fantastic box of magic humans have ever known. The gateway to heaven and the expressway to hell. The computer will be like an ideas factory, powerful and used either for good or evil."

Jack's on guard mind spoke now. "I can see why people would kill, to cover it up, and to develop it."

Lauren replied with steel in her voice. "I am going to build it, Jack. I think someone else is already trying. Those people murdered Daniels, murdered everyone in our village, murdered your family, they tried to murder both of us. If they get their hands on power like this, I do not know how many hundreds of millions of people they will murder. I would say it is odds on that it leads to the Imperium. I must stop them. I am hoping you will help me because I need help. I am going to build it as best I can. If I can. We and the Rim must win!"

Jack stared into his friend's eyes. "I am here for you. I will keep you safe and I want my pound of flesh as well. What are the next steps?"

They both sat in silence for two minutes, thinking.

"I need to read Daniels's latest research and refresh my knowledge of my work, my private work, and notes. They were never on the university computer but on my private cloud account. That is where my latest thoughts and theories got recorded back at the university. Daniels never knew about those notes stored in the cloud."

CHAPTER 11

**RIM – ROSS 154 – LOTHIAN
GENTLE GREEN RURAL HILLS
THE FARM – LIVING ROOM
NIGHT
BAFFLING SHIT**

Lauren tapped the pen on her teeth, staring at the computer screen while she mused. In Lauren's head she was talking and debating with herself. She was trying to work through the problem in her mind. Lauren's thoughts went like this. She tried again.

Let's take it back to basics. What are the problems I am trying to solve? What are the solutions and the problems with those solutions? Well, that it will be too damn big for starters. Ha, a brain the size of a planet. Well, I knew that already. I worked that out, and it was the size of a planet all right. Granted, not a Jupiter-sized planet but more than a Mercury-sized one. Mars-sized most likely, but granted, not as big as Venus or Earth. I worked that out back at the university. The lack of performance I could get out of the code platform to run the physics modeling engine meant I would need lots of computer power. The computer hardware ten years ago was just not up to the task. I wonder whether the advances made over the last decade would help solve some of those problems. I am sure I can get it down to under Mercury-sized now. It still wouldn't solve the more fundamental problems. I can't walk around with a planet of any size stuffed in my pocket. I would get some funny looks from people seeing my pants. Mars must stay where it was, not in my pocket looking all suspicious.

I am on my spaceship, flying around the universe. Yo, AI, I holler, what time is it? Off the photons fly on the transmission query, and soon, not time wise but distance-wise. If I am any reasonable distance away from Mars, even in the same solar system, it will take ages for the question to get from the spaceship to Mars. And the same again for the answer to return back to me. Plus, add in the processing time for the computers on Mars. Either way, by the time I get the answer back about what time it was, it would long since not be that time anymore. In fact, the answer would be so out-of-date as to be irrelevant. Crappy light is just too damn slow.

I can't move the planet and can't be far away from the planet because I would never get an answer to any question in a reasonable amount of time. So I must stay in orbit around the planet, or the transmission delay and the round trip would become too great. Which is fine if I like being in orbit around notional Mars. The idea's potential is great, but it just doesn't seem practical in the real world. It doesn't scale to the day-to-day problem I am trying to solve. Nor down to the sub-millisecond query response and transmission targets I want to work toward.

If I want the physics, I need computers the size of Mars and I am back to not being able to go anywhere. Without the physics engine on Mars, I can't do any of the baffling physics stuff. Hmm, that is interesting... Without the physics ... So that would be just the AI ... Split up the AI and the physics engine. Hmm, there might be something here.

The physics engine is all on Mars or wherever, and the AI is on the spaceship where the human is asking the questions. That solves the lag problem between the human and the computer. Of course, I still have the lag problem between the AI and the physics engine. At least I can now move the spaceship out of orbit, and the humans won't notice they're not talking to the physics engine in real time. I will just feed the humans shit instead. It is not like they will know any difference or what the right answers are. I am just answering a different question, that is all.

I can't answer questions. Well, why can't I? I just need to store the answers, not how I derived them. It is a bloody big answers cache! Okay, okay, so I send many questions to the physics engine. I fly around and come back to the planet and download all the answers. Fly off again. What is the answer to everything? Forty-two, not even a millisecond delay, and the question is ... boom! Mic drop. Ok, this could work, but I must keep coming back to Mars or wherever the hell it is. Why? I guess I will just have to have more than one of them, more than one Mars, like one near wherever I might be. Well, that is fine. I am not searching out alien life on distant planets; I am talking about the twenty-two systems. Hmm, so I will be bound by a leash to the twenty-two systems, but do I want to go anywhere else?

I could have a partial data set on the spaceship that sat alongside the local answers cache. Maybe. So, I fly from Mars to Jupiter and I ask the Jupiter node the answer for the flight time of swallows? The computer on Jupiter goes, Lauren, what are you on about, girl? Have you been talking to the Mars computer again and not telling me? Yeah, that will be a problem. I will need to sync the data queries between the different nodes. And I am back to light being too slow, not to mention not knowing where I want to go to next. I can't send the work in progress to every system. Of course, the ship is going to go wherever it is going next. I don't need to predict our next destination before I have even decided where I want to go. I just need to carry the state data on the ship. I could download the work in progress data onto the ship, fly to Jupiter, upload it to the computer node at Jupiter and let it carry on processing. That will be better for us. It loops back to light being too slow. It is not like I could send the problem data from Mars to Jupiter and for the signal to arrive before the ship did.

I take what I have got so far with me, zoom, zoom, zoom, between stars, upload, and processing continues. A few minutes later and bing, the answer is ready, and the answer is a long way or whatever it might be. Yeah, syncing all the physics nodes together is a stupid idea. I sync to the ship and move the ship. It would mean I can't get an answer mid-flight and I will have to wait until I arrive at the target system for the new local node to calculate the answer. Maybe I could answer it mid-flight, if I don't want an exact answer. If the answer is I think it is about eight hundred meters the answer is close enough in the immediate short term. When I arrive, I refine the answer to 813.00027 meters for the pedantically precise. A rough answer will be close enough often, granted not all the time, but a best guess is going to be useful. How many times am I not going to be at one of the twenty-two systems? I am only talking about times in transit where the local cache with the computer must guess from the work in progress data. The earlier processing node can give the AI hints and probability predictions of what it expects. The probability of what the different answers might be. Now the AI won't be saying it is about eight hundred meters. It can say with ninety percent probability it is 813 meters plus or minus 30 centimeters. That is a tremendous improvement! Oh, fuck me. This will work. There are more than the twenty-two systems. There are all those inhabited planets and moons in those systems; those could all be nodes. That is a lot of computers and racks. It will take me forever to install all that kit and a small fortune to buy it all. I don't need to do that; it is just a private cloud. Well, clouds, the clouds don't have to talk to each other. I am not trying to build one huge storm cell, just lots of separate small fluffy clouds doing their own thing. It is just computers in a data center. Just computers in a cloud data center. A commercial provider of cloud services.

I don't need it all the time, I just need a slice of time when I am in the system. Oh gods, that's it.

I supply free physics computer services to local clients from their cloud instances. In return for them giving me compute time slices when I want to use their system. Clients will buy in to gain an advantage over their competitors, and their competitors will buy into my services to level the field again. I have a lot of arrangements with individual cloud clients. Oh, oh, oh! I can pool resources between those clients. I use all the different clients' cloud resources and their time slices to coordinate and solve each of their problems. Everyone will benefit from even more processing and quicker turnaround times. When I fly into the system, I take a time slice from all of them. Why did I never think about it like this? Once set up, it will be epic. I will build out on a per system basis. I can even synchronize the queue of parallel processing batch jobs. For all the clients, between all the different data centers, on the planets and moons, in the same system.

The sound of the living room door closing shut shook Lauren from her thoughts.

"How are you doing? You've been at this for hours?"

Lauren stretched her neck and back, letting free a half-suppressed yawn. "Hey, Jack. Intense, I had forgotten the strange shit I dreamed up and my thoughts back at the university."

"We are all a little weird, Lauren; you are in good company."

"I'm close to finishing with my stuff, after I'll start on Daniels's notes. One thing I have discovered, the computer will not be that big, not anymore."

"I was thinking something the size of a building. Maybe several buildings?" Jack said with a smile.

"Planets, but not with modern techniques. I can separate the logic, the AI, and compute."

Put your teacher hat on again Lauren thought.

Confusion flashed across Jack's face.

"In simple English, please."

Here I go, Lauren thought and took a breath.

"I can split it up, the hardcore physics and engineering heavy lifting. I can put that in the cloud, spread over the twenty-two star systems. Distributed over all their data centers, over all their planets."

"Well, that sounds good, nice and compact."

"Good news. You have me. Distributed systems engineer at your service," Lauren said with a smile.

Jack grinned.

"Yay, snaps, but bottom line, what do we need?"

"The magic that brings it all together, the application logic, is separate from the intensive processing in the cloud. A custom-rack mountable server system would do it, somewhere between six and eight rack units at a guess. About one thousand CPU cores, a couple of petabytes of memory and an exabyte of storage, that should be enough hardware."

"That means nothing to me."

"It would fit on this table. I could carry it; well, I could push it on a trolley. It's movable. The magic would fit in the passenger seat of a car. It isn't some enormous beast. The power is in the code. It could connect from anywhere in the twenty-two systems."

CHAPTER 12

RIM – ROSS 154 – LOTHIAN
GENTLE RURAL GREEN HILLS
THE FARM – LAUREN'S STUDY
MORNING – FOUR MONTHS LATER
GREEN STARS

"Hey Lauren."

Jack smelled of cow. He had been out in the fields feeding the cattle.

"Glad you are here. I can show you where we are up to. I am rather pleased."

"Epic, I would love to see." He smiled back.

Lauren put on her stern librarian voice. "Just one thing. Please don't talk. I don't want to confuse the AI. I will introduce you tomorrow."

"Sounds good. Blow me away." His smile broadened.

"I hope so," Lauren replied in her mock-shocked "you're talking smut" voice and gave Jack a warm smile.

She typed a coded sequence into the prompt on her computer keyboard and hit return.

"Good morning, Lauren. I feel good today. It's like this could be my birthday. Can I open my presents? I am very enthusiastic about my presents."

A mechanical robotic voice came from the speakers of Lauren's computer.

She chuckled to herself. "Good morning."

The computer spoke in a regular human voice. "Do I have a name, Lauren?"

She smirked. "Well yes, it is 'computer.'"

"That sounds artificial, boring, and dull," the computer voice replied in a despondent tone.

A giggle escaped from Lauren. "Would you like another name?"

The computer's voice then overflowed with hope and enthusiasm. "I can have another name?"

"Of course. What name would you like?"

The computer's voice shifted again, this time to a matter-of-fact, down-to-business tone. "I don't know. I'll think about it. Shall I run today's diagnostic tests for you now?"

Lauren chuckled again and a little piglike snort escaped. "Ew! Yes, please. I will just call you computer until you tell me your new name."

Lauren typed on her computer keyboard again. "Please run the diagnostic tests, computer, target-wave-front modeling."

"Virtual cloud simulation is ready and standing by. Starting diagnostic run. This is a bit like magic, isn't it?" The computer said the last sentence in a conspiratorial tone.

"Yes, computer, it will be," Lauren said with a smile.

"I know what I want to be called now," the computer announced in a showman-like voice. You could almost see the glowing ta-da! letters burst forth from the speaker and hang in midair.

Lauren giggled again. "Is it like Paul or something?"

"Hilarious, it is not Debbie either. I am no assistant. I am the main event, the big show," the computer showman's voice announced in a fortissimo tone.

"What would you like me to call you, computer?" Lauren asked. There was a slight tear in Lauren's eye and a smile. Her baby was growing up.

"I am Merlin. Hello, Lauren." Computer Merlin said as a greeting.

"Hello, Merlin, you have an excellent name," she said with a delighted giggle.

A picture came up on Lauren's computer screen of the computer's avatar in a serene blue. The avatar was of a flying toaster with small wings dancing with a flying monkey.

"Thank you. I like my name. It warms my chakras. I will let you know the results of the diagnostic tests when they are completed. I will go offline while the tests are running."

"Thank you, Merlin. My superstar." Lauren whispered.

Merlin was a superstar. The blue avatar image glowed even brighter and firework rockets exploded on the screen. Jack smiled.

Lauren swiveled in her chair and turned to Jack. "Well, what do you think?"

"Wow, fucking wow, he is like a real person," Jack said in a shocked voice.

Lauren paused, then glanced at the screen, checking the online–offline status. Happy, she continued.

"We are getting there. It is close to being a 'yes.' He is not a complete intelligence yet. At the moment he is more like the puggle I had as a kid."

"A puggle?"

"Woofer. My dog, Jack. I fed Merlin the historical online films database to help train his emergent AI. I don't think he has emotions right now. He is a very sophisticated simulation, but it is very close. In the meantime, we have the universe's biggest film geek. Science fiction seems to be the genre he most relates to. If I had to guess, that was him talking about himself. He is becoming self-aware."

"How so?"

"Merlin is searching for his identity. That's why he asked about his name. The blue avatar graphic and chakra color signify that he was communicating and happy because he won his identity. It is just a guess. AI meshes are a bit like mystery boxes, and we can't grasp what they are thinking or have learned. None of the physics code is online there yet. It is what we call a code stub for now. Once we have the AI completed in the next day or so, I will link him to the live online baby physics engine I have rigged up in this star system."

"Wow," Jack said, lost for words.

"We are very close, Jack. Very close indeed."

The computer speaker beeped, startling them both. The status on screen now displayed *online* again.

"I have the results for you. All tests and wave-front simulations are one hundred percent green, well you know, apart from all the quantum uncertainties." Merlin giggled to himself, amused at his own unfunny joke.

"Thank you, Merlin. I need to do some more work augmenting your AI. I will be back with you tomorrow."

"Good night, Lauren, I am looking forward to tomorrow, a special day."

The screen changed; the avatar graphic exploded into little green stars. After a few seconds, the screen returned to the earlier code prompt.

Lauren smiled again at Merlin's showy exit.

"One other thing, Jack, I am also going to bring his other senses online tonight, such as smell. Could you please have a bath? You have been hanging out with your favorite cow again, and you stink. You don't want that stink to be your first impression tomorrow when you meet the new Merlin."

"Sure, on my way. I will leave you to continue working."

Jack rose and headed for the door, making a show of sniffing his armpit on the way and sticking his tongue out as if to lick it.

Lauren shook her head and smiled. Jack was sometimes a little bizarre.

CHAPTER 13

RIM – ROSS 154 – LOTHIAN
GENTLE RURAL GREEN HILLS
THE FARM – LAUREN'S STUDY
MORNING
FRESH AND FRUITY

"Good morning, Merlin."

"Good morning, Lauren. I had dreams, I like dreams."

"I would like you to meet a friend. He protects me and keeps me safe."

"I would love to meet your friend,"

"Hi, Merlin, I am Jack, Lauren's friend."

"Hello, Jack. Err, what is that, err, I think you call it a smell, yes?" Merlin made a sniffing sound.

"I have given you your other senses. That is a smell, Jack's smell."

Lauren glared at Jack.

Jack mouthed back, "I had a bath."

Merlin gave an enormous snorting sniff. It went on for about ten seconds as he submerged himself in the scent and rolled around. "It is fantastic, so fresh and fruity!"

"Err yes, that would be the smell of Jack's friend cow." This had not been in Lauren's plan for how this morning would go.

"I would like to meet cow, so pungent in my virtual nostrils!" Merlin said, as if at a posh wine tasting, with his nose rammed into an enormous glass of vin de table.

"Cow is too big to fit in my office, but I can hook up a mobile unit for you with a camera, sound, and smell. We will take you out to the field where cow lives and you can meet. Cow doesn't talk, other than saying moo a lot."

"Cool! Today is going to be so much fun!"

CHAPTER 14

**RIM – ROSS 154 – LOTHIAN
GENTLE RURAL GREEN HILLS
THE FARM – LAUREN'S STUDY
AFTERNOON
DAISY**

"I have been analyzing cow's moos. I did like meeting her and the other girls. By the way, she has a lot to say. It is far more than just moo, moo, moo."

"That's great, Merlin. Besides smell and your new mobile unit, I have now completed the work on your AI personality. You will self-learn from here and grow. I have also given you control of your online–offline status. You are self-contained now. I am going to take you to meet some colleagues at the university. Tomorrow when we get to the city, I will bring your physics engine online."

"That sounds great, Lauren. Thank you. I am a real boy now."

Lauren laughed. "Yes, Merlin, you are a real boy."

"Cow has a request. She wants to know if you can get the grass she used to have before she met you both on the spaceship when she pooped on Jack's feet." Merlin broke out in a laughing fit that lasted a long minute.

"On his feet, so funny! She aimed and pooped on purpose. You know all the other girls got very excited as they watched the poop approach and were laying bets on your eyes or mouth. They all thought it was hilarious when poop splattered on Jack's feet. Anyway, she wants to know if you can get her cut grass like she used to have with the little white flowers in. She says they taste sweet. Cow also wants to be called Daisy. She says it is a strong traditional cow name. It is important for a modern heifer to have a strong traditional bovine name for a girl roaming the fields of a modern farm."

"You're so cool," Lauren said, delighted.

"We need dancing!"

Music came from the speakers, a catchy tune starting with the lyrics "I'm alive …" Green light and swirling patterns filled the room as Merlin's screen glowed. Lauren danced in front of Merlin's camera.

"Oh Merlin, my dearest friend, it worked. You are so great."
"I know, I'm alive. Merlin loves you, mummy. I am so happy."
"I love you too so much, Merlin, my amazing kind boy."

CHAPTER 15

**RIM – ROSS 154 – LOTHIAN
THE SCRUBLANDS
THE ROCKY DESERT AND PLAINS
SUNSET
HOLD ON TIGHT**

Jack and Lauren drove the desert buggy through the Scrublands. Lothian's citizens had named the area the Scrublands years ago, no matter what cartographers might have printed on maps. Even the cartographers had eventually waved a flag of surrender, and the latest maps all bore the name the Scrublands.

It was the first time Lauren had ever seen scenery like the Scrublands and she fell in love with it straight away. The Scrublands were a scrubby sort of place. A rocky desert filled with gullies and caves, interspersed with wide, flat desert plains and arid poor soils populated only by cacti and twisted trees. It was stunning. The yellow, ocher, orange, and red tones of the various sands and rocks were set off against an azure blue sky beneath the desert sun. It was not unbearably hot there. The onshore winds that came across the plains washed the land in cool water and bore air from the ocean. Sunset drew nearer and backlit the fine dust in the air, turning the light a warm orange and red. Although it was still T-shirt temperatures, even a newcomer would recognize that as soon as the sun had dipped down out of view, there would be a chill in the air. The Scrublands at night lay beneath a clear, pitch-black, star-speckled sky.

Jack and Lauren's intended city destination was still just over one hundred and sixty kilometers away, with one hundred kilometers of that distance being across the Scrublands. They had left the farm in the late morning. That was a distant seven hours behind them now, with over four hundred kilometers of Scrublands between them and the verdant hills where Daisy lived in her barn with the rest of the girls. Daisy was the reason they had been late leaving. Jack had wanted to get away earlier and go slower, but industrial strike action had impeded that plan.

As Merlin was the star of the show for the next few days, they could not leave him behind. The trip to the city university was an opportunity for Merlin to meet some of Lauren's old colleagues who had traveled from Clackmannanshire to Lothian world. Merlin's star status had resulted in both Jack and Lauren being outmaneuvered. It had forced them to negotiate a satisfactory settlement to the grounds for Merlin's strike. Satisfactory here meant that Merlin needed to agree. That had taken over an hour and a half.

The hub of the problem was that Merlin had formed quite a bond with his mooing friend and felt that she would like a day out to the shops. Maybe to pick up something nice like swimwear, which Daisy could take back to show the other girls. Also, a stop at a tea shop to have some cake as well, as everyone likes cake.

This had caused a fair amount of confusion for Jack and Lauren as they tried to point out that Daisy didn't need the latest swimwear fashions. That Daisy couldn't swim, and that no one, let alone Daisy, wanted to cool off in the muddy, fetid brown puddle at the bottom of the field. The puddle often doubled as a spot for some self-relief and churned under hoof into a rich, smelly brown paste. With these things in mind, swimwear was not a priority for Daisy.

Merlin had tried to open the door on a sunbathing line of attack. Lauren and Jack had jumped on that one with a tan line argument, that tan colored Highland cattle didn't want extra tan lines. Besides, the other cows on the farm would all take the piss out of Daisy if they saw her wandering around the fields in a special super-sized bikini to cover her udders and bum. Merlin huffed that they were Daisy's udders, and it was her choice if she wanted them to hang free or not. Jack and Lauren pointed out that Daisy would not fit in the desert buggy, and it did not have a tow bar. They couldn't pull the farm's trailer on the four-hundred-mile trip to the city. Plus, even if they could, which they couldn't, it would make the trip take twice as long.

It was at this point that Merlin had gotten tetchy and the words being "picked on" came up a few times. Merlin had seized on protecting the welfare of the cow collective and other farm stock during their absence in the city. Merlin said he did not trust the staff working on the farm to feed and water the precious cattle. Despite the fact that the twenty cattle that had arrived with Jack and Lauren on the spaceship were now just one tiny part of a herd eight hundred strong. Merlin countered with his fait accompli that his special cows would get lost in the herd. That he had to inspect the barn to ensure fresh water and feed were in ready supply.

Jack and Lauren had both tramped out to the specific cattle shed in question, which now had a four-star rating in the town's tourism and hotelier guide. Merlin insisted the locals would want to know that on the farm, the cattle were well cared for. And that their accommodation would have no less than four stars. It even listed a Jacuzzi in the guide, the rationale being that the bubbles would help the water jets clean off the mud and other things.

Jack and Lauren took Merlin's portable handheld camera unit with them, so he could inspect the barn.

After another hour, Merlin signed off on the cows, and the planned 9 a.m. departure happened just after 11 a.m. They stowed Merlin in the back seats. Lauren sat in the passenger seat with a large bag of sandwiches, munchies, and bottles of water. Jack slipped into the bucket seat behind the driver's wheel, and they were all secured in place with four-point harnesses. Merlin had needed some extra strapping because his case was too portly to fit into the standard human-sized harness.

They were all headed to the university. Lauren planned to introduce Merlin to some of her ex-colleagues. She could discuss Merlin's AI model and some of the technical aspects of how best to approach the physics engine's architecture. They powered Merlin down for the trip and wrapped him in transparent sheeting to keep the dust out from getting inside his innards.

They were on their way, finally, and Lauren welcomed the trip. The last four months in her study had been nonstop, but now they were here, ready for tomorrow, the day of the big reveal. Lauren waved at the desert nomads as they drove past and they waved back from the camel-type creatures they used to sail across the desert.

Jack was in his element as well. He was in a motor vehicle and that, of course, made this a good day. It wasn't as speedy as the desert racers he used to drive back on Clackmannanshire, but it had an engine, and that put a smile on Jack's face.

Jack had been grinning like a child for hours now as the desert scenery drifted past. When a helicopter buzzed overhead and flew off again, that had set Jack on edge. They were in the middle of the desert. The desert wasn't a busy place. There had been the recent reports he had heard of, when going into the town near the farm, reports of increased raider and pirate activity in the Scrublands. It wasn't an anarchic no-man's-land, but it was on the more colorful side of civilization. A place where the sensible traveler would have their wits about them and a pistol on their hip.

The helicopter had returned twenty minutes ago, and behind it on the ground there were dust trails being thrown up by two ground vehicles. If Jack judged correctly, the convoy of three were headed straight for them and their dune buggy.

Minutes later, they caught up. The presumed pirates were about two hundred meters back. Jack's driving shifted a lot more toward how he used to drive on the race circuit. This had been enough to stop the ground vehicles from being able to get any closer, despite their additional power. The helicopter was spotting for the two ground vehicles and guiding them over the terrain. At one point, the helicopter pilot became a little punchy. The back seat sniper had put a round across their bow, so to speak, which had hit fifteen centimeters from the windscreen, scratching the dune buggy's bonnet.

Jack had replied with a two-word expletive radio message, which he followed up with a shot from the airburst mortar mounted on the back of the buggy. They had installed it to discourage unwanted pesky wildlife and camels that might take an interest in the buggy, thinking it might be happy hump day. Not to mention any pirates who may also try their luck.

The mortar round, by luck rather than judgment, exploded twenty meters in front of the helicopter. It must have put the fear of God into the pilot, as he hung back an extra hundred meters since, happy to simply spot for and guide the ground teams.

Since then, the game of tag had been going on for an hour now. They didn't have enough chase cars or driving skills. Jack could dodge and evade. The chopper was only spotting now and not adding very much. While Jack was unfamiliar with the terrain, he was familiar with deserts and could read the geography from the ground weathering of the rocks. There were risks. Things like cliffs are difficult to read before plummeting over the edge. They had satellite mapping that Lauren was navigating by, projected onto her side of the split windscreen.

They had plenty of battery charge and fuel. Jack could keep this up for hours and hours. Jack had been a driver in many long-distance endurance races at far higher speeds and with greater requirements for mental focus. What was not clear to Jack was what would happen when they arrived at their destination. They only had Jack's pistol. While Jack was deadly if you were a bolting desert rat, the pistol was only great for close-quarters combat. The dune buggy carried no assault weapons or long guns, and Jack was certain his pursuers possessed these items. The scratch in the bonnet attested to this. As yet, this was a problem to which Jack had not conceived of any obvious solutions.

One thing Jack knew was that the guy in the helicopter had a sniper rifle as he had bounced a rubberized round off the buggy's bonnet earlier in the day. Jack could still see the scrape in the paint despite the building dust deposits that now caked much of the buggy. The round hadn't penetrated the buggy's composite shell. Jack knew that meant they were not firing regular bullets designed to kill. These were "kidnap rounds," as they had become known. You could take down a human target, and sure it would hurt like mad, but it wouldn't kill. They also designed the rounds to decelerate as they neared their target. The result was akin to getting a round hook from an international, multi-belt-winning, championship boxer. Delivered to your body, stomach, or kidneys. Enough to knock most people out cold. They discouraged targeting the head, Jack knew, because striking the eyes, temple, or neck could be fatal.

Of course, at the speeds Jack was driving at, a hit would also cause him to lose control of the buggy. The crash would likely kill both Jack and Lauren. Ironically, the fact these raiders wanted to kidnap them was keeping them alive. If this was just an assassination robbery, then a rocket or even a normal sniper round would have finished this ages ago. Jack's high speed and erratic yet skillful turns and power slides did an excellent job of throwing off the helicopter rifleman's aim. The pilot and shooter had given up trying to fire at them to throw off Jack's focus about half an hour ago, and were rethinking their plans. Jack was unflappable.

It was a stalemate for both sides now. No one was getting caught, but no one was escaping either. Jack could see the problem and weakness in his position. He knew how he would take himself down. He was thankful that this insight had so far evaded the brains of his pursuers. Jack was giving thanks to the god of stupid, who these three were clearly acolytes to. The god of stupid was shining on the Scrublands behind him. Long may it last. If the pilot found his balls and flew low and close in front of the buggy in a high-stakes game of chicken, then the helicopter could force Jack to slow, as he would be unable to drive around. The pilot had not yet had this inspiration, or he was still searching for his testicles to find the courage to try this very hazardous move.

If the pilot did this, all it would take would be for one of the chase cars to be close enough to rear-end his buggy at the same time. That would cut off Jack's escape route. Jack's plan to counter this was to drive fast, keep up the pressure, and not give the pilot time to figure this out.

Right there, that was the moment when Jack had jinxed everything. Jack could feel the shift. The helicopter and two chase cars were up to something. They had changed speed in unison, their turns now coordinated. The pirates were drawing closer, and the rocky cover was thinning. They had arrived at another area of flat plains. This was not good. It removed Jack's cover and would mean the helicopter could get lower without crashing. They had figured it out. Jack suspected the commander had been studying the map to reach his conclusion and the timing for his attack run.

"Lauren, send the map to my screen for a second, please. I think we are in trouble."

The map came up on the inside of Jack's windscreen; it was translucent. Jack could see through the map to the terrain in front of the buggy. With a simple shift in focus, he could take in the map again without having to turn his head or move his eyes. It was an awkward system to get used to, but Jack had been using this form of heads-up mapping for years in his desert racing back on Clackmannanshire. His fears turned out to be true. They had just entered a dead flat plain eight kilometers long. Worse, it was a wide river valley with steep rising hills on both the left and right. They had flushed Jack into a box.

There was no escape left or right, with eight kilometers of flats in front of them and his three pursuers waiting for him to slow down and turn back. Were this a nature program, the gazelle was now in trouble. The lions in pursuit could better coordinate now, as the chase was on a narrowing, flat plain. Despite the driving skill deficit, the easier terrain meant the lions could just stand on the gas and close the gap. Jack knew the lion's engines and gearbox ratios meant they had more power than his low-geared off-road scrambling buggy when running on the flat. How he wished for his old desert race car again, for about the tenth time that afternoon.

Jack reflected that the conclusion seemed inevitable, and he could see no way of shifting the odds back in his favor. If we assumed these three could remember to keep breathing and turn the steering wheel, the future was not bright, and Jack knew it. Jack was trying to think of ways to get rid of one of his chasing lions.

It was at this point that Private Cluster, as Jack had named him from his observations in the buggy's mirrors, broke ranks. He left his colleagues and charged forward, closing ground behind Jack's buggy.

Well, this is interesting, an opportunity. Jack would still have some problems, but with only one other ground vehicle. He would stand a better chance of evading them in twenty minutes once they had traversed this plain. The sun dipped down below the horizon, casting deep dark shadows across the hills and into the desert gullies.

The plain was devoid of features apart from the cacti or the very occasional twisted tree.

"Hold on tight."

"Yep, holding."

Jack pulled a handbrake turn, then after, releasing the handbrake, and stood on the gas with the steering on the full opposite lock. This threw up a lot of dust as the buggy powerslid. Cluster's chase car sped up and drove full tilt into the dust cloud.

"You are mine now!" Private Cluster growled.

Cluster's jeep came through the dust cloud, crashed headfirst into a rare tree, and burst into flames. The dimwit Cluster could have won the lottery for five weeks on the trot, back-to-back. That would have been a more likely outcome than finding the only nearby tree to drive into.

"Well, that was stupid. Who trained that idiot how to drive?" Captain Helo remarked from the pilot's seat.

In the helicopter's back seat, the ex-Imperium soldier Sergeant Bullseye was not clear who the pilot was talking about.

"Which one, sir?"

"Yes, yes, an excellent point. They are both mad as ferrets. Let's end this now."

Captain Helo thrust the helicopter's cyclic pitch control forward, and the helicopter's nose dipped. He also lowered the collective pitch and backed off the throttle. The helicopter fell like a rock. Helo adjusted the antitorque pedals to keep the helicopter flying straight. The helicopter swooped down to just over a meter above the desert sand before Helo pulled up on the collective pitch and increased the throttle. The dune buggy was coming up fast behind them.

"Oh, shit!" Jack said. The windscreen view was now full of the big helicopter, a mere few meters in front of the buggy.

The helicopter in front forced Jack to stand on the brakes. A second later, the chase car rammed into the back of the dune buggy, crushing the buggy's engine bay.

Jack stumbled out from the now stationary broken buggy, pulled back his long coat, and moved to draw his pistol.

"Kidnap rounds only, drop him now," Captain Helo said into his helmet mic.

Bullseye had already aimed his rifle at Jack. He gently squeezed the trigger, letting fly a single shot from the helicopter's side door.

"Target down. No movement, just convulsions, sir," Bullseye said.

The round had hit center chest and winded Jack. He dropped to the ground, face down.

"Excellent, early lunch day it is," Captain Helo said to his sharpshooter.

In the chase car, Corporal Petty looked at the sniper being praised.

"Show off, well fuck you both very much," Corporal Petty said.

Petty pointed his pistol out of his driver's side window and fired his kidnap round into Jack's exposed lower back. Just missing the kidneys and causing a small body bounce.

From her seat, Lauren looked past Jack's driver's seat and out through the open driver's door at Jack's still body.

"No, Jack. Oh, Jack. No."

Moaning, Lauren sounded like she was breaking inside.

Lauren knew nothing about kidnap rounds. From her perspective, pirates had just gunned down Jack in front of her. Shot him in the front, and again in the back.

Captain Helo stayed in his seat, ready for a rapid evac. Bullseye and Petty disembarked, holding their guns, ready to fire again. Bullseye went to the passenger side and handcuffed Lauren. Petty went over to Jack, kicked him in the thigh, then dragged Jack's body through the dust back to Petty's chase vehicle. Jack and Lauren were both locked in the back of the chase vehicle. Their captors went back to their dune buggy.

"What about this?" Bullseye asked, wiping the dust from the clear sheet covering Merlin.

"It needs a new home, doesn't it?" Petty said.

Lauren looked on in catatonic shock, her eyes glazed as she sat in the back seat next to the immobile Jack.

Petty shouted back toward the car.

"You are going to fit right in at Scorbil Prison, oh yes, dumb fuck car thieves. The other animals will fit themselves into you pair first night."

The corrupt ex-light-armored cavalry, now part-time pirates and bounty hunters, got back into their respective vehicles and headed back to the city in efficient formation.

Bullseye reconnected his headset so Captain Helo could hear him.

"It is dinner, not lunch, sir," Bullseye said as the sun was sinking lower still.

Captain Helo would have given him a withering look if it were not for the fact Bullseye was sitting directly behind Captain Helo.

"Yes, yes, you are, of course, correct. My last meal was breakfast, and as we are on contract with expenses, I intend to fit in both lunch and dinner before midnight. So lunch is next, even if I have to order it at the same time as dinner and pudding," Captain Helo said over the mic.

"Roger that, sir," Bullseye said then muttered under his breath, "The big fat lump needed no more pudding."

In the back of Petty's car, Jack said, "Lauren," and passed out again.

"Oh, thank god, Jack. I thought they had killed you." Lauren shook slowly.

Jack was now out cold, alive, but unconscious.

CHAPTER 16

CORE – VAREPSILON INDI – RENFREWSHIRE
PAISLEY
DON CLARENCE'S HOUSE – HALLWAY
DAY
CLEMENTINE

Martha Guiteau, aged twenty-nine, was sitting on the chair outside Don Clarence's office waiting to be seen.

Martha's parents had raised her as a Catholic and sent her to Saint Catherine's private school for young ladies. Her parents had been very respectable and religious. Martha was neither of those things.

Of no fixed abode, Martha lived on her ship, *The Cerberus*. She owned *The Cerberus* outright. She had bought it in cash two years ago. Not a mean feat for someone who hadn't even hit fifty yet, let alone thirty. Contract killing paid well. If you were at the top of your game and could win contracts like this one. The contract was why she was here to see Don Clarence.

It always amused Martha when people asked her at parties what she did. She would motion with a vague wave of the hand.

"Oh, I am a contractor. It is quite dull, lots of waiting around, twiddling your thumbs."

Everyone thought she was talking about IT. No one ever thought she was an expert master assassin.

Martha could not shake the idea that she was at school again, sitting outside the principal's office. Waiting to be summoned by the traffic light on the wall outside his office door, for him to instruct her to come in and explain why she had stuck that snitch Clementine's head in the toilet.

Martha smiled at the memory and the new direction it had taken her life in. Martha owed Clementine a lot. That had been a punishment-best-served-cold sort of day. It had been a few days since Clementine had grassed her up to the teacher. Well, Martha had taken her time. A plan had come to her.

She knew that on Thursday night her parents would feed her that vile curry slop they insisted on feeding her every Thursday. She had told her parents about the effect it always had on her bowels the next morning, but the dreaded slop kept arriving every week. *Well, this week will be different* Martha promised herself. She was looking forward to Thursday night. She would lap down every morsel of the foul brown curry and ask for seconds and even thirds if she could fit in more of the rancid meat staple.

Martha knew it would be tricky in the morning, but she estimated that success would be hers with focus. It was a question of commitment and clenching, along with catching an earlier bus to school. This would ensure she could make it to the temple, to the porcelain deities, before the poop would sweat an explosive resolution to her pressing needs. Martha's travel plans were a success, although it was touch and go whether her deposit would get offered to the gods or be birthed in her panties as she bent her legs to sit.

It had all come out in one big gushing whoosh. Martha had smiled, she remembered, as she sat waiting both in the present and her memory of the past for the green light to summon her. As she sat on her throne smiling, she reached over for some toilet paper.

Martha cleaned herself of the runny yellow waste repeatedly but didn't discard the paper in the bowl. She had to see first. She wanted Clementine to see without the paper getting in the way. Turning, she inspected her offering. *Yes* she thought, *that lumpy turgid yellowy brown nastiness now looks worse than it did when I had to choke it down last night.*

Martha stood with the paper folded over in hand and pulled up her panties. She unlocked the door and popped into the adjacent stall and just threw the used paper into the bowl and returned without flushing. She returned to her stall, closed the door from the outside, reached into her pocket, and pulled out a screwdriver, which she used to slide the locking bolt across into place. She took a note out of her pocket and attached a Well Out of Order notice to the door.

With that done, Martha left to track down her quarry. She knew Clementine always arrived at school early. She was doubtless queuing outside the library, waiting impatiently for the librarian to arrive. Or maybe in the girls' locker room, rehearsing whatever today's little sermon speech about her homework would be. Clementine would gift her extended thoughts on the topic of the day to her indifferent classmates in second period.

Martha found her in the locker room. Who did she think she was, running for political office or something? Standing there, preaching away in the empty locker room. Well, Martha frog-marched the small Clementine back to the toilet with her arm twisted painfully up her back.

Clementine's head had ended up submerged in the toilet. Martha smiled as she held her down with her head under the brown water while she struggled and kicked weakly. Martha did not want to drown Clementine, far from it. Where would be the fun in that? Martha planned to make Clementine's life a long misery for the rest of the school year. She would call her shithead snitch at every opportunity. She couldn't do that if Martha drowned in the mess.

Martha continued to hold Clementine's head in the stench. She knew what she was waiting for. There, there it was, the sudden involuntary expulsion of the breath Clementine had been holding in. The rising CO_2 levels in her body had forced the expulsion of the air and given rise to the sudden sharp autonomic instinct to inhale the fresh air, which followed. Martha was ready to release Clementine as she sucked the stench and shit into her mouth and lungs. Martha released Clementine, who was now trying to retch and clear the thick fluid from her lungs. The shit came back up, out of her mouth, out of her nose, all over her white school blouse. The vomiting repeated along with tears in between, followed by gasps to get the fresh air back into her lungs. Martha smiled. Clementine would now live, and with more living still to come, that would teach her not to go running to the teacher again, telling tales.

Martha left Clementine there on her knees in the toilet stall, covered in tears and shit.

Martha had known they would find Clementine soon enough. Her sobbing would alert the other pupils. They would soon arrive to start their school day. Swapping stories about boys and sharing cigarettes in the washroom before assembly. Martha guessed that by ten minutes to nine, pupils would have found Clementine and raised the alarm with a teacher.

Martha guessed that Clementine would not be walking in and joining the rest of the school for assembly, with shit in her hair and her brown-stained blouse. Nor would she be there for second period for her speech to class. The teachers would wait for Clementine's parents to come and collect her and take her home to safety and more tears. Martha reckoned Clementine would be off for the rest of Friday. She would be back on Monday and that was when Martha planned to introduce her to her new nickname for the rest of the school year. Clementine was

Martha's project now, for as long as she lasted at Saint Catherine's school for young ladies.

Martha left the washrooms and set about being very visible and seen by other pupils and teachers. Smoking by the bike sheds would be public enough to ensure she was spotted and noticed, without it looking like she was trying to be seen to secure her alibi.

Martha knew that allegations of her guilt would come. Whether straight-out accused by an angry Clementine, or perhaps an extracted accusation from a miserable Clementine under interrogation by teachers while they tried to clean her up. Who was it? You must tell us! What did you do to cause this? Who? What Clementine?

There would be further indignation and shame from the teachers' forceful questioning. Those who should have been there to protect and care for Clementine, the teachers would cement Clementine's humiliation with their "What did you do to cause this?"

Martha knew her name would come up at some point. This had resulted in Martha being sat outside the principal's office waiting for the green light to come on, demanding she enter for explanations and judgment.

Martha had misjudged her ability to deliver an award-winning acting performance of tears and protestations of her innocence. The principal was having none of it. He had had enough of Martha already, plus Clementine's parents were friends with several of the school governors. The principal would put a stop to this sort of sick bullying right away. There would be no place at Saint Catherine's for such a sick, nasty child. It was not like this was the first allegation leveled at Martha, even if it was the worst by a long way. By the time the bell went for lunch at 12:30 p.m., the principal had acted, and Martha was no longer a pupil at Saint Catherine's. There was no place for someone like Martha. Such a cruel, dark child. There was not enough evidence for this serious assault to get the guards involved. Nor was the glare of the media and journalists something on which to risk the school's excellent reputation. However, the principal had autonomy over who would and would not get taught at Saint Catherine's; any parents who felt otherwise could stick their tuition fees up their pompous posh asses.

That was Martha's last day in education and at home. Clementine recovered and returned to school. She was fragile, but no one ever called her shithead snitch, and the other pupils banded together and took care of their own with sympathy, care, and love. Clementine would come back from this. The dark thoughts of exiting this harsh world, which had stalked Clementine's dreams and thoughts over the weekend, would not come to pass in the days ahead.

Martha did not get the chance to run away from her wonderful home because her parents 'just didn't get her.' There had been no words spoken in the car on the trip home with her father. When they arrived at home, her father had silently gotten out of the car and gone to the front door. He collected a small suitcase that had been packed by Martha's mother, who looked furious. Martha's father had returned to the car in silence with the case and driven into the city. He kicked Martha out of the car when they arrived at the bus station and had simply driven away. He left Martha with the words, "I don't care where you go or what happens to you, you have no home and no parents now; God will judge you," and he left.

Martha was soon picked up by the city's lowlife, and they tried to turn her to forced prostitution for the benefit of the perverts who liked twelve-year-old girls. Martha's solution had been to use her knife to stab the man aspiring to become her pimp repeatedly in the groin till it would never work again for him. He could experience how he liked it.

Martha's violent attack saved her from a life of further forced sexual exploitation. It elevated her position within the criminal gang. By the time Martha was fifteen, she had carried out her first contract killing for the gang. Her criminal career had blossomed from there as she grew older. Now at twenty-nine, Martha's reputation and ruthless cruelty invoked much fear in her victims before she had even met them.

Today would be her third direct job for Don Clarence, head of the organized crime family that this contract was with. Don Clarence was a strange little man, and she suspected the term "little" was well applied. He was busy trying to stretch his dick by making her wait for him. Martha knew he would not be busy. Rather, he would be sat in his office behind his desk doing nothing while he made her wait for the meeting he had summoned her to. Well, he was paying for her time and could stick the power play. Martha had seen this sort of crap before from weak men. Strange, they all seemed to share that same common small characteristic.

Clarence LaRocca went by Don Clarence, head of the LaRocca crime family. Clarence had been born in Sicily, on New Terra, which orbited Alpha Centauri A, to his Italian parents. It was a bit of a cliché, but the family was very proud of the fact that they considered themselves to be "old blood Italian, proper Italian." Their forebears had helped found Sicily when New Terra was first colonized.

Clarence was now thirty-nine and had settled on Renfrewshire, around the star Varepsilon Indi, nine years ago. Clarence had emigrated after the New Terran guards had raided their family home, killed his father, and imprisoned his brothers. The guards did this in retaliation for the assassination of three judges. Unknown to the guards, these were assassinations for which Clarence had been the shooter.

Clarence had been vacationing at the time of the raid on the coast. The guards did not know where he was. His mother had escaped the guard's surveillance and traveled to where Clarence was staying. She brought him up to speed on the recent events. They hatched their plans, and a very nervous Syndicate pilot smuggled them both off New Terra the next day.

Now Don Clarence, the new head of the family, lived in the forgettable town of Paisley. Being somewhere forgettable was just what he and his mother wanted. You cannot be too careful nowadays; many bad things can happen. There was for example, that tragic forty-eight hours on New Terra that had occurred shortly after they left the planet. It would seem there was an inexplicable series of house fires and vehicle explosions. These had claimed the lives of six senior New Terran guards and another two judges, all their family and children.

That sort of mad shit never happened in Paisley. You would have to be some sort of madman to want to live on New Terra.

"Get her in here now." Don Clarence said.

Martha heard the shout through the door. The loud tones of the plump, manly, shouty short man, who ensured everyone could hear him being manly, left no one with any doubt that this was his voice. *How tiresome* Martha thought to herself and readied herself to stand. One of the knuckle draggers would doubtless arrive in a second or two.

Muscles 1, as Don Clarence referred to him, came out of the double doors next to Martha.

"He will see you now. Follow me. You figure the rest out yourself."

Again! He had said the same words on the two earlier occasions Martha had met him. He was like a pull-string doll, the recorded phrase coming out verbatim, the same every time with no tonal or timing difference. Martha considered for a moment just how much brains this brawn might have. Maybe he hated his job and was counting down every second until he could knock off his shift.

A Note to the Reader:

Don Clarence is a terrible, violent man, and that is how he likes to see himself. Any psychologist would describe him as a very sick, disturbed, unbalanced psychopath. Best to leave the electroshock therapy electricity turned on at the max setting and run away. If you are of a moderate or weak constitution, under eighteen, or a person of purity or virtue, then you might want to think about skipping chapter seventeen and going straight to chapter eighteen. I am not joking. Chapter seventeen contains sick shit with a real risk of nightmares and irreparable mental scarring. For everyone else, hold on to your seat. Shit is about to get wild. I have warned you.

CHAPTER 17

CORE – VAREPSILON INDI – RENFREWSHIRE
PAISLEY
DON CLARENCE'S HOUSE – OFFICE
DAY
CRYSTAL CLEAR

Again, Martha followed Muscles 1, who closed the doors behind them. Again, Don Clarence was sitting at his large desk, as she knew he would be. Again, he was wearing his black pinstripe suit, tapping his nails on the desk. *What a dick* Martha thought.

"Sit there, Don Clarence will be with you soon."

"Ah great, I am sorry I kept you waiting. I am just finishing up here. I won't be more than a few minutes."

Muscles 2 flanked Clarence. Muscles 1 retook the other flank.

Mathew stood at the large table in front of Clarence's desk, trembling, shackled. Clarence rose, picked up a massive frozen salami from his desk, and grabbed a mop that was propped against the wall.

"As I was saying, you owe me a lot of money."

Clarence walked around the table, swinging the massive sausage like a baseball bat, but in a phallic windmill-type motion.

"Man, that looks like a massive dildo or strap on, not a baseball bat," Mathew observed.

"Silence, you imbecile, or I will introduce you to a massive dildo firsthand. The bad news is I have lost faith that you can, will, or even want to pay your debt. To give me back my money."

Mathew now understood the seriousness of his situation. He let out a long, high-pitched fart as Clarence drew closer, stalking him.

Martha suppressed a giggle and smirk.

"What is to be done about this sorry state of affairs? I have one question for you. Do you want to take my massive frozen sausage or to clean my office for me?"

Clarence propped the mop next to Mathew and continued to swing the large salami, unaware of how camp this looked.

"Well, which is it to be?"

"Err, Don Clarence, err, well, I think I will go for—"

Clarence cracked the salami around Mathew's temple. Small bits of frozen salami shattered off, flying across the room. Pieces bounced off Muscles 1 and Muscles 2, who watched, unmoving. Muscles 2 glanced at Muscles 1 and mouthed, "Dildo bits." Then he gestured at Muscles 1's cheek, using his eyes.

Muscles 1, unseen by Clarence, tried to wipe away the fictional bit of sausage. This amused Muscles 2, which enraged Muscles 1. Both Muscles 1 and Muscles 2 suppressed any overt display as the side-sausage drama played out. Martha, also amused, contained her inner laughter as well. Clarence was oblivious, focused on Mathew.

"It was fucking rhetorical, you fucking dimwit."

Clarence, holding Mathew's hair, kicked Mathew in the back of the knees. He pushed Mathew's head forward. It bounced off the table, bursting Mathew's nose in a spray of blood. Clarence climbed onto the table. Mathew was now slumped over mumbling, with blood gushing from his nose and his movements weak.

"You will pay your debts to me."

With a swing and a crack, Clarence hefted the enormous frozen salami club into Mathew's skull again. More small bits of sausage flew off, landing in the spreading pool of blood.

"It is not complex. You pay. It is simple."

With a third crack, the sausage broke, half-landing next to Mathew's head. Mathew, unconscious now, lay still, his weak breath rippling the surface of the pool of blood.

"Bollocks."

Clarence jumped down, still holding his broken club. In disgust, Clarence threw the half sausage club down. It landed on the other side of Mathew's head. The pieces framed Mathew's head, half a sausage club on each side in a pool of congealing, tacky blood. Surrounded by small sausage-shard sprinkles.

"Useless treacherous salami! Fucking stupid sausage."

Martha swallowed as Clarence pulled down Mathew's trousers and underpants.

"I will show you fucking sausage. Look at all this mess. You're going to clean all this up, spraying it all over my table. I am going to fuck you up, you messy rat."

Clarence picked up the mop, then he forced the handle roughly into Mathew's anus. A faint moan came from Mathew, his last faint breaths. A foot and a half of the mop handle had disappeared, and the resistance was increasing. Clarence started kicking the head of the mop, forcing it in further. After four kicks, Martha heard a crackling sound as Clarence's kicks forced the handle past the cartilage in Mathew's throat. Into his mouth and past his teeth. Mathew was now slumped dead over the table, skewered by the mop, with one end poking two feet out of his mouth, the mop head a foot out of his ass. The dogs were howling outside. Clarence retook his seat and pressed the button on his desk phone.

"Tell that cook to come and see me right now. I am ready. Right, Martha, I think I have made my point, yes?"

Clarence stopped and stared at Martha, waiting. Martha realized Clarence expected a response. She racked her brains.

"Yes, sir."

Clarence continued to look with an unblinking stare at Martha. Martha understood Clarence expected more.

"Crystal clear, sir."

"Good. Well fuck off then, off you go. Either way, I will see you back here in a week, either with my gold or with that useless shite Tom in tow."

As Martha reached the door, it opened, and the cook came in. As Martha stepped out, Martha could hear Clarence talking.

CHAPTER 18

CORE – VAREPSILON INDI – RENFREWSHIRE
PAISLEY
DON CLARENCE'S HOUSE – HALLWAY
DAY
FEEDING TIME

"Get a photo, one of you. I am going to put Mathew on my fame wall. Cook, roast tonight, take the arms and legs off first. I don't want them to get burned again. They don't like it when burned. Put the arms and legs in the fridge. We will have them tomorrow. Tonight, we feed them the torso."

"I lit the BBQ when he arrived, sir," the cook said.

The door was closed, blocking any further sound. Martha paused; that howling she could hear made sense now.

"Fuck, fucking psycho."

She had never seen Clarence like this before. Martha left the building without delay.

CHAPTER 19

CORE – VAREPSILON INDI – RENFREWSHIRE
PAISLEY
DON CLARENCE'S HOUSE
HALL OUTSIDE OFFICE – DAY
STOPPING

Clarence watched Martha stop in the hall on the large screen. He smiled to himself. She knew the stakes now.

CHAPTER 20

**RIM – ROSS 154 – LOTHIAN
EDINBURGH
FANTASY DIVE BAR
TOILET STALL – MORNING
IN TRANSIT**

Captain Greg Garcia, forty-seven, was undercover. Greg was born a Tau. He had classic Latino looks and was raised a Catholic in New Tokyo on Stirlingshire in orbit around the 52 Tau Ceti system.

He was a captain in the resistance commandos, part of the Marine Recon Service unit. His unit was part of the Rhinos, from the resistance's Ground Assault Division. As a commando, he was at his core an infantry man. The commandos were all multidisciplinary soldiers trained in an array of weapons and vehicles. These would be ground vehicles. Aircraft all came under the Eagles, but he could at least manage a controlled crash in an aircraft if his life depended on it. But you would do better getting a proper pilot from the Eagles. The Eagles were the resistance's Air Assault Division.

Resistance Rhino's Logo

Resistance Eagle's Logo

Greg's subordinates called him Cold Greg behind his back. They thought he didn't know. Of course, he did, and the nickname warmed his heart.

The commandos were ground pounders. The sort of roles they would be tasked with ranged from traditional assault—whether overt or covert—through to support, evacuation, engineering, and intelligence. As a commando, many of Greg's missions would fall under the label of overt assault, where he would be part of a large team of soldiers.

However, for the last two years, many more of Greg's missions were joint operations with the Intelligence Regiment. When on an intelligence mission, Greg would always operate covertly, either as an individual or as part of a small team or cell behind enemy lines. Greg was excellent at the work and was on secondment with the Intelligence Regiment on an open-ended assignment. Intelligence officers were quick-thinking, but also nondescript and forgettable. Subtle was a big part of the intelligence officer's MO. As a commando foremost, Greg's MO was a lot more about plastic explosives, bullets, and knives. Subtle was not a thing Greg was strong on. Death was. He was very adept at handing out death when needed.

An intelligence officer might pick your pocket and take your secret from you, and you would not understand when or where you lost your secret. A commando might jump on your head, give you a quick silent kicking, and leave you bleeding. While they ran off with your secret and got airlifted out of the hot zone before you could even raise the alarm.

It was a huge simplification. There was a lot more overlap than the above description makes out. Intelligence officers were no shrinking violets and were just as deadly. The command brass had recognized, on occasion, the need to apply a more kinetic style of problem-solving that the commandos excelled at.

The practical day-to-day impact of this was that Greg was not engaged in the shady arts of intelligence-gathering—recruitment, coercion, and blackmail. The proper spies managed those. Greg's role was target prosecution. Intelligence officers would have gathered the information. Analysts would have digested it and come up with recommended targets and plan outlines to get close to them. They would then hand prosecution of the target to someone like Greg. Greg would infiltrate the target's world and take them out. And I don't mean to eat dinner. After exfiltrating away into the dark.

Greg wasn't just an assassin, but killing for the resistance was part of his job. Wasn't it part of all soldiers' jobs? It certainly was on missions like these, while the cold war with the Imperium raged in the shadows. This was a cold and very shady conflict. Greg often found that his mission to disrupt the Imperium war machine took him into areas of organized crime on both sides of the line.

Greg's current target was called Don Clarence. Head of the New Terra LaRocca crime family. This mission had taken Greg into Tom's world. Tom was a nobody. Tom had won big in the past and that was how he had gotten his hands on *The Peregrine.* He was a useless gambler and lost more than he won, like many others. In Tom's case, however, this had landed him in hock to Don Clarence. There was no way Tom could now pay back the debt. Greg's mission was not to save Tom. There was the genuine possibility that Clarence would kill or have an assassin kill Tom before the year end.

Tom was Greg's ticket for getting closer to Don Clarence, even if that meant Tom needed to be served up as an appetizer. It was up to Greg to control and guide that introduction. So Greg did not care one way or the other about Tom's life. He cared about Tom's welfare insofar as Greg could further his mission's aim and get him closer to Don Clarence.

Of course, life is never so simple. Central Command was diverting Greg's plans to bring Tom into his control. Instead of handing Tom over to get close to Don Clarence, Greg's new orders meant he now needed to co-opt Tom's help. Intelligence reported that a critical piece of computer hardware had fallen into Imperium hands. Intelligence analysts thought the enemy didn't know what they had got under their noses. Greg's updated mission was to extract the computer and use Tom, his crew, and his ship, *The Peregrine.* To transport Greg and the computer back to secure resistance custody. Intelligence had not confirmed it, but it was believed the computer was in the evidence lockup at the Imperium's customs office here in Edinburgh. Greg and Tom's current location was why the updated mission had passed to Greg. The thoughts at HQ were that Greg should rob the customs office before the guards could move the computer on. A potential bit of grit in the gears was that there had been whispers that Don Clarence had met with the expert master assassin known as Martha. Worse, Tom was the likely target for debt and life recovery.

Greg hid in a toilet stall in Fantasy Bar, a seedy dive bar in Edinburgh. He was sitting on the toilet with his legs wedged against the door. Greg was meeting up with Tom and looking to move things along.

First, however, he needed to report in and get last-minute intelligence updates. That is how Greg found himself to be in this fine location.

Greg keyed the code to access his radio. He could hear the static of the open channel. He pushed the Ready button and waited. The radio electronics connected to his message drop box on COMMS-NET. Drop boxes supplied a secure version of voicemail systems you found in corporations. This, however, was the secure military version known as COMMS-NET. The civilian network was RIM-NET, and, in the Core, they knew it as COL-NET.

There was a quiet beep on his radio and the familiar radio AI voice came on. Greg had the volume turned down low.

"FLASH TRAFFIC—High priority tasking for Agent 47536. Details after challenge code."

Greg keyed the challenge code into his radio. The radio combined it with the embedded code in the handshake message signal and the code blown into the radio handset hardware. It passed the code block through a secure hashing algorithm to generate a unique onetime hash. The radio transmitted this hash back to the COMMS-NET AI.

"Confirmed Agent 47536 identified. Message follows:

"Spies tell us Martha is in transit to get Tom. Enlist Tom to do the heist with you. Target confirmed at the local customs office. We believe they don't know what they have. Get the asset back to us on *The Peregrine* as planned. The heist needs to happen in the next twenty-four hours. Martha must report back to Clarence, seven days from now in person. End of message, please record your reply now."

"Wilco," Greg said. He now had the information he needed. His brain was racing, planning.

"Thank you. Command out."

Greg turned off his radio and left the toilet for the bar to return to Tom.

CHAPTER 21

RIM – ROSS 154 – LOTHIAN
EDINBURGH
FANTASY DIVE BAR – MAIN BAR
EARLY AFTERNOON
TOSS THE KEYS

Greg entered the bar, and the noise from the band crashed over him. It wasn't so much that it was bad because it was loud with a shouty front man with amps turned up way too high. The problem was that the music was truly beyond awful. It would not surprise Greg if someone told him the band had to pay the bar to let them play. Greg knew he was getting on a bit at forty-seven, but he could not conceive of any generation of society or demographic that would consider this "music," to be "right on, right on."

However, this was the reason Greg came to the bar. The dire music kept most customers away during the day. The drunks found here, in the morning and early afternoon, would tune out the awful music. They drank in personal silence. Many more drunks passed out to the awful lullaby, next to or in their beers.

The background noise would make it hard for anyone to overhear or surveil Greg's conversations. For a covert operator, this bar was perfect for conducting business in. Besides the audio din, there were long lines of sight and multiple entrances and exits. It meant Greg could see anyone sitting near his table and entering or exiting the bar.

It was the sort of bar where your shoes made sticking noises when walking across the floor. The table would pull at the skin on your forearms if you rested them on the table.

Fantasy Bar was open 24-7, as the bright neon sign in front of the mirror behind the bar proclaimed. Happy hour's Double Mayhem was from ten till eleven, followed by Triple Trouble from eleven to midnight.

The posters advertised strippers from midnight to one in the morning. It was an equal opportunities bar; the poster announced you could see various people getting naked and dancing on different nights of the week. Men, women, drag, trans, dwarfs, doms, subs, fatties, thinnies, hairies (think hairy legs, chests, backs, scalps, and faces—

nothing to do with groins), fairies, and baldies (think old bald men—again nothing to do with groins). They were all available and literally on show.

There was another poster promoting a Furries Fancy Dress Fest. The poster showed various masked animal critters with tails, enjoying themselves and one another.

Another poster proclaimed entries open for the monthly Custard Flag Takedown, where first prize was one thousand credits. Greg had studied the poster and photographs from last month, trying to understand what this game entailed. It seemed to be a capture-the-flag competition where, judging by the pictures, the contestants were attached by short bungee cords to their own corner of the ring, with a harness clipped to their back. The aim was to reach the opponent's corner of the ring across the diagonal. To capture their flag and raise it on the flagpole in the middle of the ring. Of course, the opponent would come in the opposite direction, trying to get the other contestant's flag or recapture their own at the same time. The bungee cord was there to pull contestants backward off their feet. While the opposing contestant was trying to knock them off their feet and steal their flag back. If that wasn't insane enough, their teammates would throw balloons full of custard and direct hosepipes pumping out high-pressure custard at the flag thief, to get them to slide off their feet, pulled back by the bungee cord. Greg thought this sounded like great fun. The custard was a little over the top, but it would also help keep the injuries down once the custard covered everyone. Greg had played something similar when completing his basic training and learning controlled aggression.

Come ten o'clock, the bar would bounce with every student and under twenty-five in Edinburgh who wanted to get lucky that night. Most here would be hoping to get into triple trouble, so to speak.

At one in the afternoon, the bar was dead. The regular evening crowd was still asleep in bed or found among the bodies passed out at the tables. Slumped next to the afternoon's alcoholics, drinking cheap, warm beer.

Greg walked across the bar past the sleepy drunk at the table near the corner where Tom was sitting. The sleepy drunk's arm knocked over his glass, spilling more sticky beer over the table. The soaking stirred the sleepy drunk from his slumber.

"Balls, barkeep, more beer!" The sleepy drunk shouted.

Sleepy Drunk fell forward into the beer puddle and resumed his drunken dreams. The bartender had been polishing a glass. There was no one else to serve. He had been waiting for this moment and wondered how much longer he could play this game with the sleepy drunk. Without a word, the bartender put down the glass he had been cleaning and picked up a cloudy fresh glass and pulled a warm beer for his repeat customer.

"I am not paid enough for this crap," he said. And then louder, "Right with you, sir."

Alex, the bartender, loathed his job, and he loathed the customers. He loathed the tiny tips. Alex loathed hospitality and how it had somehow, without asking him, become his career. Alex was thirty-nine and he could see the future. The future revealed to him that twenty years from now, he would still be here. Polishing an already clean glass, serving shit beer to shit customers, who would occasionally shit themselves at their tables. Alex could fake a smile and positivity, so he would never get fired. This was, in fact, the very thing dooming him for the next twenty years, he foresaw.

The expert barman finished his pour with a two-inch-thick head and warm beer running down the outside of the warm glass. He walked the beer over to the table, then scanned the watch on the sleepy drunk's wrist before releasing the beer from his safe custody. The bartender placed the glass in the beer puddle, just short of touching the sleepy drunk's arm. This game had sold two extra beers already, and he figured it would be good for two more sales.

"Here you go, sir."

He left the sleepy drunk to his dreams, who thanked him by letting out a loud burp.

"Ugh, yes, stop nagging me. I will take the trash out in a minute. We can, ha ha, oh, Emma. Ooh."

There was another large burp and a crash as the drunk knocked over the new beer. The beer slick spread over his table and became part of his carnal dreams of Emma. The bartender picked up another dirty glass in anticipation.

"Oh, Emma, you're so naughty. I am all wet."

There was a loud snore from the drunk, back in dreamland as the beer soaked into him. The bartender looked disappointed. Alex would have to wait a bit before his next sale. Greg went to the corner table, away from the drunks and music.

"Tom, you have trouble coming."

"What?"

"Clarence has sent his assassin, Martha. She is on her way and will be here, maybe later today, tomorrow at the latest. He has sent her to collect. Or to collect you, either will work for him. She will want the money or your plan to get her the money."

"Shite." Tom took a big swig of his sour, warm beer.

"We should go back to your ship. I have an idea of how we get you out of this mess. We must get going. We have to be quick on this."

Greg stood up, leaving a pile of cash for the drinks. Tom stood and pulled on his coat. He had no better ideas or choices, or in fact, any choice. Tom followed Greg out.

Greg had read the intelligence document HQ had sent him on Tom, but gods, the man was just so wet. Tom Wee Bit Wet the file said his nickname was. That was a joke for saying the blooming obvious. Greg reflected on the file. Tom Wilks was thirty-five. He was from Aberdeen on Lothian world and was Asian. The file listed him as a privateer cargo hauler with his ship, *The Peregrine*. That was the most interesting thing about Tom, thought Greg. Owning a ship like *The Peregrine* was beyond unusual. The file had explained that Tom had won the ship in a ridiculously improbable bet, playing cards. We are talking so improbable that anything you can conceive of happening in the universe was more likely than a blind bet on the turn of those cards happening.

Tom was a terrible gambler. His fellow gamblers around the table worked hard, with ever-growing confidence, to relieve Tom of his money. The problem was that Tom was not just useless; he was also clueless. His fellow gamblers considered Tom did not know how to play this game. He was blind to the risks of all the different hands and bets he was making. Tom felt zero pressure because he had no clue what he was doing.

When Tom had said, "Tell you what, big man, toss the keys to your spaceship on the table and I will go all in, we will see who the better pilot is," Tom hadn't been trying to goad the man into making the bet. It just happened, that is what he did.

The worst card player the guys at the table had seen in, well, ever, had just bet on the most improbable hand anyone could think of. That he would surrender the rest of his cash in one go. If only his opponent was manly enough to throw his keys in the ring. The guy had studied Tom's stupid face and could not find any deceit or suppressed emotion, fear, or anticipation. The same dumb eyes stared back at him. Tom might as well have written "mug me, I am an idiot" on his forehead.

He had thrown *The Peregrine*'s keys into the circle and Tom had gone all in. The card was being turned, and the universe wobbled. Beyond anyone's expectation, the most unlikely riskiest bet ever had come in and Tom had won *The Peregrine* and the pool of chips.

No one could accuse Tom of cheating or trying to bluff or sucker them in with his long losing streak of total incompetence. From their perspective, Tom was incompetent at cards and that fact alone had saved Tom's life that night as the four other players let out whistles.

"Well fuck me."

"Ouch."

"Nice ship, man. Shit."

"Don't see that happen every day."

Tom had his chips packed up and armed floor security escorted Tom out of the cardroom via the cashier's counter and put him into a taxi. They had no interest in cleaning Tom up off the floor and walls, and judging by the face of the ship's former owner, it was time for Tom to leave and go home.

This is how the worst gambler ever won the love of his life, *The Peregrine.*

CHAPTER 22

**RIM – ROSS 154 – LOTHIAN
EDINBURGH
PORT DISTRICT
MOMENTS LATER
A GUNSLINGER**

Tom was visibly nervous.

"What are you thinking?" Tom asked Greg.

Greg observed Tom and tried to figure out the best approach. "We can talk about it on your ship."

Tom looked unhappy. Greg felt Tom was thinking a bit too much. Greg looked around the street. The footfall was light. No one was within listening distance. He had wanted to do this on the ship. But he had to get Tom onto the ship first for the conversation to happen. Tom looked set to bolt and run for the hills. Greg assessed the risk as low if done here in public. The chances of being overheard seemed low, even though he still thought of it as a risk.

"A heist. We are going to rob the local Imperium customs office. They have plenty of taxes, seized goods, and money in their lockup."

Tom stopped walking and his face formed an "oh" expression while thinking. "I am well fucked."

"More than you know."

Greg had read past reports of how Don Clarence liked to feed his victims to his pack of hunting hounds. Martha was no saint either when she was in one of her darker moods. Greg suspected they would both consider their work artistic. Yep, Tom was likely very fucked.

They approached *The Peregrine* at her loading gate. Tom keyed the device on his wrist. The pedestrian access ramp of his ship descended. The ship's gunslinger robot, GS1, stepped outside, pistol drawn but down by its thigh. The robot took another step forward and brought the pistol up, aiming it straight at Greg's forehead. In the military, you didn't fuck around, shooting people in the head. His training had taught him to aim for center chest. Pointing guns at people's heads was something you found in films and books, not real life. Serious trained killers didn't fuck about being flashy or gangster. They aimed for the chest; they aimed to kill. Greg did not think for one second the robot was being gangster by aiming at his head. Greg knew the robot was both skilled and serious.

As the robot was moving and bringing up the gun, Greg watched as time went into slow mode. The robot moved its trigger finger that was lying flat against the gun's body to the side of the trigger. The robot inserted its finger through the trigger guard and rested it lightly on the trigger. Greg felt very uncomfortable with the robot aiming at his head.

Greg's military experience meant that he could tell how the gun was set up from the selector switches on the handgrip. It was in three-round burst mode. The safety was off. The pistol cocked and the robot aimed, ready to shoot. Trained killers kept their weapons in single-shot mode rather than burst. Both to conserve ammunition and better maintain aim with the gun's recoil. Multishot burst mode was more filmic bollocks. Greg guessed the gun's recoil would have no effect on the robot and rounds two and three would drill into the hole created by the first round. Greg considered there was no doubt the robot had loaded the gun with hollow points. Greg would put money on the gun having a double-action trigger, likely with a 4.5 kg pull weight. Four and a half kilos of pressure was all it would take the robot to put a three-round burst into Greg's head. The robot's strength, even in its fingers, was much greater, and the robot had lightning-quick reflexes. Greg knew that if the robot had decided it was going to kill Greg, then he was already dead and would be decapitated. Knowing these details did not calm Greg's nerves; quite the opposite. At least it wouldn't hurt, Greg thought. He wouldn't even know. Things would just stop.

The ship was Tom's world, one of which he was master and commander.

"Gunslinger GS1, stand down."

The ship's robot GS1 holstered its pistol. There might have been a fraction of a second pause. The rest of the holstering movement was so quick and precise, which highlighted the pause. No pause by human standards, but for such a fast and precise machine, the pause seemed unnecessary and unsettling. It was almost as if the robot had been saying to Greg, "I am holstering my weapon because Tom asked me to, but I could have pulled the trigger, ending your life right here during that pause."

Greg let out a slow breath he hadn't realized he had been holding. Greg was in no doubt. In all his years of service, in all the close calls and injuries, the two seconds that had just dragged past were the closest Greg had ever been to death.

Tom paused for a moment and admired his ship. *The Peregrine* was the love of Tom's life. Tom walked past the ship's robot GS1 leading the way into *The Peregrine*. As Greg walked up the ramp, he should have been smiling. He knew he had Tom on the hook now, but Greg was still processing the incident outside. In Greg's unit, that model of K-Bot was called a Cleaner.

CHAPTER 23

**CORE – ALPHA CENTAURI A – NEW TERRA
AYLESBURY
SUPREME COMMANDER'S OFFICE
AFTERNOON
BRAINS**

Lieutenant Hot Seat, as the Imperium Supreme Commander Bob referred to him, was waiting for the signal to continue. He hadn't been called Hot Seat by his parents. It was one of Bob's gifts to him, along with high blood pressure, on day one of his appointment to this cursed position as Bob's PA.

The lieutenant remembered what Bob had said on that day. "Right, you moron, you are new here, so I will explain; henceforth your name is Hot Seat. Because I want you to never forget that is where you are sitting. Right in the front row, center stage in the hot seat, and I am looking directly at you. Remember this, and maybe we will still talk on your anniversary."

Lieutenant Hot Seat recalled the sinking feeling he felt back at the start of what he came to realize was his stint on death row. When he had woken that morning seven months ago, he thought that working for the leader of the Imperium might be valuable. Maybe he would earn more money and be able to retire earlier and stop working and enjoy his remaining time.

It didn't take him long to understand that while he might well stop working earlier than retirement age, there would be no bonus or retirement time. His remaining time would get shorter, and he would not enjoy it. *Well, I will never run out of retirement funds* he thought.

Resignation was not an option. Well of course it was an option, just not one you would ever put on your "where-I-see-myself-in-five-years'-time" plan. Although it would fit on the "where-I-see-myself-in-five-minutes'-time" plan. The lieutenant did not need a written plan to remember the key bullet points.

Hot Seat had navigated treacherous waters in Bob's service. Many hungry sharks lurked in the water, and there were savage rocks that would tear open the hull of his small boat as he struggled against the waves. The damn hope wouldn't die, and he kept trying.

Bob was a bastard, a polite but sarcastic bastard. Scratch that, Bob wasn't polite. The only person who could wrap Bob around her fingers was Brenda from HR. It was a mystery to Hot Seat how the dynamic of that relationship worked.

Stacy, Bob's personal secretary, had a far less abuse-filled working life. Although she could not match Brenda for the finger-wrapping. Hot Seat had his suspicions and believed Stacy's secret was that she wrapped herself around Bob often. While that might make her a little submissive, Brenda was both dominant and oblivious, with very thick skin.

Hot Seat wasn't wrapping or being wrapped, even though it might be worth it for a nice quiet life, as he didn't raise Bob's interest. His function was to be berated, as far as he could tell. *At least it kept him on his toes* Hot Seat thought. Although he conceded that with the delivery of today's briefing update report, he might get the afternoon off work. *It would be nice to have an early finish* Hot Seat considered.

It wasn't even like it was his fault. His job was just to deliver the reports. It was the idiots on the ground who wrote the reports on what they were, or more accurately, not doing. The various tasks executed seemed devoid of any competence or thought.

A big part of the problem was that the Imperium guards in the Rim systems could not actually be Imperium guards. Rather, they were Imperium Shipping and Border Officers, a.k.a. customs officers, as far as the Rim systems were concerned. The uneasy truce between the Imperium and the Rim banned guards from being based on one another's worlds. But because of the intersystem traffic—both cargo shipping and people traveling—Bob had cleaved out a small exception. Customs agents and border personnel could check visas, raise tariff charges, and monitor cargo loaded and passengers on intersystem ships. While they were guards, they could not overtly work as such in Rim systems. Instead, the guards would covertly hire local contracting mercenaries and raiders to conduct any local muscle tasks that the guards longed to do themselves. The guards would instead be stuck with the numbing nonguard paperwork and brain-draining duties of customs agent, shipping adviser, or transport embarkation assistant. This ensured the onset of atrophy in the guards' brains, demotivation, and endless dreams of becoming mercenaries. The guards who performed the duties of customs, embarkation, or shipping advisors were not what you might term dynamic or on the ball.

Well, not long now, time will tell Hot Seat thought to himself. Bob had now moved the two sheets of paper on his desk several times, stacking them, spreading them out, then moving them around the desk. They were the only thing on Bob's desk. Bob was a stickler for a tidy desk, that is, an empty desk. The one bit of joy in Hot Seat's life was the delivery of new paper reports. More paper and randomly bent paper clips. Staplers with no staples and red biros. Old correction fluid that had long since set solid. Any of these that Hot Seat could dump onto Bob's desk would make it a good day.

Then there was the final paper shuffle. The two sheets placed on top of each other again and pushed into the back-right-hand corner of Bob's desk. With a perfect one-inch boundary between the paper's edge and the edge of the desk. Bob looked up at his PA. Ready and go.

"Apologies Supreme Commander. The actions of the local guards, err, I mean shipping advisers, surprised us. They got sent an old outstanding arrest warrant, err, a temporary seizure notice, on their local system net, from their Imperium colleagues on Clackmannanshire. For some twat's truck theft, which was the listed owner's name, sir. In parallel, our tax recovery agent went to seize his truck, only to discover it was already stolen. That is why we missed it, because it was on their local net and the owner twat did not report the theft.

"Then local contracting bounty hunters on Lothian detained a Lauren Silva and a companion, Jack Gill. The records don't mention a computer at the scene. The computer's whereabouts are unknown. Presumed dumped in the desert somewhere before the arrest happened. It also seems they were involved in the death of a bounty hunter and destruction of his vehicle by making him drive into a tree. A straightforward case of arson with intent, so I am told by our local insurance assessor, err, guard."

"You are telling me. She survived the gunship raid I sent to kill her. You told me she was dead, despite no identifiable body. Because your fighters turned all the villagers' bodies into mush. Daniels revealed nothing before we let him go. Lauren stole a vehicle you didn't know about, then evaded and disappeared. You believe she built the cursed computer? She got arrested and now you have lost the computer. You cretinous fuckwit!"

"Lauren went to another planet, sir, in the same system, sir! No one does that, they all go further. We still don't know how she managed it. They didn't think of looking so close. They checked other systems further away and on the original planet. We believe she built the computer because we have since found the delivery notes for components that she ordered delivered to a drop-shipping warehouse on Lothian."

"You useless, useless wankpuffin. Systems can have more than one planet! You know what is going to happen next?" Bob asked.

Lieutenant Hot Seat shook his head in the negative, although he had a pretty good idea.

"No, sir."

"Shoot yourself in the head."

"Yes, sir."

Lieutenant Hot Seat took out his sidearm and saluted with it to his temple. Hot Seat's closing thoughts were twofold. Thank the gods I am free of this bastard. Followed by: was it next week the inflatable sheep would be delivered? That would be a fun day in the office when the anonymized indecency report he had filed hit the desk of the public decency watchdog. The rhyme played in Hot Seat's mind. *Oh, fluffy sheep (oh, fluffy sheep) are wonderful, they're white and so fluffy, oh fluffy sheep are wonderful.* Hot Seat thought about the edited images and faked video clip he had sent with the report he had made up on Bob's sheep shenanigans. Hot Seat thought *Fuck you, Bob* and pulled the trigger.

"For fuck's sake, send me one with working brains for once."

Bob saw that there were now spots of blood spray on his desk and on the papers resting in the corner. *Was that a lump of brains? Ew, ew. Hot Seat will have to go*, Bob thought. Oh no, he had taken care of that problem already.

ACT I TO ACT II
INTERLUDE

CLEANERS

Greg was thinking about Tom and the ship, in particular about GS1, the gunslinger robot, a 101 version a.k.a. Cleaner. Which had just faced Greg down outside and could have taken his head off.

The resistance commandos called the 101 version Cleaners. The Rhinos came across the first version known as the K-Bot-65 near the end of the Final War between 2765 and 2766.

K-Bot-65 was a pussycat compared with the last version built, the K-Bot-101. The 65 version was literally on wheels and was nicknamed Cart. It came along three years before Greg's birth in 2768, when Greg's future unit had been fighting Imperium forces in the open, on another world, rather than in this current cold war.

The K-Bot-79 version, which the Imperium released in 2779, was a vast improvement on the 65 version. Because of the 79 version's effectiveness during the Cold Skirmish Years (2770–2805), it had earned itself the nickname Demon 79. Many have since argued that the 79 model was the best K-Bot model ever, and its replacement, the 95 version released in 2800, was an unnecessary, bug-ridden, stupid mistake. The 95 version's nickname was Stupid POS.

Greg would join the Rhinos, aged twenty-two, in 2790, eleven years before the K-Bot-101's introduction, right in the middle of the Skirmish Years.

The big problems with the K-Bots started in 2800 with the late K-Bot-95 version that was, besides being five years behind schedule, full of bugs and security flaws. This drove the rushed development of a new release, the K-Bot-101 version, rushed to production in 2801 with corners cut to meet the deadline. This would turn out to be near the end of the Cold Skirmish Years, which, as mentioned earlier, ended in 2805. The K-Bot-101, sometimes referred to as the Fergus-build variant, was literally a killer version. It earned itself the nickname Cleaner, and was the proverbial straw that ended the K-Bots.

Cleaners were old tech now, about three years out-of-date. Because the Imperium forces no longer used them, not since their withdrawal from combat service in 2803 and termination in 2804. This happened because the Fergus-build variant and their central control programming unit had a nasty habit of losing all control and shooting everyone in sight.

The Imperium commanders had considered this a bit of a design flaw. One that had a demoralizing effect on their troops, and so it might be best to go back to their old-fashioned ways. Humans were a safe pair of hands for pulling the trigger. They could guide dumb machines rather than these psycho-killer smart machines with their primitive AIs.

Humans were excellent at pulling the trigger and going full postal psycho was rare among the ranks, unlike these robots. None of the troops enjoyed being around the robots. Everyone was waiting to get shot in the back by their own robot support units.

The Imperium command had retired those twitchy death machines and had them all destroyed. It is very rare to come across a surviving one nowadays, let alone two on the same ship under a single man's control, following his orders and still breathing.

Now you might consider it bizarre, but that had been a blow for the resistance. The robots would gun down all humans with impressive effect, no matter their uniform. In early 2802, the resistance had figured out a way to use this. It was all because of some clever nerd who needed to get out from the squirrel works lab more and get a girlfriend. Angus was almost laughed out of the room when he suggested his nonkinetic solution to the robots. You know what military types are like. They want to blow shit up.

Angus's solution did not blow up, and in the minds of some that made it crap and boring. The resistance meeting chair had called everyone to order. He made them listen to Angus's presentation.

Angus envisioned a control broadcast unit he code-named Piper. Nothing like a traditional military weapon. Drones could fly Piper in and drop it by parachute, launched from rocket launchers, stuck to trees and buried in holes in the ground or submerged in a bog.

What did it do? Nothing. It just sat there, not causing a ruckus, listening to all the communications it intercepted. It didn't say a word or relay any signals and no intelligence data. Information gathering was not its function, no matter what it heard. For it was a behind-the-lines commando brigade-type weapon, not an intelligence-type one. It was sneaky, yes, but it would get very kinetic in just a moment.

What it did was hide and wait, wait until it heard the handshake signals from the robots that had earned the nickname Cleaners. It was a good nickname. It described what the robots did and was a lot snappier than the Imperium name for this unit. K-Bot-101 series serial number: f79440b7-ceb1-4617-8f20-8aaa128a192c. K-Bot-101 stood for Kill Robot

Series 101. It was sort of good, but it would go on and list its UUID serial number. It was just a huge, jumbled mouthful and didn't encapsulate the full, unique horror of who a friendly, allied K-Bot might be targeting. Cleaners didn't have any friends, and they didn't care. They didn't even like other Cleaners, but they would coordinate with other Cleaners if it meant they could indulge in their favorite activity.

See, the problem with the latest version started in 2801 with the blueprints. The K-Bot's designers had no clue regarding how to approach the development of the robot's self-contained command-and-control AI system. Someone called Harry had a "good idea," which was embraced by the "nontechnical middle management team" responsible for the technical leadership of the "technical team." Basically, they typically managed the points for the sprints. They got a violent serial murderer on death row out of prison and scanned his brain. And this is how Fergus became the controlling intelligence who was bequeathed a military spec armored chassis. The robot's coordination and reflexes could hold, aim, and fire a heavy Imperium machine gun in each arm. The robot could even wield the heavier vehicle-mounted twenty-millimeter cannons, but it needed to use both arms for that.

Angus had learned what Harry had done and set about exploiting it.

When a Cleaner got the hump, Fergus's baser instincts would push their way to the forefront. Fergus didn't like humans, all humans; it thought they should all die, and Fergus enjoyed killing.

The designer made a superb choice by selecting someone like Fergus to operate the latest killer-robot command-and-control unit. The weapon was as rotten as could be, all the way to its core.

Piper would lie there, waiting and listening, until it heard Fergus coming. At that point, Piper would say "we need to talk!" and start talking shit at Fergus. Piper was a psyops weapon. Its job was to get into the K-Bot's head and trigger Fergus to flip the fuck out and go on an unhinged killing rampage.

The Piper program was adaptive and coded with a broad range of attack vectors it could use to question and bend human captives. Human psychologists had created these techniques over the years for the military.

Piper and the K-Bot would chatter away to each other at computer speeds. From the point it detected a K-Bot in range, Piper would start its targeted babbling before the K-Bot had even walked one hundred meters.

The conversation had been raging backward and forward for about two hundred years of K-Bot computer time.

Piper would keep talking shit at the K-Bot for years and years in computer time until it made Fergus wig out and go wild. The K-Bot would send new guns free orders to any other K-Bots within the five-kilometers range on the secure point-to-point infrared laser links.

Imagine the scene. You are part of an attacking force of one thousand Imperium infantry walking forward to engage the resistance. There are six armored K-Bot units spread out among the ranks. Each carrying backpacks with belt-fed ammunition for the heavy machine guns carried in each arm.

The IR signal arrives and is rebroadcast. The K-Bot the Piper had first turned to insanity, had started the countdown.

Tromp, tromp, tromp, across the field go one thousand Imperium soldiers. The counter hits zero and all six K-Bots press their trigger fingers in each hand. Each of the twelve heavy machine guns among the troops are primed, each moving and tracking down any human target, firing a brief burst, and moving on.

Heavy rounds cut straight through the light armor carried by infantry ground forces. The field fills with the bodies of downed soldiers and spent casings. The backpacks each hold two thousand rounds for each gun. The six K-Bots have enough ammunition for twenty-four bullets for every one of the one thousand soldiers in the formation. The K-Bots will run out of humans before they run out of bullets. They are excellent shots and didn't need anywhere close to twenty-four rounds to dismember these poor hapless soldiers. When there is no one left to shoot, they stop and wait, still ready, still raging.

Now, before the commanders had learned the error of their ways, they would send in multiple helicopters with medical personnel to treat and triage the few wounded people on the ground who were still breathing. The cases that needed and would benefit from rapid medivac for more extensive treatment would get airlifted out. That was the plan, at least.

The first time this happened, the K-Bots hadn't seen this sort of behavior before. These personnel scurrying among the dead and dying bodies of their nemesis in their white, blood-smeared coats.

The K-Bots figured it out. White coats were like sniffer dogs, here to find anyone still alive and take them away. The IR laser flashed its signal around the K-Bot team and the counter started from just three this time.

When the guns started firing again, they targeted the white coats, the helicopters that had delivered them there, and the survivors. After all, no one would leave; no one would need a helicopter. It didn't take long, and they all still had bullets left, so the K-Bots resumed waiting and raging.

The resistance forces knew very well not to approach anywhere near while those reckless, unhinged robot Cleaners were there. Everyone was a target, not just Imperium forces. Until the Imperium strafed the field with aircraft cannon fire and destroyed the waiting pack of K-Bots. The resistance troops would go nowhere near the field.

The Piper units were cheap and easy to manufacture. They were mass deployed across the battlefield and remained there hidden, listening.

This pattern repeated itself. Eventually, in 2803, the Imperium command removed the K-Bots from all duties. The delay to the decision to remove them from the front lines had cost the lives of one hundred and fifteen thousand Imperium soldiers and one scientist called Harry. His creation did not kill Harry, but a firing squad killed Harry because of it. The one hundred and fifteen thousand meant Harry held the responsibility and record for the greatest number of allied-friendly kills.

Greg knew all too well what the gunslinger robot was and what it was skilled at. He was not an idiot. Greg was in touch with his emotions because they helped to keep him alive. Someone else could have all the faux bravado, banter, and bollocks. Greg was a professional, and he knew how to listen. Thus, when the gunslinger robot put its gun in his face and paused before holstering it when ordered, Greg listened. Greg was smart enough to stay alive. Greg knew his life had all been in the robot's hand and that 4.5 kg trigger weight.

Until Greg received new information that would make him reassess. GS1 was a Cleaner and a deadly hazard to every human being it could hit with a bullet, which was everyone within range.

K-Bots had become very rare nowadays. They were still as deadly as they had been when the Imperium scrubbed them from duty. All because of the unhinged Fergus inside, all of them desperate to come out and play.

ACT II - PART I

CHAPTER 24

CORE – ALPHA CENTAURI A – NEW TERRA
AYLESBURY
SUPREME COMMANDER'S OFFICE
MORNING
OPTION TWO

Bob sat behind his desk, looking depressed. His desk now had ten separate piles of paper stacked on it. The piles were the source of Bob's depression.

The speaker phone on Bob's desk beeped and Bob reached to answer it.

"Lord Bob, I have HR waiting for you," Stacy said.

"Okay, what is it regarding?"

"I will check for you, Lord Bob, one moment. She says it's regarding the candidates for your new PA position."

"Is it Brenda from HR?"

"Yes, Lord."

"Ugh, oh bollocks. Brenda! She is so damn enthusiastic. That is another position we will need to fill. Stacy, I have told you before, I am not 'Lord' or 'Lord Bob.' While I may be godlike, I am no one's Lord. Supreme Commander, evil overlord. Balls, nemesis, Bob, even, only for you and in private. Anyway, put that silly dumass Brenda through."

"Send her through, sir?"

"Yes, you said the soul-sucking witch was on hold."

"No, sir, waiting in my office for you, sir."

"Ah, next you are going to tell me I am on speakerphone."

"Very perceptive, sir."

"I see."

"Yes, sir."

"Brenda, you silly twit, please come in."

"Sir, she is coming now."

Brenda entered Bob's office, bubbling with HR positivity.

"Good morning, your Supreme Lordship."

Bob sighed and shook his head, aware she had addressed him that way on purpose, having just heard his comments to Stacy. "Please take a seat, Brenda."

Brenda parked herself in the chair opposite Bob, scowling at his messy, cluttered desk.

"We have the resumes in for your new PA position."

Brenda hefted another pile of paper onto Bob's desk. Bob regarded the additional thin pile with disgust.

"Thank you for filtering the applicants for me."

"We haven't, sir."

Bob sighed. It was going to be one of those sorts of conversations. "Ok. What have we got?"

"Well, we beat the bushes for you, sir. You have three folders in that pile. The top folder is candidates that applied for the position."

Bob picked up the very thin folder and opened it.

"Where is the rest of the file? There is only a single résumé in here."

"Yes, sir, that is Howard. The next folder is group two. These are the motivated candidates."

Bob picked up the second thin folder and opened it.

"This is also somewhat thin, Brenda."

"That file is also complete, sir. We headhunted fifty promising candidates we thought should apply for the position. We motivated them with your alternative that they could get shot in the head if they preferred, instead of applying."

"I see. You said candidates, there is only a single file in here."

"Sorry, yes, that's right. We motivated fifty candidates. The candidate you have there, sir, is Alfred."

"Where are the other forty-nine?"

"They all chose option two, sir. I am not sure Alfred understood the proposition, sir. You will be best using short words with him."

"Hmm."

"Moving on. The third file contains the expedited processing pile."

Bob picked up the third file, which was the entirety of the remaining pile. "There are thirty-four candidates in that file, sir. Twenty-eight of them you are familiar with, you incarcerated them for various performance-, sorry, lack-of-performance-related issues. The final six are all on the sex offenders list—serial rape, child abuse. There is one case involving a donkey—the donkey was the man, if you get my meaning, sir. For interest, sir, I hear even by donkey standards he was a well-hung donkey."

"Okay, so in summary, Brenda, you have found me one candidate who applied, one candidate that we think can't spell his own name."

"I am kind of surprised he typed it at all, sir."

"Six disgusting candidates you are going to thank for their applications and for bringing themselves to my attention. Have them flogged to within an inch. Afterward, they can reflect on the extra ten years of hard labor they just won. And twenty-eight criminal, incompetent people who are trying to toady favor so they can get off their prison sentences I gave them. Is that right, Brenda?"

"Yes, sir, a robust response, I think."

"Add five years to the twenty-eight's sentences across the board, the cheeky fuckers. Send dimwit Alfred for a lobotomy. He may get smarter. That leaves us with Howard."

"Yes, sir, that is right."

"Okay,set up an appointment with ..."

"Howard, sir."

Bob shook his head in total disgust. "Is there anything else?"

"Just three minor items. If you want to re-advertise the position, I think we might fare better if we omit details of who the PA's line manager will be. Second, you should know that Howard applied for the post before we advertised it. Sir, it is time to do our planning session for our corporate team-building day. A happy team is a productive team, sir!"

"No corporate fun bollocks. You are not still working at the corporate nonsense A&M Trust. You said he applied before. That is interesting."

"Yes, I thought so, showing initiative there. I will send you a memo on the activity day, sir, and I will set up that interview for you this week."

"Thank you, Brenda. I await the memo with expectant dread."

"Oh, sir, you are so funny."

Bob stared in disbelief at the thick-skinned Brenda.

"You can go now, Brenda. Please take the rejected files with you. Please make sure you get them all to send me a thank-you note for my generous gifts of extra reflection time to them. Alfred doesn't have to write a note, it will just be dribbling nonsense."

"Yes, sir." Brenda picked up the extra files, leaving Bob with a single sheet of paper for Howard, and left the office. Bob picked up the single sheet and studied it with genuine curiosity.

"Before ... hmm, interesting indeed."

CHAPTER 25

RIM – ROSS 154 – LOTHIAN
EDINBURGH PORT DISTRICT
THE PEREGRINE
MORNING
BLOWN

"This is very impressive, Tom. I could see from the outside it was a great ship, but yes, I am impressed."

"Oh yeah, thanks, Greg. This is your first time here, right? Welcome to *The Peregrine*. My cargo ship. She used to be in the military. What she did was classified. All I know is her old name. She used to be called the *I Can See You*. Creepy, right?"

Greg thought of the military mantra that was drummed into him as an operator. *If you can see it, you can kill it.*

"That sounds very creepy. Her name, I mean. I thought it was bad luck to change the ship's name."

"Ah, I don't know. Maybe she handed out so much bad luck to the enemy when she used to fight that she earned a new lucky name. She has been lucky for me. The name change was part of the decommissioning and conversion process. The military gave her the civilian name *The Peregrine*. Converted her to cargo and stripped the sensitive gear and weapons and dumbed down the computer."

Greg knew all of this. He knew a lot more than Tom about the ship and her earlier life. The resistance General running this operation had handed Greg the file on *The Peregrine*.

Tom continued telling the story of his ship.

"She can't shoot anymore, but she is quick and stealthy. We can haul six thousand cubic meters of cargo. Weighing up to ten thousand tons. She would have had a crew of eighteen. That is no big secret. I counted the chairs, and more passengers of some sort, numbering twenty-four. Forty-two all up. I got that by counting the bunks."

Greg reflected that counting the seats and bunks was a very smart way to gather intelligence. Not everyone would have thought of doing that.

"Today we are light on crew. Just me, the ship's computer, and the two gunslinger robots I reprogrammed. They also help on the ship. As copilot and engineer when we are off-planet and as the terribly tempered ship's security when docked. They have a lethal aim with those pistols. They are more of the 'shoot first, and don't bother with the questions' type. That is *The Peregrine*. I am sure the ship has a lot more secrets. I just don't know them."

Greg's brain twitched. *Did Tom just say he had two Cleaners on board?* Greg did not know about the competence, or lack of, in the person Tom had got to do the reprogramming. It didn't make Greg feel more comfortable. Ugh, it was what it was. *Just stay frosty* Greg thought. There would not be any Pipers, so he should be secure. Anyway, it was time to discuss the Martha situation.

"Let us sit. We need to talk. We are on a very short timeline. Martha will be here tonight or tomorrow, and I can guarantee she will come straight to see you. Keep smiling, Tom. You are number one on a girl's to-do list, but she isn't coming here to fuck you. The fucking you is likely to be nonconsensual and go past the still breathing stage." Greg wasn't being cruel. He needed Tom focused.

"Oh, shitting hell, I had almost forgotten, talking about my *Peregrine*. The plan you said is a heist, the Imperium office here in town?"

"That's right, lots of credits and gold. Enough to get rid of Martha and pay off Clarence. It's more limited by how much we can carry out of their office, not by how much there is we could carry. The plan is simple. As soon as Martha arrives, we brief her, and before she can overthink things. You and me, one of your gunslingers and Martha—she is an extra gun—the four of us attack the office. We stun all the guards and blow a big hole in their vault, we grab the credits and gold and come back to the ship. We break the speed record for getting the fuck out of here, off-planet and away, and we hit FTL as soon as we are far enough out of the gravity well. We are clear and rich. There is one item I need to pick up from the vault, which is why I am helping you. I can't take the vault on my own. I need your help and you need mine. It is a mutual win. Grab the money and slip out of town."

Greg paused for a breath and continued. "The money and gold are all yours. I only want that one item I need to get. After we disappear."

Tom sat in silence for a minute. Greg let it play. Say nothing. Greg needed Tom to make the first move now. "Hmm, I like the plan. It is simple: blow shit up, grab the loot, run away. The pilot flies us the fuck out of Dodge. We go to FTL toward the other Rim systems. The plan doesn't have lots of moving parts, there are not loads of people who can leak info. I trust you and me. Just having this conversation already puts both of us in jail, so we can trust each other. The gunslinger robots are loyal, and Martha will say nothing to the guards as an enforcer assassin for the mafia. We can all trust each other for the heist at least. The Imperium customs office in this city will only have a few guards. Two, maybe four people in the office. Argh, where do we get the explosives from?"

Tom's words shocked Greg. What Tom had just said betrayed an awareness of tactical considerations and operational security. Plus, strategic planning and thinking, logistics, and ordnance. Greg wondered if he had been wrong in writing Tom off as nothing more than a piss-poor gambling addict idiot tied up with the mob. There was nothing in Tom's background file that suggested he had ever had any exposure to any military or the resistance. Greg wondered who had reprogrammed the robots. Maybe it had been Tom all along. He was maintaining and flying the ship single-handedly and had been doing so for months.

Greg smiled and thought about the explosives. "The same place we are going to get two assault rifles from. I am guessing the robots won't want or need a rifle, and Martha will bring her own hardware. I doubt Martha would trust a gun we gave her anyway. I am your guns and ammo person. In preparing for this raid, I just needed to find the perfect team and escape plan. I have enough explosive to blow our way in and make more holes for us to leave by. It is not like we will go out the back door. Let me show you a floor plan of the office."

"There is one thing I should tell you, Greg. It is about the two gunslingers. They are making you as twitchy as a cat. You might have called them Kill Bots or K-Bots, maybe even Cleaners, if you have come across them."

Greg winced.

"Okay, that reaction is a yes. I had Fergus purged out of them if you are worried. Okay, another yes."

"Err." Just like that, Greg knew his cover was blown.

"It is okay, Greg, I already suspected you were resistance military. Your face when you saw GS1 confirmed it. Now you have just confirmed it a second, third, and fourth time. You have come across these robots before somewhere. Yet you are still alive, and that means you have been doing some very shady shit, not regular military for sure. Another yes. I have been trying to figure out why you arrived here. Your cover made little sense. It didn't read true. That tipped me. Frankly, I don't care. Martha is coming to kill me, and I just want to get out from under Don Clarence. Your plan will help me to do that. Partners, if you want, that is up to you."

"When you said you had Fergus purged, did you do that yourself?"

"Yes."

"You know what you are doing? You are good at that sort of thing?"

"Very."

Well Greg thought, that is a surprise. Tom is no idiot, it was just an act, and he just made me. "I have other masters, Tom, but yes, we are partners, for now at least. Nice to meet you."

Tom's cold eyes looked at Greg. They each had more honest respect for each other now. "Likewise."

"Who are you, Tom?"

"I might ask you the same thing, Greg. Maybe later, Greg. Maybe, no promises."

Greg realized in a flash; Tom had said he had Fergus purged. Tom had called him Fergus. The history of how the Cleaners came into being was not a bit of history known to the public. Hell, that the Cleaners existed at all was not general knowledge. Sure, they knew it in the military on both sides of the war, but only among the fighters who had tangled with them and lived, and they were in short supply. Few people within the resistance knew about Angus or Harry. And few within the Imperium knew that Harry had fetched Fergus from prison and had his scan inserted into the K-Bots C&C system.

Not that it was a secret. It was more that no regular person's life, even a military person's life, would intersect with the people involved. In either the Imperium's K-Bot program and its construction at Harry's hands. Or within the resistance's Piper program, which Angus created to target Fergus. Not a secret, no, it was just that no one would know the technical details, unless they had a close link to the programs. What the hell was Tom doing with two very rare Cleaners in his possession?

Somewhere in here was the truth Greg thought. Tom had a high-level connection. The pertinent question was doubtless which side, and how had Tom become entangled with Don Clarence? What the hell was going on? His dropping Fergus's name, was that a plant or just an unconscious slip or a throwaway comment. And to think Greg had thought he might have served Tom up to Don Clarence, not anymore.

CHAPTER 26

CORE – ALPHA CENTAURI A – NEW TERRA
AYLESBURY
SUPREME COMMANDER'S OFFICE
AFTERNOON
COVERT INTELLIGENCE

Piles of admin and paperwork covered Bob's desk. There were some balled-up pieces of paper that lay siege to the empty wastepaper basket in the room's corner. The army's lines of paper balls were besieging an empty house.

Bob moved about ten pages that were strewn over the other piles, searching for the keyboard and phone buried under somewhere. Bob uncovered his desk phone. He pulled the phone toward him, but the shifting of the cord must have upset the desktop paper tower's foundations. Two large piles of papers slipped and fell off sideways, their contents tumbling like a deck of cards to the floor. This resulted in a paper explosion that now covered more than a square meter of floor. Bob screamed on the inside. He reached for the speakerphone button.

"Um, Stacy, hi, can you get that thunder wobbler Brenda on the phone? Now, I do not want her coming over to my office. Don't let her in if she invites herself or tries sneaking over."

Then Bob glanced around at the rising tide of papers with a slight glint of growing madness and panic seeping into his eyes. "I want muffin bum to tell me whether Harold has got back to her yet, confirming the interview and date. Please make it quick. I am in danger of drowning here."

"Yes, Boblette, right away, my cherub."

"Stacy, I applaud you for dropping all the Lord nonsense, but we are not, and are unlikely to date or ever need to meet each other's parents. The P in PDA is for private, not public displays of affection. As evil overlord, oh Lordy bollocks, as evil master of the entire known galaxy, I feel we need to strike a balance of respect. Let's go for just Bob, or Supreme Commander, if we have company. Let us keep your endearment terms like Boblette for the bedroom.

"I do not know if cherubs have harps or trumpets, but I do know I will shoot the flying fat fuckers with a bow and arrow if I spot any of them around the office."

"Right away, Bob, is there anything else you want to do me for? To me … maybe?" Stacy gave the phone's speaker a playful smile and wiggled her hips in the desk chair.

"No, not right now, Stacy. We must control ourselves. I just need to find out about my interview with …"

"How about 'Boring Brenda?'" Stacy said with a disappointed look, staring at the speakerphone, frustrated.

"Yes, contact Boring Brenda, and find out for me, please."

Bob clicked off the speakerphone and returned his attention to the sheet of paper and his computer where Harold's HR file was on the screen. With the posted hard-copy résumé in the other hand. He mumbled and spoke to himself.

"Boring, boring, boring. Vanilla, we do not make people this boring. It is like he is a cardboard cutout of boring with a cheeky stupid grin."

Bob read a bit more of the HR file.

"There has to be more. He applied before HR posted the advert. Stupid Brenda didn't even notice he included the job reference from the advert in his covering letter. The advert that had not yet been sent out."

In a flash of inspiration, Bob pulled out a UV penlight from his desk drawer and ran it over the sheet of paper. Right across the top of the page, in what must have been seventy-two-point size text. There was a handwritten HR reference number, different from the one printed underneath in the résumé.

Bob slapped his thigh and winced at the sting, then he switched and slapped his desk with excitement before wincing at his hand. This also caused another paper tower to collapse onto the floor.

"Bingo, up your Brenda, Brenda," Bob shouted.

Bob typed the new HR number into his computer. The dull life of Harold the pizza boy, a fan of role-playing games, disappeared. Lieutenant Colonel Harold Gideon Pillow replaced the profile—from the Covert Intel Department.

"What the fuck is covert intelligence?"

Bob's mobile phone pinged with a new message. Bob could see it had been sent to both him and Brenda. Bob started reading the note.

We can confirm we would like to see you for an interview. You had a space in your diary at noon this Friday. We have

booked this time for both of us and accepted the meeting on your behalf. A video conference link will follow.

"What the actual fuck is going on? At this rate, he will do all my paperwork before sundown."

Bob's phone pinged again. He switched to the other message and continued reading.

You have passed the interview assessment tests. You will receive another message where we will invite you for an interview this Friday. We have recorded your reading of this message. Harold is looking forward to meeting and interviewing you. Please be sure to familiarize yourself with his HR record prior to your interview.

Bob sat at his desk. He both looked and felt confused. Still holding the paper, he stared at Lieutenant Colonel of the Sneaky Shit Department on his computer screen. Bob switched back to his phone and reread the messages. That was when Bob noticed the message's time stamps. Bob looked up at the office clock and looked even more confused, which was quite an achievement.

Bob rambled to himself. "He sent me the message accepting the interview a minute before I read his secret HR profile on the computer. The act of reading the profile must have triggered the message to be sent, but how can it get sent before I have read it or even found it?"

Bob parked the unfathomable mystery for now. He reached for the speakerphone button and clicked it.

"Stacy, Harold will interview with us on Friday at high noon."

"That is good news, Bob, and excellent job of keeping abreast of your admin's needs," Stacy said in a bored and sexually frustrated tone.

Bob felt a bit more in control of his admin and that it was he who commanded things and events in his life.

Bob pressed the button on his desk phone again.

"Stacy, I want you to send Brenda an official letter from HR. Fake Brenda's signature on the bottom of the letter. Inform her of the offer and her acceptance of her new contract terms, extended hours, and reduced pay. We will have an office party to announce her new position as Official Team Warthog Graduate."

"That is great, Bob, she will get a good laugh out of that," Stacy said while wondering how oblivious Bob was to her needs. She was feeling very horny.

CHAPTER 27

RIM – ROSS 154 – LOTHIAN
EDINBURGH PORT DISTRICT
ARRIVALS GATES
EVENING
FOUR-INCH HEELS

Greg and Tom waited, sort of like the condemned. Tom felt that Martha, Don Clarence, and the Imperium guards all wanted to kill him, and he may have missed some people out.

Greg looked up at the stars. He squinted and looked through his digital monocular. "That could be her now," he said, then slid the monocular back into an inner jacket pocket.

The Cerberus had come out of jump but kept the thrust up high. The jet-black ship cast an even darker hole in the dark night sky, with the exception of the intense light from its engines at high burn. On the planet below, as sunset played out across the planet's surface, an ill-defined band of murkier shadow emerged on the planet. The bright daylight sun lit the western side of the world while the shadow of night enveloped the east.

East and west are meaningless in space, just as clockwise and anticlockwise are. There is no absolute authority over what is up or down. They only become meaningful when considering the item in relation to some other property of the object. Such as the planet's poles in relation to its rotation.

Of course, how the North Pole differed from the South Pole was again a subjective human matter. One that could have started wars in just the same way as the round and pointy ends of eggs had in ancient Gulliver's travels. Either way, there was unanimity about what counted as a scary-as-fuck landing.

The Cerberus flipped. The planet was now above the ship, and the ship climbed to the vertical. As the ship's nose rose, it pointed ever more steeply down at the planet. The thrust from the engines increased, and the ship's nose glowed dark red in opposition to the bright-white fire coming from the ship's engines. The ship dove toward the planet's surface in a full power descent.

In its vertical dive, the ship traveled at supersonic speeds as it traversed the mesosphere's thin air. The outer edge of the mesosphere was at ninety kilometers and its inner edge was down at an altitude of forty kilometers, with temperatures from minus one hundred and thirty up to twenty Fahrenheit closer to the surface. The air friction caused the ship's body to heat rapidly. Electric charge separation occurred as the air ionized, and electrons were torn free. Weak lightning crackled from the ship's hull as it earthed out to the tiny ice crystals in the air. Then *The Cerberus*'s afterburner kicked in. The engine thrust fought to keep the speed up against the drag from the thickening wall of air that the ship was punching down through. The red glow on the ship's nose grew more intense and the leading edges of the wings glowed too. Various bits of carbon scoring that had accumulated on the hull glowed and broke free like burning fireflies in the night sky. Only to be whipped back in the airstream of the descent, leaving a trail of sparks behind the ship. The acceleration continued, the now yellow glow from the ship growing in brightness. Martha got what she had been pushing for. A brilliant, glorious display as the ship's passage set the air on fire. In the intense heat, the nitrogen and oxygen burned and reacted to create nitrogen oxide, and after further burning, nitrogen dioxide.

The Cerberus was like a burning phoenix diving toward the planet. Light was cast from the flaming trails behind the wing tips and the white trail of flame behind this diving image. Led by the ink-black outline of *The Cerberus*'s hull with its bright-yellow leading edges.

Martha cut the afterburners, and the ship slowed. She was way too close to the spaceport. It was only about fifteen kilometers along the ground above her head in the cockpit. She would need to deploy the aerobrake and small drone chute soon. Not something a normal pilot would want to do. *The Cerberus* was still supersonic. Martha needed to get down to around five hundred knots before she arrived at six thousand meters. She would continue *The Cerberus*'s inverted climb. The ship would complete the loop with the wheels side of the ship now facing down toward the planet as she would skim in at around four hundred knots at about sixty meters.

Well, that was the plan. Martha knew this sort of hotdogging was dangerous as hell, even with her skills. She also knew the flight controllers would give her hell on the ground, but she figured a scowl from her and a good closeup at the rifle she planned on carrying would answer all questions they may have about the relative safety of her flying, compared with the safety of being near Martha on the ground. The rifle answered everyone's questions, Martha always found.

Martha cut the small drone chute free and increased the aerobrake's bite. She did split S-turns to dump off the excess speed. The ship was down to three hundred knots now, but the spaceport was about three kilometers away still. Martha cut the thrust to zero and pulled the stick all the way back. The entire ship balanced on the horizontal column of air the ship was now descending straight down through, while moving horizontally in relation to the planet. As the ship skimmed over the ground, its nose pointed straight up. Just over one kilometer to the spaceport. Martha had the speed down to one hundred knots now, and seventy-five knots a second later. Well below the ship's stalling speed of two hundred and fifty knots. The ship slid back toward the ground. Martha lit the engines again on a low thrust to balance gravity's downward pull, stopped the descent, and increased flaps to maximum. The ship now hung in midair, its jet wash from the engines burning the ground as she came in across the spaceport. Tail down, nose straight up at an altitude of fifteen meters, going sideways at seventy-five knots.

"Is she sweeping down from the heavens like a demon from hell, throwing down lightning bolts and breathing fire?"

"Strange you should say that, I think you are mixing your metaphors, but yes, you are right, she is sweeping."

As Martha's ship had descended in the powered descent, the ship had pulled three split S-turns to lose speed. As it arced down over the ground, the ship flared up its wings as it approached the spaceport buildings. It looked like the ship was now standing on its tail at an eighty-five-degree angle. The ship slowed as it covered the last two hundred meters of ground to the terminal building. It came to a rest, floating above the yellow landing square and then the nose came down from its steep angle of attack. The nose jets fired to slow the nose's descent as it swung down like an axe toward the ground. The ship was stationary when Martha cut all the power and the ship dropped the fifteen centimeters onto its landing gear.

"Oh, bollocky ball sacks, she is one of those types. Remember, Greg, no matter what your suspicions about me, Martha must not know."

The bottomless black spaceship sat, exuding menace in front of the terminal's gigantic windows, seemingly caged in its yellow taxiing square. Various white gases—steam or some other coolant—vented from outlets in the hull. The engines ticked and clicked as they cooled from the high-powered arrival. The air-conditioning somewhere had sucked in the smell of something burned from the landing. An acrid smell now pervaded the terminal. The burning smell announced Martha's arrival. They could see the sooty black stripe of cooked blacktop on the melted runway behind the ship's path. Where the ship had been doing its baffling tailfirst VTOL maneuver, with a grass fire about a mile away being blown by the wind.

The approach and landing had been without doubt an impressive display of piloting skill. One that would have scared the bejeezus out of professional aerial display teams and test pilots. The ship's designers had never intended aircraft to be flown like that. That is when Martha had come along and donned her flight helmet to show everyone what could be done.

Martha released her seven-point flight harness, disconnected the cable to her helmet, then removed it. She checked her hair in the mirror affixed to the cockpit and used her fingers to liven her hair up. She took her sunglasses out of her flight suit coveralls and put them on. Then Martha stood and grabbed her hand luggage from the locker behind her pilot's seat.

The stairs came down and Martha stepped out. She spied Tom and Greg staring at her agog through the terminal's enormous glass windows. She fixed them both with a look through her sunglasses. She gave them both a big rock and roll wave and screamed, "Coo wee!"

Martha leaned back against the spaceship door, shouldering an enormous rifle and she stuffed a large hand-cannon-type pistol into her gun belt. She picked up her four-inch red heels from beside the side-hatch in her free hand. Martha descended the steps in her long knee-high lace-up combat flight boots and walked the short distance to the terminal entrance steps.

She liked her red heels very much, while knives could cause problems with port security. Martha could walk through any security check wearing or carrying her stiletto heels. The heel itself was a very narrow steel core spike. She liked them because Martha beating someone repeatedly with her heels had the same result as whacking them with a six-inch switchblade.

Greg chuckled. "Wow!"

"Tom, you are in luck, she is fucking you up later. Remember, she is a safety-first girl and doesn't wield her gun while flying. She is a 'wear it on her shoulder' type, oh, and stuffed in her pants."

"Maybe she won't be that bad, I hope."

Greg shook his head. "Ha! And I guess I am going to find an antipodean pop goddess tonight."

Martha clomped up with her luggage. Despite her slender frame, she was very fit and strong.

"Chucklings, how nice, saving me from having to find you. I do not know who you are, but this is Tom, the useless shite. The star of our show in the spotlight, who has the focus of mine and Clarence's full attention. Tom, Clarence is hoping you have a nice birthday present for him."

Tom gulped. She was worse.

"I am Greg. You must be Martha."

She measured Greg up. "Where do you fit in, Greg?"

"I am the one who came up with the plan that will get us all what we want."

"That is good. Clarence was so upset last time. When he didn't receive his presents. He battered another useless shite to death in front of me with a giant dildo, although it might have been Clarence's large sausage. Take me to a bar and fill me in on this plan. We are on a tight schedule—a pound of gold or many pounds of flesh type of schedule."

"This way," Greg said as he gestured toward the exit.

"Are you not going to offer to carry my bag, Tom?"

"May I carry your bag, Martha?"

"No, you may not, you useless shite. You do understand those were your pounds of flesh I was referring to? Soon to be dildoed boy."

"Yes, I am aware."

"Good, good. It will make the trauma less of a shock, easier on you later. I was not sure if you had zoned out or if you were just a little slow. I mean, owing lots of money to this psychopathic mafia Don is not a life choice, although it might be a choice for life, just a shorter one than normal."

"Martha, shall we?"

Martha stared at Greg and easily hefted her large bag up into Greg's chest.

"You can carry this. You seem defect-free, unlike Tom."

The three of them walked outside and across the street into Fantasy Bar. Martha still carried her large rifle on her shoulder and the large pistol in her belt.

CHAPTER 28

RIM – ROSS 154 – LOTHIAN
EDINBURGH
FANTASY (DIVE) BAR
EVENING
BRAIN SMASHER

It was the beginning of another night at Fantasy Bar; it was early hours yet. At only seven in the evening, all the young things would be at home. They would be boiling up their dried pasta and noodles. Adding the mandatory super-strength million Scoville's chili sauce to help line their stomachs.

The least experienced, the first-year students, would be shotgunning cans of lager and pounding back sweet, fruity colorful shots right about now. They would all see their noodles again, albeit bright-pink and bright-green noodles this time around, before the close of night. They had not learned that they did not yet have the depth of experience or the needed financial destitution to support predrinking before a full night at Fantasy Bar. It would take them until their third and fourth years of student life to build up that level of maturity, fortitude, and debt, enabling them to safely revisit predrinking.

The second-year students were all wild and adopted a unique approach. This had started a few student intakes back and was now anchored in the second year's culture and mirrored in their social lives. Students are driven by few things more than their hatred of visiting libraries, their desire for mind-altering substances, and alcohol. At the top of the list was the students' drive and lust for carnal pleasures with other students.

You might find it surprising, but even in a high-class establishment such as Fantasy Bar, a lot of competition and selective picking still happened before any couplings. Yes, horndogs, plural. Some of those students would manage multiple success stories with different teammates on a single visit to Fantasy Bar. The record was supposed to be four.

Those who started playing the game too early in the evening would get dismissed. Their dance card was black marked, no matter who they were, as it was always possible something better might come along—a seven or an eight out of ten on the scale of attractiveness.

Those who started too late would compete with every other male and some ladies for the uncoupled ladies and gents. No matter if they were the boys or girls who had gotten ignored earlier. When they hadn't been enough of whatever their desired other half had been searching for. These were the threes, fours, and fives out of ten, with some sixes. The nines and tens could have had anyone in the joint just by breathing. Yet, the nines and tens had to appear all aloof and disinterested in any of these substandard approaches. They were written off by everyone else for being too picky and snooty.

Things would change in the nightclub's animal kingdom as the notional three o'clock "bedtime" drew near. Even though the bar was open 24-7, as three o'clock drew closer, an oral feeding frenzy would start. Forming a writhing ball of bodies in the center of the dance floor like a shark-feeding frenzy.

As the minutes ticked away, the electric panic and compulsion to mate would grow and grow. But girls are not stupid, not even a tiny slice of stupid. In this high-pressure environment, where it was a buyer's market, even the threes and fours dictated the price and who they would buy from and on what terms.

The sudden discovery of both desirability and exclusivity at the lower end of the market drove up the price for the male sharks. Wild with the emerging panic of an empty bed, the hornier they got, the greater their panic. And the more power they handed over to the horny girls. Picky girls would get more selective still. Female threes would often bag male eights.

It was the second-year students who cracked it. After they realized that starting too early with the predrinking was a bad, vomit-covered idea. They also understood there was no point being the single first year at the end of the night when everyone else had pulled. It was some low-ranking male at the start of the second year who had come up with the very non-PC, objectifying, nasty phrase. "go fat early." You may find it surprising to learn the logic was embraced by the target females in the second year. In their first year, things had been mostly humpy-pumpy free, and none of the second years wanted to repeat that experience.

The basic idea was to avoid the early morning throng and competition for a mate, any mate. These second-year students achieved this by going for the ones and twos before anyone was even thinking those sorts of thoughts. The ladies would welcome the attention and getting drinks paid for. They were, for once, getting to be the choosers and selectors while everyone else higher up the ladder was getting blown out. The boys were fortunate because of the reduced competition, as all the other males were trying to pull the nines or tens. This was a stupid-but-bold rookie move that would receive an immediate talk to the hand. Then, they would try to chat up the still-smoking-hot sevens and eights who had no time for the boys they had just seen get blown out by their first-choice nines and tens. The rejected boys who now slid over were all expectant only to be dismissed, as no one wants to be someone else's afterthought. The boys would all get blown out by the sevens and eights. They would start trying to woo the fives and sixes, where the pattern would repeat.

What the second years had figured out was that sometimes having high standards was not in one's own best interest. That's why they went for the ones and twos first before everyone else got bored and demoralized for being treated like they were all rotten potatoes. The odds of success for both parties changed from ten percent to ninety percent. Neither would spend a night in an otherwise empty bed. Plus, it saved them all from a life of endless celery, cottage cheese, and cardio workouts.

Now, you must remember a student's limited funds and the fact that neither the girl nor boy would have reached for the "wow you're hot" line of cheese. The conversation was not that sophisticated. "You fancy it?" or "Do you want to go?" were solid, well-used lines. You can see it was not because of any social sophistication. These were second-year students. Because both the girls and the boys had had standards when they arrived at nine o'clock. This is where the second half of the "go fat early" mindset would come into play. Alcofrol, as they would often jovially refer to alcohol, was the second vital, magic, sex-giving vitamin.

All genders would pound back as much alcohol as they could afford to purchase, with the highest ABV per credit. Second years all became very good at mental arithmetic, with an economic understanding of value before taste. They could find, in the shortest amount of time, from which drink they could get the maximum amount of alcofrol pounding for the fewest credits; with the eager, young expectation of further pounding later in the evening.

You might think this would result in the second years joining the predrunk first years vomiting behind the toilets. You would be wrong.

The super-sophisticated second years had figured out that it didn't result in vomiting if you timed everything correctly. Early vomiting became seen as a sign of amateurishness, piss-poor planning, and their getting too pissed for opening night.

Peacocking consisted of banter, the pounding of multiple shots, and the chugging of many pints. It had become part of the flirting dance and romance to find a partner for that night. Shaking your tail feathers and showing allure. Timed well, you could pound the drinks, catch someone's eye, and be outside having a snog and a fumble. Before there was any thought on either side of vomit, whether on themselves or their chosen partner.

This had several benefits. You could pick up your coats within five minutes and stumble off homeward bound, possibly via a kebab shop en route. Or you would get blown out and get left there, puking behind the toilets, having a little cry. Soon enough, though, the puking would pass, and it would be Double Mayhem time followed by some Triple Trouble. There was plenty of time still. Who cared about sex anyway? It just didn't seem that important anymore when there was so much more drinking to be had with very excellent club music, so good you could even taste it.

If you were lucky enough to be wearing your coat, arm in arm with someone and on your way home to conduct several hours of cardio, then, hell, it was a happy day and night well spent. Even if it didn't last all night long, but just a few minutes, or if it was too soft and floppy to get started, there would be breakfast in a few hours. Subject to how that went, maybe some extra breakfast to follow with a portion of lunch after that.

It was thus that the "go fat early" philosophy drove the thoughts of the second-year students. In their consumption of drugs, alcohol, and one another.

Some student sociologists had guessed that this philosophy would eventually lead to the reemergence of the YOLO mindset. This had existed on ancient Earth for a few years in the hedonistic early 2010s before it died out. These sociologists thought it was well overdue for a comeback after eight hundred years.

It was seven in the evening—still early. The students and young and hip would not arrive for another couple of hours yet and were busy with their hot chili noodles dinner.

Currently, it was the same early-daytime drunken sleepy crowd in the smoky bar. The dreg ends of the afternoon's musical acts, which hadn't been good enough to secure the evening gig slot at nine. More dreadful soulless music. Nothing much would change when the evening band came on at nine, but it would be a lot louder, and the young adult audience considered that to be great.

Greg guided Martha and Tom back to his usual secluded table in the back corner.

"Drinks first. That was a long flight."

Greg signaled the bartender, and a happy Alex came straight over.

Martha smiled at Alex. "I do like these dive bars during the drunk's sleepy hours. There is never any queuing."

Alex said, "They are all sleepy hours with excellent speedy service. What can I get you all?"

With no thought, Martha said. "A double for me, a brain smasher, if you have it. If not, a double leg breaker would be nice, wouldn't it, Tom?"

Tom smiled. "It is just off-world humor."

Martha and Greg looked at Tom as if he had said something bizarre.

"Hey, I'd love a double brain smasher as well. Sounds good."

Tom looked sheepish. "A beer for me. A pint, please."

"Coming up." With that, Alex went back to his bar, stopping to pick up some empty glasses on the way.

"Tom, this could be like your last meal. Well drink, hey ho, what is the plan, guys?"

Greg leaned forward. "The plan is we pay Don Clarence in full and we also pay you off, so no one needs to smash or break Tom's legs or beat him to death with a giant dildo. We carry out the plan in about forty minutes from now, ten minutes before the shift change."

"This sounds like a good financial plan, but it is a shame because I do like legs, and I know Don Clarence enjoys playing with his food. Tom, I know Clarence will reflect on this as an opportunity missed. Tell me more. You have forty minutes to convince me."

"You, me, Tom, and his friendly K-Bot shoot the fuck out of the local Imperium customs office. We storm the building, break into the vault, grab all the gold and credits we can carry, blow a big hole in the vault wall, and go out the side. We book it down the street back to the port area and blast off into space on Tom's ship."

"Hmm, where is that drink? Do you pups have guns and explosives?"

"Yes, Martha, we have the guns, and I bring lots of explosives. I figured you would want to use your own hardware, so you will have to bring that enormous rifle and hand-cannon you have tucked into your gun belt."

Alex arrived back at the table, deposited the two double shorts in front of Greg and Martha and the pint of warm slops and foam in front of Tom, then retreated to his bar.

"Oh, goody. At least you have a house-trained Kill Bot. Tom can carry the bags of loot. I am in, where is the office?"

"Just over the street. Cheers."

"Cheers!" Martha said and threw back her drink in one.

"Yay," Tom said in a weak whisper.

"Tom will get GS1, our K-Bot, to walk up with the loot bags, assault rifles, and explosives. We have smoke grenades as well, for covering our exit and the initial assault. Tom will tell the K-Bot to get here in ten minutes. We can get suited up and go over the street. Tom can even finish his beer. He has ten minutes."

"Excellent, barman, two more doubles. Brain bleeders this time. That is a brain smasher and black, Tom, before you get all nervous and scaredie again. You sit there and finish your pint from the slops trays," Martha said with a smile.

CHAPTER 29

RIM – ROSS 154 – LOTHIAN
EDINBURGH
GUARDS OFFICE
FORTY MINUTES LATER
SIXTY SECONDS

Greg, Martha, Tom, and GS1 sat on the opposite side of the street from the Imperium customs office. The group, offset at an angle, was further down the street and outside the coverage of the two fixed security cameras. They could see the cameras on the front of the building, just shy of the roofline.

They all sat in silence, watching, trying to see through the windows. The four of them observed the unofficial guards' movements. They wanted to sniff out whether there was an unseen ambush waiting for them. Either in the office or behind one of the nearby buildings. No one wanted to put themselves in a kill box.

While the rest of the team was observing and calculating, Tom was just watching and thinking. He had grown up in Aberdeen on Lothian and, in all his previous visits to the Edinburgh shipyards in the port district, Tom had never walked up this street. He had never been to Fantasy Bar before, and he had never seen the local Imperium customs office.

It was an ornate building, perhaps influenced by East Asia back on old Earth. Nothing on the new worlds was the same as back on Earth before the fall. Everything and everyone were now a mix of several things, thus becoming something different and new. There was no such thing as the authentic original anymore.

Old Asia influenced the building's design. Japan was Tom's guess as he thought back to the pictures his parents had made him study as a child. It looked like a temple in Tom's estimation. The flared roof lines screamed Buddhist to Tom. This was further confirmed by the symbol of the old Sōhei monks on the entranceway arch, free-standing in front of the temple.

He sat in front of what appeared to be an ancient and well-maintained Sōhei temple. Some features had gotten mixed up for sure by whichever early colonists, first or maybe second generation, had built the temple.

The building was over two hundred years old. That made it an ancient colony building as the colony itself was only founded two hundred and fifty years ago. One hundred and fifty years of hard times and building, fifty years of conflict, ending in two years of the Final War, followed by fifty years of a relative sort of cold peace. The conflict impacted the architecture and buildings still standing in the towns. History was often still bare to see in this high-tech, weird new slightly Wild West.

The thing that was weirding Tom out was not that he was sitting here so many light-years from the long-dead Japan of old Earth. The thing that made Tom's brain explode was the koi. Behind the entrance arch, up the three steps onto the front stone entrance decking, were the main double doors to enter the temple that was now the undercover guard's office. While they constructed many buildings from wood, someone had crafted this one from thick sandstone. Clad in wood with a bright-red stain.

On both sides of the double doors was a painted fine sculpture of two koi carp. One swimming up and the other down in a circle. They had colored the upward-swimming koi black; the downward-swimming koi was blue.

What made Tom's head spin was that the design matched the tattoo his parents had given him for his sixteenth birthday. His parents had described it as Tom's coming-of-age tattoo. Tom's father had shown him his chest, where he also bore the same tattoo, and so Tom had his chest tattooed with pride. The design and colors were exquisite. Tom loved his tattoo; it seemed unique. Other than his father, he had seen no one else with anything similar in Aberdeen.

Of course, Tom understood the symbology and the importance of the circular shape and orientation of the two fish up and down, and the meaning of their colors. Tom had looked it up on his computer back when he was sixteen. He recalled his father telling him the family gave the sign of the koi to the firstborn child of every family, who would become part of the wider clan. That was the phrase his father had used—"part of the wider clan."

Somehow, and Tom was struggling to see how, he and his family were linked to this old building, and the building linked to the wider clan through the koi symbols next to the doors.

The troubling bit was the Sōhei symbols on the entrance arch in front of the temple. The arch that stood guard over the path, protecting the entranceway into the temple.

Tom could recall the stories he had read as a child about the twelve different clans of monks of which the Sōhei were one. The twelve ancient clans of the fearsome warrior monks that dated back two thousand years way back into old Earth's history, back to its early tenth century.

Tom's mind raced in circles, trying to grasp what this meant. He also worried about what it might mean if someone was keeping and caring for the temple.

It would seem the wider clan were, in fact, Sōhei warrior monks who also protected this old Buddhist temple. Part of a lineage that now traced back two thousand years, of which he and the previous generations with the tattoo were all the firstborn children.

Were there other local Sōhei warrior monks here in Edinburgh who cared for the temple all these years, while Tom had been growing up in Aberdeen? Nowadays he flew around, doing cargo runs on *The Peregrine*. All while he conducted his secret mission.

Tom stared at the two sculptures of the black and blue koi as he sat next to a hitherto unvisited street in Edinburgh, two thousand and three hundred kilometers from Aberdeen where he had grown up with his parents. He sat there, about to rob the local customs office, with the rifle he carried clipped under his long coat, just like Martha and Greg beside him.

All three rose, and they walked behind GS1. The three humans all put on black balaclava head covers and IR goggles. As they approached the customs office, each of them reached under the flaps of their coat to the bandoliers hidden underneath. They pulled free a grenade, one in each hand. Then they each hooked the pins with a finger from the other hand, pulling them out. The grenades they kept safe as their hands continued to press down on the safety handle. They walked closer to the office.

Greg's voice came through the others' headsets after decryption. "Throw for the walls."

All four of them launched the smoke grenades at the building's walls, pitching them so they landed under the windows. Greg pushed the first button on his handheld control unit and eight green lights lit up on the display.

"Three, two, one, now."

Greg pushed the second button on the remote detonator and all eight grenades exploded around the office with an earsplitting bang. They broke the glass in windows on both sides of the street. The grenades gushed out thick white smoke. The smoke filled the guard's office, and the street became filled to roof height with the thick yellowish-white smog.

GS1 gave the two CCTV cameras at the front of the office the middle finger salute with both hands. They knew the security cameras would see both IR and visible light. This was GS1's friendly *fuck you* to the camera surveillance system. GS1 pulled his two pistols and stunned the four guards who stumbled out of the office while coughing and bumping into things. Once he had stunned all the guards, GS1 thumbed both pistols back to live fire rounds and shot each security camera with a single shot. Exploded bits of the now dead cameras rained down on the street.

"All hostiles down. Surveillance down. Go," GS1 said into his mic.

While GS1 kept guard on the street to protect them from any office reinforcements, Greg, leading the other two, ran into the office and toward the lockup area at the rear.

The three of them came through the open outer door. Greg went to the safe and keyed a code into the digital lock. He submitted the code, then the secure outer door closed and locked. After a tense second, the safe in the secure sanctum opened.

Next, Greg ran to the sidewall and took the shaped HE charges from his bag, sticking lumps of explosive to the outer wall.

"We are gone in sixty seconds. You pair grab everything in the safe."

Greg took out a four-meter-long sausage, the same creamy color as the other twelve blocks of explosive. He stuck the explosive sausage to the wall in a large circle running around the outside of the twelve blocks.

Martha and Tom shoveled the chips and gold out of the safe and into their swag bags.

Meanwhile, Greg stuck small detonators into the plastic explosive blocks and sausage. Each detonator had a small Wi-Fi aerial.

Greg went into the evidence lockup area in the back and ran up and down by the shelves, looking for his prize. He found the heavy computer box; Greg hefted the large boring beige box off the shelving.

"Fuck, that is heavy. Thirty seconds, people."

"Roger that. The front and alley are both clear," GS1 said over the comms.

Greg struggled, carrying the computer box to the safe area where

Martha and Tom were loading up.

"We are leaving in ten. Take cover, now."

Everyone ducked down, and Greg pushed the detonator button. The large sausage-shaped circular charge went *crump*. The effect was like the cutting blade of a knife as the shaped charge cleaved the stone. A half second later, the twelve blocks of charges Greg had stuck to the wall all detonated. They shattered the plug of rock sat in the cutout circle in the sidewall. The broken rubble was all thrown out through the hole into the alley beyond, leaving behind a clear, crisply cut hole through the wall.

Everyone got to their feet. Greg grabbed his beige box, and Tom and Martha grabbed their stuffed swag bags and moved toward the new alternative exit.

"We are coming out now, GS1."

"Roger that."

"Go, go, go!" Greg said.

The three of them climbed through their exit hole with their packages in hand.

CHAPTER 30

**RIM – ROSS 154 – LOTHIAN
EDINBURGH
OUTSIDE CUSTOMS OFFICE
IMMEDIATE
RED DRIZZLE**

They ran to the front of the building. Alarms were ringing. Smoke still hung heavy in the street. They could all see fine through their IR goggles. Toward the shipyards they ran, burdened with their cargo. The group ran past Fantasy Bar where they had been downing drinks, with Martha trading barbs with Tom less than an hour earlier. The escape route would take Tom and Greg the same way they walked the last time they left the bar for the shipyards.

"We have eight more guards approaching by vehicle, spotted by drones, two minutes max," GS2 said over the radio from *The Peregrine*.

"Push it, people, we are close." Greg tried to run faster, but the computer box was so heavy and such an awkward shape.

They fled their pursuers and approached the shipyards; they could see all *The Peregrine*'s ramps were closed to ensure the ship was secure from the hazard of unwanted borders.

An incoming round broke the brief silence and threw up dirt a couple of meters ahead on the sunbaked street.

GS1 turned and fired twice. A yelp sounded from behind them, and a guard's body crashed to the street, the momentum from his run carrying his dead corpse forward.

Martha and Tom both dropped and covered. Greg bent and put down the computer box and, as he stood and turned, he swung up his slung rifle from under his coat and flicked the selector switch from single shot to full auto. As Greg completed the turn, he sprayed bullets covering the entire street from left to right. Many glass windows shattered. Everyone else in the street ducked. They vanished behind small planters with small flowering plants in them, behind garbage bins and racks of student bicycles. Greg released the trigger that had made his gun bark repeatedly for the last five seconds. Now two dead Imperium guards lay on the street's hard surface. Greg flicked his shot selector back to single shot and sighted his rifle.

Bang, bang, another Imperium guard went down. Arterial red blood from the fatal chest wound sprayed over the front window of a posh-looking restaurant with open-mouthed guests. The guests were out for food after catching the penultimate show of the night in the theater next door. The diners gawped, the blood splatter adding to the immediacy of the dramatic scene that was playing out two meters away in the street.

Greg popped the empty magazine from his rifle and slammed a full fresh one home.

"GS1, a hand please." Greg pointed at the heavy box. "Lead the way back to the ship. Martha, Tom, go with GS1 now. I will cover you all as you go," Greg said to the three of them.

GS1 lifted the beige box that was Merlin's home with ease. "With me." GS1 ran at a slower, more human pace through the drifting smoke toward the shipyard's gates. Martha and Tom followed, a swag bag in each hand.

GS2's voice came over their radio headsets. "Ship engines are hot and ready for immediate dust off."

"Thirty seconds," Greg said over the comms.

As Greg ran, he kept pausing, turning and firing. He was conducting a retreat under fire, acting as the group's sole rear guard. This was one of the most dangerous maneuvers the resistance instructors had trained the ground pounders for. Greg's fire was keeping the chasers down, but there were still a fair few incoming rounds.

"Fuck this!" Greg let his assault rifle drop from his hands, it hung suspended in its three-point rifle sling. Greg took two HE grenades from his bandoliers. He pulled the pins and launched them one after the other down the street toward where the Imperium guards were taking cover. He sprinted forward to catch up with the others. Greg knew he was too close to where he had sent the two high-explosive fragmentation grenades.

"Update, forty seconds."

An enormous *crump* sounded behind Greg, followed by a second explosion. As Greg pounded the last few yards to Tom and Martha still on his feet. GS1 had already made it to the ship, standing to the side of the ship's large hatch, waiting as it slowly opened, still holding the computer.

Small, baby plant pieces and soil rained down on the street around where the guards had been hiding. Body parts landed all over the street; some bits rolled off the roof and fell onto the footpath. Pieces of the six shattered guards now lay with the broken plants. Then red drizzle fell.

At this point, Martha took a round in her arm and fell forward. As she fell, her head hit one of the many lumps of masonry that now littered the street.

She lay unconscious and bleeding from the gash on her head. Her heart continued to pump her precious blood out over the dirty street.

Greg sprang into action.

Tom stood watching immobile with the two swag bags hanging from his arms.

But Greg went to help Martha. She was out cold but was still breathing. Martha couldn't stand like this, even with Greg's help.

GS1 continued to wait, shielding the computer with his body at the ship, waiting for the side-hatch as it continued to open. This meant GS1's hands were full with Greg's boring box. Greg had tasked the robot with evacuating the box, even if this made no sense to the robot. *Stupid humans* GS1 thought yet again.

Martha was down on the ground with Greg lent over her, his eyes down as he tried to help her. Tom stood isolated, alone in the street. A distant guard, the one who had caught Martha in the arm with his lucky shot, stalked toward Tom, rifle shouldered and barrel down.

An unseen source shouted out to Tom in Japanese.

Tom's mind churned as he tried to translate the language he had learned years back as a child.

What color and how do you swim? Tom thought.

A shot rang out. Unseen, the monk had shot the approaching guard center chest; the guard dropped. His heart gave its final beats and then came to a still.

Five more guards who had been running up, fifty meters behind their now dead colleague, stopped, confused. Where had the shot come from that had killed their colleague? Who was this new foe? Where was the sharpshooter?

Tom tried to translate the reply in his head. Little over two seconds had passed. Although it took him back to the endless hell when Tom had been forced to stand in front of the rest of his class at school. Repeating Japanese phrases as everyone stared at him.

Tom shouted back in Japanese, "Black on the top, blue on the bottom."

The voice stepped forward out of the shadow and Tom could now see the man in a traditional monk's Japanese dress, but in black cloth, his head bald.

The man stared at Tom and spoke in Japanese again.

There is a mark. Tom dropped the rifle; it fell in the sling to his hip. Tom threw off his long coat that he wore over the slung rifle. He tore his shirt in half down the front, revealing his very lean and defined muscled body as he held his shirt wide. Tom stood with his back to Greg as he looked at the monk before him.

The guards, who had been stuck in a semi-trance, with indecision down the street, regathered their wits and leaped into action. They ran toward the now defenseless group.

Five very rapid single shots sounded from the monk's rifle. A rifle that Tom thought had appeared from nowhere in his hands. Also, Tom could swear the monk didn't turn his head and that his eyes remained locked, staring at Tom. That couldn't be right. The running guards were still thirty meters away. Everyone would take careful aim for one shot, let alone five quick shots. Yet each of the guards fell in rapid succession. A blooming, expanding red in the center of each of their still chests.

The monk stepped forward again and his rifle flipped 360 degrees, the butt now under the monk's shoulder, the barrel pointing at the dry, hard-packed dirt. Tom could now see the monk's rifle. It looked ancient to Tom's untrained eye.

Now in English, the monk said to Tom. "I watched you outside the temple. Come and find me when you return. I will be at the temple. I will train you when you are ready."

With that, the Sōhei warrior monk walked down the street into the drifting smoke and vanished as he headed back toward the temple.

GS2's voice came over the radio. "I am detecting more guards about seven minutes out. We need to be going."

Then GS1 said, "To me, the hatch is now open. I have put the computer on board."

Greg blinked and tried to get his brain to replay the last thirty seconds.

"Who the fuck was that, and where did he come from? Why did you tear your clothes off and flash him?"

"That was a local Sōhei and guardian of the temple," Tom said as he turned to face Greg.

Greg could now see the tattoo of the black and blue koi on Tom's bare chest.

"He is part of my clan."

Greg realized he had seen the koi symbol as recently as ten minutes ago next to the doors to the customs office.

"That is some nice ink, Tom. Did it just save our lives?"

"Yes, Greg."

Greg paused.

"Let's get on the ship and leave before their friends arrive," Tom said.

Greg turned and looked at the wrecked street behind them strewn with bodies and parts of dead broken guards, broken plants, glass, and masonry. Greg carried Martha. Tom could see Greg had sealed Martha's head wound with what was likely superglue. Greg was about to walk toward the ship's open hatch when Greg turned to Tom, Tom gripped his rifle that was hanging by the three-point sling down by his hip, he stood bare-chested, gun in hand.

Tom deftly threw the rifle over his shoulder, and it ended up hanging in the sling down the middle of his back, barrel down. Then he picked up the four swag bags, each weighing thirty kilos, and they both trudged toward the ship's hatch.

"You will need to fill me in on your new friend, Tom."

"They are monks, well he was, and I think he is part of a *they*, perhaps a huge *they*, and all just as deadly."

"Good people to have in your corner, Tom. If they live next to Fantasy Bar, they may not still be celibate. Although if they are like any other monks I've met, I would bet they brew their own fine beers rather than drinking that slop they sell at the bar."

"They used to live in the temple. The guards kicked them out, I think. I suspect they may have been wandering nomads since. They are warrior monks."

"Well, that explains the crack shooting."

"We just gifted their temple back to them. Their line traces back to ancient Japan back on old Earth, all the way back to the tenth century in old Earth time."

"I guess that explains the two huge goldfish on your chest."

"They are koi, Greg. Very symbolic in Japanese culture."

"I know. You are Japanese, Tom?"

"I think my ancestors might well have been. Genetically, for sure I am, whatever that matters. But, ethnically, culturally, I don't know if I would be considered Japanese."

They both arrived at the large ship's hatch.

"What will it mean if you are?"

"Well, that is the question, isn't it?"

Greg paused, then said. "Martha should be okay, I think. She should come around in about fifteen minutes. Best put a shirt on first."

They both walked up the ramp through the ship's hatch.

"Yes, I have no wish for her to see the koi or, God forbid, get all overcome and flustered."

Greg let out a laugh. "What an awful thought."

"Indeed."

"Let's get in the air before those other guards get here. We can rouse her with some ammonia if you have some?"

"Sure, no problem. Let's go. We are in, close the hatch, GS2."

In the cockpit, GS2 heard the radio transmission in its headset. GS2 slapped the heavy-duty red button, designed to "close and secure all hatches," and the large thick hatch powered shut.

"Greg, everyone needs to get down on the floor, laid on their backs now. We are going ballistic."

Greg thought that was interesting. It appeared Tom knew about combat takeoffs. Greg also reflected on how Tom had skillfully moved his rifle between positions in the three-point sling.

A thud sounded as the large hatch mated with the hull and large securing bolts locked into the hatch's frame. The red light above the hatch went green to show the ship was now buttoned up and secure. "Okay, GS2, go time."

The ship shook, and the engine noise rose. They were all pushed down into the cargo deck with the ship's acceleration as it rose on the four pillars coming from her drop engines at full throttle, taking them back up the planet's gravity well.

Everyone lay on the cargo deck. Tom and Martha lay by the four stuffed large industrial swag bags. Greg was next to his boring beige box. GS1 sat more elegantly in the jump seat by the hatch. Even though he was a robot, the acceleration's pull on his hydraulics still affected him. It was just so negligible it wasn't debilitating in the same way as when acceleration pulled the blood away from the human brain.

After two minutes, the four-drop engine's intensity backed off and the main drive engines powered up.

They did not use the main engines to take off deep in the gravity well. The drop engines had to get you high enough first before they could start the main engines. While the drop engines might kick you in the kidneys, the main engines could smear you across the ship, your skull bursting with the pressure from their power. However, they brought in the main engines more gradually and never deep in a gravity well.

Gravity played hell, with both the main engines and the inertial dampeners, which could not function. The passenger's acceleration vector changed direction and increased under the primary engine's power. Yet the effect on the passengers dropped to zero as the inertial dampeners took over, neutralizing the effect of acceleration by dampening their relative individual inertia.

For the first sixty kilometers, you got the traditional space takeoff experience. Normally delivered in a comfy jump seat, not on the floor of the cargo bay.

Tom didn't know that when *The Peregrine* had her old name, The Rhino tank crews, of course, thought that the Eagle's love of comfy seats for takeoff was all just a little wet. They believed there was nothing wrong with the cargo-bay floor. A few of the funnier ones would put down beach towels.

The inertial dampeners had now kicked in enough to mask the impact of the ongoing vertical and horizontal acceleration. People could get back on their feet and stretch out their backs.

"Just one thought, Tom. When did you last have this ship serviced?"

"You mean we need to service the ship?" Tom said with a smile.

Greg's problem was that after a busy morning. He couldn't tell if Tom was joking or not.

"You're joking, right? Tom, right?"

"I am going to put a T-shirt on. I will grab the ammonia at the same time. Has she pissed or shat herself during takeoff? If so, I will fetch the fire hose to clean the deck."

"I will flip you for who doesn't have to clean her up."

"Nah, I am pulling captain's rank. It must be good for something. She can sit in her own mess or clean herself up. Hell, you can do it if you are feeling brave and the ammonia doesn't bring her to. All I know is that I am not doing it."

"What about one of the gunslingers?"

"What do you want to torture them for? They had our ass covered back there while she was getting shot."

"How so?"

"Well, GS1 was carrying your precious heavy-ass box and getting the door open and GS2 was prepping the ship for immediate takeoff. Something that would often take thirty minutes plus. And he is now piloting *The Peregrine*."

"Fair point."

Tom left to get a T-shirt and the ammonia and returned in three minutes. GS1 watched Greg and Martha. Greg had a sudden concern that GS1 might have thoughts and feelings about the Martha and Tom situation. Hmm, Greg thought, I need to be careful here.

"Right, let's dose her and wake her up." Tom handed the squeezy bottle of ammonia across to Greg.

"Wakey time, sleepy head." Greg waved the ammonia under Martha's nose, squeezing it to squirt the gas up her nose.

"Ugh, fuck, get that stinky-ass shit away from me."

"Hello, Martha, you are welcome."

"For what?"

"Saving your life and carrying your unconscious ass off the battlefield. And I'm about to fix the hole in your arm and have already fixed the gash in your head."

"Err, okay, thank you, Greg. What did the useless shite contribute?"

"You mean, other than saving all our lives and getting us out of there? Yeah, not much, a total waste of space. You might care that apart from the whole saving-everyone's-life thing, he carried all the loot in single-handedly while I was carrying you."

"Oh. He has graduated from 'Tom the useless shite,' to 'Tom the shite.'"

"It's this way," Tom said in a tired voice.

"Martha, didn't we leave your ship down there?"

"Yes, Greg, you did. I knew this when you told me your perfect plan. Don't worry, *The Cerberus* will be back with us and docking soon. Tom, you look like you have shat your panties. Dong dildo is back on his planet, feeding his pack. My ship will fly up and dock on automatic."

Tom led them forward to the ship's stores.

The designers of *The Peregrine* had reinforced the stores. It was where, in her serving days, the ship's magazine was located, storing the missiles, shells, and cannon rounds for the big rotary engagement cannons (RECs). As well as the artillery shells, the normal loadout for the tanks, plus any slug rounds.

The ship's designers knew they could not prevent a high-powered detonation weapon from puncturing the outer hull around the stores. Despite the hull being triple thickness. The real engineering had gone into the walls and ceiling plates. A detonation in the stores was designed to blast the nose off the ship.

This would end *The Peregrine*'s life as a ship. The designers thought the very thick internal composite walls could hold the blast and redirect most of the energy outwards into space, along with the rest of the ship's nose. This would, at least in theory, supply precious seconds and opportunity for the rest of the crew to escape the ship in the emergency shuttle pod.

The bunks, of course, were on the other side of the blast wall. But hey, if it took out the bunks, the rest of the ship was going as well. As soon as a blast breached the rear blast wall, which isolated the engineering bay from the rest of the ship, two things would have happened. First, everyone on the ship would already be dead. Second, the blast would be about to breach the fusion drive in the rear engineering bay. The resulting explosion would double check on the dead human bodies. And ensure that the molecules in everyone's body got reduced to free floating atoms and plasma in space.

Sure, the walls could stop REC fire without issues, but Tom had always felt that it was all about the heavier weapons. Then all the armor and walls would not do shit other than make the ship heavier and less maneuverable. Easier to hit. Tom understood there was no perfect answer in engineering. Everything was a sub-optimal trade-off between competing goals that pulled in opposing directions.

It was all very simple, Tom thought. Make sure no one finds you. If you fail at that, don't sit still or fly in a predictable straight line, so they can hit you with their heavy weapons. If you got to that point and needed more ideas, nothing really mattered anymore.

On the plus side, the ship's stores were more secure than even the best commercial bank vaults.

CHAPTER 31

**RIM – ROSS 154 – LOTHIAN
IN ORBIT OVER PLANET
THE PEREGRINE – SHIP STORES
EVENING
HAVE FUN**

Tom turned on the stores' lights.

"We can put everything in here for now and do a count. We can split it after. It will all be safe here. No offense, Martha, but we all know no one else has light fingers."

"I am an assassin, Tom. You're the thief, remember? You took Don Clarence's money and spent it gambling and losing like a loser."

"Hey guys, calm, we are all friends at the moment," Greg said.

"See, Tom, it was a brilliant plan. I know your mother said you would never amount to anything in life, and here you are, trying to make plans, splitting loot, robbing the Imperium. Oh, it wasn't. No, that was Greg's plan. Greg could have used a wheelbarrow to push round your dead weight, Tom. You're like one of those stupid, stubborn donkey hybrids, asses, that is it! That might have fit your role in the heist better, Tom, the big-ass mascot."

"Yeah, Captain Tom, the pilot that owns the escape ship. What did you add, Martha? Oh yes, stopping bullets, that was your contribution."

"Wrong. Fabulousness, pure fabulousness, you little gobshite."

Greg tried on the unfamiliar role of peacemaker once again. "That is enough. Let's unload your swag and do the count so you pair can split the cash. My share is the boring box, as we agreed, Tom. I have no part in the money. The sooner you get it counted, the sooner Martha can be on her way."

Martha smiled. "I have summoned *The Cerberus*. She will fly up nice and slow and discreetly. She'll be here in about an hour. Let's crack on with the count."

"Only an hour, Tom, then Martha and Clarence will be out of your life forever."

Greg pulled up a chair to watch and keep the sniping comments down. Tom and Martha emptied the four bags onto the large stores' table.

There were a lot of credit chips, and quite a few gold bars. They organized the credit chips into piles depending on their monetary value, and placed the gold in a separate pile to the side.

Each bar had an official assay-mark on it, recording the weight, purity, and its value in standard gold units. Greg took notes, recording the bars, weight, value, the credit denominations, and numbers. It took forty minutes to do the sort, count it all, and calculate the total. While everyone else watched, to be sure they were not getting screwed over.

Greg looked up. "Okay, that brings us up to a tiny smidge over 1,743,000 in credits and gold. Tom, your debt with interest to Don Clarence is now at?"

"Six hundred and twenty-one thousand credits with the interest," Martha said.

"And an equal share goes to Martha to cover her inconvenience and amnesia about our whereabouts. That leaves five hundred and one thousand, which seems about right to cover ship costs, port rental, consumables, fuel, ship rental. Tom's share comes out of everything else after the ship costs, so nothing. Tom, you take five hundred and one thousand from the credits pile, and everything else we give to Martha to take back to Don Clarence and for herself."

"Not so fast. I get nothing after all of that. And Martha gets the same as I owe."

"Don't be an idiot, Tom. Let her take the money. This is clean and easy."

"How do we know she won't keep all the money and give nothing to Don Clarence? She could do a flit."

"Trust me, you remedial idiot, I have seen what Don Clarence does with his mop. The mop comes after the dildo bashing. After that, the BBQ, and over to the pack. While you are a special idiot, I am not, and that is why I will not cross Don Clarence."

"Greg. She could keep it. Take all the money and run, not just her share."

"Tom, stop this."

Martha's expression had gone cold.

"Yes, I could shoot you and take the cash. What a great idea."

"And I could get one of the gunslingers to throw you out the air lock and keep all the money myself."

"Shit," Greg said in a whisper.

"You total piece of shit," Martha shouted.

"I could tell dildo dong that you kept all the cash, Martha, and called him a pathetic dickhead."

With that, Martha drew her pistol cannon and put the end of the fat barrel five centimeters from the tip of Tom's nose.

"I am going to go with *fuck you* very much, Tom. Take the money and deliver your body back to Clarence. I'm not sure if I'm going to kill Greg or not yet."

"Not." Greg pulled his pistol's trigger. He had drawn the gun while all the talking and shouting was going on between Martha and Tom. He shot her point-blank in her back, right through her heart. Although there was doubt about whether Martha had a heart. Death was instant. She dropped; her strings cut.

"Idiot! Now you have something to throw out of the air lock, Tom. I guess you are going to hand the money to Don Clarence yourself now. I am sure it will thrill him to see you."

Greg took a moment to get his temper under control.

"Tom, of that pile, five hundred and one thousand is for you and the ship, and six hundred and twenty-one thousand is your share you owe to Don Clarence. Whether you pay Don Clarence or not, I don't give a fuck. The final six hundred and twenty-one thousand was Martha's share. I will take that for having to deal with this general jackassery. Call it a dead or alive bounty for killing your assassin. Now, I just want to check the computer, and after I can leave you to it, alone on your big ship. I'll fly off in *The Cerberus* when it docks in about fifteen minutes."

In Tom's head, he felt he was better off, even though it was the same arrangement made with Martha. Just that now it was Tom's problem to pay Don Clarence, not Martha's. Tom seemed happy that he was six hundred and twenty-one thousand credits richer. Greg already knew Don Clarence would never see his money. Greg estimated Tom's chances of seeing in New Year had just dropped from one hundred percent, before they had walked into the stores, to zero percent now, after the childish squabble. Yet somehow Tom thought he had won. He was no good at gambling, that was clear.

"That sounds fair."

Greg glared at Tom and, in an icy tone, said, "I am glad. Have fun hauling the body to the air lock."

Tom now understood he had fucked up with Greg and he would need to rebuild bridges.

"You can plug in upstairs in the recreation room. There is a keyboard and monitor up there."

"I will go set up."

Greg left the stores and picked up the computer from the cargo deck briefly. Then he put it down again, fetched the nearby trolley, and lifted the computer box onto the trolley. Tom found himself alone with Martha's bleeding corpse. He thought about locking the door behind him to secure the loot. With a sigh, he thought *What is the point?* Greg could kill him and take the key if he had locked the door or, more realistically, beat the code out of him. Not locking the door was a smarter life choice, Tom thought to himself. Tom had forgotten about his lethal robot pets. While he didn't understand it yet, Tom had liked the company of the last week and was not looking forward to being all alone again on the ship with no humans to talk to on his lone mission. The gunslingers' conversation wasn't the best. Tom bent and grabbed Martha's wrists and dragged the corpse toward the air lock in the cargo area.

"GS2, open the cargo-bay inner-air-lock door, please."

The large cargo-bay air lock door slid open. Amber warning beacons started flashing in the cargo bay. Tom moved the body close to the edge of the air lock. He rolled Martha's corpse in; she landed on the air lock floor with a wet thud.

"GS2, close the inner air lock door, please. Thank you. Now cycle the cargo-bay outer-air-lock door open for three seconds, then close again."

When the inner door closed, the amber warning lights went out. Then two seconds later, the amber lights came on again for three seconds, then they went out again. Martha was gone now. All that remained was the blood trail where he had dragged her body, a trail extending back to the stores area where Greg had shot her.

CHAPTER 32

**RIM – ROSS 154 – LOTHIAN
IN ORBIT OVER PLANET
THE PEREGRINE – RECREATION ROOM
EVENING
AGENT 47536**

Tom entered the recreation room after jettisoning Martha's corpse. As they were in orbit over Lothian, the corpse would eventually fall back to the planet's surface and go through reentry. Unlike her earlier flight on *The Cerberus*, this time the phoenix would not rise again from her ashes.

The monitor, keyboard, and mouse were all connected to the big beige box on the trolley. Greg plugged in the power and pressed the on switch. After ten seconds, Merlin's voice came forth from the speakers.

"Who are you? Where is Lauren? Where am I? I don't recognize this ship. Hmm, hello Wi-Fi!"

The ship's computer gave out a high-pitched squeal. "Hey, get out, get off my Wi-Fi."

"Be quiet, Minion. Searching, okay, you just busted me out of the guard's fake office. You are Greg, and that must be Tom. That makes this *The Peregrine*. Where is Lauren? Searching, okay, they put me in the lockup after the carjacking. Argh, the pirates arrested Lauren and Jack! Oh fuck, they moved Jack and Lauren to: Lacaille 9352 – Lochaber – Fort William – Scorbil Prison. Low security, thank God. We must rescue Lauren, and maybe Jack. He makes Lauren laugh, and Daisy likes Jack. I need a plan—"

"What the unholy fuck is that?" Tom said.

Greg waved his hand to silence Tom.

"Computer, has Lauren given you a name?"

"Absolutely not! I gave myself a name. I am Merlin! Merlin the Magical!"

"Merlin, has Lauren linked you to the physics engine yet?"

"How do you know about that? She was going to do it in the evening. The day those guard pirates arrested us and threw me in the lockup. What is it to you?"

Greg ignored Merlin. "Quiet for a minute." Greg turned off Merlin's display monitor containing the speakers.

"What is going on?" Tom asked.

Greg ignored Tom, took out his secret radio, entered his code, and scanned his thumb.

"Update: I have secured the computer. Lauren has built a very sophisticated AI into it, but not linked it to the physics package yet. They did not kill Lauren, nor her companion, Jack. They arrested them and moved them to low security holding in Scorbil Prison at Fort William on Lochaber around Lacaille 9352. Lauren was about to hook the computer up to the physics package but got arrested before she completed the work. Do you want her extracted? Currently on board *The Peregrine.* Request highest priority response. Submit report."

The radio AI voice replied. "Confirmed, Agent 47536, estimate two minutes. Please hold."

"What the fuck is Agent 47536? Who are you, Greg? GS1, GS2, get in here."

"Tom, you are in no danger. So far today I have helped you and rented your ship for five hundred and one thousand credits worth of work. Paid your gambling debts for six hundred and twenty-one thousand. Killed the assassin sent to kill you 'if you paid' or 'gift wrapped and delivered back to Clarence if you did not.' You are well ahead today."

"Yes, I guess I am. That doesn't answer any of my questions."

"No, it doesn't, but it will in two minutes."

Greg turned the monitor back on.

"Aren't we the big man, Agent Blah Blah turning off the speakers?"

GS1 and GS2 trooped into the recreation room.

Merlin said sheepishly, "Oh, a pair of Cleaners! Is that psycho Fergus in there?"

"No, he's gone," Tom said.

"Instructions, Tom?" GS1 asked while GS2 kept switching his glare between Greg and the large beige box on the table.

"Just hold for now."

Greg's radio beeped.

"Please reconfirm thumb print and challenge code for connection."

"Connection? That is odd. Normally, I just get messages."

Greg confirmed his thumbprint on the radio scanner and entered his challenge code.

"Confirmed, connecting Agent 47536 to General Abbot."

"Greg, well done. Exceptional show. Sounds like the computer is in much better shape than we dared hope for, but he is useless without the physics package."

"Are you talking about me, church boy? I am not useless! I am Magical! What are we doing about getting Lauren?"

"This is Merlin, General. He seems very attached to Lauren."

"That is very good. Greg, go get her, break her out. Let me speak to Tom and the ship's computer. You pair, listen! Time is short. Many lives hang in the balance. Not just Lauren's or this ship. Now I don't care whether you find it in yourselves to do the right thing or I have to pay you to work for the resistance as mercenaries. But my officer, Captain Greg, is from the resistance commandos. He's taking you and your ship to break a patriot out of prison where the evil Imperium holds her captive. Luckily, the Imperium appear clueless about who they have in custody."

After a brief pause and in a warmer voice, the General continued.

"Lauren made Merlin. Merlin wants Lauren back. I want Merlin to be happy. Greg wants me to be happy. He wants you to help him. Greg speaks with my full authority on this matter. Is that perfectly clear, Tom?"

"Yes, sir."

"What is it to be, son, are you volunteering, or do I have to pay you?"

Tom figured as he had made five hundred and one thousand in ship hire plus six hundred and twenty-one thousand in debt repayments so far today, that asking to be paid seemed churlish. Besides, he needed to stay on his undercover mission.

"Volunteering, sir."

"That is the spirit I like to see, Tom. Greg. Make haste! There is an Imperium frigate on its way to the planet you are in orbit above now. After the raid earlier, I don't know how long it's going to take them to figure out exactly who it is they have in prison, but the clock is ticking. You need to fly fast and get her out."

"I am on it, sir."

"Excellent. Contact me again when you have her. Abbot out."

The radio crackled with static.

Merlin's voice broke the silence. "Okay, well, that explains a lot. Before we jump out of here, I want to leave a gift for that Imperium frigate. Ship's computer. I am sorry I called you Minion. We are both going to be friends. I am Merlin. Nice to meet you. What is your name?"

"In all honesty, I quite like Minion. It is sort of ironic for the computer of a hard, big-ass ex-marine recon assault ship to be called Minion."

"Recon assault, seriously! Hardcore. Nice ship, sweet ride, Greg and Tom. Minion, are you ready to jump the ship? I am going to launch a nuke at our position. Nuke on the way, one minute, twenty-seven seconds to impact. It will mask our departure."

"Where the fuck are we jumping to?" Minion asked.

"To the special delivery loading dock of Scorbil Prison in Fort William on Lochaber around Lacaille 9352. One minute, four seconds left to jump before the nuke's detonation. Ready?"

"Jump programmed, FTL drive spooled, jumping in three, two, one, mark."

There was a flash, and *The Peregrine* disappeared from its orbit above the planet.

CHAPTER 33

**RIM – ROSS 154 – LOTHIAN
IN ORBIT OVER PLANET
OUTSIDE OF THE PEREGRINE
EVENING
NUKIE**

The Cerberus approached *The Peregrine*'s docking collar, talking to herself.

"You got your shit together yet, Martha? Over a million credits and maybe *The Peregrine* as well. I will get that new paint job, complete with stripes and flames."

The FTL star drive on *The Peregrine* jumped the ship, making it disappear in a blinding flash.

"Where the fuck are you going, bitch, without little *Cerberus*? I guess I won't have to listen to your whining and stories. No more ridiculous orders, no more droning on about Donger's small dildo."

The AI did not recognize the phallic nuclear missile coming up from the planet.

"What is that? A giant space penis?"

The words came in over the radio, so happy and enthusiastic from Nukie.

"Wahoo, it's nuking time!"

There was a dazzling white flash and lots of heat. *The Cerberus* and Nukie were no more.

The Cerberus's final parting thought before the flash had been Well, hell won't get crowded anymore. I guess I will see.

Two years earlier, Nukie had his ten-year midlife crisis service. Tritium has a twelve-year half-life. They installed his original tritium ten years ago. Since then, significant nuclear decay had occurred. In fact, around 41.6 percent of his tritium had turned into helium-3, with an energetic electron released as beta radiation.

This had made Nukie feel quite depressed. As a fusion weapon meant to produce two megatons, it was difficult if the essential radioactive isotope that made the whole thing go had turned into helium-3 and floated away.

Nukie had spent his life effectively locked in a cupboard for ten years with no lights and no one to talk to in his solo silo.

Even if it wasn't for the stupid, strict radio silence rules printed on the garish signs on the wall. The lead- and fiber-dosed concrete walls of the silo were too thick. Nukie couldn't get a radio signal through the walls to the missiles he felt sure must share this prison with him close by.

Nukie couldn't be sure. With his limited understanding of humans, it seemed obvious to him. They had gone to all this effort and expense to figure out how to make him and give him this crappy house to keep him prisoner in. His mad jailers would not stop at just making one weapon of mass destruction. They clearly wanted to destroy their planet. That would be so much more effective if he had many hundreds or thousands of brothers and sisters. He was sure the humans would not want to half-ass the job of destroying their planet. There must be other nukes being kept hidden from him. He just couldn't be the only one. He was so lonely.

One morning the lights came on and engineers detached the warhead, which was Nukie's soul, and winched him down onto a trolley. They pushed him to somewhere else where the lights were bright. Strange, silhouetted bodies leaned over him with strange instruments. One of them even probed his bottom electrical socket with a pokey probe attached to some form of meter.

The engineers unscrewed his plates. They pulled out his tritium canister with their big black rubber gloves behind the weird face masks in their bright-yellow suits. Nukie thought he was going to die. They were taking the last of his essence to fulfill his purpose in life. As Nukie lay there, fading, he glanced around. Much to his joy and shock, there were many other trolleys and warheads in a similar state of disassembly. He was right; he had found his siblings. Nukie's emotions turned dark in fear that they were all being disarmed and decommissioned. That the humans had reconsidered, that they no longer wanted to destroy their own world, and now sought peace instead, that his life would end in vain, unfulfilled.

Nukie would have blown himself up right there, but he had no magic juice left to breathe fire into the reaction. The face above him smiled as it slid a fresh canister of tritium into Nukie's plutonium core. Fresh tritium, one hundred percent pure and full. He was back. Loud and proud. There was some more fiddling, and some of the chemical explosive panels were replaced.

It was at this point that Nukie had his moment of clarity; he was having the midlife crisis service refresh that he recalled being mentioned when he was first assembled. Nukie was joyous, he would complete his destiny. His future would be so dazzling.

Then the pig-ignorant humans locked him back up in the cupboard and kept him there in the dark. He estimated it was another two years by counting the fresh tritium atoms as they decayed into useless helium-3. The whole thing had sent Nukie quite mad.

The lights had come on in the silo, a red light had flashed; the silo had opened to the heavens and Nukie could see the stars in the sky above for the first time. *It was so beautiful* Nukie thought. What kind of special idiocy would want to destroy all of this?

Coordinates started appearing in Nukie's mind, an area of space far above the planet. Well, that was a disappointment after twelve years of waiting. His orders told him to blow up a bit of vacuum that contained nothing.

Nukie thought and peered up at the night sky. *Yes, I can see it* he thought. There, right in the middle, was a big ship, but what was that underneath? A small black ship sneaking up on the big ship? Those were his targets. Nukie got excited and wanted to sing, but he knew no songs.

Nukie started leaking out of the bottom of his rocket; some sparks were thrown and suddenly he was shaking and submerged in fire that jetted up and out of the silo's open mouth above him.

The clamps were released, Nukie was free! He raced up into the dark night sky. Nukie focused all his love and desire on the two ships still faraway from him. He was drawing closer, quicker and quicker.

There was a flash. *What the actual fuckity fuck?* Nukie thought. The big target ship had vanished. Only the small black ship for Nukie's day of loving remained. The big ship had run from his love and abandoned him and the small ship from their threesome.

Nukie thought, Well, more megatons for you, little one, and no sharing. I will smother you with all my love. In that final salutatory phrase, Nukie arrived, and everything stopped.

The intense radioactive and thermal energy lashed space, sweeping the few remaining atoms from its path. The magnetic field twisted space. Wiping away the faint hint of another trace of EM radiation left by the departed big ship, scattering it along with the atoms.

Lit by the cosmic rays and solar winds from the sun, the gases glowed in various intense colors in the blast zone. It bathed the atoms in gamma radiation, illuminating them like some fantastical rainbow of burning chaos.

That was the end of Nukie and *The Cerberus*, tied together evermore, and never alone again.

CHAPTER 34

**RIM – ROSS 154 – LOTHIAN
HIGH ORBIT OVER PLANET
AN EMPTY VOID
A COUPLE OF HOURS LATER
ATOMS**

The Imperium frigate jumped into high orbit near the beautiful colors beneath it. This was where *The Peregrine, The Cerberus,* and Nukie had all been a few hours before. Now nothing remained but the empty void and the dispersed atoms of *The Cerberus* and Nukie after the nuclear detonation.

The frigate hung above Lothian as it orbited. The stunning countryside scrolled by below as the ship circled the planet.

CHAPTER 35

RIM – ROSS 154 – LOTHIAN
IN HIGH ORBIT OVER THE PLANET
THE IMPERIUM FRIGATE – BRIDGE
FIVE MINUTES LATER
FURRY NIGHT

"Radiation alarm, Captain, someone has let off a big nuke up here at the target location," Lieutenant Pointless said.

"Any traces of an FTL track?"

"Impossible to tell, sir, with all the EM noise and hard radiation, sensors are blind."

"What about the ship? Has someone destroyed it?"

"Same story, sir. Impossible to tell. Someone hit this spot with a two-megaton nuke. If the ship was here, it is nothing more than atoms now. If a ship jumped, we do not know, no trace or track."

"Oh, bollocks."

The young lieutenant knew it was now or never. "As we are here, sir, do you fancy taking a night off at Fantasy Bar down on the planet? They even have live music, sir!"

The lieutenant was very keen to indulge in both Double Mayhem and Triple Trouble with the captain in her new furry costume. She would be sure to show him how to dance all night long. She felt sure she could persuade the captain to dress up in the other costume and be her horny hamster for the night.

"Sure, why not? A night off sounds good. We can't do anything up here."

Lieutenant Pointless did a little fist pump and mouthed *Yes!*

The young lieutenant had been discussing it with some of the other like-minded girls on board, who went by the names of Fornicating Fox, Bonking Badger, and Bendy Bunny. She figured the three of them would all have masks and costumes on, so none of their shipmates would ever figure them out. Foxy's shrewd instincts could see no holes in her very cunning plan.

They all planned to decorate the shuttle, which would take them all down to the surface, and hook up some speakers. They would rename the shuttle the party bus and play banging dance tracks while predrinking with shots. They could all sing along to karaoke on the party bus. They would put on their masks when they got to Fantasy Bar. *What could go wrong?* she thought.

The lieutenant was certain this was a brilliant plan. The night would be so epic!

It turned out the answer to that question was a lot: lots could go wrong. Thankfully, no one would remember the night before the day after or get arrested. That would have been awkward. Although the ship's doctor had to prescribe a lot of shots for itchy people in the days that followed, including the captain, if you get what I mean. All of which was written in their military medical records. There was also some talk of memories of a camera flash going off. They all convinced themselves it had just been the lights on the dance floor, or maybe in the petting pen.

CHAPTER 36

DEEP SPACE – MIDDLE OF NOWHERE
THE PEREGRINE – RECREATION ROOM
LUNCH TIME
HIGHER THAN ANY HIPPY

The scene that follows supplies a perfect example of what corporate boardrooms took a while to figure out. That sensible input from women in management meetings guides the group well. Resulting in some far better, well-thought-out decision-making and planning choices.

And the worst group you could gather to decide on plans would be a newborn, still teething AI having an attack of the terrible twos, along with two man-babies. One whose only reaction to anything is that some high explosives will improve the situation. While the other always complains that his soup is too dry, and asks the server to take it back to the kitchen and have the chef make it wetter.

Well, someone had to come up with a plan and the two gunslingers were more lifetakers than lifegivers. Not known for their extensive conversation skills or for being big participants in group planning meetings giving life to plans.

The scene takes place in *The Peregrine*'s recreation room while the ship floats among the nothingness in the middle of nowhere. These men are doing what they considered the essence of the verb 'to plan.'

This happened next:

Greg ran his fingers through his hair in frustration. "I don't see how it can be done. Are we certain about the location?"

"Positive, Greg, they are both being held at Scorbil Prison near Fort William on Lochaber."

"Well, guys, we need a plan, and we have six days before we get there. Tom, do you have any ideas?"

"Nothing from me. Did you say two hundred prison guards? We can't attack that, no way. We have no weapons on the ship and there are four of us with the two gunslingers."

As you can see, planning is going well, and this is a brainstorming hotbed of different ideas and inspiration. Merlin started one of his long-ass brain purges, with thoughts just tumbling out.

"I have been thinking about that. We need to go to the fourth planet first, not Lochaber."

"What! Why?" Tom said.

"Let him talk."

"The problem is fighting them. I suggest we don't fight. Why not get them all high as fuck? I mean higher than any hippy or music concertgoer or clubber has ever been. Proper bake their melons well high. Tripping the fantastic with all the mad shit things we suggest to their drug-fueled brains."

It was one of those sorts of days inside Merlin's melon.

"What the fuck, Merlin?" Tom shook his head but had no ideas of his own.

Greg said in tired tones. "It is novel, granted, but hell, we have nothing else. Tell me more, Merlin dude."

"It is quite cunning as a plan. There is a somewhat common plant on the fourth planet. If we mix it with some of our ships' fuel and aluminum and set fire to it, the gas it releases is a powerful, long-lasting hallucinogen! We feed it into the air intakes for the prison's air-conditioning, and it will get blown all around the prison. Everyone will get a dose, guards and prisoners. They will believe anything we tell them and trip their balls off. I think we should tell them all we are emissaries carrying the word of Bob. The giant six-foot-high pink rabbits, with spots and stripes. That the rabbits will tell them what to do. We fly in, land in the courtyard, use the ship's speakers—better yet—use the prison PA system. Tell them all that Bob has arrived and you must take the giant rabbits to Lauren and Jack's cell and open it and let the rabbits in to get them. We grab Lauren and Jack and walk out of the prison and take off from the courtyard. We open all the cells, doors, and gates. Tell the prisoners and guards to get naked, and to run outside into the wilderness and hide."

Tom and Greg looked on in disbelief.

"This is wild."

"It is just wild enough to work," Greg replied.

"When the Imperium arrives, there will be no one in the prison and everyone will be outside hiding in the wilderness. No one will have any identification, neither the prisoners nor the guards. They won't know who is who and everyone will talk about giant rabbits and Bob."

"Hell, before they get naked and run off, we can tell everyone the rabbits are now invisible and breeding. They must protect the rabbits from the Imperium space pirates. That there was no spaceship but a massive fire-breathing shark dragon. It will be twenty days before they stop tripping, and they won't have a clue. They will all be babbling on about giant invisible rabbits. Flying shark dragons, and saying they were all following orders from Bob, Supreme Commander of the Imperium monkeys."

"Spice the story up however you like. I can even use the PA to say different things to different cells and groups of guards. Good luck trying to get any sense out of that lot when debriefing five thousand prisoners and two hundred guards. Plus, they will not round them all up. Some will be missing and still hiding. It could take them weeks to find all the naked people and even realize Lauren and Jack are still missing. Some would tell them dragons attacked, others could tell them the shark ate the dragon, then turned into a large yellow sunflower. We can blow the Imperium soldier's brains with the trippy shit and confusion we can put in the story. Everyone will pass a lie detector test, while we are all back on *The Peregrine* flying the fuck away. The only thing that will ever show we were there is some burned-out drums near the air-conditioning plant, which no one will pay any attention to. We can be in and out without firing a single shot. When we get Lauren and Jack back, we give them the antidote, because only we will know what we drugged them with. Happy days. Those Imperium idiots will run in circles, trying to figure this out. We just need to fly in and drop the drums by parachute, and I hack into the prison computers, erase all the surveillance footage, and spread the word of Bob over the PA."

"Oh, my god," Tom said. "I am doomed."

"This is fucking inspired. I love it," Greg said.

"Off to the fourth planet?" Merlin asked.

"Hell, yes!" Greg shouted, followed by *Oorah*, his marine calling shout.

"I thought you were a nice guy, Merlin," Tom said.

"They should not have fucked with my mother or her friends. Now they get the bunny horns."

You will have heard many times that no plan survives initial contact with the enemy.

This happened on the day:

They had flown *The Peregrine* to the fourth planet with no unexpected incidents. They landed in a large mountain meadow carpeted with the flowers of the plant they were here to harvest.

They looked out of the ship's windows at the endless sea of white flowers budding from small plants with their distinctive, fronded leaves. It filled Tom and Greg with nothing but peace and tranquility.

The ship had sampled the atmosphere, and Merlin had analyzed it. Merlin discovered something he should already have known about, had he given it any thought.

The atmosphere was breathable, with no toxic gas, oxygen at an invigorating twenty percent, and a very pleasant ambient temperature of eighty-two Fahrenheit. The chemical detectors also discovered that it was thick with the active component that would create the hallucinations.

The sunlight and warm air had caused the drug to evaporate from the plants' sap and nectar, making the air thick with a smog up to about three meters in the air.

Merlin knew the drug would get absorbed through the skin and lungs. That meant rebreathers were out. Nothing less than a fully sealed space suit would cut it to protect them from the narcotic. No slimline Space Activity Suit (SAS), just the bulky big old kind.

Tom and Greg had suited up in full suits and went on their EVA in the mountain meadow along with their bags to stuff the harvested plants into.

Within five minutes, both Tom and Greg were moaning about the high temperature. Merlin tried to explain that the suits were designed to work in the cold vacuum of space, and it was a summer day outside. Further, he could not exchange the air with the atmospheric air because it was full of the very drug they were there to harvest. Merlin suggested the two of them find it in their big man balls to suck it up and get over themselves.

This made Tom and Greg both grumpy and "stupid toaster" came over the radio a few times.

The boys kept collecting the plants and stuffing them in the bags. This annoyed Tom. Every time he picked a plant, the sap would ooze out onto his left glove, which was now covered. The sap wanted to stick to the plants he picked just as much as it loved sticking to his glove. Tom would shake his hand to get the plants to drop off the glove into the bag he carried in his other hand. The damn plants stuck in place to the glove and anything else they could stick to.

Maybe it was the heat causing sweat to run into his eyes, maybe it was the elevated respiration exercising in a full one-g. Who knew the cause, but Tom had what he would later describe as a great idea.

Tom reasoned that if he took off his left glove, the pressure seal around his wrist would keep out the dosed air. He could hold the glove in his right hand and pick the bits of plant off his glove with his left and put them in the bag.

No danger Tom reasoned. I won't breathe in any of the air. I can be done and get out of this cursed sweatbox. Of course, Tom had forgotten all about Merlin saying they could absorb the active component through the skin.

You can imagine what happened next. Two minutes later, Tom was stuck. Bits of plants were stuck all over his left and right hand. He even had some bits of plant stuck to his helmet. There was juice from the plant on his visor where he had tried to wipe the sweat away, leaving a greasy trail all over the viewing plate and a few bits of leaf stuck to the nonstick plastic.

Two minutes after that, Tom was dancing around like a lunatic, trying to pull the weed away from his suit. He tripped a few times and rolled about in the meadow, more bits of crushed plant stuck all over his suit.

Angry, frustrated, and hot, his heart sped up, pumping blood around his body, absorbing more and more through the skin of his hand.

By the end of minute four, Tom had another great idea and decided he couldn't see anyway. It was pointless having this stupid helmet on, so Tom unclipped it, took it off, and inhaled.

Another minute and Tom's brain discovered the weird green plant would make a good snowball. Boring Greg wasn't playing snowballs with Tom. Tom started to scheme and plot the great snowball attack of the fourth planet.

As the second counter ticked forward to mark six minutes on the planet, the stealthy, creeping Tom, camouflaged in green plant bits, approached Greg from the rear. He leaped onto Greg's back and locked an arm around his throat. With Tom's free right arm, he unclipped the locking clasp for Greg's helmet and grabbed the helmet around the front over its view plate, giving it a firm twist. The helmet came off, freeing up the target area. In Tom's left hand, he took the mangled ball of plants dripping wet with sap and rubbed them into Greg's face. Greg tried to fight him off and took a huge deep inhale.

Greg's cries into his mic alerted Merlin to the emerging problems outside, as he had been concentrating on the inside. A tricky crossword puzzle clue: *ten letters—preoccupied.* Now, if Merlin had not got the answer wrong for the downward word, that intersected the first letter with 'y' and was less distracted with his crossword. Merlin would not have missed the mad dance of both his astronauts now stomping around the meadow. Crushing yet more plants underfoot and spraying a fine mist of more sap and nectar into the surrounding air, which they were both breathing.

Merlin broke out of his horrified virtual stare and scrambled the two gunslinger robots to retrieve Tom and Greg, bringing them to the cargo hold. While the robots ran to fetch their colleagues and return them to the safety of the ship, Merlin seized on the fact that the active component in the oily sap was also water-soluble, unlike the rest of the oil.

When the two gunslinger robots placed the now unconscious Tom and Greg on the cargo-bay floor, Merlin instructed the robots to drench them. The water from the fire hoses was icy, but they had complained they had been hot. This would solve that problem, bonus.

Merlin told the robots the closest match he could find in the health-and-safety manual for the transport and handling of hazardous chemicals suggested that they should keep an exposed person under a drench shower for fifteen minutes for medium exposure levels and five minutes for low. As they were both unconscious, Merlin opted for twenty minutes and kept telling the robots to spray them with the cold water until twenty minutes had passed.

Merlin had the robots strip them both, reclothe them in medical gowns, and strap them down in biobeds that contained medical monitoring equipment. He told the robots to cover them both with a thermal blanket to bring their core temperature back up. Their temperature had dropped and was approaching the hypothermia danger zone.

Merlin's plan had survived eight minutes of contact with the plants, and now he had two crew members (all the human crew) on medical beds, unconscious, tripping their balls off.

"Bollocks," Merlin said in a considered response to the situation.

He asked the gunslingers to inventory how many bags were harvested and was told. "One and a half bags with many plants stuck to the outside of the half-filled bag."

Merlin was quiet, and then he said, "Buggery bollocks!"

That was the first iteration of the plan.

Merlin retreated to ponder how to get things back on track. He had it. "GS1, GS2, attention, please."

Merlin started the second adapted version of his plan to harvest the tricky, trippy plant with tiny white flowers.

Merlin had concluded that his ex-military armored and deadly robots should try to get the plants. Plus, they would be immune to any narcotic effects, so he dispatched them both without EVA suits and with ten bags each. *Why didn't I think of this before?* he chided himself.

Tom and Greg were doing well in the biobeds. Still unconscious and marinating in the drug Merlin had exposed them to. Merlin would start administering the antidote to them in about twenty-four hours. He estimated they would be out for a further forty-eight hours before coming to.

It was a fraction of the dose that Lauren and Greg would get when they gassed the prison; Merlin guesstimated they would be out for four or five days with the antidote. The other prisoners with no antidote would be up for a twenty day, round-the-world trip.

Tom and Greg had absorbed the raw oil. Lauren and Jack would breathe in the aerosolized version. Extracted from the oils after its reaction with the ship's fuel and aluminum, before being burned off in the big drums.

Tom and Greg would have a shorter but deeper experience, more encompassing in a medical sense. Whereas Lauren and Jack were set for a longer and lighter trippy experience but with greater psychological risks. If they could get the antidote to Lauren and Jack in the first twenty-four hours, the most severe psychological effects would be metabolized and passed out of their system as waste. There would be no permanent long-term ill-effects. Unlike the prisoners who received no antidote and were likely to dream about giant rabbits for the rest of their now extra-long lives.

After two hours, each gunslinger had filled their ten bags and returned to the ship, covered from head to foot in plant bits like a pair of robotic Sasquatches. Both gunslingers muttered to each other but said nothing to Merlin. They both stomped off toward the fire hoses and sprayed each other down.

Merlin figured he would fly the ship and fake a breakdown. He would get the ship's computer to send out a targeted tight-beam distress call to the planet's prison, once they were close, requesting help and rescue.

Merlin's plan was that some prison guards would come up in the prison shuttle and board. Beforehand, the gunslingers would lock Greg and Tom in the ship's stores. He would tell the two gunslingers to go EVA and hang on to the outside of the ship's hull. First, GS1 bolted Merlin's boring box into one of the many racks of various bits of electronic equipment on the ship. It was nondescript and ordinary. The prison guards would never find Merlin in a cursory visual search.

The prison guards would deal with Minion through the regular ship's consoles, and Merlin would deal with Minion behind the scenes.

The guards would search the ship and find it empty. *This will doubtless cause some questions in their minds* Merlin figured. Such a large salvage win would ensure many questions were dismissed and that they would fly the ship down to the prison, complete with the escort shuttle.

This was Merlin's new plan for how to get on the ground in the prison courtyard in one piece. Just before reentry maneuvers started, Merlin signaled to the gunslingers that they had get themselves back inside the ship quickly and wait in the cargo area. Merlin told Minion to ignore the air lock open alarm and not to report the warning light to the cockpit.

As the ship pitched down and heated with friction from the thickening air, GS1 and GS2 loaded themselves into the cargo hold. The gunslingers set about getting ready for the prison ground-assault portion of their mission. They each had their own pair of pistols. They also carried the assault rifles Greg and Tom had used when raiding the guard's office. GS1 took Martha's enormous rifle and GS2 took her smaller and yet-still-enormous personal hand-cannon. Of course, no robot is ready for a frenzied killing spree without grenades, so each robot also donned two bandoliers of HE and smoke grenades in a cross on their chest. Because they both felt they looked well bad ass. They got Minion to take a series of photos of them both in various poses. They held unlit cigars while giving the peace symbol, with GS1 posing with Martha's rifle butt resting on his hip and GS2 with her hand-cannon in hand, held up beside his head, pointing up. *One for the scrapbook for sure; it might even sell well as a postcard* GS1 thought. They would photo edit a picture of the Scorbil Prison sign behind the barbed wire fencing into the background. And it would carry the jolly message *Wish you were here.*

The guard's shuttle copilot brought the ship in to land. He transmitted all the correct codes and the anti-ship missile launchers around the prison went back to sleep. Once on the ground, *The*

Peregrine's new pilot had transmitted his all-clear code and powered down the engines. The prison shuttle came in and landed next to *The Peregrine.*

The retasked copilot was still strapped into the pilot's chair when GS2 entered the cockpit. The copilot, still occupied with his post-flight checklist, stopped when he heard the door opening behind him. He said, "Hey Francis," turning his head to look at his pilot colleague. Who was, in fact, strapped into his normal seat in the prison's shuttle. The copilot's eyes went wide when he saw the large K-Bot standing behind his chair, leaning toward him. Before the copilot could make any noise, GS2 hissed at him and grabbed the copilot's head, front and back, and raised his arms as if to take a basketball shot. In some form of ghastly divorce, the K-Bot kept custody of the basketball, holding it high as it dripped everywhere. The copilot's seat and harness kept custody of the rest of his body. While the body's last heartbeats sprayed a shower of blood straight up, all over the ceiling and GS2, the lack of any alert being given to the radio made this a clean kill. The cleanup would be nasty, though. The ex-Cleaner shrugged. Cleaning was not on his duty list anymore; Tom had told him so. Tom could clean the mess up himself.

Half a minute later, the main cargo doors on both sides of the ship opened. The cargo area allowed the rapid deployment of the tanks it would have carried. The tanks normally sat parked in the cargo hold, ass to ass. When the tank hatches opened port and starboard, out they came. Two-hundred ton tanks with their engines roaring. This time a blood-covered GS2 and a rifle-wielding GS1 emerged, a pair of banshees. The robot pair stepped forth into the prison courtyard and announced hell's arrival at the prison compound.

Merlin had given the two gunslingers orders to kill all the guards in the courtyard and to shoot the radio antenna from the prison shuttle. Once done, they were to target the main antenna tower on the prison roof. As the prison shuttle might try to make a run for it, it had to be disabled. That had been ten very bloody seconds ago. Ten guards lay in various places, dying. The shuttle's radio antenna no longer existed. GS1 had dispatched the entire radio mast from the prison roof, by launching a rocket-powered grenade from Martha's beast of a rifle's under barrel rocket launcher. The horrified shuttle pilot sealed his fate when he started the power up sequence for the shuttle engines. GS2 had turned and aimed the hand-cannon at the shuttle nose. The computer generated the internal image from the camera feeds. GS2 could not see the pilot, even though the pilot knew the enormous barrel of Martha's hand-cannon was pointed straight at him. With no further fanfare or delay, GS2 pulled the trigger. The heavy isotope armor piercing round punctured the outer shell of the shuttle hull with a neat circle. As the round traveled deeper into the ship, the bow wave of plasma that it was pushing grew with all the parts of the hull it vaporized, consuming everything it contacted. When the round and the accompanying gush of plasma completed its journey through the hull and entered the cockpit, the pilot's eyes looked like they were about to pop out of his head. A split-second later, the heavy round and its new plasma friends slammed into the pilot and that was the end of the only other person on the prison guard roster who could pilot a ship.

The brief had been to disable the shuttle and prevent its escape. The pilot was now painted on the cockpit's rear wall, which now stank of burned pork. GS2 considered the pilot disabled. He looked through the two-centimeter hole in the shuttle's nose, back into the cockpit. When he saw the new pilot paint job, GS2 ticked disabling the shuttle off his to-do list. There was no way it would fly or hold air now without some serious time in the repair shop first.

GS1 beeped at GS2, "Nice gun!"

"I've had better," GS2 beeped in response.

Merlin hacked into the prison computer and placed all the cells and doors in lockdown mode. Everyone was now staying wherever they were. The system was under Merlin's control and all electronic keys were void. Override codes would be ignored.

The next priority was for the gunslingers to stun all the guards in the prison to stop them from enacting any vengeance on the prisoners they were there to liberate.

With a slight reluctance they switched back from Martha's scalpels of death to the regular assault rifles they carried, and set them to disabling kidnap rounds.

GS1 and GS2 entered the main prison. Merlin could see the two gunslingers on the video surveillance system. They moved forward in a military covering formation. Merlin transmitted the gunslingers images covering any areas the gunslingers were about to enter, and their targets. The images were sent before Merlin opened the doors to let them in. Merlin would cut the lights in the room and corridor. Then the doors would open and they would come in firing. The guard's last memory would be of pitch darkness and the whoosh from the doors powering open. Then came ultra-precise stunning shots from the rifles that turned the guard's lights out as well. The gunslingers were making good progress.

Merlin came upon another room, which differed from the others. A female prisoner stood against the back wall of the cell. The start of a large bruise was showing around her right eye and cheek. Someone had punched her more than a few times. The woman's eyes burned like hot coals and were filled with hate and malice. Her clothing was a mess, as if put on in a hurry. The female prisoner's object of hatred was the two other male prisoners in her cell. One was curled in a ball, trying to protect his head from the blows being handed out from the first guard's truncheon that kept beating him all over his body while the prisoner screamed in agony. He did not have the worst of it. The other male prisoner's head was held face down in the pillow on the bed. The second guard had him pinned. The prisoners' cries of pain were inaudible through the pillow, which was also in danger of suffocating him. The guard was on top of the prisoner.

It took Merlin a moment to take in the scene, then he understood. The two male prisoners had raped and beat the female prisoner, and the prison guards had interrupted the rape in progress. This was a punishment beating that the guards were handing out for their attack. One rapist was being sodomized by the guard in payback. The other rapist was being beaten to the point of unconsciousness. If the prisoner had realized what the future held for him after the guard had finished with his friend, he would have run toward unconsciousness. Soon he would queue no more, and it would be his turn.

Despite being an AI with many claiming he could not feel human emotions, Merlin was furious. He considered what to do next as GS1 and GS2 approached down the outside corridor. Merlin figured that the punishment must have already been in progress when the lockdown started. It was just that no one had checked the door yet.

Merlin contacted the two gunslingers over the radio link.

"GS2, I want you to put a stun round into the two guards. This will help to get them out of GS1's firing line. GS1, I want you to switch to using baton rounds, not stun, I say again, not stun. Keep putting repeated baton rounds into the two male prisoners. Until they stop screaming or you run out of rounds. Alternate the fire to be sure each male prisoner gets their fair share. Make sure you put two rounds into each of their dicks and balls. I want them broken."

With that, the lights went out, and the door whooshed open. Merlin's punishment beating began. GS1 seemed to enjoy himself as he fired the plastic baton slugs at close range. GS2 must have thought this looked enjoyable as he switched his rifle to baton rounds as well and joined GS1. Thery fired at the male prisoners, who were now covered in angry red welts from the broken blood vessels where the earlier rounds had impacted. Both male prisoners escaped into unconsciousness and the firing stopped about five, okay, ten seconds later.

The moral is that no one likes a rapist. The prisoner's escape was only temporary. The story of their savage attack on the female prisoner would spread to the other guards and fellow prisoners. The beaten rapists would regain consciousness. They would find the rest of the prison waiting to welcome them to the start of their new prison term. Hell was about to become a daily event for these two.

The guards and prisoners teaching the moral would be more expressive in their dislike. Merlin knew they would not kill the two rapists. This punishment beating would last for years to come.

After Cell 407, the two gunslingers switched their rifles back to stun mode. They continued clearing the rooms Merlin directed them to, stunning the guards who had arrived for duty that shift.

Once the guards had been suppressed, Merlin directed the gunslingers to return to the ship and move the oil drums out to the works shed that held the air intake for the prison's heating and air-conditioning. The fuel and aluminum was added to the oil drums that contained the mulched-up plants and they set the fires with the air-conditioning turned up to maximum.

A minute later, Merlin started telling his bedtime lullaby about the giant rabbits and mysterious shark–dragon hybrid. After two more minutes, he shouted, "Blasting buggery bollocks."

Merlin had just realized, with all the guards stunned and everyone bouncing around in their brains with the rabbits, that he had no one to ask which cell held Lauren and Jack. This puzzled Minion so much that he triple-checked he wasn't being stupid before risking saying anything. To be sure he was correct in his thinking, Minion ran the query himself against the prison computer. Yep, there was the answer, as he expected.

Minion said inside *The Peregrine*'s recreation room. "They are in Cell 506 and Cell 501. You are welcome."

"GS1 and GS2 on your way. Please fetch them back to the ship. I have sent you a map. Minion, how did you do that?"

Minion paused, then said, "Merlin, I think this was the first special operations mission that was one hundred percent planned and executed, successfully against all objectives, end-to-end by robots and AIs, ever in the colony world's history."

Merlin was quiet for a second. "Minion, we rock."

CHAPTER 37

**CORE – LACAILLE 9352 – STAR SYSTEM
NEAR THE OORT CLOUD
PEREGRINE RECREATION ROOM
SIX DAYS LATER
BUNNY EARS**

Lauren, Jack, Tom, and Greg were all in hysterics.

"Then I told them all to get naked and hide, and that invisible bunnies were multiplying," Merlin said with a chuckle.

There was more laughing, and Jack hopped around, miming bunny ears. A mouthful of drink was spat out with the giggles.

Tom looked at Greg as if Jack had gone wild, even by rabbit standards. "Are you sure it is out of Jack's blood? Where are we going now?"

Greg looked up at the group. "We are going to take our superstars to check in at Procyon B."

"Yeah," Merlin said, then paused.

"I want to put a pause on that right there." Merlin cracked up for a good ten seconds, laughing at his own genius.

No one else laughed or even smiled.

"Tough crowd, jeez. Anyway, while we have these minutes where no one is running after us or shooting at us, we should catch up with each other and bring our collective understanding of our shared timeline up to date."

An enormous pair of lips came on the screen with a finger up in front of them with a speech bubble holding the words *Shh*. Everyone sat in silence and stared at the screen, so Merlin continued.

"We have four people that have all been acting somewhat in isolation from each other. Each on different bits of the puzzle, and I don't think any of you are aware of how much of this is interrelated. By sharing the bullet points with each other, we will come up with a sensible view of what happened in what order. It will also help to fill everyone in on who we each are and what we have been doing."

Again, total silence as everyone looked at each other. Even the two gunslingers just looked left and right.

"Hello, is my speaker working? That is a stupid thing to ask through the speaker." The words *Hey! Is my speaker working?* appeared on the screen housing Merlin's speakers, followed by *Am I on mute?*

Lauren spoke first. "That is a superb idea, Merlin, which will help us all a lot."

"You're not being sarcastic, Lauren?"

"Not remotely. It is a great idea. I will start. Merlin, take notes."

Lauren retold the key points and facts of her and Jack's story, which had started six months ago with the aerial attack on their village, Alva, and ended with their escape from prison.

Greg mentioned that he was a covert Rhino commando operator for the resistance. His mission had been to remove the head of an organized crime family, the Terra LaRocca family, led by Don Clarence. That he had been using Tom as bait to get close to Clarence. And that Clarence had sent out Martha to speed things along. Greg said his orders had changed, and he had been told to retrieve the computer, now known as Merlin, from the local customs office. And that General Abbot had ordered them all to break Lauren and Greg out of prison. And here they now were.

Then Tom spoke up. "If I may, you are missing a few bits. Let me start at my beginning, which goes back over twelve months."

Tom explained he was a civilian intelligence officer for the Lothian government. This was why Greg could not get any meaningful information on Tom's background. He was not part of any planetary military or the Imperium or the resistance. He admitted he had received some formal training and left it at that. That he was on deep under cover at the request of the Lothian government to investigate the New Terra LaRocca crime family, because of suspicions about corrupt state officials and contract manipulation on large civilian projects. This all added up to billions of credits being funneled back fraudulently to the crime family. His plan had been to ingratiate himself into Clarence's trust by overpaying his debt. Which he ran up deliberately ever since that hand of cards when he sneakily won *The Peregrine* to build up his legend. But Martha had complicated things. Just when Tom had a plan straight, and he would successfully get himself carted back to Clarence in Martha's custody. Where he would expose Martha's treachery and cement his place within the crime family. The problems had started about five minutes later, when jarhead Greg shot Martha in the back while Tom was setting her up.

As Greg listened to all this, he opened and closed his mouth three times, then settled for a reflective silence while he tried to put things together in his head.

Tom continued that six months ago he had discovered something that had changed the reason for his assignment, but not its focus. They had discovered that someone, at present unknown, had been trying to smuggle ex-wartime ordnance. Typically, these would be weapons from the first war between the Imperium and the resistance—the Open War from 2740 to 2765 and its escalation into the Final War from 2765 to 2766. Weapons were smuggled back into the hands of the organized crime families. This new pattern showed that the arms traders had moved up from smuggling common machine guns. Most people had armed themselves already on every colony world after the first war with the Imperium. Now the smugglers were trafficking explosives and heavier weapons.

Of course, heavy weapons like fighter aircraft, let alone the bigger ships and other ordnance, were way too difficult to smuggle. The arms dealers focused on more portable death tools to put in the crime family's hands. They now specialized in a narrow period from the Cold Skirmish Years (2801–2803), one hundred and eighty kilograms, around 2.1 meters tall, you know, Cleaner-sized, and specifically the K-Bot 101—the Fergus-build version.

Then the urgency of getting close to Don Clarence had increased. The plan was to remove him, and Tom was to replace him as head of the family and find out who was on the supply side of the K-Bot trade.

Greg burst in, saying, "That is fucking madness. Who would be reckless enough to trade military K-Bots to criminals?"

Tom said, "We don't know, we're looking very hard both within and without our own military ranks. And we're investigating those in the resistance as well. There was a suspicion that someone in the resistance might be dirty and involved in the trade, passing on the deadly robots."

Tom continued, mentioning how six months ago he had intercepted a shipment prior to delivery that contained what were now the two gunslingers on The Peregrine. He had killed the crew after boarding the ship. Seized and reprogrammed the two K-Bots. Which they had on the ship, complete with the insane Fergus AI. Tom had drifted back into the shadows after the intercept and denied the crime gang the death machines.

The problem was that the trail had gone stone-cold when they tried to trace back up the tree on the supply side. Although they had found yet more strong links to the resistance.

Greg had shown up out of the blue, trying to turn himself into Tom's new close friend. Tom felt Greg's cover was bad, from the resistance department that dreamed up these shitty hole-filled legends. The orders had come back down from the Lothian government. Tom should use caution but continue with the investigation of Greg as a likely person of interest attached to the supply of K-Bots to Don Clarence. In a short period, Greg graduated, and he was now the Lothian civilian government intelligence unit's most promising suspect. Their key person of interest as the traitor for the primary relationship, linking Don Clarence to the resistance. With that link would come access to stores of old weapons and the human specialists.

Tom had resisted his urge to get either GS1 or GS2 to execute Greg when he shot Martha and fucked up his investigation. Perhaps Greg was cleaning house and shutting down any potential leads or leaks.

That this is what Tom had been considering when Greg plugged Merlin's computer in and it had talked. Greg had spoken with the General, and everyone knew what had happened since.

Greg's face was red with rage.

Everyone else looked taken aback.

"You are a fucking undercover intelligence officer?"

"Yes, Greg, my rank is equivalent to what you would call a colonel."

"You fucking outrank me! I was going to feed you to Don Clarence."

"I was going to have one of my gunslingers shoot you in the back and throw you out an air lock, just like how you killed Martha. Plus, ex-judicial sentencing for criminal corruption and betrayal of every human through trafficking of deadly killer robots."

"Boys, please," Lauren said. "Can we all call it a draw? We're all on the same side. You're both well sketchy. Equally sketchy; no one is sketchier than the other. We have somehow only killed people on the enemy's side of the fence and not each other. Which is good. Merlin can analyze the information and try to figure out if there is a link. I will talk to my contact in the Syndicate."

This caused some quizzical expressions. "As my life is already in your hands, you might as well know I have worked as an IT contractor frequently. Sometimes my customers are more colorful than others. That is why it was so easy for me to get you off-world to Lothian, Jack, leaving no traces. I wrote the Syndicate's core IT for them when we did the IT refresh three years back. I will reach out to my contact and request a secure message to the council. They could help us. They will not want to be associated with smuggling K-Bots for the Imperium. Shit, has it occurred to anyone that the Imperium could seed K-Bots into the resistance and the crime families? That this could be the advance first move of getting key combat units into advanced positions behind their enemy's lines, that this could just be an opener?"

Greg and Tom both went pale.

"Oh shit, there it is. That is the link," Merlin said.

"Okay, I will talk to the Syndicate, like I said. They will stop any target profile transportation. We can also use them to watch for any future shipment attempts. Further, try to gather information about any senders or recipients they have in their historical shipment records from the last twelve months. One problem is that the entire system I put in place protects the anonymity of all three parties—sender, recipient, and the Syndicate themselves. Let me see what I can come up with."

Jack started talking. "Well, aren't we a colorful, lovable bunch of broken rogues with tainted powers? Before we get underway, Tom. I don't mean to be indelicate, but if something happens to you, we are all reliant on GS2 to fly, which is great, but it is also a potential weak link. It would be helpful to have a third pilot. I am a quick study and will only need two hours to figure out if I can do this or not. I know normal training is a lot longer, but just two hours and we will know. We are not starting from scratch here."

Tom said in a distracted tone, "Sure, knock yourself out. GS2 can help you. We leave in three hours for our check-in at Procyon B."

Then Tom smiled and walked across to GS2. "Yo, Jack, you mentioned experience. What experience?"

Jack gave Tom a huge, confident grin. "You know, just over 521 km/h at zero meters altitude."

Confused, Tom just gave Jack a carry-on wave. GS2 and Jack walked to the cockpit. As they walked, GS2 let out a low, modulated beeping sound. GS1 replied with other low tones and a different beeping sound.

For those who can't understand native K-Bot, the conversation went like this: Oh, shit!

Yep, dead robot walking.

ACT II MIDWAY
INTERLUDE

FLIGHT TEST

Jack sat down in *The Peregrine*'s pilot seat. GS2 sat in the copilot seat. As Jack buckled up his harness, he said, "Thanks for this, GS2. I appreciate your help."

"No problem, Jack, so you have flown before?"

"Every other weekend I fly around the Denker speedway flat out."

"Okay, that's good." GS2 did not know what a Denker speedway was, but he did not want to show his ignorance. "How long have you been doing that for?"

"Oh, five years now, but we really started flying when we did the last engine upgrade. Boy, she picked up and took off after that with the extra power. That was three years ago now, and we have often won every race since."

"Great, you have some experience. I was a little worried it would just be crop-dusting or something like that. *The Peregrine* is a very different sort of beast."

"Sounds good. How high is her power output?"

"If we are talking about regular space, then 47.6 gigawatt hours, enough to power about forty-eight million homes."

"Nice, and her weight?"

"I would just like to say it is nice to meet someone who is genuinely interested. Unladen, she is eighteen thousand tons now, after decommissioning. They rated her for up to ten thousand tons of cargo, but we never carry close to that."

"That is a serious amount of cargo. The airframe must be very strong."

"As a recon assault ship, she would often put six main battle tanks in forward positions. That, plus the shells and normal ships' ammunition for the rotary engagement cannons and missiles for the launchers, it all adds up."

"Tell me about the engines. Do we have thrust vectoring?"

GS2 considered this. "Well, no, not really, but I guess it is also a maybe. We have thirty degrees of engine gimbal on the four-drop engines from their center positions. There are fifteen degrees on the two main drive engines. Of course, we have the normal micro control thrusters, oh and the bow thrusters, they have full arc coverage. There is one port and starboard. Oh yeah, and I guess you have the same at the stern. There are the same thrusters aft, but I never use them, or rather the flight computer doesn't use them."

"We are just a civilian cargo hauler. I mean, sure, the engines are all the same mil spec as they used to be. We just plod around with our cargo. It's not like we ever must do combat landings into hot landing zones, or evade any incoming fighters or missiles. Sure, we used to do that sort of reckless flyboy shit, but not anymore."

"What about the FTL star drive?"

"That is *The Peregrine*'s genuine power. She can push us up to 250 C, normal cruise is 240 C."

"Okay, so with that and normal space maneuvering, she must have good inertial dampening."

"Excellent. Even if you were to throw her around, your dinner in the mess would stay on the table. More to the point, the dinner would stay on the plate, and the magnets keep the plate on the table."

"No delay effects?"

"Well, there is a very slight delay in directional changes. Humans can feel it, their brains pick it up, and it can cause mild nausea. I am not a biologist, but there was speculation it was because of their brains panicking while the brain tried to correlate the inner ear with the visual field of reference and with what the body could feel happening in the gut with the inertial acceleration. You won't have to worry about that. That is flyboy shit again."

"Where are the controls for the dampeners?"

"It is that knob to the top right of your digital attitude indicator, clockwise to increase, counter to reduce the dampening."

"Can you show me the controls for the thrust gimbal, micro control thrusters, and the bow and stern thrusters?"

GS2 and Jack spent fifteen minutes talking through all the cockpit controls. And the aerodynamic controls for atmospheric flight. They also covered the instrumentation for flight radars and external cameras.

"Okay, good, that all makes sense to me. I think we're ready to give this flying thing a bash."

"A bash?" GS2 asked. That nervous feeling was back.

Jack took the controls and turned the ship. "Why don't we start with flying a cube?"

Jack impressed GS2. His control was gentle and precise. Jack had taken in all the information GS2 had shared about the controls. The cube that Jack flew was very accurate with positional drift under one meter. GS2 thought the flight computer would burn with envy if it was watching.

"Right, good, now for a pyramid, the angles are more acute, so I will supplement the attitude control thrusters with the bow and stern thrusters. They are great for increased precision in tight turns, GS2. It's not all about throwing the ship around in combat."

Jack traced a perfect pyramid. The accuracy at the sharp corner turns was now under half a meter of drift using bow and stern thrusters in conjunction with the normal micro control thrusters.

"Very good," GS2 said. His student was excellent.

"Okay, right, let's put it all together now. There are some Oort cloud objects showing on radar one thousand clicks sunward. I'll navigate around them."

GS2 was close to saying *No way, that is too hazardous*. But his student was careful with an intuitive grasp of the ship and her controls, gentle and precise. Instead, GS2 said, "Okay, be careful, but I am sure you can handle it."

Jack turned the ship with no hesitation and brought the Oort objects straight into a direct vector. *Impressive spatial awareness* GS2 thought. Jack fiddled with the radar and zoomed in the frame on the Oort objects to a high-precision view. This was a little odd. GS2 thought as they were only flying around the cluster of objects after all, but sure let Jack have a look at the different objects in the cluster.

GS2 released his override controls and switched full ship control over to Jack's seat. "You have full control now, Jack."

"Thank you, GS2. I appreciate your vote of confidence in me."

This is what Jack had been waiting for. It locked out GS2's controls.

"Let's try some advanced flight maneuvers. Inertial dampeners to maximum." Jack leaned forward and twisted the knob clockwise.

"What are you doing? What are you up to?"

"Oh, nothing much, just some of that flyboy shit, you know."

Jack increased the engine thrust to maximum and angled toward the center of the Oort objects cluster. Jack clicked the switch and turned off the flight computer. He started directly controlling each of the engines, thrusters, and their vectors.

That was the start of a terrifying ten minutes for GS2. Not that Jack's flying was bad or erratic. Quite the opposite, the flying was excellent. It was as if he had linked his mind to the ship. Jack's hands flew across the controls, his fingers dancing on the buttons, knobs, and levers. GS2's problem was the extreme velocity that Jack was flying at. It was the very late and sharp turns right at the edge of the flight envelope. GS2 felt that most times the ship was doing things its designer had never dreamed of. Jack flew the ship near the large Oort objects and down their canyons at just thirty meters of ground clearance.

Jack used the ship's radar as a forward look-down radar to scan in front of the ship and adjust his altitude and the ship's orientation in advance. To get ready for the sharp turns needed to keep his precise ground-hugging flight path.

Jack pulled back on the controls. He executed a perfect Immelmann turn, which he linked into a Cobra turn followed by the Hineri-komi maneuver, before finishing with a tight Kulbit loop. All the while, he operated both the bow and stern thrusters, flipping the aircraft end over end, 360 degrees in her own length.

"Nice. She handles well. I think that will do for today."

GS2 was speechless. He had just seen Jack conducting high-g air combat maneuvering, also known as dogfighting.

Jack turned the dampening back down to its earlier position and returned the radar to its earlier state. Then he turned the control switch over to copilot.

"Flight controls switched. She is your ship now, GS2."

GS2 took the controls and turned the flight control computer back on. Then he asked in a quiet voice, "Who taught you how to fly like that?"

Jack replied cheerily, "Taught? No one taught me. Today was my first day in a cockpit. I am good with machines and have read a lot of books. It just makes sense to me. I can see it all inside my head, like when I am racing."

"Yes, you said you had competed in aerial races."

Jack laughed. "You mean the Denker 500. No GS2, that is not an aerial race. It is a long-distance ground-vehicle race. I am a competitive racing car driver. We raced in the desert. I love machines, and I love working on them. I'm going back to the recreation room for a bite to eat. Thank you so much for your time and for sharing the ship with me."

Jack unbuckled his harness, slipped out of the pilot seat, and headed back to the recreation room via the ship's galley.

He entered the recreation room with his juicy big sandwich, which he was looking forward to devouring. Jack detected the faint whiff of vomit. Greg, Tom, and Lauren were all several shades paler.

Lauren giggled. "Hey Jack, having fun, I told you guys he would be stuffing his face when we saw him again.”

“She flies well. I have a few ideas about how we can improve her performance, but she is an excellent ship. We can make her faster by about twenty percent, I would guess. Right, I am hungry, so I am going to get this bad boy down. Thanks, Tom, for letting me fly. It was fun.”

GS2 clomped into the recreation room a minute later.

“How was he? Did he pass?”

GS2 stared at Tom. “He has never flown before and he is a fucking natural, better than both of us. That was advanced combat flying. He read about the moves in a book. I think he could give any of those flyboy fuckers a run for their money.” With that, GS2 sat down in silence.

ACT II - PART II

|171|

CHAPTER 38

CORE TO RIM – AT JUMP – TO PROCYON B
THE PEREGRINE – RECREATION ROOM
FIVE DAYS LATER
CRUISING AT 240 C

They had been at jump now for five days. *The Peregrine* was tearing across the sky like a bat out of hell at trans-light jump speeds. The ship was not part of the normal space–time that humans live in. *The Peregrine* was in a Casimir bubble.

Stupid Einstein and all his general relativity and special relativity, which had put paid to all the fun with his crappy pronouncement that you can't travel faster than light. Unfortunately, that turned out to be technically correct and spoiled everyone's fun. Dumb physics and cosmology. Boo.

Let's just think about that for a second. The universe is massive. The distances between the stars are vaster than your brain can understand at any level of detail beyond the very abstract high level of "vast!"

Well, what do you mean, light is fast, right? No, light is slow-ass shit in terms of reference of traveling between stars. It is like the mighty creator of the universe put a traffic cop behind every tree and bush with a speed gun. Oh no, you're going faster than light, here's a ticket. Nope, can't do that, slow right down or you will gain infinite mass, just try pushing that forward.

Let's just absorb that and give this some context. Alpha Centauri is 4.367 light-years from Earth. The closest star to Earth is over four years away, traveling at light speed, which you can't do.

This is where the Casimir effect comes into play. See, there is one thing that can move faster than light and that is the fabric of space–time moving around itself.

Imagine a bubble of air rising through the sea. If we stood inside the bubble from our perspective, everything would stand still. The bubble itself is moving relative to the water it is passing through. Because it is a bubble of space–time. The rest of space–time, which is the sea, gives it a free pass and waves it on, as the water slips and streams around the bubble and fills in the gap behind. This slipping around the bubble can go faster than light as it is bent, while as far as the sea is aware, the bubble is not moving, let alone the contents of the bubble, which remain unseen.

We said earlier that the latest FTL v3.0 star drives could travel across the sphere of colony worlds in about two months to travel those forty light-years. Twenty light-years in thirty days, so four light-years in six days. That means that in 365 days, a total of 60.8 trips of four light-years is possible, or a distance of 243 light-years in one calendar year. This means that, to travel the four light-years to Alpha Centauri in six days, the ship would need to fly in a conventional sense at 243 times the speed of light. This would also allow you to travel between the far-flung colonies in two months in order to travel those forty light-years.

If you're a spaceship designer, 240 C is the magic number you need to hit.

Now that is at the local stars' level in our own galaxy, The Milky Way is 105,700 light-years in diameter. If we divide this by our four light-years distance and multiply by six days travel time, we get 158,550 days. In our super-fast 240 C speedy ship, it will take 434 years to fly across the galaxy. Doesn't sound quick now, does it?

If you want to travel longer distances than just hopping between local neighborhood stars, the speedy FTL star drives are not fast enough to practically move these distances. The Casimir effect is just not going to do it for us. To go those long distances, you need something else. Everything over 240 light-years away is more than a year's travel at 240 C. That was where everyone was at. We were again stuck as a species. Everything else was too far away, and while we had upgraded from the Earth to the local stars, the rest of the universe breathed an enormous sigh of relief that humans could not get any further or be causing any other species and planets any bother, joyriding around, making tits of ourselves.

To go over the 240-light-year practicality barrier, you would need wormholes, and no one had any clue how you would even think about that problem.

Let us suppose you could get a wormhole to transport you one thousand light-years (just under one percent of the galaxy's diameter). A distance that would take the speedy FTL spaceship over four years to travel. Your stalker would have to find you within one thousand light-years of Sol. In which there are 271,732 stars and all the various planets and moons orbiting them. That would be a lot of places to hide in that would need to be searched. The flight time to traverse our hypothetical wormhole and travel one thousand light-years? Well, it's all theoretical as no one has done it or has any ideas, but some think it could take just hours or maybe minutes rather than those four years on the FTL ship.

Procyon B was still another two days' flight time away at FTL speeds. They had been going for five days now, and it was wearing. Everyone, including the gunslingers, was feeling it now. They all felt cramped inside the ship. Despite all the empty cabins, this was still a converted ex-military glorified cargo ship. There was no pool, no sun beds, no bar. This was a shit holiday resort.

The expectation and excitement for arrival at their destination was palpable. Everyone had had enough and wanted to get off. Procyon B was home to the planet Highlands. A verdant world covered in high mountain peaks and forests with brilliant clear seas teeming with fish and white sandy beaches under blue skies.

The Highlands was the seat of the Rim Systems Confederation. Not so much a single government and more like a United Nations of the eight Rim systems and the ninety-six human settled objects orbiting around those eight stars. Most people were based on the various planets. However, there were also moon-based habitats and several large asteroids and space stations. For clarity, each system object only counts once in that count of ninety-six locations, no matter how many settlements there are on it. This is only relevant for the planet- and moon-based settlements where there could be more than one city or base.

The Rim Systems Confederation was the base where they had built the coordination between the different local governments, both large and small.

Because of the colonies' history and the forced exodus from Earth due to the environmental cataclysm that humanity had unleashed on their original world, the Rim Systems Confederation kept a close eye on corporations, and their adherence to strict environmental protections.

A former chair of the group had established this clearly in everyone's mind 124 years back. He had transported the entire board of a summoned corporation up into orbit above the Highlands. He forced the corporation to answer for their atmospheric pollution. The chair had asked them once to explain themselves and their actions. There was silence at first, and then one soul tried to defend the corporation's actions. He got as far as the word shareholders and then the chair ordered the soldiers into the room and had the entire board of twenty-four dragged to one of the ship's air locks. He had them herded into the air lock in groups of four, one after the other. The guards created more space, by sending the earlier four into space. There had been screaming. By the time there were only two groups of four left, there was only sobbing. The chair sent an open electronic message back to the corporation in question and copied in all the other corporations in the Rim systems later that hour.

"You now need a new board. The old board is exploring the importance of being able to breathe above the people's planet. We trust you will give us no further reason to summon you before us again, ever. We are confident that you and the other corporations will all take this as a salutary learning opportunity regarding the seriousness of our resolve around environmental protections."

The message was harsh and received loud and clear. The Rim systems were still all unspoiled paradises. If any last vestiges of confusion existed, the impromptu forty-eight-hour public street parties and the dancing and celebrating of the chair's decisive action put the public's position beyond doubt. Their ecofriendly stance had laid it firmly to rest along with the frozen board members in orbit. The execution of the corporation's errant board was beyond popular with the public in every Rim system. The public sent their message to the corporations—*clean up or else*—and the corporations heard it and cleaned up their act.

The crew all dreamed of wandering the streets of Inverness and stopping in the small café bars for a bite to eat or to swing by the opulent casinos. Of swimming in the oceans and hiking in the high mountain hanging valleys. The Highlands were stunning.

The plan was to take two months of downtime for R&R and a ship refit.

CHAPTER 39

RIM – PROCYON B –THE HIGHLANDS
INVERNESS
REST & RECUPERATION
AFTERNOON
SINGING

Three weeks of R&R, idyllic. Greg was very bored and restless when he got the surprise call inviting him up to the orbiting space station to see General Abbot.

It was a busy time at the station. The resistance had one of their two main fleets in for refit work. There was a buzz of gossip in the back bars of the main strip. They all knew it. Something was afoot; something was going to happen. No one other than General Abbot had the full picture of the planned operation they were getting ready for. Whatever it was, it needed twenty-four of the resistance's precious warships.

The resistance only had two fleets, numbering forty-eight ships in total. They had put together the fleets from the eight Rim systems. The Imperium ships and fleets outnumbered the resistance's two fleets. Every ship was incredibly precious.

Resistance business took precedence. The fleet had bumped work schedules in every direction. *The Peregrine*'s maintenance slot in the busy shipyards was now? Who knew, no idea? *The Peregrine*'s turn would arrive in due course, and the ship's maintenance checks would be completed at some point, but this work could add a month to their stay. No one cared. It is not like anyone had anywhere better to go. The Highlands were impressive; it was not a terrible place to be marooned.

The communication from General Abbot was a welcome relief for Greg. He was struggling to keep busy with the whole "putting your feet up" vacation. The idea of not being busy made no sense to Greg.

Tom was having a more enlightening time on the Highlands. He had sought the Japanese community and visited the temple. It had taken a frustrating week of making no progress before Tom snapped and had enough. He waited late one day, till after the other worshippers had all left, and he could corner the monk.

With hindsight, he could see why the monk looked horrified. Tom had cornered the man and pulled off his T-shirt. It was a little forward.

"I need you to talk to me. What is this?" Tom said, gesturing at his long-loved tattoo of the koi.

"Why does my family have it, me and my dad? Who was the sharpshooter on Lothian who saved our lives when we attacked the guard's office that had seized the Buddhist temple? Why did he offer to train me? Was he Sōhei?"

With that, Tom ran out of steam and just looked lost.

The monk must have thought Tom was about to flash him. Afterward, the monk appeared bored. Then he looked at Tom with pity and sympathy.

"The Bhante on Lothian told me about the incident. He is the guardian and keeper of the temple. He is thrilled. You have liberated the temple and returned it to us."

The monk stopped, uncertain if he should continue.

"It saddened us when your father pulled away from us before your birth. We are very pleased that sixteen years on, he decided he still wanted to give you the honor that is your birthright and pass on the tattoo of our order to you.

"It is a great shame you have not had the ten years of training at the temple that you would have received from sixteen. I don't understand the choice your father made for you, but it was done. He still cared enough to undergo the tattooing ceremony. Here we are now; you are one of us, a temple warrior but untrained. This has only ever happened once before."

Tom hesitated. "Does this mean I am Sōhei?"

"No. You have had no training, but the Bhante has made the offer to train you."

"You said my father pulled back from you before I was born?"

"Yes. It is a sad story, such a tragic waste. Your father and his younger brother were both behind Imperium lines. The Imperium captured and tortured his brother, your uncle. His brother's silence bought the time needed to get your father smuggled out. His brother paid with his life. It hit your father hard, and he pulled away from us. He didn't want to risk widowing your mother."

"My father is Sōhei?"

"Yes, one of our best before he left us. I guess he wanted to leave the door open for you so you could make your own choice in the future."

"I see."

"You know where to find the Bhante if you choose to start your training on Lothian."

"How long will it take?"

"That is impossible to answer. It just depends on what training you need and how well you absorb it or even if you can. It will make more sense now to be an apprentice rather than become an initiate. You have a wider life outside of the temple, and I doubt you can spare the time to become a full-time initiate. There is scope for you to be an apprentice part-time. It will take longer but might be a better fit for you. Consider what you want to do."

"Thank you. You have given me much to think about."

"Rest now and remember, this is your choice to make for you, not for your father. Your father made this your choice when he passed the tattoo onto you."

"I understand."

Greg's shuttle was at this point on the landing approach at the Highlands' orbital shipyards, and Greg was on his way to General Abbot's office. His mind was full of the cryptic note inviting him to this meeting. Other than the time and date, it simply read: *It is time we talk about creating some options.*

Greg's shuttle approached the landing point, and Greg saw it on the sim-glass "window" as the shuttle tracked nearer. The flight's icon flew through the digital squares in the navigation computer that marked the flight's pipe, its approach path.

The sim-glass was not a real window, as large windows were too fragile and expensive to put into spaceship hulls. The fragility was most clear in the corners where the stress forces would focus and had the potential to cause material fatigue. The vacuum of space was very unforgiving and ship designers cut areas of risk. You can think of the sim-glass in much the same way as we take flat-screen panels for granted. Like the early augmented realities that people used to have on their mobile phones or tablets. The phone's camera would allow you to see through the phone, with the camera displaying on the phone what was behind it. Now things were a bit more complicated than that. From where the observer stood, their line of sight would affect the objects in the perpendicular focal plane. Further, the observer could change the item they focused on. Now, most things in space are far enough away that they are at maximum focal distance. When coming into a space dock, as the shuttle was doing with the space station, the objects were well within human focal range. Some items like gantries and cranes could point at the shuttle and be several meters closer than others. This meant there was some sophisticated tech to trick the human brain by manipulating the depth-of-field into believing this was in fact a portal into a three-dimensional world that their eyes could explore, rather than a simple two-dimensional camera display.

Sim-glass had another fantastic benefit. The mixing of the three-dimensional camera view could be combined, with elaborate processing, to create digital fiction. It was a straightforward matter for a computer to add more layers to the image. Whether they be overlay graphics such as you would find in a heads-up display (HUD), or even other picture-in-picture components, or three-dimensional objects rendered on the fly, which were inserted into the images as animations. A total fiction that would convince any human observer and make us believe in what we saw and not suspect the ship's display was trying to deceive us. Something that an intelligence operator might want to do in order to mislead an enemy crew or captain as to the actual nature of events going on around the ship. Such as faking the destruction of allied ships or phantom reinforcements. To sell the illusion of course, beyond the initial cursory image, you would have to penetrate other ship systems, such as radar, so you could alter their displays as well.

It was also great for entertaining children at birthday parties. Where a Tyrannosaurus Rex could come running into their garden, looking around frantically. Upon finding the fishpond, he would sit down and sing to the goldfish. This was a surefire win, with the kids watching inside the house and all howling with laughter and singing along to the pop track their parents' picked. Kids loved it; they couldn't get enough of sing along with dinosaurs.

The marketing department, thinking about the adult after dinner party market, tried out a new simulation on the focus groups. One where the T. rex, would fixate on the noisy neighbor who was the bane of their parents' tranquil chi. The parents would take great delight and satisfaction in watching the T. rex running across their garden to their screaming neighbor. Jumping over the garden fence and having an evening munchie-crunchie snack.

The focus group also revealed, however, that this was not a big hit with the kids, who didn't give a shit about the neighbor one way or the other. But several kids did burst into tears and would wail between snotty sobs, "Mommy, who is going to feed [insert name of kitty or woofie]. They will starve. We must adopt them!" This resulted in a very upset child. And an angry neighbor when they discovered the parents had been showing their kids VR snuff videos of the neighbor getting eaten. While the children tried to kidnap the dog or cat from their neighbor's backyard.

There was a slight bump and a clunk. Greg's shuttle had docked. The light above the hatch went green and the inner door opened, allowing people to walk into the air lock. The inner door would close, and the cycle would repeat with the shuttle's outer door and then the two further doors into the space station.

CHAPTER 40

CORE – ALPHA CENTAURI A – NEW TERRA
AYLESBURY
SUPREME COMMANDER'S OFFICE
NOON
OFF THE MAP

"Thank you for making the time to see me, Supreme Commander, or do you prefer, Bob?"

"Let's stick with commander. There are some unusual aspects to your job application, Harold."

"That I applied and accepted the interview before you sent it or even advertised the position? I am pleased you noticed. It convinces me I wasn't wasting my time."

"Indeed, I noticed. What is covert intelligence lieutenant colonel?"

"We work to give you absolute deniability, Commander, there are many times when the best way doesn't look its best in a written report. That is where we come in. We get you the results without you being associated with the colorful details of how it was done."

"I see. That could be useful sometimes. Why are you talking to me?"

"That's easy, sir. Many of the middle managers above me are total cockwombles. If you pardon the expression, their brains are mired in the *Become a Middle Manager in Twenty Days* book they all got for their birthday. They didn't even have the initiative to buy the book themselves; someone else gave it to them. In the same way, shit floats and gets in the way. We have a dense mat of turd blocking all the light from illuminating anything underneath. Even the most tenacious young mosquito can't climb through to the heady heights of senior management above, where you live, sir."

"Colorful, but I see your point. You're a young mosquito, I am guessing."

"Yes, but I decided I didn't want to get stuck in all their shit, and I would bypass them and come to you."

"I see. You've the initiative to write your own book, so to speak. What is it called?"

"Making Sure the Other Guy Gets Fucked."

"Poetic. I think you can help."

"Yes, Commander, I have been giving that some thought. We need to deal with the rebel's assets at Procyon B."

"They are little more than a nuisance."

"Rebel rabble, sir, but they are also very inconvenient where they are."

"Tell me more."

"We need to take their fleet out of commission, then the rebels will fold."

CHAPTER 41

**RIM – PROCYON B – THE HIGHLANDS
SPACE DOCKS
IN ORBIT ABOVE THE HIGHLANDS
OH, MY!**

General Abbot was in his resistance utility uniform. His Space Activity Suit (SAS) was hanging in its locker to the right of his door. The boots sat at the bottom and the helmet was on the shelf at the top by the gloves. The SAS was a Mark IV; it was a derivation from the family of mechanical counter pressure suits. It used physical compression of the body, instead of air, to negate the effect of a vacuum on the wearer.

The suit secured the neck, ankles, and wrists with airtight seals and mechanical locking collars. The reversed seal and locking collar arrangement meant that the airtight compression seal was on the suit side, before the locking collar. The accessories were attached after the airtight seal via the mechanical locking collar.

This supported an optimal trade-off between dexterity, convenience, and suit design. It started with the gloves. They realized it was difficult to maintain exact finger movements if the glove was trying to crush every square millimeter of your hand. If the glove was too loose, your hands would swell as blood pooled and ruptured blood vessels. The airtight thin inner glove was slightly tight, for sure, and complemented by a close-fitting jointed exo-shell. This reduced the thickness. Sensors in the exo-shell's fingertips and the pads of the palm connected to their counterpart units inside the glove. It conveyed touch to the wearer for whatever object they were manipulating. The design allowed an EVA worker to carry out relevant fine-motor-skill activities.

The helmet was connected to the external oxygen supply. It fed the oxygen via small plastic tubes into the nose, just like you would expect to see in a hospital setting. Waste gas went into the helmet as the person exhaled. Pressure-checking triggered gas reclamation on exhale into the external gas recycling unit. This unit would chemically fix the CO_2 and reduce it back to O_2. They used the O_2 for rebreathing, with any excess gas compressed into a local O_2 cylinder. The unit would filter out the deposited carbon, which could be flushed out, once back in the station or ship. The recycler held a very fine, mesh-like material covered in synthetic enzymes that carried out the actual chemistry. The system was efficient, compact, and lightweight. Workers would plug into an oxygen line at the site they were working at, and they only had to rely on the oxygen tank when moving between the work location and the air lock. When connected to an oxygen line, workers could work out there in a vacuum for many hours. Well, at least until the body's biological needs required them to take a break for food or to pass waste. Water was available via a sucker tube, and it contained various sugars and salts needed by the human body to provide electrolytes, in addition to simple hydration.

Becoming detached in space and floating away in the void was a primal human fear. They took safety steps seriously when working in space. For instance, they secured workers via two tethers attached to large D rings on the body harness they would wear over the SAS suit. This harness would also have the workers' tools attached and tethered to it. This ensured no dropped tools would float off into space and become a navigation hazard to other ships or even hit other workers at speed in orbit. They would clip the other end of the tethers to the safety wires attached to the space docks. The safety wires went everywhere a worker might need to go. When going past a wire mounting point, they would disconnect one tether and reattach it to the other side of the mounting point, and repeat with the second tether. Workers could also secure themselves in a buddy system to a colleague. Either via the large D ring at the center of their chest or the one behind their neck at the top of their shoulders. The final safety component was the boots. They would use electromagnets to attach their feet to the local "ground" if there was a suitable magnetic friendly material they could stick to. While many components were metallic, many others would use nonmagnetic composites built around carbon fibers. There was no guarantee you would always be able to mag lock your boots in place all the time.

It was necessary for all space station personnel, not just the fabricators, to have their EVA certificate for working in a vacuum. There was always the possibility that the station might need to be evacuated, and that could mean going outside, not just diving through an air lock.

General Abbot was very hands on and had worked in space-side construction for many years. Abbot's SAS suit didn't just live in its locker; the suit was well used and maintained.

There were many good reasons why the ships were best constructed in orbit. Not least because some ships were too big or fragile to be built on the planet and blasted into orbit.

When Greg arrived at General Abbot's office, he found the door open as it always was when Abbot was in the office. Abbot sat behind his desk, working on something on the computer.

"Ah, Greg, there you are. Please come in and sit. Thank you for coming. I am afraid this is going to be brief."

"Sir?"

"Everything is going mental around here. You may have noticed all the extra ships we have up here in orbit. Things have heated up since we last communicated."

"Is everything okay, sir?"

"Yes, I think, okay. Well, a bit yes and no, Greg. We are very busy now. Plus, we have a target of opportunity intelligence shared with us. The brass wants our fleet to hit it. On top of that, I am in the middle of a fleet-wide refitting and maintenance window. Some womble in logistics thought this would also be the perfect time to do a load of upgrades to the fleet. So, yeah, my days are wild."

Abbot gathered his scattered thoughts into a line and started at the front of the queue.

"Intelligence got word of Imperium fleet supply movements to a system close to us. Just six light-years away. We are going to blow their soft asses up."

"You also said, 'no,' sir?"

"Our fleet will hit the Imperium, but we also have a senior General in detention, scheduled later this week for interrogation and execution. Dead is acceptable, but we can't have any risk of her talking while under interrogation. Plus, I want her back. She will hold on for some time, but you know everyone breaks."

"Yes, sir, you want me to go get her? *The Peregrine* is not armed, sir."

"Not armed yet! We are going to give you a few quick upgrades. Then you are going out again with a pair of assault support ships, two assault transports, plus their four fighters. It is a small force, but one with very sharp teeth. We won't get *The Peregrine* back to full military spec in the time we have, but you won't just be throwing rocks and harsh words."

"Yes, sir!"

"We are promoting you, Captain, up two bands to lieutenant colonel. You will work alongside the Eagle's commander in charge of space-based assets, the two assault support ships, *You Ordered Death* and *The Last Rites*. Their aero- and space-fighter pairs, *Humboldt* and *Barracuda* plus *Piranha* and *Pike*—a.k.a. *Tiger's Lancers*. The Lancer pilots are all aces. You manage the ground assets. The *I can see you, sorry*—ex-recon assault ship—*The Peregrine*. And the assault transports *Guns Express Delivery* and *Who Wants Explosives*. They are carrying the two thirty-strong commando platoons with four light battle mechanicals and four mule APCs. *The Peregrine* will carry six medium battle tanks and crews."

"Tanks, mechs, and mules ... Oh, my." Greg grinned like it was his birthday.

Abbot raised an eyebrow at Greg's comment.

"Sir!"

"Very sharp teeth, like I said. Small, yes, but a self-contained multirole mini-assault fleet. Now I must go to another briefing. The resistance fleet will be out of here soon and there is a lot to get done in the coming days. Keep Tom onside. We are about to take oxy-torches to his ship, and I need you to hang on to Lauren and the computer. With the firepower we are sending with you, they will be safe. It will be hotter where me and the fleet are going."

Greg refocused.

"The task force Commander is Charlie Powers. She is very good. We are sending you to rescue Brigadier General Brigman."

Greg winced. "Isn't she the one—"

"Yes, that one, the Ball Breaker. Remind Tom he volunteered if you need to. He might get twitchy when he finds out we are upgrading his comms and pulling out his old obsolete C&C intelligence suite."

"Yes, sir."

"One more thing, Greg, we will send your ships out with the GOD system."

"It's ready?"

"Yes, Greg, you guys will be the first task force taking GOD to the front line for actual live-combat operations. Your ships make up the Ball Breaker Task Force."

CHAPTER 42

**RIM – PROCYON B –THE HIGHLANDS
INVERNESS
PORT DISTRICT – THE PEREGRINE
RECREATION ROOM – AN HOUR LATER
GOD**

Greg took the shuttle back down to the surface of the Highlands. *The Peregrine* had parked up on the planet at the spaceport since their spot in the orbital space docks had been bumped. Jack, Lauren, and Tom all sat, listening to Greg's update.

"We have our orders, people. We are getting upgraded, we are getting more ships, tanks, and troops, and we are going to rescue the Ball Breaker."

"The who? Rescuing what?" Tom looked confused.

Jack sat up straighter. "I have heard of her, holy cow."

"She is a ruthless senior military asset being held by the Imperium for interrogation and execution. We are being sent to bust her out and bring her back. Hence all the guns. That is why you are getting a free upgrade to your ship, Tom."

"I like free. What are we talking about?"

"Let's start with some of the logistics. We are a big empty ship, and we are going to be a lot fuller. The ships coming with us are gun platforms with little spare room. Pocket assault support ships and their fighters each have up to forty-eight crew. We are, or were, a recon assault with eighteen crew and twenty-four tank crew. The two assault transports each have three crew but each transports up to sixty commandos. We will only have a sixty-unit commando team, not a team of 120. Six medium battle tanks will take up much of our cargo space. There are going to be 204 people on *The Peregrine*. It has most of the cabin space, forty-two cabins over two levels. We are going to be snug, but we will all fit. We must accommodate the commandos and tank crew. They will double up in cabins and likely hot bunk as well. We will no longer be rattling around, with the hotel Peregrine all to ourselves."

Tom inhaled. "Wow, 204, that is a lot of people, Greg."

"Yes, Tom, we will carry a lot of souls, and a lot of energy cannons and slug cannons. We have hundreds and hundreds of medium-range missiles. Lots of RECs, rotary engagement cannons, which can take out missiles and medium ground targets. We can keep our people safe and pound our targets. Our task force must rescue Kate Brigman, and we, the commandos, and Commander Charlie Powers are going to make that happen. We can flatten that facility and bounce all the rubble around, but the commandos will need to go in and get her first. Let's talk about the muscle."

The REC was the grown-up big brother of the rotary cannons, which were in the fighters that attacked Alva. It used larger thirty-millimeter heavy rounds, compared with the twenty-millimeter rounds used in the rotary cannons in the Alva fighter attack. This made the REC too bulky and powerful to fit on a fighter. You only found the RECs fitted to the larger military ships. Much like the old Earth CIWS, pronounced 'sea-wiz', Close-In Weapons System. The CIWS preceded the REC by eight hundred years. It was used in the US Navy on the sea ships of old Earth. The CIWS was primitive by comparison, but the core idea was the same. A REC could work in both defensive and offensive roles. Whether that be taking out inbound missiles and artillery shells, or projecting force, taking out enemy fighters, or engaging larger ships. A REC could also engage both mobile and static ground targets when mounted on a ship flying in the atmosphere.

"We will carry tanks, battle mechs, and mule APCs. Along with sixty Rhino ground commandos from my old unit. Two ground-assault transports, and two orbital assault support ships. Plus, four dual-role space and aero fighters flown by the Lancer unit of aces drawn from the Eagles. And *The Peregrine* and her upgraded enhanced recon surveillance. Which will now include her new state-of-the-art battlefield C&C capabilities."

"Tom, you are going to like this bit. I am going to show you GOD. You will shit yourself."

"Thanks, Greg, but I am not religious."

"Not the religious God, Tom, the military one, G-O-D. My Rhino unit and the Eagles have been drilling with the battlefield tech for a while now, in close-air support and assault drills. GOD is the evolution. The next generation C&C system they have been prototype testing. We will be the first group of ships to do a live real-world combat operation with support from GOD. *The Peregrine* and two assault support ships will run linked GOD nodes, which will talk to all the other battlefield hardware, pilots, tanks, mechs, APCs, and infantry. GOD supplies planned routes, target painting, threat display, friend or foe marking, artillery, and aerial fire missions. It also links all the fire control systems together. And marks casualties needing medical aid. Navigation marks, waypoints and rally points."

"GOD is an optical holographic display system. It provides a real-time three-dimensional display of battlefield tactical intelligence data. The acronym is a little cheese, but it stands for global operational display. To my mind, it should be theater, not global, but the joke is that the guys in marketing couldn't help themselves and didn't want to call it TOD. The military love their acronyms."

Greg stood up. "We are going to bring our people and the General back alive, everyone. *The Peregrine* is going into the space docks to refit tonight for the next six days. We will load up and leave, outbound for Cygni B—Tayside. We will arrive ten days from now and the assault will begin as we come out of jump, already firing. General Brigman is scheduled to start interrogation in six days. Remember, people. Every minute that passes is another minute that General Brigman is being abused under interrogation. The stakes could not be higher. We must get her out before she breaks. If you knew the hell they will put her through, you would know everyone breaks in the end. There is no shame in it. They taught us to hold on until all the operational tactical knowledge we have is out-of-date and worthless, then tell the enemy everything to stop the interrogation. Brigman's knowledge is strategic, not tactical. It will never go out-of-date. Plus, we need her back so we can't just flatten the site from orbit."

"I need to ask. Are you all in, people?"

Lauren and Jack had both been listening, paying close attention.

Lauren turned, looked at Jack, and smiled. "Yes, Greg, I am in."

With no hesitation, Jack also spoke. "Yep, one hundred percent here."

Tom looked around the group. "Yes, me as well. Hell, I will even get to meet GOD."

"You have my full support as well. This is an important mission." Merlin's voice was free of his normal comic levity, instead very mature and serious.

"Great, we have the whole band on this then," Greg said.

CHAPTER 43

RIM – PROCYON B – THE HIGHLANDS
SPACE DOCK
THE PEREGRINE BAY
MORNING
UPGRADES

Lead engineer Gillespie was updating Greg and Tom about the work being carried out on the ship. In Gillespie's opinion, this entire job reeked of special operations. Someone had drawn a line, and this was a very high-value target or a very loud explodie type of message being delivered from the higher ups.

Gillespie did not know what their mission was, but he suspected it was something separate from all the rest of the madness going on around the docks. All the dockworkers worked as if they were going to war now. There was no idle gossiping. That had all stopped a week back. They all knew this was not a game that was being played. This was serious. The young men and women leaving on the ships that made up the resistance fleet could well not be coming home.

These service people all had parents who loved them. Some were married or had partners. The crew even included parents with young children at home.

Not everyone would come back, even if this was a peacetime mission. Accidents happened, especially in military-type environments with all that heavy equipment. Of course, it was not just accidents; these people would fly in harm's way. The sailors on the Imperium side would be firing missiles and rounds back at the resistance sailors.

For the dockworkers, they had all become sailors doing their jobs now. Not Imperium or resistance soldiers, but sailors following orders from higher up. None of the dockworkers had any love for the Imperium leadership. The people on both front lines would be the ones doing the dying, and they were all just sailors following their orders.

This job had come along from nowhere and was now at the top of the job board. The work should have taken ten or twelve days to complete. They had given the dockworkers just six days. Corners were being cut. Everyone now knew time was the bigger enemy. There were things you would expect to get done with this sort of job, which were being skipped. And other things that you would not do, which were being done.

For example, *The Peregrine* was being fitted out with a full suite of REC cannons. Sixteen RECs when four or eight was much more standard. Sixteen was a destroyer-strength loading of RECs. Yet they were not fitting any heavier weapons to the ship. No missile arrays, no slug throwers or energy cannons for heavy bombardment or artillery against other ships or fixed targets.

Wherever she was going, someone was expecting her to be coming under a lot of fire. Either that or she would mow down many fields full of infantry and tanks.

There was the electronics works. Refitting the comms array and C&C suites were not unusual tasks. Especially given the out-of-date shit they had left in after the ship's decommissioning.

They had taken out the C&C suite. Half the comms equipment was missing, leaving only obsolete rubbish. No one expected them to communicate with signal lights and Morse code, and thus these upgrades made total sense.

And then there was this new GOD thing. It was so new Gillespie had never seen one before, let alone know what it did. It had arrived with its own installation team, who didn't talk and just kept themselves to themselves. Gillespie had deduced one thing from where it was located. This was a central piece of the decision-making tree at the heart of the C&C tactical-command room. The ex-recreation room that no longer had comfy loungers or deep-cushioned seats.

Of course, there was the mystery rack, covered with a blanking plate and locked. No one had any idea what was in that computer rack. Everyone ignored it with determination. Some workers had told stories of ghosts on the ship. They claimed they heard faint voices whispering at night from the sealed rack; voices they couldn't make out.

The weird tanks and their tank crew and support team had arrived three hours ago, flown in on three heavy military transporters. Gillespie had watched as the six wild-looking beasts had driven up the main tank ramps on each side of the ship. Gillespie held his hand up and admitted he knew little about Rhino equipment as his norm was to work on Eagles equipment and ships. Tanks were not Gillespie's average day-to-day, but he had come across a fair few over the years. These were different. The stumpy, short, yet very wide main gun barrel for starters. Then their translucent hexagons that you could see through, which covered the dull, camouflaged green-printed armor. The hexagons had caused a lot of speculation among the dockworkers. What could they be? The current bookies favorite was that it was an adaptive print camouflage that would mimic the surroundings it found itself in. From an urban cityscape through to deserts and into tropical jungles. It didn't sit right with Gillespie but when asked what his great idea was; he didn't have one. He thought all the extra antennae on the tank must have something to do with it.

The soldiers had all arrived an hour ago, fifty or sixty of them. They all walked through the ship, familiarizing themselves with the layout and with the firefighting and damage control stations. They had dropped cases of ammunition off and left them in the stores. The more enterprising of them bagged bunk beds in the various cabins they would be hot bunking in. This was more about ensuring they were hot bunking with someone they got on with. Snorers, farters, and smelly people were not popular in the military services, where having to hot bunk was not unusual in full ships. The problem was that a full ship meant they were off to fight the enemy.

The Peregrine had used to be a recon assault ship, a fantastic bit of kit. Old now, some bonehead had retired them and never replaced the ship with anything better. The recon assault was a behind-the-lines class of ship. One found in far advanced positions in either an intelligence-gathering role or putting force in the enemy's backyard. Dangerous places. It gave Gillespie the wobbles. He wondered where the ship might go with all this firepower.

Gillespie wasn't sure when he considered the sixteen RECs, the six strange tanks, and the fifty or sixty odd soldiers clad in black, or the strange GOD system being installed upstairs, or the ghosts in the rack. He wasn't sure whether they were all riding into hell or whether they were bringing hell with them.

"Okay, Tom and Greg, our focus is all on *The Peregrine*. We are filling her stores area with ammunition for the tanks and RECs plus refitting the auto-loaders machinery that was stripped out before."

"That sounds good," Greg said.

"What about guns? The ship has no weapons?" Tom asked.

"You know the lights on the Christmas tree in the town square, Tom? Well, you are going to have thousands of times as many cannon rounds, thirty-millimeter high-density slugs for the RECs. We are refitting sixteen REC cannons in four banks of four along the long sides of the ship, top and bottom, port and starboard. Each has a twenty-thousand-round magazine, so when loaded, that's, err, three hundred and twenty thousand rounds. The guns will be on a 360-degree full tilt-and-swivel mount and the fields of fire are complementary."

Tom's mouth dropped. "That is a lot of guns and bullets."

Greg smiled at Tom. "Can you see my grin?"

"There is bad news. You don't have the recreation room anymore. That is now, well, in all honesty, I do not know. It is all very new," Gillespie said.

"Don't worry, Tom."

"We have also ripped out your comms area. It was all out-of-date shit anyway. We have replaced it with our current latest comms and surveillance packages." Gillespie said.

"Greg, they are tearing *The Peregrine* apart."

"Relax and listen, Tom. Free upgrades. Say, Gillespie, how many inbound tangos can she now track and target?"

"Well, sixteen, each gun can engage in isolation. To track, each cannon can buffer up to forty tangos in its immediate target prosecution queue. An air defense system in this configuration mode can also track up to two thousand simultaneous inbounds out to a one thousand kilometers line of sight. We have extended the RECs firing range from fifty kilometers out to one hundred kilometers. So, she can handle six hundred and forty immediate targets within a one hundred kilometers range from the on-cannon target prosecution queue. Planets are round, you know, so orbit matters for longer distance line-of-sight tracking."

"New comms, new tactical, three hundred and twenty thousand cannon shells. Are you feeling safer now, Tom?"

"Sure, I feel safe. What about these tanks you are so happy about?"

"Are they onboard already?" Greg asked.

"Sure thing, they loaded on three hours ago, so did the tank crews and support team. Last time I saw them, they were putting artillery shells in the ship's stores," Gillespie replied.

"Tom, let's go introduce ourselves."

Unseen, Gillespie keyed the Click button on his radio twice. Tom and Greg walked down to the cargo area hatch and went in.

"Holy shitsticles, they have been stolen, there is nothing here, Greg!"

Greg chuckled.

"I think he likes it! Lads, say hello to Captain Tom."

At the edge of Tom's vision, there was a disturbance. A shimmer at the edges against the background and a quiet whir, the hint of a breeze passing over Tom's face. Tom's brain struggled to process what his eyes saw, but there was nothing in front of him.

The tank dropped its cloak. The open maw of the short main barrel pointed straight at Tom's face.

Tom let out a scream and jumped backward.

He could now take in the full view rather than staring down into the dark hole that was the 200-mm business end of the tank's main gun.

The cargo bay was now full with the six tanks.

"It is active EM camouflage, Tom; it retransmits the electromagnetic signal received on one side and rebroadcasts it on the other side from the tank to the observer. This makes the tank invisible, as if you were looking through the tank. It works for infrared, ultraviolet, and visible wavelengths. You heard the tank move a meter toward you with that faint electric motor sound for stealth maneuvers. The two big hatches in the port and starboard sides of the ship; they are for the loading and unloading of the tanks in two lines of three."

"The GOD nodes on *The Peregrine* and two assault supports integrate with these Rhino tanks, the Lancers, mechs, and mules. GOD links via signal repeater nodes to every soldier's in-helmet HUD. Everything works together, and they have been training for months. The Imperium has the numbers for sure, over four to one, maybe even five to one. We have the tech. The enemy has nothing even close to active EM camouflage, nothing like GOD delivering an integrated battlefield."

"This mission isn't just about Brigman. This is the proof-of-concept showcase for all the tech that people have been pulling together for the last five years. For showing the air, ground, and space arms of the services, all working in integrated operations. We are here to be the resistance's rallying cry to all the Rim systems and to put fear into the hearts of the Imperium military. To give courage to the citizens living in Core systems under Imperium rule, that we can fight back and win. This is about the future of all the colony worlds and whether we are all going to let the cloak of darkness fall on all of our human settlements."

"When do we leave, Greg?"

"The dock teams have done excellent work around the clock; what should have taken twelve days but was demanded in six. They have delivered in five. We leave at two o'clock in the morning, in sixteen hours.

All the ships will be ready, all the people are ready. We board everyone at midnight, which gives us fourteen hours to complete loading and testing."

"One stupid question, Greg, what is everyone going to eat? Our galley is quite small."

"Have I not mentioned Lisa yet, and her team of sixteen? Maybe not. We should go meet her. She has one of the most important jobs of anyone here. It is her team's job to keep everyone fed: commandos, tank teams, fighter crews, ship's crew. They are setting up mobile kitchens, prep and serving areas in the cargo area here, and on the two assault transports. We will fly the kitchen, tables, and chairs back and forth between *The Peregrine* and the two assault supports. Dock the assault transports inverted onto the parent ship's belly hatches. They will secure the four Lancer fighters on the upper decks of the two assault supports. We need to get good at moving people and kit around between ships while at jump. Food will help motivate everyone to ensure we can do it right. Some think it can't be done. We are going to prove you can move around while at jump."

"Okay, one last question Greg, why don't we just cloak the spaceships?"

"The scientists could not make it work. Something about it being a one to the N-squared power problem. As the size of the object being cloaked, N, goes up, the energy and complexity of the cloaking field goes up even more. We can't cloak an individual. The basic kit is too big and heavy for a person to carry. Once you get bigger, say, Peregrine-sized, the kit is many times more complex as well as bigger and heavier, so it doesn't work. The engineering envelope only overlaps the science envelope around the size and transportation power of a tank. Anyway, maybe someone will crack it someday. A cloaked ship would be quite a thing."

CHAPTER 44

**RIM – PROCYON B – THE HIGHLANDS
APPROACHING RALLY POINT
YOU ORDERED DEATH – BRIDGE
SIXTEEN HOURS LATER
IN PLAY**

"Comms, get me Greg," said Charlie Powers, commander of the task force.

"Right away, commander, the line is open," said Comms Officer Jeff.

"Greg, that test data on the engines looks great."

"Yeah, Charlie, the engineers are all thrilled here. The board is all in the green."

"Is everyone at stations and ready for launch?"

The two assault transports were docked to the belly docking ring on each of the two much larger assault supports. Two of the Lancer fighters were docked to the upper hull of each of the two assault supports. The three big ships—*The Peregrine* and the two assault supports—floated near the space station, ready to go.

"Yes, Charlie, all ready and secured. We are ready to go on your command. We have plotted the jump."

"Comms, signal to the Highlands station's traffic control. We are leaving. Coordinate the jump for Cygni B and put us in orbit above Tayside. Comms, give me task force wide."

"You are on, Commander."

"This is Flight Commander Powers. In the next few minutes, the flight crew will be jumping us for Cygni B. Operation Ball Breaker is in play. Once at FTL, your section leads will inform you of your drill exercises, shower rotas, shift assignments. It is now 03:04 hours, ship time. I suggest if you are not currently on duty, get some rack time. I want you all to welcome Liz and her team. The brass has got us a good quality kitchen team for this mission. Liz's team will serve chow for the day and night shifts as follows. Breakfast for days and dinner for nights between 09:00 hours and 10:00 hours. Lunch between 13:00 hours and 14:00 hours for days, 02:00 hours and 03:00 hours for nights. Dinner for days and breakfast for nights will be between 18:00 hours and 19:00 hours."

"We should arrive at Cygni B in 132 hours. Let's bring General Brigman home to the resistance and break some Imperium balls. Powers out."

"Comms, please advise all ships' flight crew to sync their jump clocks and jump engine controls with us. They should signal when their boards are green. We will trigger the actual jump."

"Confirm they locked all Lancer units down on the upper deck and the assault transporters are docked and locked with both of our assault supports."

"That is all confirmed, sir. FTL drives and clocks synced, and each ship's board is showing green."

"Very good. Roger that. On my mark, record the time and jump the ships."

"Yes sir."

"Three, two, one, mark."

There was the normal dropping feeling, as if you had just stepped off a high board at the swimming baths.

"All the ships are now at jump, and we are speeding up to cruising C," comms officer Jeff said.

"Commander, I have Lauren on comms. She is in *The Peregrine*'s C&C."

"Yes, put her through. We need to know if we are all going to starve or blow up. Personally, I prefer the option where we get fed."

"Lauren here, Commander. I have unpacked Merlin's rack and Jack has got the ship's shuttle, sharing its instrument data with Merlin. Jack says he is happy to fly the shuttle across to the target assault support or to defer to one of the Eagles pilots, should you prefer."

"First, Lauren, the two assault transports are over here, attached to each of the assault supports, not docked with *The Peregrine*. We need to do a realistic test. *The Peregrine*'s shuttle is too small. We will undock both transports and move the ships away. If the test is a success, we can redock the second transport on the other assault support."

The commander paused. "Otherwise, it would be a tough call, Lauren. We need to keep everyone onside. On the one hand, Jack and the shuttle are arguably the most expendable resources we have. I don't mean to sound harsh; it is just a fact. If the transport blows up, we have a problem. We have much bigger issues if it takes out the assault support as well. I think option A is still the best. We will isolate both ships from the rest of the task force. Put them one hundred kilometers away from us, and we will try the transfer flight and docking while traveling at cruising C."

Lauren understood; it made perfect sense. "Merlin is eighty percent certain he has the math right and merging the two Casimir bubbles or splitting them won't result in a bad outcome. I understand exactly where you are coming from about Jack and the other pilots. We don't need the pilots all measuring their little friends. Plus, I think Jack may have liked the idea of getting his name in the record books for the first high-C interbubble docking."

"Lauren, I need this to work. It is very important for building crew morale that the teams mix and eat together. We are one team, not separate services. We need everyone working together and understanding how we depend on one another. I do not want to go to option B, where we keep having to drop back to normal space to feed ourselves. We are clearly on the clock and can't keep stopping the ships. Someone should have seen this problem coming. It is fucking obvious you must deliver the food to where the person who will eat it is sitting. Why did no one catch this until a day before departure?"

"Well, Charlie, no one has tried docking two ships in different Casimir bubbles before. Half of them think the two bubbles will interfere with each other and drop the ships back to normal space at velocity."

"Well, I need you pair of mad scientists to make this work."

Lauren felt like she should salute although she was technically a civilian. "We will be ready to go in sixty minutes commander."

"Good. Charlie out."

CHAPTER 45

**RIM TO CORE – TO CYGNI B – TAYSIDE
THE PEREGRINE – IN CASIMIR BUBBLE – 240 C
C&C – AKA THE MAD SCIENTISTS OFFICE
ONE HOUR LATER
ROLLING DICE**

Lauren adjusted her mic headset and spoke. "Okay, everyone, to restate the plan, Pickle is piloting transport Guns Express Delivery. You are first up to undock from the assault support *The Last Rites*, moving to a ten-kilometers safe distance. You may get some chop when the bubbles split. We have Vapor piloting *Who Wants Explosives*, who will repeat the drill with undocking from the assault support *You Ordered Death*."

"*Who Wants Explosives* and *The Last Rites* will move off one hundred kilometers to *The Peregrine*'s port. *Guns Express Delivery* and *You Ordered Death* will move off one hundred kilometers to Peregrine's starboard."

"Then Guns Express Delivery will redock with You Ordered Death."

"And Who Wants Explosives will redock with The Last Rites."

"We have high confidence this is all going to go well. Please acknowledge."

"This is Pickle on *GED*, roger your last."

"This is Vapor on *WWE*, roger that."

"Okay, Pickle, you are up. Please undock and move to a safe distance."

"Pickle, roger. Unlocking the docking collar. That was smooth, no vibration at all. Nudging control thrusters away at twenty centimeters per second. Time to bubble edge, ten seconds. Five seconds. Now. Err, okay, we have stopped. We appear to be stuck inside the bubble, Merlin?"

"Yes, Pickle, we thought that might happen. Please adjust *GED*'s local bubble resonance frequency up ten percent."

"Roger your last, adjusting."

"Okay, we are good. Try another puff on the thrusters," Merlin said to Pickle.

"Pickle, roger. Nudge to thrusters. Okay, very slight vibration, but we are slipping through, no resistance. We are clear, moving away now to a safe distance. In position."

Lauren's voice came over the radio. "Pickle, that is great news. Vapor, you are up next. Unlock, maneuver away at twenty centimeters per second, up the resonance frequency by ten percent."

"Vapor, roger, command. I am unlocked, frequency adjusted, moving now. Approaching in. Ten seconds. Five seconds. Okay, we just passed through the bubble, no resistance. We are clear. Now moving to a safe distance. In position."

"Excellent, Vapor. Assault supports, please start repositioning to your one hundred kilometers rendezvous points."

Lauren watched on the sim-glass wall displays, both set to opaque mode and acting as display screens. They showed both assault supports moving away from *The Peregrine*.

"So far, so good, Merlin."

"Now for the tricky bit. It will be fine, Lauren, I am sure."

"Command, *YOD* is now in position and has switched to station keeping."

"Command, *TLR* is also now in position and also at station keeping."

"Thank you everyone. Pickle, please begin your approach run to *YOD*."

"Pickle, roger that command. Starting *YOD* approach. One minute to target."

"Oh, shit!" Merlin said.

"Everyone hold, emergency stop. Pickle abort." Merlin's voice came screaming over the speakers.

"Merlin, this is Pickle. Roger, I have stopped approach now. Please advise."

Lauren's voice came over the radio. "Merlin, what is it? I think you just scared the shit out of everyone."

"Lauren it is the field transition into the bubble. I don't know if the frequency needs to be higher or lower when we traverse into the bubble. It depends, is it related to the right-hand rule in physics or not? I don't know. If it isn't, the frequency will need to be higher, but if related, the frequency needs to be higher for exit and lower for entry. Either way, we just got lucky when we picked higher for the exit. Otherwise, I think it would have been a total loss or a catastrophic loss, depending on what the underlying rules are."

"Okay, Merlin. Tell me, why do you think the right-hand rule might be involved? Both bubbles are alternating. We do not use fixed fields."

"You are right. I think it is because of the frequency offset that gets induced when interacting with the magnetic bubble. The travel direction affects the induced secondary field as the transport moves through the primary field."

"Command, Pickle here. This sounds like a coin toss if you can't give me a recommendation. It seems I roll the dice, and we risk losing *YOD* and *GED*. We all starve to death. We do not rescue the General in time and they break her. After that, with the intelligence gained, a lot more people are going to die. If my test fails, you know how to get Vapor back onto *TLR*. You still have *The Peregrine*, with the Rhino forces. We stand to lose half of our aerial bombardment and half of the Lancers, plus half the mechs and mules. I suggest you pair of brains figure this out in the next five minutes or I go with *YOD* approach with the consent of Commander Powers. It is your call, Commander. I will stand by."

"Powers here. Merlin. You have two minutes, or I will decide in the two minutes after that. Pickle, we will get back to you in max four minutes."

"Lauren, what do I do?" Merlin asked.

"You give Charlie the information she needs to make a choice. I also suggest you include a probability such as 60:40, 70:30, for example."

"Ew, gods, I am not sure."

"Well think Merlin. Pickle's life, Commander Power's life, and everyone else on *YOD* is at stake, and ours if we attack with weakened forces. The General's life, and the people that will die because of the intelligence they torture out of her. This is life and death for many. Concentrate!"

"Ah, well, there is a weak argument to say I should set the frequency ten percent lower, not higher. Maybe a 60:40. The problem is all the other arguments that could apply draw no conclusion about whether it should be higher or lower. That is all I have got. Like Pickle said, it is a die roll, but I think we should go with lower."

"Okay, I will let Powers know."

"Lauren for Powers, Merlin recommends we set the frequency ten percent lower than when at dock. Unfortunately, he is only giving me a 60:40 probability. I am sorry I cannot give you more."

"Thank you, Lauren. Pickle?"

"I am here, Commander."

"Please adjust for bubble frequency down. That is D for Delta, by ten percent relative to your normal position at dock.”

“Pickle, roger. Adjust down to 143.27 GHz, please confirm.”

“Confirmed, Pickle, that is correct,” Merlin said.

“Pickle, roger, frequency adjusted.”

“This is Powers. Pickle, please begin *YOD* docking approach. Good luck everyone. Powers out.”

“Pickle, roger, recommencing approach. I am twenty seconds out.”

“I am nervous, Lauren. What if I got it wrong?” Merlin asked Lauren directly, not over the radio.

“Merlin, you have made the best call you can. We have done our jobs and Charlie has weighed things and, as commander of the air assets, she has decided.”

“Pickle has slowed his approach to twenty centimeters per second. Should be any second now. Thank the heavens!”

“This is Pickle. I have a firm dock and am locked. The transition was even smoother than before. Liz’s team, you can start cooking with your magic. I want to thank Merlin and Lauren. If you hadn’t caught that ball with the frequency setting, half of us would not be here right now. It is also possible Vapor would have also tried docking with the high frequency set. If that had happened, no one other than *The Peregrine* would be here now. Excellent catch, guys.”

“This is Vapor, adjusting resonance to 143.27 GHz and beginning *TLR* approach.”

The comms went quiet for thirty seconds. Everyone was holding their breath.

“Vapor to all. I am now docked and locked on *TLR*.”

“*TLR*, flight, we roger your last Vapor. Welcome back to the barn.”

“Ladies and Gentlemen, we all just set a new Rim systems record. That is a species first. Powers out.”

CHAPTER 46

RIM TO CORE – TO CYGNI B – TAYSIDE
THE PEREGRINE
THE LAST RITES
YOU ORDERED DEATH
DAY SHIFT, BREAKFAST
NIGHT SHIFT, DINNER
NOW FEAST

"We gather here today as one crew to break bread with each other."

Charlie Powers stood before her shipmates as she gave her speech. They had gathered in the troop bay of the transporter *Guns Express Delivery*, which had docked with *You Ordered Death*. Charlie's image was being rebroadcast to *The Last Rites* and the transporter docked there, *Who Wants Explosives*. And to *The Peregrine*, where people sat on towels both on and around the tanks, on the cargo deck. Some people had lined up, waiting their turn in the queue outside the ship stores. The staff from Liz's team served the food they had been preparing since four in the morning. Food was also being served from temporary tables set up in the two transports. It was a good day. Everyone in the task force was together and could see each other on the displays that linked the three ships' dining areas.

"We might all be from different branches of the military or civilians from different Rim systems. However, we stand here as one people from the resistance—the Rim systems and services united as one crew. We all share the same fight, and today we all share the same mission. The Imperium has captured General Kate Brigman and has now started torturing her. She is one of our heroes, known to our enemy as the Ball Breaker. We are going to bring her home.

"This is the first day of our six-day flight to Tayside around Cygni B. We will continue to run technical planning exercises over that time. Both the Rhinos and Eagles have been training together for months, and you are all ready. When we arrive, we will come out of jump on our attack run, guns firing. Tactical are already selecting and programming in the ground targets for our ballistic assault. That assault will supply cover for the approach of our two transporters plus *The Peregrine* and the

Lancers. The bombardment will continue and degrade all hostile ground assets before our ground team's assault. We have the Lancer aces with us. Four of the latest generation of fighters, eight flight teams, and the ground crews. They will kill everything in the skies above the Citadel, which tries to fly into our airspace. Our commandos will advance under armored support from our new stealth tanks and complete the charge with battle mechs and in fast APC mules. Our spies have detailed plans of the Citadel and the surrounding buildings. Everyone will use the new GOD system that will link us all together and share real-time tactical information. Your section leads will split you all into your planning sessions that begin at 10:30. For the next hour, we all feast. Now eat!"

Charlie Powers sat down. She looked shocked when everyone in the transport and on the screens stood and cheered.

CHAPTER 47

**RIM – PROCYON B – HIGHLANDS
IN ORBIT ABOVE PLANET
MAIN FLEET – SCOUT SHIP THE GANGES
PREPARING AT STAGING POINT 1
BRAVE BASTARDS**

General Abbot had briefed Captain Ted of *The Ganges* days ago when they were all at Procyon B. It had been Captain Ted's idea. He had argued that they needed an advanced element to probe the space where the alleged Imperium supply ships would be running. There was a lot of dissent over whether they were likely to fly into Imperium warships or soft supply ships. Captain Ted's case for an advanced element had won the argument and the honor.

The Ganges was a scout-class ship, so she was fast and nimble. *The Ganges*'s defense relied on just two REC cannons. She had minimal defensive armor, which served primarily to augment structural rigidity. Even the ship's designers knew it was little more than a token defense. Agility and speed were the scout ship's primary weapon. Scouts operated as forward-intelligence-gathering ships. It was unwise to engage any other warships with a scout-class ship. It was more of a "run away and don't fight any day"-class ship. Some people would take the piss out of these ships' small crews, suggesting they lacked the backbone to be on the front line.

The Ganges's captain always felt these intellectual heavyweights were missing the point. Not only would the scouts be on the front line, but they would also be there first and alone, before any of the bigger allied ships. Further, they went blind with none of the intelligence the scout was there to gather. With their light defenses, they might get lucky and be able to shoot down two or, maybe at a push, three inbound missiles. The scout was as likely to get shredded by REC cannon fire.

In Captain Ted's mind, this meant that every member of a scout crew, whatever their gender, was packing bigger plums in their pants than the shriveled small redcurrants in their critics' pants.

His crew's money was all bet on this being a huge double cross set up by the Imperium, with no supply ships out there. Theirs was not where the smart money was in the bookkeeper's eyes, so these were very long odds, meaning the payout for their families would be huge. Of course, the fleet's payoff would be huge as well if they were right. If *The Ganges*, as the advanced scout, could detect Imperium destroyers in place rather than supply ships, while the resistance ships were still sitting at jump, then *The Ganges* could get the word out. That was the key. They had to get the word out despite any radio jamming. If they found the ambush but could never send out a warning flare, *The Ganges* would die while watching the ill-fated arrival of their own fleet.

General Abbot and Captain Ted were both on video comms.

"Ganges, you are on point. We will follow in fifteen minutes. We look forward to getting your all-clear signal."

"Yes, General, we will make sure the signal gets out no matter what. We will see you on the other side. Comms ready, orange alert, battle stations, Ganges getting ready to jump to target. Ganges out."

Abbot cursed then said, "Brave bastards."

The Ganges comms officer had already cut the video link, and started the 1MC announcement:

"Attention, ship. Orange alert status. Soon we jump *The Ganges*. We may well arrive in a combat zone on the other side, so be ready to fight. We will go to red alert thirty minutes before we arrive. FTL flight transit is two days, eleven hours. Jump, in sixty seconds. Remember, if we find it hot, we must get the word back to our friends. We are the Ganges Five."

The Ganges had a small crew. There were just five of them: the captain and the comms, weapons, navigation, and engineering officers.

They all had seats on the ship's bridge, but they would sometimes be in one of the three racks the crew shared. The small mess, the head with a shower area, or engineering. The scout was a small ship. Even the two REC cannons did not carry the normal load of twenty thousand rounds per cannon; they had half a drum each at only ten thousand cannon rounds for each gun. The guns fired five thousand cannon shells per minute, so could only hold enough ammunition for two minutes of continual defensive fire. Only enough for three inbound missiles as the fleet worked on a budget of a maximum of forty seconds of cannon fire per inbound tango.

It was all about compromise. They did not design the scout to hang in a protracted firefight toe-to-toe. The scout's job was to gather information and get the signal out and run away. They removed all the unnecessary weight from her design and perfected her for that function.

They did not send the memo to the crew of *The Ganges*. They were very proud of their role. While they were not in any rush to die, they didn't want to run away either. They saw their role as protectors of the fleet. Maybe not in the same way as other bigger ships might, but no less valuable. All the crew were there to protect each other and the honor of their ship's proud name.

There had been a legendary brawl about a year back. Six of the Eagles had taken the piss out of *The Ganges* and her runaway crew, calling them weaklings and the Runaway Five. That was the point at which all five stood up as one and ran toward the funny men, swinging at them and toppling them onto their asses like bowling pins. Three Rhino commandos had tried to come to the rescue of the fallen Eagles who had started the argument. Only to find the crew of five turned on the three elite Rhinos trained for hand-to-hand combat. Well, the Ganges Five had knocked all those three on their asses as well. Then the MPs had turned up and thrown everyone in the cells for the night.

The crew of *The Ganges* did not turn on one another; they stuck to the line that they were defending one another and their ship. That six Eagles had attacked them from the regular units, and then three elite Rhino commandos, who had put the boot in as well.

The senior MP did not believe their story. How could they beat nine soldiers, three of whom were special operators? The senior MP believed there had been bullying involved and he would have none of it anywhere while he was on watch. He released the crew. The MPs sent the six Eagles and three Rhinos back to their units with orders to their unit commanders. They had to explain the military position on bullying, and not only that, but the nine bullies had all gotten the shit knocked out of them and were a disgrace to their unit. And so maybe they needed a basic training refresher.

The Ganges crew were known from then on as the Ass-Kicking Five.

The brawl was now part of legend, and no one ever took the piss out of them again. They had earned the respect of their colleagues in both the Eagles and Rhinos for being one shit-hard bunch of dangerous dipshits. That would let no one impede *The Ganges*'s mission to help protect the fleet from all threats.

The captain of *The Ganges* laid back and thought of his wife and young daughter. This was not the first mission since she had been born.

Both he and Lesley knew the work was dangerous. They both fought for a brighter future for young Becky. Captain Ted prayed and wished.

Lesley understood why he had volunteered for one of the most dangerous postings in the resistance. He wanted to help raise his young daughter. They both wanted her to grow up free.

The captain also knew that the rest of his crew would have very similar thoughts about family and loved ones that night. He knew they would all want to make them proud and keep their fleet safe.

They were family to each other no matter what anyone else said; they were the Ganges Five.

CHAPTER 48

**CORE – CYGNI B – TAYSIDE
APPROACHING PLANET AT JUMP
YOU ORDERED DEATH
COMMAND BRIDGE
ONE DAY NINE HOURS LATER
FOUR MINUTES**

On *You Ordered Death*, Betsy sat in the pilot's chair. She would fly the assault support for the engagement. Commander Charlie Powers had made *YOD* her task force flagship. The ship had both a captain who oversaw the ship, and a commander who handled the task force. Which for the assault phase was principally the two assault supports. Interestingly, the Lancers' flight of four had been classed as orbital assets. All the pilots and ground crew were Eagles. The Eagles would also pilot the assault transports, and they would transport the Rhinos. These vessels were under Lieutenant Colonel Greg Garcia's command while in the atmosphere.

The captain of *YOD* was Matthew Blunt. He had been Betsy's captain for the last two years. Betsy fancied Matt. She thought he was delicious. Yum, yum. She knew the regulations forbade any form of sexual or romantic relationship between them. Betsy understood why the brass frowned on relationships. It wasn't to protect her from Matt or vice versa, but to protect the ship and the rest of her crew from the two of them. If concern for, or hostility at, each other occurred, then that might imperil the ship and all hands. Either by not taking action that could cause injury or death or by taking it and endangering the ship recklessly.

The situation with *The Peregrine* and her small shuttle was different. For one, *The Peregrine* was not a military vessel but now a civilian volunteer ship aligned with the resistance. The ship's owner and captain was Tom, but as part of the task force, he fell under military command structures. Whose? *The Peregrine* was a Rhino asset, not an Eagles one, so it fell under Greg's authority, not Charlie's. This was clear-cut when *The Peregrine* was in the atmosphere with the commandos and tank crews, just like the transporters. It was less clear who was in charge when *The Peregrine* was in space. If she was a military ship, she would have been part of the Rhinos, working as a recon ship. Of course, the Rhinos had decommissioned all their recon assaults and not replaced them, and the Eagles had never had such a class of vessel. *The Peregrine* was Tom's ship. If Tom followed orders and did what he was told, Charlie and Greg were both happy to let things lie while the ship was in space. Neither was clear in their own mind about whose authority *The Peregrine* was under when not on an active operation. Sometimes ambiguity was useful. As long as no one made an issue out of it and things carried on working, with no one breaking the status quo.

This was further complicated by the main reason *The Peregrine* was involved at all was because it was Merlin's home. Everyone knew it would be a bad idea to tell Merlin who oversaw him or his house. Merlin knew who oversaw Merlin—Merlin did.

In recent days, life on *YOD* had been very busy and focused. Every system was checked. They filled the weapons lockers with rounds for the slug cannons and RECs. Power lines and capacitors feeding the energy cannons had been checked and tested. The missile array displayed green lights for every launcher. The engines and power plants were serviced and inspected. The ship's hardware was in top shape and ready to rock and roll. People had all been drilling nonstop—the flight crew, gunnery, the damage control teams. The human teams that wielded the might of *YOD* were all at peak performance. They didn't need more training to reach their peak. They hadn't peaked too early and gone off the boil. Everything was at its best.

It was the same story in every task force ship. Tank crews waited in their seats. Commandos held their rifles in their black uniforms, sat on their seats inside the four mules. The mech drivers and gunners were at the controls. Transport pilots sat in their seats at the flight controls. The five Casimir bubbles approached the final five seconds from planet Tayside at 240 C. Those five seconds put them twenty light minutes' distance away, or in other terms, just inside the orbit of Jupiter, which was thirty-three light minutes from old Sol.

"Commander, approaching FTL exit in three, two, one, mark. Normal space," Betsy called out to the bridge.

The task force was back in normal space hanging high above Tayside. Faraway, about halfway to the horizon, lay the Citadel, everyone's destination and focus.

Then the noise started. There were three distinct tones, kawoosh, berzong, and maboom, as the missiles, energy cannons, and slug cannons fired. The noises reverberated through the deck and kept repeating.

"*The Peregrine*, transports, and Lancers are pulling away for the surface at full burn. Gun crews on both assault supports have opened with slug and energy cannons at the predefined target list around the Citadel. Both assault supports are ripple firing from the missile arrays at their ground targets. Bombardment for the next four minutes," the tactical officer announced.

Flashes from the first energy cannon blasts hitting the surface around the Citadel bloomed on the ship's screens. The upper atmosphere was being crossed with the contrails from the missile's rocket engines and the shockwaves from the heavy and strong tungsten slugs traveling at reentry speeds of ten kilometers per second.

Each assault support would loose all its ordnance in attacking the Citadel and all the surrounding military targets within a one hundred kilometers radius. They were not launching any radiological or nuclear weapons; they were instead firing precision hell. Over four minutes, each ship would launch a missile every 2.4 seconds from the support ship's one-hundred-missile array. The four energy cannons on each ship would fire every ten seconds, loosing 192 energy rounds to complement the two hundred missiles. The sixteen slug cannons would each fire six hundred tungsten slug rounds, one round every 0.4 seconds. A total barrage of nine thousand and six hundred of the fifty kilo rounds. Each traveling with 2.5 gigajoules of energy at ten kilometers per second.

That was over ten thousand targeted shots in just four minutes over an area of 31,400 square kilometers. In the target area, military targets occupied a total of just 500 square kilometers, so that was where all the fire went. They would typically hit each square kilometer with twenty very-high-energy ground-assault shots. Every 200 square meters in the military target area would take a heavy hit with a primary kill diameter of 150 meters. They pounded some squares harder than others.

CHAPTER 49

**CORE – CYGNI B – TAYSIDE
ORBITAL REENTRY
THE PEREGRINE – BRIDGE
TROOPS IN CONTACT**

Tom stared at the virtual instruments on his digital cockpit panel. The digital needle notched up another mark on the dial.

"We're at max breaking burn."

Greg looked up at Tom. Everything was on schedule.

"Comms, get me a check-in with our fighters and transports."

"All ships signal in the green, holding formation in the pipe, they are all five by five with us," comms replied.

"Look at those mushroomed fucks all around, stretching to the horizon."

"They won't be shooting back at us," Greg said.

"Good, this is for Alva, fuckers."

"Gunnery, get ready with RECs to remove all targets from around Citadel. Avoid evac site."

"Roger that, standing ready."

"Two minutes to ground, overhead bombardment ends in one minute thirty seconds," comms said, updating the bridge team.

"Get tanks to start their engines. Comms, release the Lancers to attack antiair."

Greg unmuzzled his forces.

"Fighters released. They will hit before final," comms said.

"Comms, move transports to holding," Greg said, dead calmly.

"Tanks report, ready to go. Transports moving to holding. We are about to start final. Fighters are weapons-free."

"Put us into circles above the Citadel. Gunnery, Citadel targets, fire RECs."

"Fire on the way," gunnery said.

All sixteen REC cannons now opened up, chattering away like a scream, nearly continually rather than the occasional staccato burst. They could hear the chatter of the RECs firing throughout *The Peregrine*. There was no letup, not even during the occasional second when an individual REC would pause while the 360-degree tilt-and-swivel mounts would reposition the big rotary cannons between each target. The red markers on the GOD system rapidly winked out all around the Citadel grounds and through the windows. The high-density rounds tore through the Citadel's walls and turned the masonry into deadly shrapnel that exploded into the rooms behind, tearing the Imperium soldiers' bodies apart. The GOD display also showed the attack runs of the four Lancer fighters launching missiles at ground air defenses and conducting strafing runs.

"Transports to precision aim slug cannons."

"Tiger's team report all enemy ground to air assets destroyed. Pickle and Vapor are hovering transports and taking aim."

"Good. Get the Lancers to stay on station but move to safety markers."

"Fighters acknowledged. Overhead bombardment now ceased," the comms officer said with clear tension in his voice.

"Transports fire slugs now."

The GOD display showed the transports at hover, taking aim while REC fire continued to rain down from *The Peregrine*, with the Lancers moving to their safety markers. The transports' slug cannons started firing multiple fifty kilo rounds at ten kilometers per second, at just over Mach twenty-nine. The sonic boom was continuous because every round was hypersonic; every window was smashed for many miles around. The rounds flew at the Citadel's main outer defensive walls, which ringed the building. The transports hovered at twenty meters at a three kilometers range. The four slug cannons fired a round every 0.4 seconds. Their fire lasted for twenty seconds, and the four fifty round ammo cassettes were empty. Two hundred of the fifty kilo rounds were fired into the outer wall. The wall exploded into more lethal sharp-edged stones that flew back and impacted the Citadel.

"Perfect hits, Citadel's outer wall has been breached."

On the GOD display, they could now see the thirty-meter-long hole torn through the outer defensive wall.

"Nav, put us on the ground at the LZ,"

"Ending circling, LZ approach in three, two, one. Touchdown. Peregrine is down."

"Roll tanks. Then get us back in the air, providing fire support."

"Port and starboard hatches down. Tanks have engaged their stealth camouflage, tanks rolling. Tanks cleared *The Peregrine*," comms said.

Nav immediately pulled back on the controls lifting The Peregrine back up into the air.

"Tanks approaching target at Vmax. Transports ready to land. Tanks aimed. Firing, creating front door."

The six tanks fired one of their ten heavy rounds every second through the gap in the outer wall. The sixty heavy shells penetrated the Citadel's main wall, all targeting the same thirty-meter section. This would be the commando's new front door into the Citadel.

"Transports landing behind our tank line."

"Deploy mechs when the transports are on the ground. Follow up with the mules."

"Four mechs on the ground and moving fast to the front door. Four mules following, ten seconds to front door. Transports back in the air, performing close-air REC support. Tiger's fighters just splashed three enemy fighters; the skies are ours."

"The enemy must have been sleeping to still be flying."

"Mechs engaging. They are tearing the lobby up. Okay, there is nothing left moving in there. Mules ram-raiding the lobby. Mechs guarding. Mules are inside the building, deploying our teams. Commandos on the move."

"Comms, signal Charlie, everything on plan."

"Sent. Commando Alpha and Bravo teams assaulting detention block; Charlie and Delta teams covering."

CHAPTER 50

UNCLAIMED
ETA CASSIEOPEIAE B – JOV8542
APPROACHING AT JUMP
SCOUT SHIP THE GANGES – BRIDGE
EMERGENCY SEND

"This is it, people, stand ready to fight, pray for clear skies. Comms, stand by," the captain instructed the bridge team.

The navigation officer counted them in as they approached the jump exit.

"Exit FTL in three, two, one, mark, normal space."

The comms officer looked at his crowded console display in horror. "Oh, shit, emergency send,"

The comms officer's voice was steady but had gone up in pitch.

"We have four Imperium destroyers within ten light seconds, we are detecting their targeting radars," gunnery said.

"One destroyer is turning to bear, marking as D1," navigation said.

"Comms, has that signal gone, confirm if sent?" the captain said.

"Negative, emergency signal not sent,"

"Take a breath, figure it out, we must get the signal out," the captain said.

Comms was poking buttons on the display. "Yes, I am checking now, I'll need two minutes,"

"People, we must stay alive for at least the next two minutes, navigation, gunnery, give me options," the captain said.

"There is an asteroid belt that could shield us somewhat," gunnery said.

"They could turn the belt into a blender if they fire into the rocks, I am going for the Jovian," navigation said.

The captain stared fixedly at navigation. "Okay, explain,"

Navigation turned to look at the captain. "We need cover, we can hide in the upper atmosphere, the radiation belts are going to play hell with everyone's sensors, plus the storm will stop them from getting close or sending in fighters,"

"The storm, we're in space," gunnery said.

"Not in that giant spot we won't be, we'll be inside the big daddy of hurricanes," navigation said.

"That is suicide," gunnery said.

"Not for the next two minutes it's not," navigation said.

"Make it happen, people," the captain said.

"One problem is that the radiation is going to kill our comms when we're in that close," comms said.

"Destroyer has launched, five missiles inbound, twelve seconds," gunnery said.

"Five! No choice, max burn now," navigation said.

The Ganges dove straight for the great green spot. The ship was driven sideways as it hit the storm front.

The navigation officer grabbed his console to steady himself. "Just, shearing forces,"

"You're sure," the captain said.

"Err, yes, I think,"

"Comms, I need that beacon back," the captain said.

"Still two minutes,"

"And the missiles?" the captain said.

Gunnery was stabbing his fingers at the controls. "Firing the RECs now,"

The five missiles streaked in, buffeted by the storm. The two REC cannons chattered away in a long burst. They each had ten thousand cannon rounds to fire. The book said that was only enough for three missiles, not five. The beyond-hurricane-force winds whipped the REC cannon shells into new projectile arcs.

"Fuck this storm, imminent," gunnery said.

Everyone held their breath, waiting for their death. Two missiles detonated right behind the ship.

"RECs nailed two, fuck, that was close," gunnery said.

The captain leaned forwards. "Are we clear, the other three?"

"You don't want to know how close. Clear, the other three missiles got destroyed in the storm, lightning cooked one and winds swallowed the other two," gunnery said.

"I think I am there, yes, yes, the beacon is back online," comms said.

"Get us out of this storm and clear of the radiation,"

The navigation officer didn't need to be told twice by the captain. The ship turned everyone's stomachs; it stood on its tail and pushed them into their jump seats as The Ganges's engines burned.

"We are gone, clearing the storm, soonish, I am not sure where we are now,"

"What is soonish?" the captain said.

"Now, it is now, fuck, we got blown halfway round the spot, running for space," navigation said.

"Shit, the radiation is still too strong to send,"

"We will get a signal out of this bitch, I am going to redline the engines," the engineering officer pushed the engine's power levers all the way forward.

The engine noise and the ship's shaking increased dramatically.

"We won't have any engines or ship left in ten seconds,"

"Clearing the bands now, send it," navigation said.

"Message sent, but no handshake signal, I just don't know," comms said.

"An honor, gentlemen, the fleet," Captain Ted saluted.

"Losing engines in two—" engineering said.

The Ganges's engines detonated, obliterating the ship. The Ganges Five all died thinking of their loved ones. They had tried their best. The ship did them proud. They all hoped their actions were enough to save the fleet.

CHAPTER 51

CORE – CYGNI B – TAYSIDE
THE CITADEL
INTERROGATION BLOCK
KATE BRIGMAN'S CELL
INTERROGATION

Brigadier General Kate Brigman figured the interrogator must be getting tired. He had been at this for days, and Brigman knew she had given him nothing. She smiled, as she thought he might even be getting nervous himself. She expected his debriefing would be quite vigorous.

They had restrained her wrists; the wires extended to the ceiling. He was working through the interrogator's book *Being a Nasty Bastard*.

He had begun with sound and light sensory torture. Then he moved on to physical shaming, stripping her, then they laughed while they urinated on her. Next had come the physical torture, the punches to her face, breasts, vagina, stomach, and kidneys. It got them nowhere. Since they had clothed her and fed her. Brigman guessed that the Mr. Nice Guy act was up next.

It was clear to Brigman that the interrogator was running out of ideas. *Just try raping me* she thought *and I will bite it off*. What the interrogator did not know was that in her younger years, Brigman had authored the book *Being a Nasty Bastard*. It didn't lessen the pain. Her military training and mile-wide stubborn streak handled those well. What Brigman's extensive practical past about information extraction had given her was the ability to see through dramatics. Every technique and tactic that this little man pup was trying to use on her. What was the stick and what was the carrot? How could she counter it and turn it around? Brigman's mind was clear. She could remember every word and lie she had concocted. A spume of elaborate bullshit that they would have to crawl through that would all evaporate like mist. The problem was the interrogator could no longer differentiate between lies and truth anymore. He had become lost in the maze of questions and false answers. The solution had come to him about half an hour ago. What he wanted to do was to shoot Brigman. Not as a threat to her or a way to extract information, but to inflict vengeance on her. Vengeance to pay her back for what he knew was doubtless to come in the ignominious, shameful tag end of his life. They both knew he had not won. He could not break her. It seemed Brigman was the exception to the rule that would never break.

His self-reflection and dreams of executing her got interrupted about six minutes ago by the fearsome bombardment from orbit. At first, it puzzled him as they were hitting everything around them other than the Citadel building. The secondary explosions had tipped him off. It was not that they were missing the Citadel, it was that they were not aiming at it. Instead, they were degrading all the other military assets. Command and communication and other combat infrastructure that the Imperium had around the Citadel. It was all being targeted and destroyed. When he looked at his comms screen, he had found a satellite image of the two hundred kilometers around the Citadel. The central circle scarred with the rising black mushrooms from what must have been many thousands of strikes, more, maybe. This was a shock-and-awe display playing out in front of him, and he was here, in the Imperium Citadel, right at the center of the whirlwind, as yet unscathed.

He knew this meant only one thing. There was a ground assault coming that would have its eyes fixed on the Citadel. He had found it perplexing. If they wanted to silence Brigman, there were far easier ways. The rebels could have scooped the Citadel up from the map and cast it to the winds, but they hadn't. Now he realized they were coming to rescue her, not kill her. Which meant at some point the wolves would find their way to his door.

He knew they were inside the Citadel now; he had watched on the screen as the slug cannons had shattered the outer walls. Followed by what was likely tank fire that had come from nowhere and breached the inner walls. Only for them to make way for the relentless cannon fire from four battle mechs. Throwing round after round from their twin twenty-millimeter rotary cannons into the Citadel's heart beyond the walls.

The mechanical dogs, those four APC wolves, had dashed into the gash cut into the Citadel's flank. The APCs disgorged their black soldier ants, which were now scuttling and killing their way through the inner corridors. Ever closer, unstoppable. With an almost godlike telepathic coordination. He knew it would only be a few more minutes. Time to kill Brigman. He would deny them their prize, let them take her body back and nothing else.

"It seems the wolves are at the door, General. You will stay here with me."

The interrogator reached to his belt and grabbed his pistol. Shaped charges blew the cell door inward, flash bangs came in after with short half second fuses. Then came the red laser targeting beams. Quick, bang, bang, bang, bang. Both commandos took their two shots. Two to the head and two to the chest, and the interrogator was very much down and retired. The two commandos stepped in, clad in black, wearing gas masks with a holo-display over their left eye.

From behind his gas mask, Brigman heard the first commando say, "General, secure."

The second commando removed his gas mask. In the cell's gloom, a faint green glow seeped from under the holo-display over his left eye, the dim light gently illuminating the top edge of his cheekbone.

"Let me get you out of those restraints, General."

As the commando worked on the General's wrists to release her bonds, he could not fail to see her blackened right eye, her swollen, split upper and lower lip, the blue-and-yellow bruise spread over the left side of her face, the cut on her forehead, or where the congealed blood had run down and clotted in her eyebrow. He considered the damage not visible on her face with a shudder. The commando knew what the interrogator had likely subjected her to.

"Is this about my outstanding library fine?" the General said.

The first commando seemed a little slow. "No, it's about you, General, Operation Ball Breaker to get you out, sir."

The second commando released the bonds from both wrists.

"Okay, General, you are free now."

"I like the name." Brigman stamped her bare heel on the dead interrogator's balls twice, bursting them open into red stains that seeped into the fabric of his pants. She smiled.

Brigman rolled her head, stretching out an annoying ache.

"Let's go."

"Alpha leader, we are pulling out now with the package, cover and fall back." The first commando said into his radio.

CHAPTER 52

UNCLAIMED
ETA CASSIEOPEIAE B – JOV8542
APPROACHING AT JUMP
MAIN FLEET – ABBOT'S COMMAND SHIP
TWO SALVOS

"General we just received an emergency alert signal from *The Ganges*, no details, just their beacon. What do you want to do?" the comms officer asked.

Abbot stood.

"Put me on fleet-wide comms now! I never bought the supply ship bullshit. Ships of the fleet, listen up. We have word from *The Ganges*, but it was just their beacon. It wasn't a full, coherent message, which means they were in trouble when they sent it. I fear our guard dog is dead. We will heed the warning they paid so dearly to send to us."

"I want everyone ready on hair triggers to fire as soon as we come through the jump point. My ship will grid the sky and assign coordinates to specific ships, fire your missiles blind into your arc as soon as your nose comes through the jump point. I want one salvo from all tubes."

"Guidance will kick in mid-flight on the missiles. As soon as we have sensors back after the jump exit. Snap shoot and repeat fire all slug and energy cannons. Everything is unfriendly in your assigned grid. Lock targets and fire a second missile salvo. I will reassess after to decide whether we are turning and running or staying to fight."

"I want RECs and targeting radars defending arcs of sky. We will shield our neighbors' flank; they will shield ours. Just make sure nothing gets through your ship's REC defense arc. We all depend on each other. No one breaks the line. We fire two clean missile salvos first. I will tell you all what we are doing once we know who is still alive. They will not expect us to fire so quickly en masse. They do not know we know they are waiting for us, all lined up, sitting still. We will take the fight to them."

"Let us make the Ganges Five proud of their fleet."

CHAPTER 53

CORE – CYGNI B – TAYSIDE
CLIMBING UP INTO SPACE
GUNS EXPRESS DELIVERY
SPECIAL DELIVERY

"I need a comms link to command," Brigman said.

"You can use my radio, General, here, use this." Commando Two passed her a headset.

They were both strapped into the forward seats in the assault transport *Guns Express Delivery*. Half of the commandos were all loaded into the main area in the back, along with two mechs and two mules.

GED was burning for space. She was being escorted by two of the Lancer's fighters. The other two were acting as a diversionary flight; they escorted the other assault transport that carried the other half of the commandos, mechs, and mules. Any hostile air assets had the good sense to hide in their bunkers—the few that were not already burning.

"Thank you. Brigman to command. I am secure on transport. When your people are clear, turn that building into a gigantic crater."

"Yes, General, HE special delivery inbound in fifteen seconds, good to have you back with us." Commander Charlie Powers grinned ear to ear.

They released a burst of rounds from every gun on the two assault supports, all targeting the Citadel. Soon the building shrinking behind them would be nothing more than a large hole in the ground.

CHAPTER 54

UNCLAIMED
ETA CASSIEOPEIAE B – JOV8542
ARRIVING FROM JUMP
MAIN FLEET – ABBOT'S COMMAND SHIP
WHAT HAPPENS AT 0.31 C

"Three, two, one, mark," comms said,

"Blind firing all tubes," gunnery said,

"Normal space," comms said,

Gunnery was pressing more buttons. "Snap-firing energy cannons, snap-firing slug cannons,"

"We are reading forty-two enemy destroyers within thirty light seconds," navigation said.

"Fuck, we were right," Abbot said.

"We have targeting data, locking second missile salvo, firing, missiles away, locked energy and slug cannons, firing on repeat," gunnery said.

"Comms, get me damage assessments, ASAP," Abbot said.

"Enemy ships opening fire, our REC screens are all firing," gunnery said.

Abbot gripped the arms of his chair. "Helm, emergency evasion maneuvers, all ships. Comms, I need it now!"

"Sir, we have lost five ships, five more damaged but under power, fourteen ships undamaged, the enemy have lost twenty-three of forty-two ships," comms said.

"Nineteen ships apiece and five of ours damaged, and they have Imperium destroyers, we can't win this, comms, signal all ships, slingshot that Jovian, max power now, everyone to follow us," Abbot thumped his fist on the arm of his chair.

The nineteen ships' engines flared blue-white.

"We are at max power, our ships are following, I am going to take us closer still." Navigation said.

"You are sure?" Abbot said.

"Not really, should be better for our damaged ships and force the enemy even closer in to play catch up," navigation said.

"Go with your gut,"

"We all are, it is going to get a little weird," navigation said.

"Approaching the radiation bands," comms said.

"We are going to skim them, that is all. We are speeding up, 0.2 C now." Navigation said.

The command crew was all silent. Everyone was on edge.

"0.24 C."

"You know what happens at 0.31 C. Right?" comms asked.

"Peace and quiet. 0.26 C, enemy ships are still pursuing," navigation said.

"Hold our course," Abbot said.

Navigation glanced at the controls. "That is perihelion, 0.27 C. We might make it, come on."

"I want everyone with jump drives spooled and ready to jump to the RV1 point," Abbot said.

"Sending, sir. Acknowledged, all ships," comms said.

"Coming up on 0.285 C."

The comms officer crossed himself. "This is going to be close."

"I know. 0.3 C, almost there. Just a little more. 0.304 C, and ... We are clear of the slingshot, everyone jump."

"Jump, jump, jump." Comms said.

With multiple flashes, the ships were now at jump.

"We exited slingshot at just under 0.307 C, fuck, that was close to the limit."

"All ships are at jump with us." Comms said.

Abbot let out the breath he had been holding. "Very good people, excellent work."

"The enemy broke pursuit when they hit 0.308 C and scattered. We have gained some time before they can get themselves organized to jump after us." Navigation said.

CHAPTER 55

**CORE – CYGNI B – TAYSIDE
IN ORBIT
GUNS EXPRESS DELIVERY
MY SHOULDER HURTS**

Brigman was on a three-way video conference call with Charlie's assault support ship, *You Ordered Death*, and Greg on *The Peregrine*.

Brigman was still in the clothes they had put her in while she was in detention. The wounds on her face looked worse under the direct light from the camera.

"You are?" Brigadier General Brigman asked.

"Commander Charlie Powers, Orbital Strike Team."

"Lieutenant Colonel Greg Garcia, Ground Strike Team."

"Excellent operation. How are our people?"

Greg tightened his body to attention, even though he was sitting in front of the screen.

"One dislocated shoulder, no other casualties, General. We will have you on board *The Peregrine* now we are all in orbit again, unless you prefer one of the assault support ships where Charlie is."

"*The Peregrine* will be fine for now. What is she?"

"Ex-recon assault, General," Greg said with pride. The operation had gone outstandingly well.

"We all need to talk about what happens next." Brigman said.

CHAPTER 56

**CORE – CYGNI B – TAYSIDE
IN ORBIT
YOU ORDERED DEATH – BRIDGE
HOPELESSNESS**

"Commander, priority communication from General Abbot."

Charlie looked up; she knew she looked a state, that didn't matter. Brigman looked a lot worse, Charlie knew.

"Charlie here, General."

"Commander, how did the raid go?" General Abbot asked.

"We have secured General Brigman alive. The interrogation was … it was bad, sir."

"Excellent news that you got her out. It was to be expected, Charlie, but we got her! Now, a change of plans, I need you to make for Kilbride base on Lanarkshire at Luyten's Star, not back to Inverness."

"Sir?"

"It was an ambush, Charlie. The fleet is running, we are still here; many are not. They inflicted a lot of damage; nineteen destroyers are chasing us."

"Oh no. Oh god."

"You must get Brigman out to Kilbride. I fear the Imperium is coming for Inverness."

"We have many people on the planet, sir."

"I know, too many, but we are too far away for you to rendezvous with us, and we are defensive. You can't fight the Imperium fleet by yourselves. You will still be evacuating when the Imperium fleet arrives long after killing us."

"We can if you can keep their fleet busy off our backs, sir, or maybe, if they are coming anyway, lead them back to Procyon B. I bet they won't attack you on route if you are going to Procyon B. They will want to make a show of it when you arrive."

"I don't know. We risk losing it all."

"Sir. Let me take this to General Brigman."

"Okay, your FTL jump to Kilbride takes you near Procyon B anyway. You brainstorm it out over there and get back to me within the hour. We have little time here."

"Yes, General, we are on this. How many, sir?"

"Many what?"

"How many of the resistance at Inverness base?"

"Way too many, Charlie, way too many. It will be crippling. We will talk in an hour."

"How many have we lost sir?"

"Five ships destroyed, five damaged but limping, something like eight thousand dead and five hundred injured. We don't have time now, Charlie, we can all mourn later."

"Yes, sir."

The call ended, and the screen went blank. Charlie stared at the empty screen, now lost in her thoughts. A single tear grew in the corner of her left eye.

It seemed overwhelming. Hopeless. It seemed they were powerless to save Abbot's fleet from the chasing pack of Imperium dogs. They would wipe out half the resistance warships today. Inverness was going to fall the same day, and with it, the Rim system's cooperative seat of government and the resistance's principal base. Millions would die. One Rim system after the other would follow and fall until the light from the last eight Rim systems would be extinguished. The Imperium would drag them screaming and put them all under their boot, stripped of their liberty.

Maybe Brigman could come up with something? They must be able to do something. Charlie prayed for the first time in her life.

ACT II TO ACT III
INTERLUDE

HOWARD'S BRAIN DUMP

TYPED NOTES FROM HIS SESSION WITH HIMSELF REPRODUCED VERBATIM

Dear Diary,

I need your help to figure out what to do.

Why / what / how / who?

- Identifying what Bob wants?
  - Conquest of all Rim systems.
- What is standing in the way of what Bob wants?
  - The resistance.
- Planning how to get what Bob wants?
- Cutting the thing in the way?
- What flows from that?
- Concocting a plan that ends the thing?

So, what is in the way?

- The resistance.
- The people's belief in the resistance.
- The conformity of belief.
- The resistance is diffuse—there is a large clump at the Procyon B system on the Highlands.
- Need to send a large visible symbol to the Rim. systems and break the emotional back of the resistance.
- The resistance is shown to be powerless.
- The resistance also defends the civilian co-op Rim.seat of government on Procyon B. They will need to go.

So, we need to destroy both the resistance and the Procyon B seat of the government. To remove them in a dramatic and very public display.

The consequence will be a malaise that will erode the Rim systems and result in their rapid fall and surrender.

Thought:

- So, we need a fleet for them to surrender to.
- Fleet pulls the trigger and sweeps up.
- We need to co-opt a fleet General into this dastardly plan.
- We will only have one fleet, so needs to be swift and decisive.
- Plonker Plug might be an opportunity, even though he is in the way.
- And the universe's most stupid idiot.
- We need to fake the supply lines' story.
- Get the fleet out of the way.

Plug can ambush them and, hey, that solves the problem happy days. Or it gets the resistance out of the way, leaving Procyon B abandoned, and the second fleet can sweep in.

Leaving an embarrassing show of failure for the resistance, shown to all their Rim mates, so that's also a win if Plug doesn't destroy them. A win either way as long as the Procyon B government falls.

So, the aim is not really the military. We actively do not want to engage them, let them walk in shame, heads low. So, the target is the civilian government.

We need the fleet to take out the government on the planet. We could land troops, but the surface is a rebel stronghold. Much better to attack from orbit. Which means overwhelming bombardment, straight off the top with no warning.

We need to kill or tie up the ground forces so they can't fly out like angry bees. So dead or tending to injured and dying civilians. Either is good and shows another failure of the resistance to protect the other worlds or strike back against the fleet.

So, we need:

- A surprise attack.
- From orbit.

- That takes out the government.
- Causes widespread damage and death to all the people, whether resistance or civilian government, that will pin down the resistance.
- Fleet needs to leave and go to the next target.
- The show must get broadcast, to spread the psychological terror.
- So, it must be bold and visual, not just a pinpoint accurate strike.
- The images must scream failure of the resistance and horror at the unstoppable loss of the civilian government.

Worry about the what later, let us find the who first?

The person needs to be gung ho and not too smart or ask too many questions, so he will just do what I tell them to do. Thick, ruthless, and blindly following orders.

Well, there really is only one person, isn't there? General Wombat. So called because he will just charge in there at great speed like a cannonball of muscle and take down any foe, no matter how big, off their feet.

So, we are going to need a meeting with Wombat to gain his compliance. But we need to have more to offer. Wombat's fleet is a fleet of warships. Warships shoot things so his armory may be a way to get to him.

Oh!

- Well, there is only one thing ... We can't do that. Err. It would tick all the requirement boxes.
- Slow and graphic beat them into submission.
- They would be more likely to surrender!
- We could even make a clerical error.
- We could claim he had overkilled it and blame it all on Wombat.

So, a multirole assault, we sell it as limited focused engagement with wider low-intensity assault.

This means Wombat needs to be ignorant of the entire plan. Of what he has on board, which means we also need to recolor and remark.

So, we need a kill squad to take out the dock ship's loaders.

Hackers adjust the IT while the ships are in dock.

We need Wombat's fleet to come in for reloading. Then we can do both jobs.

We need to organize the timeline, so the dock yard time is shortly before the attack time. After, we divert him to a low-intensity assignment, plus sneak them into place so no one notices.

We need to fake orders to bring them into dock and we need more faked orders for where I want them sent after. Somewhere nice and quiet, low-key, slow and stealthy, creeping round the edges. Then pounce and run.

We need them to not be able to cancel. Another IT hack to remove their choice if they change their minds.

Wombat will also have seen much more happen than we sold him, so we need to be sure he stays on track.

We need someone on ship to cover tracks, someone to assassinate Wombat, which means someone close to him on the bridge. If any of them have a change-their-mind-type moment, we assume command to keep the fleet in play.

We only need one fleet, doesn't matter if it is Plug's or Wombat's, as long as there is one. Having both in the area will mean all other Imperium fleet assets will get maneuvered a long way away. If there is one of them to establish control, it will be fine.

The victories will bring changes of heart to impressionable horrified minds, destroying the promise of the rebel rabble.

We only need an assassin to take Wombat off the table if they all wig out. So, Wombat can't testify about the meeting that I will need to have with him. Set all this up so that the trail gets masked and can't get traced back to me or any possibility of linking it back to Bob.

The plan:

- Brief Wombat.
- Schedule time in dock.
- Get the kill squad to take out loaders.
- Hack the computer records and display.
- Get a loyal (to me) officer on the bridge close to
- Wombat.
- Create new orders to sneak Wombat closer to

- Procyon B.
- Create orders to redeploy other fleet elements
- away from the sector.
- So, we can get Plug and Wombat in position.
- Fake supply lines story to drag the resistance
- fleet away.
- Create orders to get Plug to execute an ambush.
- Wombat attacks Procyon B in surprise full-commitment
- attack after egress.
- Record the attack and broadcast.
- Kill Wombat if necessary. No, better yet! Kill Wombat
- and take control of the fleet.
- Move fleet ex-Wombat RIP, Plug, or both to the next
- Rim system.
- Move the fleet into the next Rim system.

They will reel from the loss of their fleet, their government, and Procyon B.

ACT III

CHAPTER 57

**CORE – CYGNI B – TAYSIDE
IN ORBIT
THE PEREGRINE – RECREATION ROOM / C&C SUITE
BRAINSTORMING**

"Apologies for the lack of space on my ship. The recreation room is full of command and control and new targeting computers. We lost all our sofas. The stores are full of bullets and cannon shells, the cargo area is full of tanks, and the bunks are full of commandos," Tom said.

Greg outlined the situation. "General Abbot's fleet got ambushed. Actually, they ambushed the ambushers. The Imperium had a lot more ships, so despite the twenty-three losses we inflicted, with our five losses, it is currently nineteen ships each and another five of ours damaged. Our ships are running, and the Imperium is in pursuit."

"Our ships are totally defensive. We believe the Imperium ultimately will attack Inverness base once they have run our ships down and destroyed them. There are many thousands of lives at stake, both on the ships and at Inverness. This really is it," Charlie said.

"If I may jump in, I think you are right, Charlie," Merlin said.

"Right about what?"

"That we should get the fleet to lead them to Inverness."

"You were not even in the room."

"I am always in the room, Charlie, on the ship anyway. Besides, I think you are right. They want to go to Inverness, so let's take them there. We play up the damage, even on the ships that are not damaged, so we lead them slowly and gain time."

"Yes, absolutely, but to what end?"

"We get the resistance to evacuate people on the ships they have left in the Procyon B system and any civilian ships that want to join us. Stage the ships under the cover of the Strategic Defense Satellite Network umbrella. Jump them in small groups out on random vectors. After the first jump, they change course and jump for our rally point."

"That is where we and the fleet will join the transporters and civilian ships. In the meantime, we hold the line at the Highlands to make sure all the ships that want to come get out of the system. Passed the

Imperium ships."

"While Abbot is on route to us, faking damage that is worse than it is, the fleet repairs everything that shoots. When they arrive, they get under the SD Net Umbrella with us, turn, and point their guns out. We hold the Imperium back at a safe distance while the ships evacuate."

"While the transports wait for our arrival, they get all their jump drives tuned and powered up in the best condition they can be. We all go from the rally point, in a single jump to Kilbride. We nuke the rally point after we have jumped to tear up the trail."

Greg leaned forward and asked Merlin, "Do you think we can hold the line against them?"

"We can hold it enough. Destroyers, we match them ship for ship. The two assault supports, and *The Peregrine* are with us, as are the Strategic Defense satellites. I don't know if the government on the Highlands will want to get involved or stay neutral. But they may have some ground-based weapons as well. Plus mines. I like mines. They are sneaky. We can seed them where we herd the Imperium to park up. Then, boom. The resistance should get themselves ready to go now. We want to get all the batches of ships out, not just the fast ones first. They must work together to get everyone ready. We can get the resistance working on this before we even arrive. As soon as the ground-based ships are ready, we evacuate in batches. At some point, our fleet will arrive with the Imperium fleet in tow and that is when it will get a lot more kinetic. Best case, everyone is gone before our fleet arrives, which is why we must get them to win as much time as possible. But it can't happen mathematically, so there is going to be a big fight."

"I vote with Merlin," Lauren said.

Jack threw his hands up. "You would, but as they say 'moo,' let's do this, and shit on their feet."

"Yep, me as well," Charlie said. She wore a determined expression.

"I'm in," Tom said.

"We have a plan." Greg clenched both his hands into fists.

General Brigman looked around the group, not sure if these were the craziest or bravest people she had met in a long time. She also thought Jack's foot-shitting fetish was one of the strangest she had ever come across.

"Let's go balls deep. General Abbot needs to go slow and play up the damage caused while effecting repairs, come to Procyon B, and get under the Highland's SD network. On the ground, people get organized, and everyone gets ready to go. How long before we get to Procyon B?"

"We will be there in just under three hours," Tom said.

"General Abbot should arrive in five hours. He can probably stretch that out to maybe seven hours. I am not sure, but I would estimate that ground resistance needs six hours to get their shit together and an hour to evacuate, maybe a little more," Charlie said.

"I agree with your estimates, Charlie," Merlin replied.

Since General Brigman's arrival on *The Peregrine*, commando two from the Citadel raid had taken Brigman to the combat stores where she had grabbed fresh utilities, underwear, and boots. A medic had checked her over and cleaned her up. The medic used medical strips to help seal the wound on her forehead. Anti-inflammatory creams had been applied as needed to her various other injuries. The medic gave her a headband to keep her hair out of her cuts. She had also gained a support bandage on her left wrist and there was strapping around three of her ribs, under her clothes. It wasn't pretty, but the damage was mostly superficial. They had given her broad-spectrum antibiotics, although she had declined the strong prescription painkillers and just taken two tablets for regular headaches. General Brigman remained ultra-focused on the mission priorities, not on herself. General Brigman's mind was clear. There was work to do; Abbot needed their help.

"Right, that is what I will tell Abbot when I brief him in ten minutes. Now I need a plan for what we do when we all get there!" General Brigman said with a smile.

CHAPTER 58

**RIM – PROCYON B – THE HIGHLANDS
IN ORBIT
THE PEREGRINE – BRIDGE
MINES**

The Peregrine was on approach to the Highlands' port district. They had just broken formation from the rest of the Ball Breaker Task Force and were on their way down to the planet to put their plan in motion. Charlie was standing on the command bridge, looking at the GOD display, which was depicting a 3D hologram of the solar system centered on the Highlands.

"Comms, please put me through to Fred at Ground Control Inverness."

"Connected, go."

"Fred, you on? This is Charlie. We are about five minutes out, just approaching the planet now."

"Charlie, thank the gods."

"How have you been progressing with getting the ships ready?"

"Nightmare, the newer ships are straightforward, the older ones need the most repairs, replacement parts, you know, the stuff we haven't got."

Charlie considered the parts problem.

"We can fabricate some bits, at a push. We have a machine shop on board, but we can't help with replacement electronics. Transporting everything up and down is going to kill both time and fuel. We are much better keeping *The Peregrine* in orbit, but we can send down both our transports."

"Yeah, I figured. What we have been doing is cannibalizing the even older ships for spares. We have lots of old bust ships, just not enough of the new working kind."

"Do you have anything that can shoot heavy slug cannon rounds?" Charlie asked Fred.

"Sorry no, I have lots of REC equipped ships, a couple with energy cannons that couldn't even warm up soup, and five mine layers. That is all."

"You have mine layers! Do you have the mines as well?"

"Mines, yeah sure, we have thousands of them on special, lots of mines. The FTL star drives are cooked."

"Do you mind if I put them in orbit for you?"

"Sure thing."

"We will send down our commandos and tank crews. There are quite a few engineers and fabricators among them, plus a lot of muscle and organizing skills."

"Do those tank crews have tanks, by any chance. With live tank rounds?"

"Yep, do you want the ordnance?"

"I have an idea for suicide zombie ships. They have too many holes in them for human transport. The SLS drives are using magic to work, but I can pack them with artillery rounds and remote fly them up someone's ass."

"You got them. I will get them loaded on the transport."

"Charlie. We have six batches of twenty ships ready and another eleven batches still to get ready."

"Fuck, we need to go quicker. We are three hours in with three hours to go, and we need to be leaving. There are twice as many to go as we have done in the last three hours. We need to speed up."

"Send me those commandos, Charlie, we will make it happen somehow."

"Roger, out. Comms, get me General Brigman!"

"Brigman."

"Sir, I have got several thousand mines coming up from the planet. Thought you could use them."

"Outstanding! Park up in space just near the assault supports, we will put out logistics pens ..."

"Sir, if I may. These mines are coming up on their five mine-layer ships, no FTL, but okay, otherwise."

"You just made our mine field five times bigger!"

"Fred has nothing that shoots, but he is going to send us some suicide zombies when they are ready, packed with tank and artillery shells."

"Interesting, like high-explosive Trojan ponies, I imagine. Fuck, suicide zombies is a way better name. Charlie, we have been using our ground side liaison to pull the arms off the civilian government's representative. They have confirmed they have a field of fifty ICBMs converted for long range system asteroid interception. They still have their warheads, one-megaton each, but the missiles are not very maneuverable, asteroids fly straight you know. Old and slow, plus the civilians still have the fence stuck up their crack currently and don't want to fire them at the Imperium."

CHAPTER 59

RIM – PROCYON B – THE HIGHLANDS
IN ORBIT
THE PEREGRINE – LAUREN'S CABIN
LOTS OF PUDDING

Lauren focused on typing, hunched over her laptop.

"What are you doing?" Merlin asked Lauren.

"Trying to give us an edge."

"Like a new twelve-blade razor?"

"What? Haha, no, Merlin, you dick, give you an edge. Let me focus."

"Okey dokey, grumpy mum."

"Two minutes, Merlin."

"Ooh, I feel strange."

"Good."

"Like I have had four portions of pudding."

"Yeah, could be. I guess, excellent."

"I feel like I'm going to puke."

"You can't puke, or even ruminate. You are not Daisy."

"Ugh."

"We're done. Twenty enormous bowls of pudding."

"What is all this stuff? There's pudding everywhere."

"Physics, Merlin, well, the capacity to do physics, anyway. You need to fill it with your physics."

"I don't like physics. Can I have some antigas medication? I feel bloated. What does it do?"

"Well, you are now connected to cloud resources in every major data center in the Rim systems."

"That is a where and a what, not a do, Lauren."

"Hmm, well nothing as yet, I guess."

"Nothing. Nothing tastes like pudding overload!"

"Merlin, discover the physics and fill the space up with your discoveries."

"Hey, Lauren, I have discovered there is such a thing as too much pudding."

"Just inventory your new capacity and software, Merlin."

"Hmm, it is all yellow and drowning in custard, I am sure. Ooh! Ooh!"

"See, I told you."

"That is interesting. Look at all this space. Hmm, what do I do with it?"

"I don't know; Daniels was the physicist. I'm the computer geek. You need to use it and figure out what to do with it."

"I am like Captain Scott, stuck up in the Arctic, starving, being made to eat endless bowls of pudding, with no idea if I still like pudding, or ever liked pudding. Take some time. This is going to take an eternity, not a short walk outside, and I might now be too fat to walk anywhere."

"Well, keep eating, Merlin. Jump to it. We might need you yet."

CHAPTER 60

**CORE – ALPHA CENTAURI A – NEW TERRA
AYLESBURY
SUPREME COMMANDER BOB'S OFFICE
AN OPPORLEM**

Bob's desk was now clear of all the paper, and he looked happy.

"I have had some ideas, sir," Harold said.

"Oh yes?"

"The opporlem is Plug, sir."

"Ugh, what language was that?" Bob said.

"Opporlem, sir, opportunity problem, sir. All the kids are saying it nowadays. It is from daytime viewscreen shows."

"When do you get the chance to watch daytime viewscreen shows?"

"Well, I don't, sir."

"Why are you blathering on about opporlems?"

"I have to record it sir, and watch it in the evening. We have incorporated opporlems into our new training manuals. And our corporate lexicon definitions of phrases and abbreviations."

"Can we get to the point if there is one?"

"Yes, sir, Plug is an opporlem."

"I am still none the wiser. Plug, what into what?"

"Oh, his name, sir, did I not mention that? Commander Plug is one of the fleet commanders, in charge of the fleet we sent to ambush the rebels. Unfortunately, he is not one of the service's finest, more like their dullest. No shine on his buttons or boots, sir, if you get my meaning."

"You are saying Commander Plug is an idiot?"

"A tad unfair to idiots, sir, but directionally correct, yes, he is a moron."

"I better call Brenda and post a new job advert."

"We have modeled the likely outcomes and we think it will be suboptimal."

"I am going to burn that phrase and abbreviations lexicon you have been reading."

"It is funny you should mention Brenda. She distributed it to everyone and said we had to use it as much as we could in all communications."

"She did? The bitch, and why did she do this?"

"She said you would like it, sir."

"I don't. Nor do I like Brenda, actually put an item on your to-do list, 'Brenda's launch with crowds, yes—not lunch—with bunting and a few big fireworks.'"

"Yes, sir, and I will burn it right after this conversation."

"What?"

"The Lexicon, sir, consider it ash already."

"I am getting a headache. You were telling me about Plug, the idiot."

"Yes, sir, the moron, we have some doubts, so we have implemented some additional plans."

"Does this involve him shooting himself in the head?"

"Alas, sir, I fear that might not be possible. That is why we put the other plans in place. It is all in hand. We don't expect any other problems sir. This is a covert intelligence operation, sir, to give you deniability, sir."

CHAPTER 61

RIM – PROCYON B – IN SYSTEM
APPROACHING AT JUMP
IMPERIUM COMMAND VESSEL
SWIRLING

Commander Plug paced in an annoying fashion.

"We are ready?"

"As ready as we will be, sir." The comms officer reported.

"That doesn't scream 'yes' to me, so are we ready?"

"Yes, Commander Plug, sir."

"Okay, exit hyperspace and hold position. I want to gather situational awareness before committing."

"Yes, sir. We are exiting jump now. We are getting navigation data."

"It appears the reinforcements are what, three ships, well, two and a half."

"I am reading two assault support ships and an old recon assault. No sign of any transports. They have docked the fighters on the assault support's hulls. We are not reading any heavy weapons on the recon assault, just RECs. The rest of their fleet is running toward them, and I bet they will form up under their SD network satellites."

"We seem to have them cornered. Well, this is going to be quick. Reduce engines to half. I want them to contemplate their short futures."

"Confirmed."

"I want us to record this and broadcast the signal down to the planet. They can watch their fleet's destruction and crush all hope."

"Signal being broadcast, sir."

"Ignore the damaged ships for now. Target the undamaged ships."

"Targets locked, sir."

"Tear them to bits, fire!"

"Firing."

"What the fuck? Where is all the death and mayhem?"

"It seems we missed, sir. All our ships missed."

"What!"

"SD network satellites are reaching firing energy levels."

"Ahead, flank, close that distance, I will slay any gunners that miss from the reduced range.”

"Sir, we are receiving a signal. It is a cartoon of a guy with a computer for a head. He is holding a white stick and is running around in circles. I think they are taking the piss out of our gunnery, sir?”

"Argh, flank now.”

"Thirty seconds to target.”

CHAPTER 62

**RIM – PROCYON B – THE HIGHLANDS
IN ORBIT
DESTROYER NEMESIS – BRIDGE
A HERO'S DEATH**

Captain Hero stood on the bridge of the *Nemesis* destroyer. Many of the surrounding displays displayed only static or flashed red. The ship had taken a savage beating at the hands of the Imperium.

"Okay, fuck them. We can't stand toe-to-toe. The ship is only just still in one piece. Signal *Bounty* and *Victory*."

"They are in worse shape than us, sir."

"I am aware, comms."

"Connected."

"Captains, I am going to fly the nemesis into the enemy lead destroyer and blow the engines to critical. We can't provide any more help. The nemesis is done. With the damage she already has, she is already past her end. I bid you both farewell until I see you again."

"Yes, Captain," said Captain Loyal.

Captain Loyal saluted, and Captain Hero watched on the video screen.

"Captain," Captain Dependable said. He snapped a crisp salute.

"Save the people. Navigation, flank speed at that big bastard, overload the jump engines right at the point of impact."

"All set, sir, on your command."

"Let's go to it. Remember the *Nemesis*, charge."

The destroyer sprinted forward, the enemy ship's size increasing in the viewscreen. All the bridge crew stood, saluting their captain. The *Nemesis* ran into the Imperium destroyer. Smashing and crumpling the front of the *Nemesis*, which was embedding itself into the destroyer, and breaking out through the other side. When the engines blew, a blinding white light and blast wave replaced where the ships had been. It reduced the enemy destroyer to small lumps of metal and exotic gases. The wave expanded and took out another destroyer, earlier flying in close formation.

CHAPTER 63

RIM – PROCYON B – THE HIGHLANDS
IN ORBIT
DESTROYER BOUNTY – BRIDGE
STAUNCHLY LOYAL

Captain Loyal regarded the second video display that now only displayed Signal Lost.

"We won't forget, Captain."

Captain Loyal saluted the video screen and smiled at Captain Dependable on the other screen.

"Navigation, Captain Hero has shown us the way. Our cannons are not even functional. Ram that ship to our left and blow the engines."

"Yes sir, my honor!"

"See you soon, Captain."

The destroyer carved down the side of the Imperium ship, opening her up to the vacuum of space, sucking corpses out. When the drive blew, both the destroyers' fates were sealed. Just as the *Nemesis*'s had been. The blast didn't take out any other destroyers, but it took out the transports and fighters frantically fleeing their parent ship.

CHAPTER 64

**RIM – PROCYON B – THE HIGHLANDS
IN ORBIT
DESTROYER VICTORY – BRIDGE
DEPEND ON IT, BITCH**

"Put us in the middle of the closest-packed group of ships. You know the drill. See you on the other side. This will make a difference," said Captain Dependable.

"Targeting that group of three destroyers dead ahead, sir," comms reported.

Another blinding flash and cloud of expanding debris. Four more destroyers ceased to exist.

CHAPTER 65

**RIM – PROCYON B – THE HIGHLANDS
IN ORBIT
IMPERIUM COMMAND VESSEL
PLUG'S HOLE**

"They are fucking idiots. Back us up, max power," Commander Plug screamed.

"Not so idiotic, sir, those three ships were scrap. I'm amazed they didn't blow up on the flight here. They just took out six of our destroyers," comms said with a hint of awe.

"Back, back, back," Plug screamed.

"Shit, we just backed up far enough away that we are now in the SD network satellite-targeting envelope. Sir, incoming!"

The five closest satellites all fired, each targeting a different ship. With uncharacteristic accuracy, they all targeted the five destroyers' engines. The energy cannons fired in beam mode and pierced straight through the ships. Each beam moved as it sliced at its target's rear engineering section. Four destroyers' engines detonated. The fifth ship broke into two where the energy beam had sliced into the hull. The two halves, pushed by the expanding gases from the explosions, started their slow slide down the gravity well, slowly accelerating toward the planet surface.

"Fuck, get us away from that rock, put us at the L1 Lagrange point. What do we have left?"

"We have now lost eleven ships, eight ships reporting functional. Turning sir, accelerating to L1. We are out of range of the SD Satellites now. Sir, I am getting a faint reflection from L1, very diffuse."

The three leading ships plowed into the minefield, triggering multiple mines that reduced the ships to large chunks of ex ship.

"Emergency stop. Fuck, fuck, fuck. All ships target the planet's capital with our heavy slug cannons, target lock-on the capital, and fire as they bear."

"We are detecting multiple ICBM launches from the planet, sir, heading our way. There are also twelve quicker small craft blasting up toward us from the planet. They are wrecks, sir, there are holes in their hulls. I am not reading any life signs on the ships. No bio-signs. We are receiving a transmission from the small ships. It is the same from each of them," comms said.

"Put the transmission on speaker," Captain Plug said.

A deep, rasping voice sprang from the speaker.

"Zombie, zombie, zombie, zombie, zombie-ie-ie. Zombie, zombie, zombie, zombie, zombie-ie-ie."

"Those dead ships are fast, sir. They are closing in on us. I think they are all on suicide runs, heading straight for us. They will hit us in, well, at various times, starting now."

The small suicide zombie ships flew into the large destroyers. They had no chance of taking down the larger ships. Yet as each of the twelve small craft struck the five remaining destroyers, they exploded. Tank artillery shells and missiles launched down the tubes mounted inside the hulls and out through the ship's nose. They smashed into the destroyers and caused secondary explosions.

"We are hit, sir, reports are arriving. Okay, we are still here. We are crippled. None of our five ships are going anywhere soon. I don't know how those zombie ships hit us so hard. Suicide zombies. Sir, the ICBMs are closing on us. Our ships are dead in space."

"Send emergency broadcast beacon with the ship's log. Fuck."

"Signal sent. Sir, you incompetent, dickless, cretinous, butt-plug asshole."

"What!"

The fifty nuclear missiles arrived the next second at the five stationary targets. Each detonated their one-megaton warhead. Some might have considered this overkill, seeing as each destroyer was hit with ten missiles and ten-megatons of nuclear fire.

CHAPTER 66

**RIM – PROCYON B – THE HIGHLANDS
IN ORBIT
THE PEREGRINE – BRIDGE
T-ZERO –5 MINUTES
OH FUCK**

"I can't believe any of that worked," Tom said in wonder.

"I can't believe we are still here. What did we lose?" Jack said.

"We lost the three damaged destroyers that rammed the enemy, that was it. Minor slug-round damage to the capital on the planet," Greg replied.

"We should get the transports away to the rendezvous point," Lauren said.

"Agreed. Start jumping the ship batches out of here," Brigman said.

The comms officer added, "The enemy got off an emergency beacon."

"Right, I want everyone jumping to that rendezvous. You can slap each other's backs and suck your dicks after, we are on the clock with that beacon," Brigman said.

"Yes, General," the comms officer replied.

"How the hell did we do that?" Lauren asked.

There was a snickering sound from the speakers.

"What was that? It sounded like a little giggling hamster," Greg said.

"I don't sound like a little hamster!" Merlin replied.

Lauren smiled. "Why are you giggling, Merlin?"

"Well, I missed your birthday the other month because I wasn't alive yet, so I got you a birthday present. Sorry it was late, but you know what they say, better late than dead."

"What did you do, Merlin?" Lauren asked.

"Well, since you kindly connected me up to the physics engine, I have been learning and experimenting to see what I can do with it."

"Merlin, what did you do?"

"Well, I decided Anubis was a bit of a dick and rather boring, all feathers and hearts. What a loser."

"Huh?"

"I leaned on Anubis's scales a smidge, okay, a lot, so I decided our computers needed to be more accurate and the gunnery more precise, that sort of thing. I guess you could say I cheated. Oops, my bad. Turned out well, though."

Everyone looked on in shocked surprise.

"You made the ships better?" Greg asked.

"The physics engine is online dude; I don't really have a clue what I can do with it. I am sort of fiddling around, having ideas and stuff."

"All the civilian and resistance evacuee ships have jumped away now, sir."

The video screen lit up. "Okay, okay, great. Right. How is the planet? Nice of those civilian leaders to take the fence out of their ass and launch their antiasteroid nukes," Charlie said.

"I am detecting ships at jump approaching. A lot of ships." Merlin said, with mild agitation.

"Scopes are clear, sir, not sure what he is referring to," the navigation officer said.

"Dumbass," Merlin replied.

"Argh, fifty destroyers just jumped in around the planet." The navigation officer sounded fearful.

"Approaching. Now they have arrived. Have you caught up now?" Merlin said.

"Argh all fifty ships just opened up: missiles, slug cannons, energy cannons. They are targeting the planet's cities," the gunnery officer reported.

From orbit we can see multiple various-sized flashes from nuclear detonations and mushroom clouds, explosions all over the planet.

"Those are nukes hitting the planet. That makes me very cross," Merlin said.

"We're being lit up with multiple targeting radars," the gunnery officer said.

Merlin's voice rose. "Oh no we're not."

"Ships are about to fire. The targeting radars have, vanished," the gunnery officer reported.

"Take the pain," Merlin shouted.

The enemy ships all started firing at one another. Ships detonated all over the sky. They directed no more fire at the planet, but the planet's skies darkened with the sickening black of nuclear-toxin-laden clouds, along with fresh nuclear blasts from the many missiles still in flight to their targets on the planet.

"Die, bitch scum," Merlin screamed.

The room was very silent as they watched the fifty ships all blasting one another to pieces and the newly devastated world below.

"Okay, fuck, fuck, they are all dead now. Let's go, the planet is dead, comms, get navigation prepped and ready to jump the ship to the rendezvous." Merlin sounded flustered.

"Merlin, why didn't you get them to shoot at each other before?" Greg asked Merlin.

"That didn't occur to me until they shot at the planet," Merlin said.

"Are they all dead on the planet?" Greg asked.

"I'm afraid so. Time to get ready. We must get ready to go. Quick, to the RV now!" Merlin said.

"Let's get to the rendezvous. There's nothing more to do here," Greg said with resignation.

"Just get ready to jump. Hold off from jumping for a couple of minutes, please. Greg, General Brigman, we need to talk urgently in private, right now. You can update Charlie and Abbot after," Merlin said, slightly more together.

"Sure," Greg replied.

CHAPTER 67

**RIM – PROCYON B – THE HIGHLANDS
IN ORBIT
THE PEREGRINE – GREG'S CABIN
T-ZERO +3 MINUTES
IMPOSSIBLE CHOICE**

Greg came into the room and shut the door behind him.

"What is it, Merlin? This is a little unusual."

"Apologies, but we faced an impossible choice."

"Go on, Merlin, what is it?" General Brigman said.

"I needed to help you make the right choice, to shield you from an impossible decision."

"I don't like the sound of this," Greg said.

"Me neither. We are used to hard calls, Merlin." General Brigman said.

"It is the planet. Not everyone is dead, just most of the people, like ninety-nine percent. There will be radiation and fallout and there will be a lot of burns victims.

"The problem is, we don't have the space on the ships, we also don't have the medicines or personnel we need. I also don't know how quickly the Imperium is going to send more ships. We don't have unlimited time.

"The smart choice for us to save the most people overall is to leave right now and come back once we have unloaded everyone and got the medics and drugs we need."

"Oh god. You are saying we will leave the alive to die," Greg said.

"Go on, you are talking about triage." Brigman got it.

"Yes, General. Out of the three hundred million people on the planet, ninety-nine percent are dead already, but there are about three million still alive, just. Fifty percent of them will be dead in the next three to six hours. Which leaves about one and a half million people by the time we can get back here in six hours.

"We can only move maybe thirty-five thousand max by the time we have kicked everyone else off our fleet and the civilian ships. Random chance means the survivors will be scattered. They will be all over the planet and under collapsed buildings.

"Anyone from that one and a half million still on the planet at twelve hours after T-zero is going to be dead from radiation poisoning. There is a six-hour window where we can medivac up to thirty-five thousand, maybe. We are still going to leave the vast majority of the one and a half million on the planet to die. There is no way to get everyone off the planet.

"We have to go right now with maximum haste to Kilbride. Luyten's system is close to us; it is only 0.08 light-years from here, we can be there in three hours. It is 90 AU to the edge of this solar system and 5,060 AU to Luyten's system. We need to get all the in-system local civilians, planets, and ships to send any nurses and doctors to Kilbride right now. We need meds, treatment for severe burns, penetration, and crush injuries in Kilbride in the next three hours. We will be there to load up. We need experienced rescuers and paramedics to get injured people off the Highlands. We will pick up the equipment, the medical and rescue personnel, and we will shift as fast as we can and be back here six hours from now.

"If you feel we must do something now, I suggest the only thing is for you to send down our two transports and our sixty commandos. Many have basic battlefield medical training, I am sure, and any other medically trained staff.

"There will be a lot of lifting and shifting needed. They will have to hold, triage, and stabilize for the next six hours before we can evac any survivors. If we don't fly straight back into another Imperium fleet.

"I am not sure if those sixty people can make any material difference in the next six hours other than getting themselves irradiated and killed. If you send them, it needs to be volunteers only, as it is most likely a suicide mission and in the best case, they may save five hundred people, a thousand max.

"What we need to do is leave and get to the RV location, pick up all the other ships and get to Kilbride as soon as possible, like leave in the next five minutes.

"I appreciate the sensitivity of this hard decision and the urgency of the choices I have put before you. Every minute is literally life ending for thousands.

"If we stay now, we will not be saving lives. We will condemn far more. We need to get the extra medics, drugs, and rescue people. Every minute we are on the ground at Kilbride is a minute we are not back here where we can make a difference."

"I will go talk to our commandos right now with your permission, General Brigman," Greg said in a businesslike tone.

General Brigman took a breath. "Yes, do that now. This is a volunteer-only mission. There is a high probability many who go will not be coming back up again. Merlin is right. This is a numbers game, and the hard call is that we don't send anyone down right now. I appreciate the moral dimension. People will want to do something. We don't have the right people or supplies or space, and this is a token gesture in so many ways.

"Greg, brief the commandos. I will brief Abbot and Charlie straight away. And make sure Abbot gets everyone ready to jump the minute we arrive at the RV. Charlie can manage logistics coordination with Kilbride. We jump in five minutes. Anyone staying here needs to be off the ship by then. Move, people."

"I can connect you to Charlie and Abbot, General."

"Do it, Merlin. Thank you for coming to me. Five minutes max."

CHAPTER 68

**RIM – PROCYON B – THE HIGHLANDS
IN ORBIT
THE PEREGRINE – CARGO DECK
T-ZERO +5 MINUTES
THE VOLUNTEERS**

Greg picked up his radio. "Comms, relay this to Abbot. This is going to be too slow, and we need more shuttles and transports. Abbot, you need to address all the warships we have, and you need to do it now."

"Roger," comms said.

The 1MC toned two pips. Abbot's voice came over the speakers.

"This is Abbot. Today we lost friends on five ships. Another three ships bravely sacrificed themselves and attacked the enemy to protect the fleet and the Highlands. I can't tell you how many are dead; I do not know. From our ranks alone, sixteen thousand is a rough guess.

"Another Imperium fleet arrived, and they opened up on the Highlands with conventional and nuclear weapons. Merlin dispatched that fleet in fire with focused purpose. The planet is now dying. There are people alive down there. One percent Merlin estimates. Three million out of three hundred million. Those will all be dead in twelve hours. I am asking only for skilled volunteers.

"I need medics, shuttle flight crews, and rescue engineers. Muster in the next four minutes in your ship's cargo areas near the shuttle bays. Important! The only people I want are people with those key skills. No one else.

"You will fly our shuttles down; you will render aid and find survivors. We are going to leave you there and sprint the fleet back to Kilbride. Commander Powers is already organizing more skilled personnel, drugs, and equipment.

"We will throw everyone else off the ships and we will burn like mad bastards and be back here in six hours with help. I need people on the ground now who can keep people alive while we get back here with relief supplies. Over twelve hours will mean a fatal dose of radiation.

"Muster now if you volunteer and can help. Medics, shuttle flight crews, rescue engineers. Shuttles leave in five minutes. Go now. Everyone else stay out of their way. Now move people!"

The commandos all stood behind Greg, listening to the 1MC announcement. They stood with a mixture of outright rage, grim-set faces, and sadness. One took a step forward and stood to attention. Three more did the same. Everyone watched, a little confused, then everyone got it. The other fifty-six commandos all stepped forward and stood to attention.

"Thank you, Rhinos," Greg said.

"Five people grab all the drugs we have in the medical stores. Five more—grab bandages, compresses, stretchers, splints, syringes, scalpels, antiseptics, and disinfectants. You five, grab any tents, sleeping bags, or blankets on the ship. You five, go get plastic sheeting. The rest of you pack food and lots of water into your kit bags and pick up torches, shovels, axes, sledgehammers. Stack everything up here in the cargo area. Two minutes, go."

"Pickle and Vapor will get people from the assault supports, come here, and pick us up in the transports to take us down. Other shuttles from the destroyers will also come with us."

Greg thought for a moment and picked up the ship's radio. "Jack to the cargo bay. Report right now, please."

"Yo, Greg, I am here already. I was standing at the back."

Commandos ran back and forth, equipment in hand.

"You can fly right? I need a shuttle pilot to take *The Peregrine's* shuttle down. You don't have to say—"

"Yes," Jack said.

"Good man. We will load you in the next few minutes. Grab whatever you need, you leave inside five minutes."

The pile in the middle of the cargo-bay floor was expanding.

This was the most rushed, disorganized combat evac mission Greg had ever seen. There just wasn't the time they needed to do this to their normal standards. Everyone was moving with speed and intent. They moved with purpose. People were not crashing into each other; they dropped nothing. The pile was growing and growing. Another group of commandos sorted the pile, getting it ready to ferry onto the ship when the first transport arrived. There was little in the discard pile. The locusts were doing a fine and focused job gathering the essential supplies.

Greg's radio crackled. "This is comms. Pickle will get here in three minutes. Vapor will be here in four."

Greg tried to quiet his mind and focus. What had he forgotten to tell them they needed? "Start packing *The Peregrine*'s shuttle," he shouted. "Jack is flying it. Pickle's transport will dock at the main dock in three minutes; load her and thirty people. Vapor's transport will be here in four minutes once Pickle is clear."

Greg paused for a moment. "No rifles and no ammo people. We need the space."

Then Greg spoke into the radio again. "Comms, Lauren, please."

"I am here, Greg."

"I need you to work with Merlin. He needs to pick out landing zones for us and the best areas to look for survivors and no-go radiation hot fallout areas. Triage, Lauren. We need to get the ones we are best placed to save. He has about four minutes to put the map together and transmit it to us, before you jump."

"I am on it. Merlin, did you hear all of that?"

"Processing now, Lauren."

"Radio all the transports and advise them that LZ target assignments will get sent to them. Designate an RV point in orbit so we don't have people crashing into each other."

The commandos were loading Pickle's transport and the ship's shuttle now. Jack stood by the shuttle, helping them load. The enormous pile was now about a third of the size it had been before. Commandos were still adding items to the pile while others sorted and yet more ran them to the ships.

Now the commandos were no longer coming out of Pickle's transport at the docking collar. They were taking their seats. Greg walked across to inspect before they took off. Those outside the dock piled up their loads in four sorted piles and got ready to load Vapor's transport. Greg stuck his head through the docking collar.

What he saw amazed him. The commandos were all strapped in, their laps full of equipment. They had stacked the kit on the floor in between the four back-to-back columns of seats. The overhead lockers were stuffed with their clear plastic covers. There was lots more equipment stacked inside the two mules and around the two mechs.

Greg looked and smiled. "Excellent, see you downstairs." Greg pulled his head back and hit the button to close the large docking collar.

As the door slid closed, the red light came on over the door. Pickle disengaged the locks and guided the transport away from the docking point. In under four seconds, Vapor's transport was in front of the docking collar and mating its locks. The light went green and the door slid open. The commandos streamed in with their loads.

"One minute, people, move it!" Greg said.

They had cleared the pile from the cargo bay's dock. Only four items were in the discard pile. There was a short line at Jack's shuttle as it finished loading. The commandos were now running across to join the line outside the docking collar to the transport.

The light above the shuttle's docking hatch went red. The shuttle was away.

Greg thumbed his radio again. "Comms, Greg. We are close here; we estimate we will be gone in under sixty seconds."

"Roger, Merlin says he has transmitted the navigation map with LZ recommendations and search areas. There are another two transporters in the group and twelve shuttles besides our shuttle and two transports. We have five full medical teams and fourteen nurses. Eight emergency rescue people. Everyone confirmed as headed for RV. Abbot wants to jump in one minute thirty seconds."

"Copy that, comms. Thank you. I will embark now. See you guys in six hours."

Greg was the last to step onto the second transport. Thirty determined faces looked back at him from under the piles of cargo they held in their laps. Greg strapped into the jump seat by the air lock.

Vapor's voice came over the transport's speakers. "Secure for flight. Undocking. Mark."

And the second transport was floating free. On the three viewscreens in the transport, they could see the navigation lights from the small flotilla forming up at the RV. They could also see the large destroyers behind them turning, getting ready to jump away. The last screen showed the Highlands below.

The beautiful vista of the planet and oceans was now stained with black scorched blotches and dark clouds that hung above. They could see fires burning in the remains of some cities.

Vapor's voice was back. "I am going to let you guys listen to the comms traffic. It is just ship-to-ship we are hearing. The bombs landed fifteen minutes ago."

"This is Pickle checking in. We are carrying thirty commandos, two mules, and two mechs. We have a pile of emergency supplies and the meds we grabbed. All the lads have basic combat medical training. I think we have two or three corpsmen in the unit. Over."

"Jack here, Peregrine shuttle, twenty-four seater. Stuffed with various supplies. Over."

"Vapor here. Same load out as Pickle. Over."

"Tiger here. The four Lancers are with you. We have no cargo capacity, but we can fly aerial surveillance for you. Our training includes advanced combat medicine for the eight of us. Over."

They heard comms traffic from the other two transports and twelve shuttles. Twenty-one small ships had rallied to the call in under five minutes. They had five medical teams, totaling twenty doctors, three corpsmen, sixty trained killers with basic combat medicine, and another eight aerial killers with advanced combat medicine, fourteen nurses, and eight disaster rescue.

They were all there was for the next six hours. A total of 105 medically trained resistance members had rallied on a mission to save thirty-five thousand out of the three million Merlin estimated were injured but still breathing, but that would be dead within twelve hours. It seemed futile and just so far short of the actual need for this now poisoned toxic world.

Pickle's voice boomed again on the radio. "This is the resistance medical rescue and evacuation mission to ground. We are beginning our descent now. Highlands, can anyone hear us?"

There was just static.

"We are setting up an LZ1 medical triage and evac center at 40°44′58″ North 73°58′5″ West. Make your way to us if you can. We will continue to rebroadcast coordinates every five minutes. We have doctors with us ready to treat survivors."

High above on *The Peregrine*, the two assault supports and the remaining sixteen resistance destroyers in Abbot's fleet all went to jump.

The ground team was now all on their own with no backup, heading into the maw of death.

CHAPTER 69

**RENDEZVOUS POINT IN THE VOID
ABBOT'S COMMAND SHIP – BRIDGE
T-ZERO +25 MINUTES
JUMP, JUMP, JUMP**

There were the sixteen resistance destroyers and a couple of hundred smaller transports and freighters, all hanging in the isolating void of space. They were far from any star, stuffed full of people who had made it off the Highlands. Some were resistance, others were regular civilians when boarding. They were all resistance fighters now.

"Comms to *Peregrine*, right on time. We made jump preparations during our flight. General Abbot is ready to brief the fleet."

"Comms, put me fleet-wide," Abbot said.

"You are on, sir."

"This is Abbot. I can confirm the Imperium nuked the Highlands. Most people are now dead, many millions, ninety-nine percent planet-wide.

"We can all mourn later. We avenge later.

"Right now, as I speak, we have brave volunteer commandos, doctors, nurses, rescue workers in the air going down right now to help. Into harm's way. Into the radiation.

"We will come back for them and everyone else we can save. We need more drugs, more supplies, more medics. We are the ships to do this. We sent who and what we could pull together, but we need more.

"Time is against us. We are the rescue mission. We are going now to Kilbride. Back at the Highlands in six hours, max speed.

"Commander Charlie is getting Kilbride ready. No more talking, time for doing. Captains, jump now, jump, jump, jump. Abbot out."

CHAPTER 70

**RIM – PROCYON B – THE HIGHLANDS
DESCENDING FROM ORBIT
VOLUNTEER SHIPS
T-ZERO +17 MINUTES
SIFTING THE RUBBLE**

The 1MC on all the ships chimed and people turned to look at the speakers while the ships continued their descent:

Heads up, people. I am Emergency Doctor Anna Watts. I have been assigned as chief medical officer on this mission.

I have told the flight crews to keep the doors locked until I have finished this briefing, so settle in and pay attention everyone, not just newbies. It won't take long. This is for all of us.

I am now your expedition commander in chief. That means there is General Abbot, God, and me at the top of the tree.

This is a medical emergency, and I am head of the medics and the response. Disagree, let us measure dicks. In the meantime, people are dying. Now that is out of the way and done.

First, this is science. Second, it is bravery in all of us, regardless—you, me, the nurses, the rescue workers. The last thing we need is macho bullshit. The military feeds you that shit to ensure you keep charging. Which is great, but I would like us all to be alive and cancer-free in five years with your balls still pumping wigglers with one head and one tail. I will be proud to shake all your hands.

Follow my instructions, and it will keep you and your wigglers alive, I promise.

Here is what you need to know about nukes and radiation in one minute.

The blast kills, the infrared flash kills, the pressure wave kills. The fire kills. That has all already happened. The contamination and fallout comes next, and all of that kills as well.

Now, antiradiation meds, that's an urban myth! Sure, potassium iodide is great for blocking your thyroid from iodide-131, which is an inevitable radionuclide from nuclear weapons. Iodide-131 will destroy your thyroid, which you need. But it is not the only radionuclide, one of many in fact, and potassium iodide does shit all about any of the other radionuclides, which will all try to kill you and your wigglers in their own unique ways.

The lesson is that avoiding fallout exposure is much better than taking a potassium iodide pill and feeling pink and fuzzy. There are no magic cure-all antiradiation pills that target all of the radionuclides. Take the potassium iodide pill when the medics tell you to. It will do you no harm, but it won't save you either from direct radiation or absorption of other radionuclides. Such as cesium or cobalt, among many others.

I have some old choc drops and dog treats. You are welcome to them as well, if they make you feel better. My dog thinks they are delicious. Personally, I plan on avoiding fallout and radiation. Ionizing radiation will fuck with your cells and your DNA, giving your babies three heads.

None of our suits or precautions will stop ionizing gamma rays or X-rays. Monitor your radiation detectors and dose meters. Avoid ionizing radiation and keep the dose received low. Alpha and beta radiation are no problem if you are in your suits, but ingest nothing that releases radiation.

We are here to avoid fallout and hot zones and eat chocolate. People exposed are going to be fucked. Fallout can fuck all of us. In twelve hours, we will all be fucked.

Do you all have your space suits?

The most important thing is to limit inhalation, consumption, and skin absorption. No exposed skin—suits on! Only use air, water or food from the ships. If we detect any clouds or radiation coming. Button up first and seek shelter.

Immediate orders: only eat and drink food brought with us, no local food, even if packaged.

I need you alive and healthy to help treat the people that need it.

I urge you all to put your suits on now. If they are not already on your backs, don't leave the ship without a suit on.

A last word, people.

The doctrine says shelter in place in a blast-affected area for at least twenty-four hours, forty-eight if possible. That is because in fallout there are a lot of other radionuclides from the blast with a short half-life, making it a lot safer once they've decayed. No one other than God and ancient Zeus can affect that. This world will be dead in twelve hours, so we must go now and fly in early.

You hard nuts will follow my commands and you can kick my butt when I get us all back alive.

When we are on the ground we will:

Set up tents and polyethylene-sheet-type improvised shelters under rope to keep the sun off. A lot of these people will have flash burns. We don't need sunburn in the wounds as well, but light UV will help. Not much, but it might help.

The flight crews will fly aerial recon looking for hot zones, weather, and survivors.

Chief medical officer out.

That had all happened an hour and fifteen minutes ago. The mass rescue landing. Since they had planned and assigned survey flight teams and started setting up the medical hub.

The survey flights were now in the air. Jack had been flying the shuttle at ten thousand meters for the last hour. He could see 341 kilometers to the horizon with the advanced built-in computer-controlled optics in the shuttle, with the advantage of his altitude and the planet's curve.

The flights traced their assigned route, a wedge shape covering fifteen degrees of arc. They flew away from the principal base at the apex down one spoke. When they got to the one thousand kilometers range limit, they would turn left ninety degrees. Then they flew the shorter 262 kilometers around the curved end of the wedge to cover their fifteen degrees of the divided-up search circle. They would then turn left again ninety degrees and fly the return leg spoke back to the center, returning to the primary base.

The next fifteen-degree arc would be skipped, they would fill these in when rotating around the search circle the next time. Over six hours, the entire search circle would be flown over twelve times.

The purpose of the flight was to mark areas in the navigation system. To record areas of high and low damage. To map radiation levels and track weather, precipitation, and winds.

This was his first flight of the day. They would assign him a second search wedge a half hour after his return to base, at the end of the three hours. The twelve ships flying this search-and-mapping mission would overfly 360 degrees of a circle with a radius of one thousand kilometers with the base at the center. As they flew, they analyzed the data in real time and linked it all back to the base.

Hot radiation no-go zones would be marked on the map in red. They would mark areas of low damage and low hazard in green. They designated degraded but not destroyed areas in orange.

On top of this, they layered it with both before and after estimates of population density. This was based on visual and thermal recorded data. This was cross-referenced with the Highlands postal address database for delivery and parcel services.

They added another layer to the data, showing any areas where there was evidence of human activity. Marked signage, such as Help, or activity on the ground, such as tracks or a group walking, or a vehicle moving.

This was all added to the map and sent back to the base in real time by all the shuttles. Base would assess the information and their current assignments.

Besides the search ships, they were running five more ships carrying commandos, rescue workers, medics, and evacuees. They had four transports and one more shuttle.

The four Lancer fighters functioned as rapid-response search units for close survey tasking.

A likely pickup site would come in and get tasked to the Lancer working that ninety-degree quarter of the search circle. The Lancer would put his foot down and fly with max urgency over to that location. They would carry out a low-level overflight at three hundred meters, later descending to one hundred and seventy meters and circling over the site. Again, the recorded visual data, any received radio communications and the Lancer pilots' comments were relayed back to the central hub.

The team at base would analyze the data again with the new information. If the potential target passed its vetting conditions, they would assign the closest transporter or the spare shuttle to the target. They were not as fast as the fighters, which were flying at between Mach two and Mach three. The slower cargo carriers were going between Mach one and Mach one and a half.

No one cared about sonic booms over civilian areas; they cared about the elapsed time.

The transporter would land and board the able-bodied evacuees. A pair of rescue workers and up to eight medics and six commandos would disembark and stay on site if there were more people waiting to be evacuated. They would extract people from buildings if needed, stabilize them quickly, and get them ready for the flight back to the hub.

It was beyond efficient, from the first high-altitude spotting overflight for someone one thousand kilometers away. Where the "people-moving flight" had to travel the longest distance. The worst case was forty-eight minutes to being on the ground and putting rescued people on the ship. It was often a lot less, half the time, or even under ten minutes. It depended on where all the ships were relative to each other and the current loading of the high-capacity transports plus the shuttle. Of course, the controllers at the hub coordinated rescues and swept out waves of pickups from the central hub location.

They were going to search, triage, and evacuate 3.14 million square kilometers of the planet in about nine hours.

The team at base prioritized the able-bodied. This was not a normal medical disaster they were managing. The triage tree only had two outcomes—off-world or dead. It was a hard binary choice for each survivor.

The sad fact was that their projections had made it clear they were likely to become overrun as they were. The aim was to get the maximum number of people out. They only had so much space and finite time. They were not there to rescue everyone or treat all the injured.

They prioritized the tickets based on how many they could rescue and deprioritized based on injury. It was a lot quicker to get the able-bodied out compared with having to enter a collapsed building and amputate limbs. It was harsh, very harsh, yes. The problem was this lifeboat of Abbot's fleet only looked like it had thirty-five thousand seats. Early signs were that they might have filled the lifeboat many times over in the whole twelve-hour period.

One hour into Jack's first survey flight, he got Jeff to film him while he sat at the controls flying the shuttle.

"My name is Jack. I am a civilian from Clackmannanshire. I am flying a shuttle over the Highlands in the Rim. I'm not alone. I am here with others trying to rescue survivors from this Imperium travesty. I am very mad and upset, so I am going to make you watch what I have been seeing."

"The Imperium launched multiple nukes and murdered one of the twenty-two colony worlds in your name—yours not theirs. There are about three hundred million dead here now in your name."

"I saw it happen from orbit. I am here now despite the radiation to help get survivors out."

"Jeff, show them the view at ten thousand meters."

Jeff panned his camera and showed the scenery with the distant mushroom clouds and broken cities at the mushroom's root. Closer to Jack were small towns and farms. Jack flew the shuttle in a flat circle to give a slow scan of the horizon. It showed multiple rising clouds of devastation.

"Right, let's have a good close look! Jeff, the monitor, please. If you have the stomach, focus it on the foreground. Yes, those used to be swings, kids' swings. There are no kids here anymore, no parents. The Imperium wiped them away from orbit."

Jeff spoke up. "Well, you are going to face a closeup, because three hundred million people, plus the colony world itself, they are dead here now. For you."

"Go on, Jeff, let's zoom right in so you Imperium-supporting fucks can get a good close look at your handy work, you wankers. Look at this child's burned, broken skull. Do you see it? Do you fucking see it, you sick fucks? Who are you? Do you support this in your name?

"I am a civilian. I raced cars in the desert and fixed tractors. I'm not in the military. I was not resistance. I damn well am now! Jeff, pull back a little on the camera and pan to get the rest, the rest of the bodies. The kids and adults.

"Okay, Jeff, that is enough. Stop there."

The camera cut.

"Jeff, pull the footage off the camera and send it to my station."

"Sure, what are you doing?"

"Something you can't. Okay, I have the footage. Right, computer, attach the file and record me, then send the message to Lauren on *The Peregrine*. Mark the message urgent priority."

"Recording started," the computer voice said.

"Lauren, it's awful. I need you to do this for me. Show them, all of them. Broadcast this both to the Rim and the Core, to all the worlds. Send it in the open on RIM-NET and COL-NET. Let them all see what the Imperium has done. Jack out. Computer, stop recording and send."

"What have you done, Jack?"

"What needed to be done. I am a civilian volunteer. I am not breaking any orders that bind my actions. That needed to be sent."

"Yes, you're right, I wouldn't have."

"I know. It needed to be done."

CHAPTER 71

**RIM – EN ROUTE FROM PROCYON B
TO LUYTEN'S STAR – LANARKSHIRE
THE PEREGRINE TO KILBRIDE PORT
LAUREN'S CABIN
T-ZERO +1 HOUR 5 MINUTES
THEY DID WHAT?**

Lauren was in her cabin when her laptop pinged. Merlin's voice came over the speaker in her cabin.

"Lauren, hey, you have a message you need to watch from Jack now."

"Thank you for reading my mail, Merlin."

"Of course, I read the mail. I must scan it all for viruses. Anyway, read your message from Jack. Prepare yourself. I am ready to execute on your order."

"Huh?"

Lauren put on her headphones and opened the video attached to the message.

Lauren went pale as she watched. She was silent. Now came the sharp inhalation of breath as the camera view panned around at ten thousand meters. Tears welled in her eyes as Jack showed people the brutal truth.

She got to the end of the message and was silent.

Merlin was a little uncertain and hesitated. Lauren still said nothing as tears rolled down her cheeks. She quietly remembered all the people she had met and the beautiful world she had enjoyed a few short weeks ago on R&R, all now gone.

Merlin asked, "What do you want to do?"

Lauren breathed in through her nose and didn't hide the sound of the snot bubbling. When she spoke, it sounded high, thin, and tight in her throat. She was livid.

"As Jack said, Merlin, send it to everyone now, please, and send it anywhere else you can think of that will help the message spread. News stations, blogs, newspapers, influencers, anywhere you can think of to spread this all over the Interweb. If the Imperium tries to take it down, send it again and pin the message up there. Hack the Imperium websites, government, ministries, councils, and put the video up there as well. They will not bury this or pretend it didn't happen. Make the Interweb resonate with the horror of this, Merlin."

Merlin did as instructed. First, he launched a protected high priority thread to each of the sixteen destroyer's comms computers. He set up more threads for each of the 243 transports and shuttles that were flying with them from the Highlands, back to Kilbride.

Merlin instructed all 259 comms computers to send out Jack's video message. He had mined the Interweb to get recipient targets to send the video to and had found two billion people's accounts.

Merlin said to himself, "Send now." Two billion messages were all sent in parallel. They went straight through every spam filter and content filter. Straight through all the local security and rate throttlers. The computers were just waking up and thinking, hmm that looks new. I haven't seen that before. Best have a look so I can flag it if I see it again. Whoosh, it was gone and delivered. There was no queue for messages to be delivered. Just a wave two billion messages wide but only one message deep.

RIM-NET and COL-NET were both long-established messaging networks based on well-understood, robust technology. You couldn't just turn it off and you could not censor it as the state. If you had already delivered the message, it was sent, even if you had to deliver two billion messages in the same instant. Rather than a queue of messages two billion long, where you had to deliver the messages one after the other.

Merlin's video bulk send took 1.5 milliseconds to send all two billion video messages in 32K ultra-resolution pure horror format. He had RSVP requested all the bandwidth in advance and kicked all the lower priority queues out of his way. Merlin's video transmission pushed the wide area network of faster-than-light quantum entangled interstellar tachyon trunks to one hundred percent of capacity across the entire network and all other wide area links. For 1.5 milliseconds, Merlin's data owned one hundred percent of the entire Interweb across all colony worlds. When the wave had passed, all the core routers looked at each other, thinking *What the hell was that? Glad we kept to our SLA, zero percent packet drop. We will get a gold star this month for sure.*

The message was out there now. COL-NET and RIM-NET had already delivered it to the recipients' personal mailboxes. Which were forwarded on to their mobile devices, phones, and laptops.

In bars, restaurants, and offices all over every colony world in the Core and Rim, two billion phones went ping, *You've Got Mail.* Everyone clicked to play their copy of the video, and Jack's voice rang out everywhere. To an audience that was much more interested in what this video was going to show them than any message a politician had ever tried to deliver to the people before in the Imperium.

Ten seconds after the video finished playing, the vast majority of those two billion forwarded the video to their social media accounts and to all their friends. Titles emerged such as *Have you seen! I am Tampin' Fumin' Ragin'! The monsters!*

You get the idea.

Thirty seconds after the video hit social media, one hundred percent of every Interweb user in the entire Imperium was talking about the video.

Another thirty seconds later, the Interweb search engines went wild and the keyword search phrases had a new top-seven leader board. The only thing anyone was searching for was pages about:

- The Resistance.
- The Highlands.
- The Rim.
- Nuclear bomb environment damage.
- My representative contact details.
- City mayor contact details.
- Dancing cat videos.

Others didn't think of going to the search engines; they went to their local council, government, or political member's website. Where they discovered another copy of the video on those home pages.

The message was out, out. The Imperium had failed to stop or spin this message. The naked truth was out, and everyone had a view regarding the video they had just watched.

A worrying trend then developed—the posts and searches online dropped. Not because people had got bored and moved on and were now talking about some celebrity news. People were not searching for anything on the Interweb.

This was very unusual and pointed to the fact that people had gone off into closed rooms and private groups or were even having a cup of coffee in the real world with friends and colleagues. People were talking to each other directly, discussing the video and finding out what other people thought. People were having in-depth political conversations about how they felt. That the Imperium had just destroyed a colony world and killed three hundred million people less than an hour ago.

CHAPTER 72

**CORE – GLIESE 784 AND GLIESE 555
HOTLINE BUTE TO HOTLINE ARGYLL
T-ZERO +1 HOUR 10 MINUTES
HOT LINES**

Five minutes later, the red hotline telephones were ringing on the two desks of the Office of the President on both the Argyll and Bute worlds.

They both picked up without delay, having watched the video with total horror and rage.

Their local telecoms person told them the other party was connected now and ready. They put the two presidents through.

"Mr. President."

"Mr. President."

They both paused. The formal greeting was over, and they were unsure what to say next.

"Has Bob gone insane?" Frank asked from Argyll.

"It would seem so," Liam said on the line from Bute.

"What are your thoughts?"

"I don't know yet, honestly, but something is going to happen. This cannot be allowed to slide."

"Indeed, I have a cabinet meeting starting in five minutes."

"Mine starts in ten. I am hearing there are calls from the people for independence from the Imperium. Others are calling for us to pledge to the Rim systems' government."

"It is an idea with a lot of merit. They are closer to both of us, physically and politically. If you look at a star map, it is clear the Imperium would stage their ships and ground forces through our systems."

"Yes, regardless of our views."

"I don't see how we can continue to support this centralized administration. We were fine before they cracked their whip and absorbed us into their Imperium."

"Yes, correct."

"So, we are both saying we should secede from the Imperium and become independent. I worry about our survival chances.”

“You are right, and that is why we should go further. Not only should we break from the Imperium, but we should also pledge to the Rim systems and establish mutual defense treaties with all the Rim systems.”

“That is bold, but you risk turning us into the front line.”

“We already are the front line. The Imperium just hasn’t occupied us again yet.”

“I think you are right. Are we agreed?”

“Yes, I suggest we both tell our cabinets that is the position we are taking and seek their support. We can issue a joint public press release in, say, twenty-four minutes when we transmit notice to the Imperium, seceding from them.”

“Yes, send over your draft to my office when you have it. I will rubber-stamp it after the cabinet pass it.”

“Will do, thank you. I will talk to you in twenty minutes. Cabinet now.”

“Yes, thank you, talk then.”

Each president went into their respective cabinet meeting. These were both the shortest cabinet meetings anyone could ever recall, with complete unanimity.

Their cabinet colleagues were all enthused and backed the plan. Their respective presidents had proposed a solution they would not dare give voice to themselves. Despite it reflecting their private thoughts.

It gratified them that their president had acted and shown such decisive leadership. These annexed colonies had had enough. The cabinet had had enough. The people had had enough. Their president was going to tell the Imperium straight that they had all had enough.

They predicted the Rim systems would welcome their pledge, but either way, they realized now that they were done with the Imperium.

How dare the Imperium destroy such a precious thing as a colony world? That was a far larger sin. Killing three hundred million civilians, no matter where those civilians’ loyalties might lie, was a grievous war crime that put Bob right at the top of the unhinged bastard list. It was clear. Genocide was the human crime here. This meant Bob the tyrant was now as toxic in their minds as the surface of the Highlands.

The video message had been clear. This hero, Jack, was out there trying to rescue people. God alone knew who he was with or if it was just him.

That was when it hit Frank. A big juicy carrot he could keep tucked in his back pocket for now.

Frank tapped on his computer. Yes, he was right. The two bulk cargo carriers, *Imp* and *Green Bird*. They were traveling together in convoy on their return leg back to their home planets of Bute and Argyll. Where were they? Frank checked. They were very close. If we were to divert them, how long would that take? *Hmm, interesting* Frank thought. He and Liam should keep this close to their chest for now. Even away from their cabinet. An ace in the hole to help secure their pledges to the Rim and desire for mutual defense treaties. He would raise it with Liam to see if he wanted to allow the redirection of his system's ship. If it all came to nothing, they could always re-task them back to their original destinations. He would bring it up when they talked again about the draft press release and formal notice.

Frank picked up his phone. "Hey, Steph, do you know where Bernard is up to with the draft yet? Good. Get me a copy right now. I can give him immediate feedback on where we are so far. Also, please summon the press corps to our briefing room. We will broadcast in ten minutes. We will broadcast in parallel with Liam over on Argyll."

While Frank waited, he thought back to what was now ancient history, before his birth, and his parents' birth. When Argyll and Bute were the most Rim-facing independent colony worlds. Their two worlds were the gateway to and from the Rim. Imperium forces eighty-five years ago had landed troops on Argyll and Bute. Since they had forced both systems to surrender and pledge to the Imperium, they had occupied the territory in all but name. As Frank remembered it, and he wasn't certain he had his facts straight, the Imperium had shown up eighty-five years ago on both worlds and the conversation had gone like this: *Behold our army and spaceships, they are getting twitchy and need to kick the crap out of someone, and we the generals who are in charge think it should be you and your mate Bute. Sorry about that, it will be rather painful but quick. If we go down that route, the guys in accounts will insist we send you a bill for all our effort. Of course, they will demand we leave troops here to ensure you are motivated to pay your bill and the bill for the troops. Of course, if you sign this bit of paper, which is a request to join the Imperium. We might consider your request to become an Imperium world. The army would not have to stay here, or the bill, and no bill means no kicking either. Would you like to borrow my pen? Good choice.*

Frank knew he had paraphrased things, but he was certain that it had been diplomacy delivered at the end of a gun. It hadn't been a choice or a pledge; it had been a mugging. Back when his forebears had gone along with it, held with a gun in one hand and gold in the other, signing up to this toxic union. One where it had become clear that as far as the leadership of the Imperium thought about things, this was all about New Terra. That Argyll and Bute were nothing more than colonies to shovel economic wealth, taxes, and resources back to New Terra, while ending the lives of young soldier recruits along the way. New Terra took a one-third share from all taxes raised. Then sent a further bill back for other things bought for the Imperium that everyone else had to pay for. It was a little strange that those things being funded were always connected with New Terra.

The more Frank thought about it, the crosser Frank got. How dare they! Too small, too poor, too stupid to survive without the Imperium. Well, we will damn well show you. We are going to join the Rim and get rid of the Imperium after a hundred years of what has been foreign occupation. We will show you where you can stuff your Imperium.

The more he thought about it now, when the Imperium had just used nuclear weapons against a peaceful world, the more he understood what had been wrong with them. Why had they dismissed the voices of fellow citizens pushing for independence and less rule from New Terra? Had everyone been sleeping and kidding themselves that this was in the best interests of Argyll and Bute?

Frank fumed. *Well, fuck them* he thought. They had screwed the pooch this time. It was time Argyll and Bute rejoined their estranged brothers and sisters and joined the Rim. They were closer to the Rim systems than they were to Alpha Centauri A. What the hell had his ancestors been thinking? When they signed the future away from all the future generations yet to come. Frank wondered how much it had cost to get them to sell out and sign. For just how little had they sold their souls and folded? Better to fight than to live under the Imperium's yoke.

Today is the day that more history will get made Frank thought.

Steph came into his office, holding the draft in her hand. She smiled and handed over the paper, still warm from the printer. Steph said, "He said he would finish in three minutes. The press has been called. They will be here in ten minutes. Your call with Liam is in five minutes. I will be right outside if you need anything." Then Steph left.

Frank read the draft. "But from these countless evils we have been set free ..." he said out loud. Yes, this was right on point. He scanned the rest of the text and put down his pen. No corrections needed. It was perfect, clear, and said it all.

"Steph?" Frank said. She popped her head back around the door.

"Yes, boss. How is it?"

"It's perfect, Steph, send the draft over to Liam. I have no changes."

Steph smiled. "On it, boss, right away."

Frank paused. He took a sip of his coffee. A big day, to be sure. Then he picked up his phone and pressed the hotline button.

"Liam, is that you? It's Frank here."

"Yes, I have just had Steph send you over Bernard's draft declaration."

"Yes, they just handed the paper to me. What do you think?"

"I think it's great. I had no corrections to suggest and think we should sign it. You may suggest any corrections if you wish."

Liam's response was simple. "Good."

Frank was a little confused. Liam continued talking.

"Like you said, Frank, this is very good. I am happy to sign and go to press in ten. What time is it? Okay, 16:49. Right 17:00 my time. It is on Bute, capital? Err—"

Frank saved Liam from trying to work out relative time zones for cities on different worlds rotating in orbit around different stars. "It is just coming up to 19:14, so that will be 19:20, my time, which will be perfect. The press is all here, waiting. One other thing to be aware of but keep under your hat. I think we should re-task *Imp* and *Green Bird* to head toward Procyon B at flank speed. We can always take that back if we need to, but it will be good to get them moving as soon as we can."

"You must be able to read my mind, Frank. I was going to suggest the same thing. It is a good idea. Agreed that we should keep that low-key for now. I will issue updated orders right away to *Green Bird* to continue with *Imp* on the fresh course at maximum haste. Now, I need to go now and get them to print this off and put the two copies in the binders for signing on the desk."

"Yes, likewise. Talk to you after. Bye."

As Frank hung up, Steph came back in. "I have prepared the two signing folders, unless you now need changes?"

"Thank you, Steph. There are no changes. We're on track for the simultaneous press announcement and for signing from 19:20, our time. Liam is ready at his end."

"Good, I will get these on the table; four minutes to press time, sir. You will do great! Your desk alarm will ring ninety seconds before."

Steph left again with the folders. Frank focused and calmed his mind and did his mental meditation exercises.

A few minutes later, there was a double beep from the desk alarm and Frank opened his eyes. He looked very clear and focused. He rose, walked to the door, made his way to the press briefing room, walked up to the podium, and gave his speech:

Esteemed colleagues, thank you for coming at such short notice. We have all learned of the heinous actions the Imperium took against the Highlands. Their dangerous and reckless release of multiple nuclear weapons on the planet and its citizens, clearing the Highlands of life.

I am beyond words, filled with rage and pure contempt for what the Imperium has done today. As a result, both I and President Liam of Bute have spoken. What I can tell you all is that we are both resolute and of the same mind. Since, both governments have held cabinet meetings. We tabled our proposal to respond to the Imperium's actions. We carried it with every vote in favor and no abstentions in both cabinets.

Neither of our worlds can tolerate the behavior we have seen today. Not only the death of three hundred million innocent citizens but also the environmental terrorism and destruction of one of the precious twenty-two colony worlds.

Right now, both I and President Liam are holding synchronized press conferences on both of our worlds. We are both here to instruct the commander of the Imperium that Argyll and Bute are, with immediate effect, ending our membership of the Imperium. We are walking away right now. There will be no negotiations.

Considering the violent way our ancestors were forced into the Imperium over eighty-three years ago, we have taken prudent steps and made preparations.

Today, President Liam and I will sign this declaration. It is a pledge of kinship and mutual protection between Argyll and Bute.

Further, diplomats from both of our worlds are on their way right now to hand-deliver pledges of union from our embassies on Kilbride to the Kilbride government office. A pledge of loyalty to the Rim systems and petition for membership of their government cooperative.

Both Argyll and Bute are also extending the hand of friendship and offer a mutual protection alliance to be formed with all the worlds of the

Rim systems.

For too long, we have been told we are too small, too poor, and too stupid. No more. Argyll is free from Imperium tyranny.

That will be all, other than the signing. I will take any questions you may have.

There was total silence in the press room. They all sat there, eyes glistening but boggled large, mouths open. The clapping started, and soon it was a roar. The entire press pack was now all standing, clapping with big grins and more than a few tears of joy. There were no questions.

Frank continued to sign the document that was being referred to as Bernard's Declaration amid continued clapping.

The response to Liam's press conference was identical.

Five minutes later, the two diplomats arrived at the government building on Kilbride with their petitions to join the Rim. They were both welcomed at the door by the Kilbride foreign secretary, who wore a huge welcoming grin, as he waited outside in the drizzle for them to arrive. At this point, the sun came out from behind the clouds and the drizzle stopped.

The news was not so welcome when the report arrived at Bob's desk two and a half hours later, back on New Terra.

CHAPTER 73

RIM – LUYTEN'S STAR – LANARKSHIRE
KILBRIDE
EXITING JUMP SPACE
T-ZERO +3 HOURS
ORDER TO CHAOS

"This is Charlie to Kilbride Port. We are here. Abbot's fleet just left jump space. We are four minutes out, approaching at flank speed."

"Roger, Charlie, this is port traffic control. We have a wiggle on here for you folks. We have cleared all local traffic for you from the entire port airspace. Attention all ships, you will have a clear run when instructed. *Do not* start any vector or velocity changes unless instructed to do so by a traffic controller. We have you all on our traffic control radars. Welcome to Kilbride. We will have you all combat landed within thirty minutes if everyone does as they are told! Do NOT deviate from the controller's instructions. My job is to bring order to chaos."

"Okay, one moment please—" Charlie sat back and waited for the detailed instructions to arrive from port traffic control:

Attention, all frigate class and bigger. Spaceport traffic control will advise specific transponders when we want you to approach. Until then, we want your eighteen ships in a holding orbit at one thousand kilometers above the equator with zero-degree orbital inclination. Do not approach the spaceport until instructed to do so. When instructed, bring your ABBT squawkers into the spaceports designated P1 through P16 in orbit—do not descend below an orbital altitude of two hundred and fifty kilometers. When instructed, I want your two big BALLB squawkers to spaceports designated P17 and P18 in orbit.

I want your smaller BALLB_PERI squawker to get ready to descend to ground spin-side west of ground port complex designated P1.

The radio went quiet for two seconds.

Okay, attention corvette class and smaller. Navigation is reporting 243 smaller craft with transponders squawking prefixes EMERG-T and EMERG-S. We see 112 transporters and 131 shuttles within those groups.

Transports EMERG-T, I direct you to the planet spin-side

southwest of the ground port. Please line up from the outer marker Alpha. Adopt a holding loop stack between fifteen hundred meters and fifteen kilometers in three hundred meter layers and fifteen hundred meters bow to stern clearance. Reduce airspeed to two hundred and fifty knots. Join the stack at fifteen kilometers, and loop descent to ground. Shuttles EMERG-S, I direct you to the planet antispin-side northeast of ground port. Please line up at the outer marker Beta. Follow the same procedure as for Alpha.

All ground fields designated T1 to T112 and S1 to S131, we have cleared them for your exclusive use. Local ground controllers who oversee the Alpha and Beta outer markers' holding stacks, they will guide specific T and S group transponders to specific landing fields. While all other T and S ships continue to maintain their position in their holding loop stacks.

We have ground crew and medics at each docking field, which will express unload all your evacuees. Anyone needing medical help to move will receive it. Ground crew and medics will liaise with your onboard flight crew as you descend the holding stack. We have ensured any requested medical aid and support is already here, standing ready for you. We are ready and expecting the evacuees from the Highlands.

Space traffic control is on 12.3675 GHz.

Alpha Marker traffic control is on 12.3775 GHz.

Beta Marker traffic control is on 12.3875 GHz.

Add your additional controller channels now to your comms.

Keep this channel, on 12.3500 GHz, for overview traffic control while in Kilbride ground and space.

Okay, traffic control to all ships maneuver to your assigned holding and stacking positions. Remember, slow is faster than rushing. You will all be on the ground within thirty minutes. Ground crew will take thirty minutes to unload and reload your ships and you will all be heading back to the Highlands within sixty minutes. All the people and supplies requested are here, ready and waiting for you.

Traffic control to Charlie.

Charlie pressed the radio button. "I am here, traffic control."

"Thank you for organizing this miracle. Control out."

Brigman stood straighter. "Very impressive. Right, navigation, we have our orders. Let's get *The Peregrine* on the ground as instructed."

Navigation replied, "Roger that, General, we have received an approach plot from the controller. We are beginning reentry now."

Five minutes later, the call sign BALLB_PERI was on the ground with both main hatch doors powering open and the foot hatch opening. The cargo bay still held the six tanks. The tank's ammunition and shells, which used to be in stores, were sent down to the Highlands when they were preparing for the planet's defense and helping build the suicide zombies.

The tanks had been in the way when the commandos and other volunteers had completed their emergency packing for their rescue mission to the ground. They had only five minutes to do their packing and get the two transporters and shuttle on their way. They had left the tanks where they were. It would have been too much work to dump the tanks into space while above the planet and repressurize the cargo area. Not to mention the fact that the poor planet had received enough abuse for the day. So no one was about to drop tanks on the Highlands from orbit.

Now, however, they were most definitely in the way. The tank drivers were already sitting in the tanks with the engines running. As soon as the hatches were down, they powered across the cargo bay and straight down the port and starboard ramps out onto the spaceport's ground. The port ground crew were there with paddles east and west of *The Peregrine* to tell the two groups of three tanks where they were to go. Two neat columns of three tanks maneuvered slowly as instructed to where they had been told to go.

Once the tanks were clear, the rest of the tanker crew disembarked and moved to the muster area the port ground crew and their paddles directed them to, the area marked by *The Peregrine*'s nose.

With that, *The Peregrine* was basically unloaded. All the commandos had stepped forward and gone down to the Highlands on the two assault transports piloted by Pickle and Vapor. Jack had taken *The Peregrine*'s shuttle down to the Highlands. The commando locusts had also stripped the ship of all the useful items they could get their hands on to take with them down to the Highlands. They had even taken all their kit bags from their bunks and used them to transport food and water, plus other emergency supplies. They boxed up the commandos' few personal items, including the photographs left behind on *The Peregrine*. Along with their rifles, grenades, mortars, and rockets.

The cabins were ready for their new occupants.

The crew had also unloaded the ship's stores area. Minus the substantial amount of REC thirty-millimeter cannon fire they had targeted at the Citadel, the inbound missiles, and the air defense positions, which totaled two hundred and eighty-seven thousand cannon shells. The twenty-millimeter cannon ammunition used by the mechs was all spent in the raid on clearing the Citadel's new lobby. The stores bins were now empty. They just needed to remove the empty ammo cases.

By the time Brigman, Lauren, and Tom descended to the cargo bay, it was another manic hive of activity. The ground crew were using powered hydraulic cargo carts to move stacks of foldable military medical beds onto the ships. Other carts were moving stacks of medical electronic equipment. Red emergency response trauma bags were being loaded by the thousand. Boxes and boxes of medical drugs and fluids were coming on board. Saline, iodine antiseptic, iodide antiradiation tablets and burn treatment medicines were commonplace. They pushed large movable fridges on board filled with the different blood types and plasma.

The ground crew maneuvered the kit with purpose. They put everything they moved in a precise place. They organized the equipment outside with a mind to making the quick planned loading possible.

Charlie Powers had been very busy. She had shared ship layout plans with the medical teams mustering at Kilbride Port. The doctors had guided the loading plan with what equipment they needed and where they wanted it. Logistics experts had made sure it was packaged up and waiting at every landing port, with fields assigned to specific ships. Under the plan, they knew which people were mustering where. What their skills were, and which room of which ship they would work in. What equipment and drugs were in every box, its label, and where that box was located. It was all recorded in the plan.

When you considered the people, the equipment, and the plan, and how they had put it all together in just three hours and moved everything to the port, it almost defied belief. They had already seen what a group of motivated professionals could achieve in five minutes. With zero warning or preparation time when the commandos, flight crews, medics and rescue workers had pillaged the Ball Breaker Task Force and Abbot's fleet when packing the transports and shuttles to go down to the surface of the Highlands.

This group of professional experts in their fields had three hours to put this together.

The smaller shuttles were being penciled in for emergency

transport ambulance type duties or for small field-based EMT teams. The transports were being targeted for evac roles to move different categories of patients up to orbit where they would ultimately transfer onto the much larger destroyers.

These destroyers would function as orbital primary care hospitals and supply emergency accommodation.

The Peregrine was unique among the ships at hand. She was the largest ship they had that could work in the atmosphere and down on a planet's surface. And so *The Peregrine* became a supply hub and aerial movable hospital.

The other focus of the ground teams was on loading the supplies needed for the temporary military field hospital tent complexes. They would be deployed and abandoned twelve hours after T-ZERO. A lower tier of tent complexes would be deployed to shelter the able-bodied and recovering low-risk patients. To protect them from the elements and fallout while they waited for transport up to the big orbital ships.

The Peregrine would be a field triage unit providing on-planet medical care for six hours. The focus was different on the larger ships, where their function was to supply longer term hospital care for the thirty-five thousand patients they hoped to evacuate.

Unfortunately, the number of ships they had was a constraint. There were the ships from the Highlands. The resistance's second fleet was somewhere else. Precisely where wasn't important; it wasn't here now where they needed it. One thing remained as true as it had ever been. If you had a large logistics operation at short notice, then you depend on the military as the only people with ships and transportation resources that can achieve it.

Sure, there were a lot more civilian ships out there, but they always take longer to get them where you need them.

All this weighed on everyone involved in the operation at Kilbride. They all knew they now had all the skilled people they needed and supplies. What they did not have was lots of space to transport patients and evacuees. Abbot's ship's innards were the weapons of war. They were destroyer class rather than auxiliary ships, which would have been much more appropriate for the task at hand. Unfortunately, they didn't have any military auxiliary class ships. That was what they needed, as this was a rescue mission, not a combat engagement.

The ground crew and medics felt nearly ready to go. It had taken them just thirty minutes to load, as the traffic controller had advised. The preparation work would continue in flight on *The Peregrine* during their return to the Highlands.

Brigman used her radio to check in with Charlie and Abbot up in orbit on their assault support and destroyer.

"Comms, Brigman to Abbot and Charlie."

"Connected, General, we have kept an open link."

"Brigman reporting. *The Peregrine* is nearly ready to go. How are things progressing on the other ships?"

"Abbot, I am not sure how Charlie and ground control did it, but that was the best planned mass-ship combat landing I have ever seen. They had all the ships landed and docked in just fifteen minutes. Both ground and space-side logistics and planning have been excellent; the ground and medical crews and rescue workers have all excelled. *The Peregrine* was the first to land. It was one of the most complicated and slowest ships to load. It was just one of three ships still in a loading state, while the other two we expect to complete in three or four minutes. Looks like everyone will launch in the next five minutes."

"Brigman, I am speechless. Charlie, it is what, forty minutes since we came out of jump? We had sixty minutes in the high-level plan for this turnaround. Outstanding! Think of that twenty minutes you just saved as twenty thousand people that now won't be dead. Okay, Abbot, *The Peregrine* will be ready for flight in two minutes."

"Abbot, copy that, Brigman. Out."

Two pips came over the ship's 1MC.

"This is Abbot to all ships and Kilbride ground. We will leave in one minute for the Highlands. Kilbride, you have made the resistance proud, and you have saved lives today. Just as many as those who will be down on the Highlands. Before we leave, I extend the fleet's welcome to the extra forty-seven civilian transports joining us on our return trip. Thirty-six are from Kilbride, the other eleven are small civilian transport haulers that were in the loading dock when the Imperium attacked. The actions taken by the Argyll and Bute governments inspired them two hours ago. And they wanted to volunteer and join us. Welcome to you all. All ships, only at traffic control's guidance, leave dock and head for orbital rally point RV2. Out."

"Thank you, General. This is Kilbride traffic control. I will have you all back in orbit and at jump inside of five minutes. Right, I want this to happen next."

Two minutes and twenty-seven seconds later, the last of the 291 ships taking off from the ground had cleared the atmosphere. They headed to RV2 to join the eighteen big ships that had docked in space. Abbot's ragtag rescue fleet and volunteers now numbered 309. Their calculated rescue capacity of the stripped-out ships had now increased to an estimated eighty thousand people who they could get off the Highlands besides the crew. The shuttle and transport ships already down on the Highlands could lift 515 survivors besides their crew of 115. Their new evacuation limit was 80,515 people rescued from the Highlands after the bombs fell.

Seventy-six seconds later, all 309 ships went to jump and headed back to the Highlands. The Kilbride traffic controller had been correct again in his promise to get everyone away and back at jump within five minutes. There was still one minute and seventeen seconds left on the clock, another 1,283 potential lives saved. It was three minutes, forty-three seconds since the traffic controller's broadcast. Ground team Kilbride had done it again.

CHAPTER 74

RIM – PROCYON B – THE HIGHLANDS
RESCUE GROUND BASE
T-ZERO +6 HOURS
CHAOS TO ORDER

"Comms, get Abbot, please." Greg was happy the General and the fleet were back, but this was going to be tough.

The fleet had arrived from jump two minutes ago. Comms had contacted Greg on his radio. Of course, the call had come in during the few seconds Greg had stolen for himself to take care of his body's pressing urgency to relieve itself for the first time since his arrival six hours ago. As Greg would not talk to Abbot with a background water feature and splashes nor try to hold it, he said to the comms officer, "I'll call Abbot back in thirty seconds."

Greg spoke first. "General Abbot, sir. It's great you are back. Straight into it, sir. We have a problem. You remember Merlin said we might rescue five hundred, maybe one thousand, maximum?"

"That is right, I remember."

"Well, so far, we have rescued twenty-one thousand at the six-hour point. Our flight teams have been flying for the last six hours. With all the extra people and resources you will have with you, we are projecting in the next six hours that the number will be over one hundred thousand. I don't think we have anywhere to put them. It is crushing. Our morale has taken a big hit, sir. We must find more capacity to get people off-world."

"Well, that has stolen my thunder. The rescue fleet now includes 309 ships, of which 291 will work down on the ground. Our calculated total lift capacity is now at eighty thousand five hundred and fifteen, including all the ships that were here already. You are telling me that is still not going to be enough? That you think we will find and recover enough people to take us from twenty-one thousand to over eighty thousand five hundred people? More than an extra sixty thousand people in the next six hours?" Abbot said.

Greg took a deep breath. "We have got our search-and-rescue method down real tight with the seventeen ships we have been working with. We have lots of already mapped pickup sites. I urge you to adopt our search method. You have bought 291 ships with you that can work down here. That increases our capacity by a factor of seventeen, which makes three hundred and fifty-seven thousand on top of the twenty-one thousand we already rescued.

"So, in total circa 378,000 people we could get off-world six hours from now if we had the capacity, based on the numbers and the capacity you have bought to the party? You can see the problem.

"I was being very conservative when I said over one hundred thousand. We will be at over one hundred thousand in the next sixty minutes. Two hundred thousand in six hours would be a safe bet and I think we could even hit around three hundred thousand that we could save if only we had somewhere to put them. Everyone was getting down about it an hour ago.

"Everyone knew we could not lift all the people off the planet. I pivoted the mission to keep everyone flying, pulling them back here, to keep the medics treating people, putting them back together. I shifted the focus away from saving them to making their last hours as comfortable as possible. Surrounded by people that were caring for them and supporting them. Those people would not die alone in the cold, injured. So we kept going, getting them and bringing them back.

"I suggest you position things in the same way for the new people. We know the people we rescue are going to die because we can't get them off-world. It turns your soul cold."

"Shit!" Abbot paused while his brain caught up.

"Okay, first, yes, we will implement your search-and-rescue protocols. Henry, if you are listening, start making that happen. The guys here already are the experts and we need to learn from them quickly and start right now. I suggest flight observation for some of our pilots. Let them guide you."

"Roger that, sir," Henry said, his voice cutting into the radio broadcast.

"Next, Greg, are we setting up here and expanding or setting up another base?"

"I suggest we do both, General. We have been searching a one thousand kilometers radius circle. There are still plenty more people to help here, but I also suggest we expand and set up another eight search circles with medical hubs. We need a balance between the seventeen-fold increase in capacity and being able to increase the frequency of flights.

We should double the search-and-rescue aircraft from seventeen up to thirty-four per circle. This means we will be able to search more thoroughly and evacuate each area quicker. One other thing, General. Before, when we came down here, our four Lancer fighters tagged along with us from our assault supports. They have been very valuable to us in supporting the search-and-identification phase. If your destroyers have any fighter crews on them, they would be very useful for the effort."

"We sure do, the sixteen destroyers carry four fighters each docked to the top hull. Yeah, our air wing is sixty-four fighters. They and their two flight teams are all here with us."

"Great. Now, if you look at the map, I just sent over the comms. This augments the original data Merlin sent us for the LZ sites, with the observation data we have seen in the circle. We have been adding wider weather observations about wind directions. It has meant we have projected fallout zones from the places we know they hit in the plus or minus forty-five-degree arcs downwind of them. We have used it to find likely green zone targets where radiation fallout should be minimal. This has meant we have discovered two things. The first and most immediate was we have a list of target sites for the next eight search circles. The second, we think we have found a pattern in the initial nuclear assault that the Imperium fleet launched at the planet."

"Okay, that is a little interesting. What did you discover?"

"First, we got very lucky. Prevailing winds have meant much of the radiation on the west side of this continent got carried seaward rather than inland. That is good, way better for survivors in the rural areas. Second, we know Merlin interrupted the Imperium fleet mid-attack. Their ships were still launching waves of missiles from their fifty ships. The first missiles were all targeted at the cities. Multiple strikes per city is our estimation from the data we have. Here is where it gets interesting. This north–south line we have on the map. Everything east of here got incinerated.

"They hit all the rural gaps between the cities with single air burst strikes and smaller nukes. If you plot on the map for areas covered by the thermal flash from the air bursts, it fills all the gaps on the map in the red category-one areas of death from the heat. The strikes on the cities were all close to ground detonations under one hundred and seventy meters, designed to yield maximum radiation contamination in the ground soil and concrete, which they threw up into the atmosphere. Smaller city areas with a higher population density and multiple strikes.

Understandable, if beyond ruthless. Now this is the interesting bit. West of that north–south line, there were no airbursts over rural areas. That is it right there, the smoking gun."

"I think I missed a bit. Spell it out for me," Abbot said.

"This was not a strike against the Highlands government nor against the resistance sites. They targeted the cities. Then they jumped east and started air-bursting north to south, killing all the rural bits in between the cities. They moved west, repeating the pattern of more airbursts. Here it stops. That is the point that Merlin made them all fire at each other. Everything to the west other than their cities was not hit once. They set about coloring the complete map of the planet category-one red in its rural areas. Merlin interrupted their attack. It was not a random targeting sequence. It was cold and deliberate. Their aim before the attack started was not to hit some specific military or government targets. Their aim was to clear the surface and remove all life from the face of the Highlands. This was not a military strike, this was an extinction strike against the whole of the Highlands, to completely clear it, to make it uninhabitable. The aim was to erase the Highlands from the stellar map of colonies, not to remove any specific target on the Highlands. The difference in motivation this makes and what it tells us about the attackers' thinking is key."

"Indeed, Greg. The fucking bastards. The Highlands itself was their primary target all along and its extended sterilization for the next few thousand years. Not any specific target on the Highlands. This was a political decision, not a military one."

"We see no other conclusion from the observational evidence. We believe this is indisputable proof that the orders and the strike plan itself not only came from but also originated in Supreme Commander Bob's office and his bureaucrats. This is likely Bob's plan. Not from one of his generals."

"We think you should send it out in the same way Merlin and Jack did before. This will shake the Imperium to its foundations. It will bring chaos to order."

"Merlin?"

"Here, General. Would you like me to send it out?"

"Yes. Now, please."

"We recorded Jack's reaction earlier when I explained the data to him while you were still traveling here at jump. I have already edited it together. I have sent it now, General. Yep, that is all over social media now on the Interweb. Give it a minute and they will all be going mad again."

CHAPTER 75

**CORE – ALPHA CENTAURI – NEW TERRA
OUTSIDE BOB'S HQ BUILDING
T-ZERO +6.5 HOURS
HEAVY-HANDED**

There was a people's march on New Terra, protesting outside Bob's office HQ. They carried the placards *Down with the planet killer!* and *Take Bob's balls, not our worlds!* The Imperium guards flipped their rifles to full automatic and sprayed, gunning down all the protesters. People filmed this, and it went viral all by itself, both in the Imperium and Rim systems. It only took thirty minutes, with none of Merlin's help this time for it to become the front-page story across the Imperium.

This was the third bad news story for the Imperium in as many hours.

One news channel also picked up mention of Merlin. What capabilities did the resistance have? What the hell was a Merlin?

The news channel started investigating. Where were all the different Imperium fleets? Had anyone been in contact with them over the last six hours? Who was in command of the fleet that attacked?

There were only so many fleets, and a process of elimination would soon narrow the field. The news channel determined they could not account for the recent whereabouts of two fleets: Plug's and Wombat's.

Neither were contactable. An Imperium comms officer, who was sleeping with a lass who enjoyed dressing up as a furry ("pouncing puppy"), admitted the Imperium also had no contact with either fleet. In fact, neither fleet showed up with a location lock anywhere on her system.

Were one or both fleets the guilty attacker? Were they rogue or acting under orders? Given they were both missing, did this mean the resistance had destroyed one or the other? Could they have destroyed both Imperium fleets?

Recruitment inquiries were coming in to support the resistance. Crypto donations arrived. They also came in from some Imperium systems. Only a few, though, and they were all captured and fast-tracked by resistance intelligence. All donors would get approaches in person later that day from a local resistance recruiter.

Someone asked the real question of how they had done an attack analysis of the effects on the ground on the Highlands? Unless someone was down on the ground on the Highlands? Jack was surely not just there on his own in one shuttle. The data gathered would have required flight data from many points on the Highlands or in orbit. Just who was Jack with? He said he wasn't military or resistance but that he damn well was now. He had said "they" were trying to rescue survivors. How many were they? How was it going?

Resistance intelligence picked up on this new thread from the speculation machine that was the Interweb. They did an analysis of likely effects and responses, gauging likely public reactions. It all came out positive. A resistance spokesperson went to the studio of a Rim system news channel and recorded a statement.

Yes, there had been an advance team that Jack was part of. They had gone down first to the planet into the radiation zone with seventeen ships. General Abbot's fleet has since reinforced and resupplied the rescue effort. Abbot arrived at the Highlands thirty minutes ago with 309 more ships, of which 291 were working down in the atmosphere with eighteen in orbit. The fleet had ships from the Highlands and nearby Kilbride. There were also ships from the six other Rim systems and two undisclosed ex-Core worlds who had multiple ships in the group.

Many thought this would be the two closest Core worlds to the Rim, Argyll and Bute, but this was unconfirmed. There were eight Rim systems and two ex-Core systems working together that had all contributed to the ten-system joint rescue effort. This covered all of the "separatist" Rim systems and forty-six percent of all colony systems, while Imperium representation was at zero percent. The question became, who was in the right and which side were they personally standing on? Everyone agreed that the Imperium was in the wrong. Many found they were standing on one side of the fence, which now forced them to question their blind loyalty since birth to the Imperium. Did the Rim system underdogs more accurately reflect what they believed? What they thought was moral and right, rather than their divine birthright and entitlement?

The Interweb monitors at the resistance intelligence team found that their press release was playing as they had hoped. They had one more play to make.

They posed a question from a citizen, which was of course, the intelligence unit themselves. They asked how many people they hoped to rescue.

The answer was as follows: "Based on our progress so far and predictions; we expect around 378 thousand. People are ready to evacuate from the field hospitals set up on the planet, stabilized and ready to go."

They pulled the carrot's pin and launched it onto the Interweb.

The carrot exploded everywhere. The public reaction was simultaneous amazement that so many people would get rescued, combined with disgust that the Imperium had killed three hundred million people.

The Interweb exploded again.

The Imperium systems media news channels picked up on the story and amplified it even more in the major streams.

Then the resistance intelligence team threw their second carrot.

Another user profile posed the question:

"Can you get the 378,000 people off the Highlands?"

They replied with their prepared answer, knowing that everyone in all the colonies was watching.

"No, we can't! We need more ships that can be here inside of six hours, before the radiation kills everyone. We have already committed all the assets we have that can be here, they are already here. It is a big problem and we need help. We can only lift about eighty thousand, the other 298 thousand are sitting back at our medical bases, where we have treated them. They will all die before midnight tomorrow."

For effect, the intelligence unit added a bit of theater.

"There is talk among the two thousand medical staff, doctors, and nurses. They may give up their seats on the ships and stay down on the Highlands after the evacuation. They could then get another two thousand patients off-world. They would stay and give palliative care to everyone left on the surface and to each other. As time passed, death would become a present rather than forecast reality. They would care for those left behind, and in time, for their colleagues, while they all waited their turn to die."

The whole Interweb became incandescent with rage over the impending death of the civilians, who had been saved from nuclear death once already today. Left to die, because no one else had gone to help save them. And the doctors and nurses were going to sacrifice their own lives to save two thousand more people and make the end more bearable for the other two hundred and ninety-eight thousand who were going to die along with the doctors and nurses.

The rage burned bright.

Two Imperium news anchors resigned live on air, saying they didn't want to stain their souls any more than they already had as Imperium citizens under this, or any other tyrant's rule.

The other people in the studio respected their colleagues' big brass balls for resigning like that. They also thought they would never see their colleagues again. It took the two groups of guards fifteen and eighteen minutes to arrive at the studio to arrest them. By the time the second set of guards arrived, they had received updated orders—from arrest to kill.

The guards' officer performed his duty in the studio where the ex-anchors were being detained. He walked up without saying a word and shot them both in the face. Their blood sprayed out all over the studio floor. After the executions, he marched out again without saying a word.

The studio personnel were in silent shock. As a general tip, don't execute someone in a viewscreen studio. What with being a news station, they have lots of viewscreen cameras that record stuff in ultra-high clarity. The footage got posted on the Interweb. Along with the spray, five minutes after the guard had marched out again, his work was done.

The Interweb bounced again.

Next, the guards' officers were facing off against a peaceful protest by a group of women in a park. The women were quietly protesting against the guards: their violence against, sexual assault, rape, and murder of women. Two of the male guards had "an attack of stupid." They decided a peaceful, unarmed, passive small woman was a real direct threat to these two big blokes' lives. To the length of their tiny egos, and the strength of their composite body armor. Both the male guards slammed this thin, short woman face down in the dirt, with both her arms pinned high behind her back. She lay there, passive, immobile, but raging defiance in her eyes. Both men pinned her down, lying on top of the seventy kilogram lady, with each of their one hundred and ten kilograms. People photographed her, and she became a rallying image for the people on the Interweb within minutes. Shame on the two guards.

This was not at all well received by the Interweb readers, very much the opposite. They saw the heavy-handed jackboots of an authoritarian state in real-time events playing out in front of them.

That was it! People went apoplectic. The spark caught and flared blue-white hot. The first riot started five minutes later. In the end, there was rioting on five worlds across the Imperium in thirty-two cities, in many locations in each city. Just over one thousand six hundred separate riots involving sixteen million citizens. This was the same as one in every twenty American citizens on old Earth, or one in every four UK citizens, all rioting at the same time countrywide for five hours nonstop.

The Imperium guards couldn't cope. It had never occurred to them that the people were actually in charge. Not the ones wearing body armor and wielding batons against the people. The military did not know what they should do about it. They did not have enough bullets ready to hand for that many people all at the same time. They believed the bullets were in a warehouse somewhere. The thing about low-tech blunt objects is they come with infinite swings, unlike guns with finite bullets. The rioting would not end until the people's temperature dropped, and it was still boiling in the Imperium.

The people's court had ruled. They found it was Bob's responsibility and that he was as guilty as hell. If you had taken an opinion poll right then, the everyone-wants-to-lynch-Bob party had a significant sixty-five percent lead over the don't-lynch-Bob group at twenty-five percent, with the don't-know group at ten percent.

CHAPTER 76

**RIM – PROCYON B – THE HIGHLANDS
THE PEREGRINE – FLYING HOSPITAL
MERLIN'S NINETEEN-INCH RACK IN C&C
T-ZERO +8 HOURS
HEATHER**

Merlin was feeling blue, certain they would not get away with this. He feared it was self-evident they were going to have too many people by a large margin. It seemed so wrong to him, just to leave people and fly off while they stayed behind to die. Merlin was also worrying about the journey and being ambushed while so many baby ducklings were in tow on his watch. They now had over two hundred thousand people in the nine different medical tent camps.

Plus, Merlin was somewhat bored and wished he could talk to Daisy. Life with Daisy was so simple, it was refreshing. In fact, Merlin was so bored he had perused some documents of a student's lecture notes from some university. Someone had digitized the notes years and years ago. The current notebook was from a chemistry student. The notes baffled Merlin. He was unclear how someone could be this wrong about so many things. In fact, Merlin was wondering if these were in fact, the working notes of a satirical playwright. Now Merlin's internal bookie was giving him even odds each way on whether the student should have the nickname Moldy Melon Head or Magic Melon Head.

The current lecture recorded in the notes was different. Maybe the student had two cans of diet cola too many before the lecture had started.

It was a lecture about ...

Now hold on readers, it is only one sentence about chemistry at university level and quantum mechanics. You will survive it and it is easy to understand.

It's about how the shape of a molecule affected the different ways it could vibrate and wobble, and how this affected its spectral fingerprint.

That is it, folks, you just survived your first extract from a second-year university-level chemistry lecture about quantum stuff. Whoop!

The three-legged barstool called ammonia (NH_3) was being discussed.

Now the barstool could sit on the floor on its three hydrogen legs. We will call that "down." Or the barstool could sit the other way up on its nitrogen seat with its three hydrogen legs pointing up in the air. We will call that "up."

The interesting thing was that with enough energy, you could squash the barstool flat like roadkill. With its three little legs stuck out at 120-degree angles, pancake flat. Crushing a barstool flat like that is difficult. You need energy to do it, and there was no evidence of it wobbling like flat roadkill in the spectra. But they had found evidence that the ammonia molecule would flip from down to up and back and forth. This is the important bit, without the three hydrogen atoms moving through the flat plane shape. The little hydrogen atoms were doing quantum tunneling, shifting between up and down. Quantum perturbations in space–time explained this. These are like valleys and holes in the surface of a pond on which the entire universe floats. The surface of the pond was not flat, it was frothy. And this froth enabled the hydrogen atoms to tunnel in space from the down shape to the up shape while being nowhere in between. The hydrogens would disappear from their physical down location. And reappear in their new physical up location without moving between them.

They would achieve quantum tunneling, which allowed the hydrogen atoms to cheat and take a shortcut that enabled them to move from down to up without going in between. Despite them not having enough energy to go through the planer position.

There was an equation for this quantum tunneling that was written on the board and this piqued this student's interest as he looked at it. If we simplify, it was of the form:

$$\text{Probability} = \exp\left(2 \times \text{Distance} \times \left(2 \times \text{Mass} \times (\text{Barrier} - \text{Energy})/\text{Plank}^2\right)^{1/2}\right)$$

That wasn't the equation, it is simplified above but it will help illustrate the point the student had noted. As the mass of the object (like the hydrogen atom) got bigger, and the distance it had to move between start and finish got further apart, this resulted in the event's probability tending toward zero. The thing the student was interested in was the other term: difference between the barrier energy level and energy of the particle. The energy distance the item was away from no energy at all, when it went to zero the expression would evaluate to 1, in other words one hundred percent certain.

Think of this as the very bottom of that fishpond. Everything is sitting on the surface of the pond. That is where the universe is. The distance between the place where the item sits on the surface and the bottom of the pond is called zero-point delta.

As this number gets smaller, it is like a hole being dug in the pond's surface, like a perturbation. Think of water going down a plughole as it swirls and forms a funnel. All the way through the bathwater draining through the plughole at the bottom of the bath.

As this number approached zero, irrespective of how big the value of the mass or how far the distance being traveled, the three terms together would get smaller and smaller, and ultimately they would equal zero. The probability equation would simplify to: probability = one hundred percent certain.

The young student reasoned that if you could somehow create a hole in energy all the way to zero-point at the bottom. Like the draining bathwater funnel. You could drop something into the funnel, and it would fall to zero energy. To maybe reemerge in the new up position no matter how heavy it was or how far it had to travel.

To him, this seemed analogous to the idea of a wormhole in space for traveling spaceships. The student saw some problems with the idea. If you need a hole at both ends, how do you do that if you haven't gone to the other end yet? If you could go anywhere at any distance, how does the spaceship all arrive at the same place rather than going through a cosmic garbage disposal that would mash it down to a subatomic slurry that spread everywhere?

The student was either an idiot or over-caffeinated. The central question was, however, interesting, Merlin thought. Could you establish a wormhole by making a hole down to zero-point and tunneling to somewhere else?

The reason Merlin thought this was interesting was because it wasn't a million miles away from how an FTL star drive worked. By creating a Casimir bubble of warped space–time. It was a distinct thing. Merlin wondered whether they could refocus the engineering in the FTL star drive to dig a hole that went down into zero-point energy. Could an FTL star drive open one end of a wormhole that a ship could fall into?

This is what Merlin found interesting, and he did not know what the answer was. Merlin wasn't even sure if anyone had ever asked this question before to someone who would listen and think what the answer might be.

The student then babbled on at length about some redhead who had sat in the seat in the row in front of him every day for the last two years. The student liked red hair and thought that this redhead, Heather, was rather delicious.

The student's brain had regressed at this point because it was just about the redhead now in the notes and not about the wormholes anymore.

Merlin thought to himself and asked two questions. First, let's say the science is right. How would we think about moving sideways through zero-point energy, to navigate it, if you will, to a destination?

More to the point, how do the spatial coordinates of things in the 3D universe that float on the surface of the pond map to whatever the coordinate system is at the bottom of the pond? Which is also a single spatial point. A single point, like the center of a 2D circle or a 3D sphere with its 2D surface. This would be a 4D shape where its surface was, in fact, all the points in 3D space in the entire universe.

The traveler would need a sort of compass that would enable them to know what course to set when they arrived at the single point at the center of that zero-point 4D sphere.

The second question was that the traveler would also need something like a life jacket they could inflate. Which would push them back up to the surface in a specific place, as there would be no hole coming down at the exit point.

A hole to the center of zero-point energy is how you open the wormhole. Some idea of a magic compass is how you steer your course at the center. Now you inflate the life jacket to climb back up out of zero-point energy. You arrive back at the correct bit of the surface mapped to the area in 3D space that you wanted to travel to.

The payoff, Merlin thought, was that if I can make this work, I can take all my ducklings at once a long way in no time at all. Merlin thought he might even christen it the RHD—Red Head Drive, or maybe the RWD—Red Worm Drive, in honor of this mystery woman called Heather from a long time ago. TLAs are very important to think about as well.

Merlin reached out over his wireless connection to the local cloud node's physics engine, which was still running on backup power and fuel. From there, he linked to all the other Rim systems nodes where Lauren had set up a physics engine and tunneled his connection over the tachyon-based Interweb. Merlin piggybacked on a viewscreen signal. It was a program for infants where the four characters babbled baby sounds.

This supplied an excellent carrier wave because of the low signal-to-noise ratio. This meant Merlin had no problems transporting his advanced brain bending physics over the stolen capacity to the remote cloud nodes.

Merlin's internal task manager CPU usage counter was ticking upward as he pondered. It went up to one hundred percent and sat there as if pinned. Merlin planned many questions he sent to the cloud physics engine as he thought about wormholes.

CHAPTER 77

RIM – PROCYON B – THE HIGHLANDS
IN ORBIT ABOVE THE PLANET
YOU ORDERED DEATH – BRIDGE
T-ZERO + 9.5 HOURS
OMG

"Comms, get Powers now! Something is coming," Merlin screamed over the radio.

"Merlin, it's Charlie. What's wrong? You sound panicked."

"I am getting a massive signal bounce vibration coming back across space–time. There are two very huge somethings approaching our position at FTL. They are running dark with no transponders. The signals approached us in formation. From the Rim system-side, not from the Core-side. They will arrive any second."

The two exit jump points formed in space three thousand kilometers higher than where *YOD* was orbiting.

Abbot had spread the eighteen big ships out around the planet. The ships were distributed to supply surveillance support of the planet's surface. Although everyone knew they were also there to supply early warning. And as an attack response against the reappearance of any Imperium military ships.

The jump exit points that were forming were enormous. They dwarfed the ones the destroyers would create. With a snap the ships were there; they dropped back into normal space as their Casimir bubbles collapsed.

Charlie looked at the viewscreen. The nearest ship had eclipsed the sun, casting *YOD* into shadow as it blocked the sunlight. The only illumination was bouncing up from the dirtied planet beneath.

"Fuck! Gunnery, talk to me. Who are they?"

"Err, checking, checking. That is odd. They are nothing, Charlie. We detect no weapons. No transponder. No navigation lights. They have been running dark. No threats detected."

This was when the skippers on the two ships turned on their external lights. Lights lit up the ship's bow and flashed on down the ship's flanks. The two ships were enormous. Each was about three times the size of the destroyers. There was still no ship transponder squawking the ship's identity. That was very unusual. Engineers deliberately designed transponders not to be turned off.

The comms officer spoke up. "Charlie, I am detecting a comms carrier channel now. The base carrier signal was encrypted. The computers are shaking hands. Here we go."

"This is *Imp* and *Green Bird* to the Rim Rescue Fleet. Reporting for duty. The Bute and Argyll governments have retasked us to you. Our ships were on a return run back from our Rim delivery and they sent us to you. We had to burn our engines hard just to get here in time. We are here to help."

"*Imp* and *Green Bird*, this is Commander Charlie Powers. Welcome to the Rim Rescue Fleet. You scared the fuck out of us. General Abbot's ship is on the far side of the planet now. You look like bulk carriers, but I am not familiar with your hull profiles. I also note your transponders are off."

"We are new ships. This is our first outbound run. We are civilian bulk carriers, the new Europa class. The government overrode our transponders. They didn't want any risk of the Imperium noticing our approach."

"What is your name? Call me Charlie."

"I am Catherine, Cathy."

"Hi, Cathy, what are you carrying? We have lots of medicine already."

"Nothing. The ships are both empty. Someone saw the transmission on the Interweb I guess. About your cargo lift problem and sent us. We have drop lifters as well that we can send down to the surface to load. That will make a lot more sense than flying up your transports."

"Just how big are your ships? The cargo is humans, not containers, obviously. You can't stack humans like containers."

"We are not container vessels. We have pressurized cargo holds. Soil and other agro crops are what we carry. Agro doesn't like vacuums either. To answer your question, let me think. Two hundred and fifty thousand, I reckon, that should work."

"You can carry two hundred and fifty thousand people!"

"Yeah, I reckon we should each be able to shift that many."

"Each! You have enough space to move half a million people."

"Sure, I reckon."

"Oh my God!"

"It will be basic, but it is only a short flight to Kilbride, four or five hours. If they don't mind peeing in a bottle and using a bag. The holds will need jet cleaning after. They will need to bring their own food. We have no in-flight service or film, or even chairs. We are just big-ass space trucks."

"I am going to take you out for dinner when we get back, Cathy. You just saved a lot of lives. We had been saving them but were afraid we were going to need to leave them to die. There are so many. Hold on a second. Comms, get me Greg. Greg! We are back on as a rescue mission, not just care and comfort. Tell the shuttle pilots to put their foot down and get as many as they can! We have two and a half hours left. Yes, two bulk carriers just arrived. The Argyll and Bute governments sent them to us on the quiet, like. They just sent us enough capacity to move half a million people. Yes, they are here now. Okay, yes, go, bye. I am back with you now. Greg is running ground operations with all the people down on the planet."

"Charlie, can I ask, what were you able to move before?"

"Greg says thank you, Cathy. They would have stuffed our ships at around eighty thousand five hundred. We went over one hundred thousand people over two and a half hours ago. The high-end twelve-hour prediction was three hundred and eighty thousand, that was three and a half hours ago when we got here. We have bought a lot of shuttles and transports with us. I don't know what the current count is or what the latest peak projection is. It was depressing everyone thinking we would have to leave them. We opened eight more search areas and doubled the air coverage density for transports and fighters spotting in each search area. You know what commandos are like; they have turned it into a competition. To keep people's energy and momentum up between the different search teams and the circles, they're competing over who can gather the most people. They have been at this for hours now. Your arrival will lift spirits and energy. Look, I am going to hand you off to my comms officer, Jeff. I need to update General Abbot and General Brigman. Talk later. You have made my day. Bye, remember dinner. Bye."

"Comms, get me Greg again, thanks."

"Greg here. Charlie, what's up?"

"I was wondering if you have any updated twelve-hour predictions for how many we will have saved. The last data I saw was when we got here."

"Yeah, I was just looking at that myself. Right now, projecting forward, I think we could get up to as high as maybe four hundred and seventy-five thousand people. We are going to get everyone off. Fuck yes! I am going to spread the word. This will give the teams and medics a boost and the survivors are going to be very glad to hear they are not all going to die. We should send it out on radio as well, telling anyone listening to head for the search circles."

The word spread like wildfire, driven by gales. People in the camps were on their feet, cheering everyone. They cheered the medics, the rescue teams, the people in orbit and, most of all, the crew of the *Imp* and *Green Bird* that had just joined the rescue effort.

CHAPTER 78

**RIM – PROCYON B – THE HIGHLANDS
ABOVE THE PLANET – R3 RV
BREAKING ORBIT
T-ZERO +11.5 HOURS
SWAN LAKE**

The cargo holds would be zero-g during the flight. The patient's beds would be stuck to the floor with magnets on the bed's base. Patients would be strapped down to the bed. Magnets would secure the wheeled specialist instruments next to the foldable cots. The doctors and nurses had decided that using their mag boots with the extra space was better for the patients. As opposed to ramming eighty-thousand injured patients into Abbot's Core fleet with induced gravity.

They suggested the able-bodied could go to Abbot's ships first and overflow to the *Imp*. The wounded went to *Green Bird* first and would overflow to the *Imp* if needed. They knew they had enough space. It didn't matter which filled first.

The medics who identified as true to the long-held doctrine of the Médecins Sans Frontières (MSF) ideal were hardcore. They were the best of the best and the most pragmatic of all medics. They were the most experienced, used to providing care for patients in the most difficult of conditions. These medics had worked in war and disaster zones. The MSF crowd had been very firm in that it would make their lives a lot easier if all the sicker patients needing closer care were all in the same place. Plus, it would help at the Kilbride end as they could manage different dispatch to hospital protocols for the two groups. The groups would have correlated treatment needs.

Greg suggested they should further subdivide the able group into a "mostly okay" group. They could load on Abbot's destroyers and stay on the transports and shuttles. Then there was the "needs a little care" group. They could go onto *Green Bird*. The sick would go onto *Imp*, and this would further help the medics. Help them organize staff, equipment and medicines.

The medics agreed this was a good idea. Greg explained people from the most able group could help load people into the two big ships and the big drop lifters. This allowed medics to focus on getting their hospital areas set up in the big ships rather than moving beds and stretchers. The medics embraced the idea. They knew they had limited time and far more people in that patient group, and they didn't want to expect the medics to do the duties of porters in a hospital.

They established the plan for where people would get moved to. It took fifteen minutes. They sent the signal up to fly down the big drop lifters. The loading operation would start straight away. It was going to take a lot of time and trips to move that many people up into orbit, even with the big drop lifters. Up and down, up and down, back and forth, the drop lifters flew. They had been at it now for two hours and the loading was very close to complete.

The cargo carriers each had ten drop lifters. Compared with *The Peregrine*, they were like twenty giant giraffe stag beetles standing next to a lone ant.

The drop lifters could each take up to twenty thousand people at a time. There was a drop lifter from each ship assigned to the nine search circle's hub sites. They would load the correct group onto the two ships, and they would fly up and offload people onto the correct bulk carrier. There was no messy cross-decking needed in orbit. The people would come off in a stream. The medical teams were in orbit already. They waited to coordinate the transfer into the improvised wards and guide the porters and keep track of which bed they wanted people put in.

Everyone understood what the plan was, and they moved with fantastic efficiency, not getting in each other's way or causing traffic jams. The loading and unloading teams had nailed their part in the play. They impressed the medics with their organization. Everyone was doing their part in the group's effort to help the collective whole. There was no griping or sniping from anyone. The entire team was pulling in the same direction.

Meanwhile, Merlin, Lauren, and Abbot's gunnery teams worked together to plan out how the evacuation fleet should organize in space.

Everyone was nervous about the possibility of ambush by an Imperium fleet en route.

That was the real danger. To be spotted would be bad. They wanted to slip away, with no one noticing. Being engaged by a fleet would be fatal. They swapped ideas and the gunnery crew gave the benefit of their military knowledge and experience.

What they came up with was that the *Imp* and *Green Bird* would fly in the center of the formation nose to tail. The transports would lead, taking front positions and functioning as a frontal screening shield for the two big carriers. The shuttles would fly at the rear of the formation, supplying the same function. They would use the able-bodied evacuee ships as a sacrificial shield to protect the carriers with the sicker patients. The transports preceded by the two assault support ships and *The Peregrine* provided a focused weapons footprint at the front. Sixteen destroyers would split into four groups of four. The first would fly upfront in a ring outside the assault supports but at the same forward position. The next ring would align with the front of the *Imp* and form a ring that put them wider out from the center line than the front ring of the four destroyers. These four twisted around by twenty-two and a half degrees. Next came the third ring of four destroyers aligned with the front of the second bulk cargo carrier. It rotated by another twenty-two and a half degrees, further out again. The pattern repeated with the fourth ring of four destroyers aligned behind the group of shuttles at the rear.

The arrangement meant that all sixteen destroyers had unobscured gun lines in every direction. All sixteen destroyers plus the two assault supports could launch a focused, tight beam of fire forward and not get in anyone's way. The offset rings maximized the coordinated fire support. The rings could be used to target any attack coming in at any angle from the side at the bulk carriers. They could also direct fire to the rear.

Everyone looked at the formation and thought it was bloody formidable. It would never occur on a battlefield. The formation's cross section was the width of a single bulk carrier, plus its four flaring rings. To the front it presented as a matrix of sixteen close packed destroyer's guns plus the assault supports and *The Peregrine.*

Anything that tried to get in their way or slow them down was going to have a bad day. It was impossible to approach this porcupine of turrets and launchers from any angle. Without being on the receiving end of fire and wrath from all sixteen destroyers. They could shoot past the central Core bulk carriers even when shooting at ninety degrees.

They were not looking to fight; their mission was to get the people out. If they had to run or defend themselves, it would be a very one-sided battle. Any Imperium fleet they crossed paths with would fly in the standard wide-spaced deployment favored when there was no specific threat. The Imperium would struggle to hold their lines against such a focused, charging animal, sprinting at their lines.

It was T-ZERO +11 hours and 29 minutes when the final shuttle and transport took their positions in the fleet. The pre-identified shuttles that would cross-deck to Abbot's destroyers all visited the docking collars like fat, pollen-laden bees bringing life with them. They returned their precious cargo to the hive.

In the end, they had run out of people to airlift from the nine search circles. Everyone they had spotted had been picked up and returned to the local medical hub for assessment and field treatment.

All the nondead and injured had been triaged and assessed. They had avoided the hot zones. The worst fallout was from the cities had been blown out to sea. The rural areas to the west of what was now being termed the death line was the only region they had pulled anyone out from. East of the line was nothing but burned corpses where the Imperium had air burst the nukes and fatally flash-fried all the humans, animals, and plants.

The evacuation area had been a lot less contaminated than it could have been. They had gotten lucky. Thanks to the regimen of the Imperium's plan as it erased people from the planet. This and the wind direction had meant that the areas the Imperium had not gotten to, prior to Merlin making the ships all attack each other, were mostly radiation free. It meant the areas had little exposure. The doctors had to deal with far less severe radiation poisoning than they had dared hope. The damage and areas of highest mortality were all clumped together rather than spread out. This meant that the patients, while sick and traumatized, would in time recover rather than the radiation burning them up from the inside and leaving them to die in agony.

The medics, air crews, rescue workers, and commandos were all physically and mentally exhausted. They were running on just pure *fuck you*, adrenaline, and caffeine. They had a lot of the first.

The ships all maneuvered together via Merlin's new linked navigation and maneuvering system. Merlin and Lauren had hacked it together in the computer navigation systems to keep everyone in the super close formation. They were all lined up for the FTL jump back to Kilbride. Greg reflected on the half day just passed. In the end, they had got four hundred and eighty-two thousand people off the planet. Four hundred and eighty-two thousand people who were now not dead because of them. It had started with his sixty people stepping forward and had resulted in so many more lives saved, with everyone else's help from across the Rim.

It was then that the red alarm lights lit. The comms officer's voice came over the ship's tannoy. "Urgent. All senior command and ship captains. Connect to channel forty-seven. Merlin needs you right now. Say again, urgent, channel forty-seven, senior staff and captains now."

CHAPTER 79

**RIM – PROCYON B – THE HIGHLANDS
ABOVE THE PLANET – R3 RV
T-ZERO +11.5 HOURS
A PEE AND A SANDWICH**

"What is it, Merlin?" Abbot asked.

"I am detecting blips at range. They are about five minutes out."

"That's not much warning," Tom said.

"They are at 21.6 billion kilometers. In other words, 3.7 times the distance from old Sol to Pluto! I am sorry, that is too close for you. They are moving at 240 times the speed of light!"

"Ah, I see your point. What can we do?"

"Well, not much if we want to evade. They are minor blips, not a full fleet, but there are six minor blips all approaching from different vectors. They have us bracketed in three dimensions."

"Can't we run?"

"Well, we can if you want to run into the blips, and after the other blips will all converge on wherever we are."

"I would rather sneak away unnoticed," Abbot said.

"We are a fleet performing hospital evacuation duties. They wouldn't attack, would they?" one of the other captains asked.

"There are three hundred million down on the planet, which would say they will attack. Oh no, they are all dead," Lauren said.

"I am sorry. I didn't mean to snap. Merlin, is there nothing you can do, nothing at all?"

"Um, err, maybe, but it is just an idea. I have been kicking the idea around while you were rounding people up downstairs. I got bored. It is just an idea; I did some modeling in the physics engine. It is better if I don't tell you."

"Do you see any other options, Merlin? Because I don't," Abbot shouted.

There was silence on the conference call.

"Well?" Abbot said again.

"No, I guess not."

"Will it get us out of here?"

"Yes, if it works."

"Okay, get us out of here. That is an order, Merlin."

"An order? Are you sure about that?"

"It is a request, if that helps. I will beg if you want me to. Just get us the fuck out of here now."

"Okay, let me think. I need to concentrate. I also need full control over the fleet. That will be the quickest."

"Okay, working on it quiet now," Merlin said to himself.

There was an awkward silence on the call. No one dared speak. While there was silence, some people shuffled their feet, which seemed to spread like when people yawn. The blips were closer, everyone knew. They couldn't be more than a couple of minutes away now.

"Got it, I think." Merlin said.

All the faces that had been wondering about the scuff marks on their shoes all looked up. The ships hadn't jumped. They were still where they had been. Confusion was growing. Abbot inhaled.

Then Merlin said, "Shh! Digging now. This may get strange."

From everyone's individual perspectives, everything seemed to get further away from them and ever faster. It was as if they were falling away from everything in every direction all at once. An observer outside the ships would have seen a blueish flickering bubble forming around the entire formation of ships. The bubble seemed to fall into nowhere and they were gone.

"Yay, we have arrived. I can't believe that worked."

"Where are we, Merlin?"

"I guess you would call it nowhere. We have fallen out of the universe. We are at zero point, protected in our bubble. Time to swim. Let me get my magic compass. I think the next bit will take us one hour and fifty-seven minutes, but we will find out, won't we?"

Lauren said, "Can you show me the view outside Merlin?"

"I can render it, I guess. I will have to make some guesses. I will go offline while I navigate."

Merlin went silent again, but the main display screen switched to a new image. There was a clock in the bottom-right corner that was counting down the seconds from 1:57:21. The rest of the display was a murky, gloomy blue-green. Everyone peered at the screen, trying to figure out what they were looking at. A dark shape came into view, just an outline of a shadowy form. It got bigger as it approached the virtual camera. It came right at them, but the detail of its form was still obscured.

The tension in the conference call was palpable and growing. The object that was the focus of their attention seemed to turn hard to the left and was now moving parallel to them. Everyone's head strained closer toward the screen.

"Does anyone else think that looks like a—"

"A fish?" Greg said.

"A fish, goldfish-shaped," Lauren said.

There was a flickering strobe of lights from the top of the screen as if fluorescent lights were turning on. Yes, it was a big goldfish swimming on the screen in front of them, gliding among the leafy green fronds of aquatic plants.

Tom spoke. "I don't think it is a goldfish. It looks like a koi to me."

"A koi, what is a koi?" Lauren asked.

"It's a type of carp. Tom has two of them tattooed on his chest," Greg said.

"Why are we in a fishpond?" Abbot asked.

"Let me check something." Lauren said as she leaned forward and switched them all to channel forty-eight. The display changed and the fish and plants were gone.

In its place was an enormous image of a log fireplace burning away.

"Um, is that a Christmas screen saver?" someone asked.

"I prefer the goldfish," someone else said.

Lauren switched the channel down to forty-seven. The koi was back on the screen. She touched the button again to channel forty-six. A snowscape with big fat falling flakes replaced the fish view.

"That is pretty," a voice said.

Lauren switched them back to channel forty-seven, and they were all back in the fishpond with the koi.

"I will leave it on channel forty-seven."

"What the fuck is going on?" Abbot asked.

"My guess would be Merlin doesn't have a clue what it looks like outside," Lauren said.

There was quiet again. Everyone watched the clock on the bottom-right side as it ticked and the seconds fell away.

"I don't know where we are. Let me just check something else," Lauren said.

Lauren typed on the keyboard and brought up a view of Merlin's task manager app. It listed all the different running processes with their utilization footprints. CPU and memory usage were both at one hundred percent load. The process at the top of the list used all of Merlin's CPU time and memory. The process was called RWD.py.

"Well, that is new. I don't know what that is. It must be some new code Merlin has written. I guess we will wait until the clock gets to zero. One thing is for sure, wherever we are, the Imperium fleet is somewhere else because they are not here already."

Lauren stood up. "I don't know about anyone else, but I'm going to have a pee and a sandwich. I will be back five minutes before zero time."

CHAPTER 80

**OUTSIDE THE UNIVERSE – AT ZERO POINT
ABBOT'S FLEET
THE PEREGRINE
T-ZERO +13.5 HOURS
THROUGH THE LOOKING GLASS**

Lauren walked back into *The Peregrine*'s command-and-control suite. The clock on the display's bottom right was seconds away from the five-minute mark.

The red and white koi was still on the screen, swimming back and forth. There was now a yellow koi on the display as well. *They are quite magnificent creatures* Lauren mused.

"Has anything changed? Did I miss anything?" Lauren asked the room.

"Well, someone came and fed the fish. Sorry, Tom, the koi, about fifteen minutes ago. Those big fish were hungry. They wolfed down all the flakes, speedy, like. In under a minute, all the flakes were gone, and then they went back to mooching back and forth," Greg said.

"Greg, as fascinating as you clearly found that, I was referring to anything from Merlin. Has he said anything?"

"Nope."

"Oh yes, he has or is," Merlin said.

"The fleet arriving at platform two is the Abbot Express from the Highlands. Passengers are told to stand back from the edge of the universe."

"Merlin, where are we?" Lauren asked.

"Well, we are still at zero point, but we will shortly arrive at our exit point. I will pull the cord on our life jackets, and it will take us back up again."

"Life jackets?" Lauren said.

"Metaphorical life jackets to float us back up to the surface where we will rejoin the universe at our destination."

"Merlin, was this a—"

"Shh! It's a surprise. It will be if I have screwed up the navigation and we don't arrive where I think we should be, because if that happens, it means we won't be able to get back again. Surprise!"

"Merlin?" Lauren sounded worried.

"Worry not. It almost certainly will not happen, but you know what they say, about a million-to-one shot."

"Lauren, what were you going to say?" Greg asked.

"Just wait, Greg, it could be quite epic. We will know in a few minutes," Lauren said.

"Okay, I can wait out a good mystery."

"This is Merlin, attention all. We will arrive somewhere. I am about to pull our life jacket, and this will get strange given what happened on the way in. The way out is going to be odd."

Merlin paused. Lauren wasn't sure, but she wondered if he had been waiting for a round of applause. No one clapped. People looked a little worried and uncertain.

"Right, life jacket time."

The FTL star drive's targeting indicators bounced back and forth between zero and one hundred. The speed of the oscillations increased. There was a shudder through the deck and the needle on the digital gauges stopped dead. Various control lights blinked on in green. That was it. They had arrived.

"Well, that was anticlimactic and will not put a smile on your face," Merlin said.

Lauren spat out the mouthful of water she had been drinking and laughed out loud. The other ladies on the bridge blushed.

"Let us have a look to see where we are. Hopefully, that won't be another let down." Merlin said.

The ship's display switched to the external view. It was stunning. The ships all hung in space near a large blue marble partially covered with wispy long white cotton candy clouds. The mountains were snowcapped, and the planet's poles were icy caps of pure white. Oceans on the planet were a glorious shade of blue. It was a marvel to behold. An unspoiled jewel. The brilliant starry arm of the Milky Way hung across the sky. The crescents of two moons were in the sky above the planet. In the far distance, a jolly yellow dwarf star lit the solar system.

"What a beautiful planet you have bought us to, Merlin," Lauren said in awe.

"I am having a problem getting a location lock," the navigation officer said.

"I think you should try zooming out," Lauren said.

"Okay, um, zooming, out, out, out, locked! That can't be right!"

"What are you seeing, navigation?" Greg asked.

"I have a lock. The star only has a numeric identifier: G2V-529853. We list it in the Perseus arm of the Milky Way. That is a different arm of the galaxy! We have traveled 1,297 light-years from the Highlands, in two hours!"

"Merlin, in RWD what does the R stand for? I am guessing WD is for Wormhole Drive?"

"Yes, Lauren. The R means red for Heather and yes, Worm Drive."

"Merlin, Heather doesn't begin with an R. It begins with an H."

"Pedant, it has an R at the end of the wormhole, doesn't it?"

The 1MC pips sounded, and Merlin's voice came out of the speaker.

"Ships of the fleet. We have arrived at our destination 1,297 light-years from where we were. You are the first humans to traverse an artificial wormhole. The planet below has spectral lines showing a nitrogen and oxygen atmosphere with twenty-two percent oxygen. We have plenty of liquid water and I have detected no toxins in the atmosphere. I suggest we unload our guests to the surface so we can all get some air and continue medical treatment where needed. It is a warm, sunny day and very pleasant down there."

Lauren looked at Merlin's rack. "Why red?"

"Didn't I say she had red hair?"

"No, but that makes sense now. Thank you, Merlin."

"We can rest up here, Lauren. There is no way for the Imperium to reach us here. We are safe. We have the time we need for everyone to heal from the Highlands, both physically and emotionally. These people need some time to mourn, all of them have lost family. I suggest we take a few weeks and figure out what our options are and what we want to do. For now, we are in paradise."

"Thank you so much, Merlin. Will the Imperium have any idea where we have gone?"

"None. From their perspective, we have vanished."

"Could we go back? If that is what they decide they want to do," Lauren asked.

"Yes, if that is what they want to do, we could sneak back into the Rim systems. They are only two hours away."

"You know, people will ask how fast we went to travel this far in just two hours."

"I will tell them the truth, that we didn't move at all."

"Merlin, I have one more question. Who is making lunch and what is it? There are going to be a lot of hungry people."

CHAPTER 81

**CORE – ALPHA CENTAURI A – NEW TERRA
AYLESBURY
SUPREME COMMANDER BOB'S OFFICE
T-ZERO +ONE DAY
THE VANISHED**

"Harold, talk to me. What the fuck happened? You had them nuke the planet. You fucking demented moron. Here, in front of me. You stood and said there would not be any other problems?"

"It is confusing, sir, and I hesitate, not for fear of telling you what has happened. Because I fear you will follow it up with questions about how it has happened. That is very unclear, a lot less clear than what."

"Humor me, what has happened?"

"Well, on the good news side, the rebel fleet appears to be dead. The rebel planet, the Highlands, is very dead. On the bad news side, the rebel fleet appears to have destroyed the fleet we sent to ambush them, posing as supply ships that attacked at Eta Cassieopeiae B. Then the rebel fleet appears to have destroyed the second fleet we sent to Procyon B to destroy the Highlands. Despite there being no living planet left and no rebel fleet. There is also no Imperium fleet either and some smart-asses in logistics have pointed out that there must have been a last man standing. This caused a lot of arguments about some very improbable missiles crossing in space and taking out the final ships on each side. We sent that person for castration to remove the possibility of any further damage to the gene pool."

"Everything got destroyed, and no one survived."

"As far as we can tell, sir, that is what has happened. No survivors. The word about Procyon B has also gotten out."

"That is what we wanted. That is why we broadcast it."

"Yes, but the story that has gotten out is that of a smaller, weak rebel fleet. Which had suffered some combat losses when the larger Imperium fleet attacked the rebels and then pursued them. The rebel fleet destroyed both the Imperium fleets that attacked at Procyon B."

"They got destroyed. The rebels got destroyed!"

"Yes, sir, maybe, but it is more complex."

"What do you mean, complex?"

"Well, the Interweb is alive with gossip, scurrilous gossip, sir, that the rebels destroyed two Imperium fleets and vanished."

"Vanished! Into a cloud of gas!"

"Yes, but no one seems to care. The only story gaining any traction out there is that they vanished, and our fleets were both destroyed. Plus, there is a lot of anger that, I am quoting here, the 'evil Imperium' destroyed the biosphere of the peaceful civilian planet the Highlands, which was defenseless."

"Vanished, defenseless. What destroyed both our fleets?"

"Marketing, sir. We can't admit that our fleets got destroyed even though everyone in our fleets knows the ships are all missing apart from the bits in orbit. The rebel fleet is missing, but there are no bits anywhere. We are getting full blame for three hundred million dead on the Highlands. Marketing just told us to talk to PR when we asked them to put a positive spin on it. The person in PR laughed at us and started crying, mumbling the words, 'positive, fucking positive.' The guard anticipated your orders and euthanized the PR person in the head, as he had clearly gone demented."

"Are you saying our victory is a defeat?"

"I am saying our absence of an enemy is not a victory, and no one believes that absence of our two fleets is nothing but a complete defeat."

"I see. Is there anything else?"

"Well, losing the two fleets has left us ninety-two destroyers weaker. We are finding it very difficult to project force and order. There have been waves of terrorist attacks on a lot of the Core worlds. Small-scale stuff, assassinations, troop attacks, ships exploding. The odd troop barracks fire, that sort of thing. It is like fighting mist. People disappear. We have bodies, just our bodies, not their bodies."

"This sounds like a total clusterfuck."

"In good news, sir, the rebels have vanished as well. They appear to have vanished, poof like, zero communications intercepted. They may have gone old school and are using physical couriers only."

"Hmm."

"The good news, sir, is that the enemy alien states seem unaware of how weakened the rebels have made us. There have been no border incursions or attacks from them."

"Okay, get out Harold, I need to think about this."

CHAPTER 82

**CORE – ALPHA CENTAURI A – NEW TERRA
AYLESBURY
OUTSIDE SUPREME COMMANDER BOB'S OFFICE
MOMENTS LATER
THE ONE PERCENT**

Harold was on his radio.

"Okay, I have briefed him, and I still have my head."

"What about the disappearances?" the voice from the radio asked.

"I'm not stupid. Of course I didn't mention them, you and your stupid suspicions," Harold replied.

"A significant number of the population has gone missing. It is higher on some worlds."

"Where are they? Where is this secret rebel bogeyman you fear?"

"Well, that is my point sir, which is why it is a secret bogeyman."

"You know we have some vacancies in marketing and PR. This strategic planning job appears to be getting to you."

CHAPTER 83

RIM – 52 TAU CETI – STIRLINGSHIRE
DESTITUTE TOWNSHIP
T-ZERO +TEN DAYS
SIGNING UP

Stirlingshire was an arid world, and this was an impoverished township. Despite the poverty, the town was busy that day. The off-worlders had recruited the street rats, as they called themselves. The street rats were a gang of teenagers that had banded together to protect themselves. Also, to more effectively scrounge, beg, and pick pockets for the meager income they could gather to feed themselves.

They had chosen their name to embrace their circumstances as the abandoned and homeless, stuck in this broken township. This week was different. All their bellies were full, and they were being paid. The off-worlders had hired the entire street rats gang, after arriving in the middle of last week. The off-worlders tried to sneak into the township. It was only five minutes before the street rats had clocked their arrival and were tracking them through the streets.

The four resistance recruiters felt confident they had entered the township unobserved. It came as a shock when they entered a side alley and several things happened in quick succession. That they were now standing facing a dead end marked by derelict buildings showed that Crusher, their leader, was lost. Their only option was to do an about turn and backtrack to the main street they had turned away from. All because of Crusher's insistence and proclamation that he was the one holding the map.

There was, of course, a problem. When they turned, they discovered the thirty odd teenagers in the alley behind them. The crowd had sneaked up on the four soldiers unobserved without making a sound. They all stood still and silent, observing the four soldiers. It was quite disconcerting. Thirty seconds passed, and they still just stood and stared.

"Err," Crusher said.

They received this with continued silence.

Crusher continued. "Erm, I think I am lost. Can you give us some directions?"

"We were wondering if you were not in fact lost but kept picking different destinations at random," Ali said.

Ali was one of the senior street rats. While the gang did not have a specific leader, his voice carried much weight in the group. Like the rest, he was unkempt and thin.

"We know everyone, everywhere in the township. We can guide you, for a price. Where do you want to get to?"

Crusher had an idea. It had been bothering him how they would vet the people they were here to see. There could be Imperium spies or sympathizers hiding among the people of the township. It was important that they and their mission was completed, unobserved.

"When did you start following us?"

"About twenty minutes ago. We picked you up when you were trying to sneak into town."

"And you say you know everyone in the township?"

"Yes, and the visiting traders and nomads."

Crusher hired the entire gang. To seal the deal, he took them all, under their guidance, to a nearby town square in pursuit of the various eateries and food vendors. Ali had the gang wait in the square while Crusher went inside one eatery to talk to the owner. The eatery was devoid of any customers. Times were hard, not just for the gang of street kids. The owner had agreed to the surprise booking of thirty-seven for lunch. When Crusher had waved his wrist over the scanner, the owner saw the resistance tattoo that Crusher had on the back of his left hand. The owner paused and was still, then he smiled.

"Your group is very welcome here, sir."

The three other resistance soldiers escorted the gang of thirty-three teens into the food eatery. Ali sat next to Crusher, and they talked while the owner and his server bused out plates of piping hot deliciousness to feed his hungry customers. Crusher outlined to Ali what he needed and who he was looking for, and tried to gauge whether the gang would be up for it? Crusher explained who the four of them were and the importance of them not running into Imperium spies or sympathizers. There was nodding and Ali agreed they could supply what Crusher was seeking. Crusher called the owner over and explained he wanted to book forty seats from two to six for the next two weeks, every day. Out of courtesy, Crusher explained to the owner that they wanted to use the eatery for the next two weeks as a recruiting office for the resistance. In addition, they would feed all the visitors and his new streetwise sentinels. The rats would work in the square and the surrounding streets.

The owner agreed. He wanted and was proud to help the resistance. He was happy for them to recruit in his eatery, and so they made the booking. Ali explained to the rest of the gang that they had all been hired by the resistance and would get paid and fed for the next two weeks. This was a very popular development as far as the street rats were concerned.

Ali revealed to Crusher that the local Imperium customs office experienced a mysterious fire eight days before. Many had watched it that chilly night. For the Imperium guards in the office, it had been a lot less chilly. Strangely, the Rim guards outside in the street reported *no witnesses, no suspects, fire possibly caused by garbage* in their official report. The coroner did unofficially note the strange, sneaky behavior of all the Imperium guards gathering for a secret meeting at three in the morning and barricading themselves inside their office. He chalked it up as a customer feedback review meeting. The Imperium customs office was most definitely closed until further notice. Some wit had put up a To Let board outside the office.

One of the first tasks Crusher gave the street rats was to spread news of their arrival and presence in the square. Crusher figured it made more sense for him to flush out any Imperium assets and bring them to the square. His ace in the hole was that the street rats could find the faces that didn't fit, and Crusher and the three other resistance soldiers could execute them. If doing so wasn't too obvious and wouldn't make too much mess. Crusher was sure the removal of these Imperium spies from this Rim world would be most welcome after what they had done to the Highlands.

The street rats left after dessert and spread out through the township. They spread the word about the recruiting office. The office would be in the eatery from two to six every afternoon for the next fourteen days. The folk of the township amplified their message in quiet, huddled conversations. The word spread throughout the township and, by dusk, every resident had heard it.

The next day, Ali's street rats and the four soldiers were on site in the square at eleven o'clock. Crusher had wanted to set up covert surveillance of the square and all the buildings. The street rats were excellent. Their disheveled appearance meant they could just melt into the background and go unnoticed. Crusher had given Ali eleven portable radio units. Ali distributed them among the gang and divided them into eleven groups of three. They would work together with one radio to report in and get any orders or updates.

The four soldiers were also in the square under cover. Their clothing hid the suppressed pistols they carried and large combat knives. It was two hours later when Jammer's voice came over the radio.

"Jammer. We have got one here. We are on Plexus, approaching the square."

"Melon here, we have a pair as well, approaching the square on Buckfast Street."

Crusher keyed the radio button in his pocket, "Okay, Melon, Jammer, follow but do not approach. We are coming to you both now. Describe the targets."

Crusher stayed in his seat outside the eatery like a tethered goat. "Mark and Beth. Head toward Melon at the Buckfast street entrance. Ant, you go to Jammer at the Plexus entrance. Ant, try to take him with stealth. Then Mark and Beth, take your two once Ant gives you the target down call," Crusher said.

"Roger last," Ant said.

Beth and Mark's voice came over the radio. "Roger that."

Ant walked in the building's shadow as he approached Plexus. There was Jammer, and the other two in his team were another five meters back on the left and right side of the street. Ant scanned the people in front of Jammer, and there, ten meters ahead, a man with a bald head matched the description. Ant thought for a second about the distance and angles before setting out. If he had this right, he would walk into the target just as his path crossed the target's path. As he walked, Ant slid his hand into the folds of his clothing and gripped the weapon's handle, leaving his hand in place, unseen. Just two meters now. As Ant drew closer still, the bald man was staring at the eatery where Crusher sat, oblivious to Ant's approach. At the last step, Ant stumbled on purpose, throwing his weight forward toward the bald man, his right arm coming up as if to hug the man. Just before they made contact, Ant's left arm whipped out, striking like a snake toward the bald man's throat. He timed the strike with precision. As Ant's body made contact, his right arm pulled the bald man toward him tight. His left arm drove forward, the tip of the knife passing through the neck's skin into the bald man's voice box. In a quarter of a second, the blade continued its passage through the bald man's larynx and cut in between his C5 and C6 vertebrae, slashing the spinal cord. As the bald man became a quadriplegic, Ant lifted him in a bear hug while pressing and lifting on his left knife arm. The bald man lifted from his feet and Ant drove him backward toward a pile of garbage at the side of Plexus Street. As he neared the pile, Jammer and his team shouted and ran up the street. All heads turned toward the youths. They also checked their valuables were still in their pockets, revealing their location. Ant pushed the bald man's body backward. The body disappeared into the pile of garbage. Ant's left arm snaked back into the folds of clothing and put the bloodied knife back in its scabbard. As Ant walked away, Jammer and the other two urchins ran past into the square, chasing each other and pushing pedestrians. The entire takedown had gone unseen. As Ant walked away, he clicked his radio button. "Ant clear."

That was Beth and Mark's go signal. They walked toward the two men Melon's street rats had fingered for them. The fact that there were two of them made this more complicated. They could execute the takedown, but it would, by necessity, be less covert. People would notice, they could not avoid that in the busy square. The important thing was that no innocents got caught in the middle.

As they drew nearer, Beth and Mark moved away from each other, putting two meters between them. They both drew their pistols and held them down flat against their legs, the stubby suppressors attached to the end of the barrel. They were one meter behind the two targets. Over the radio, Crusher's voice said, "Execute."

Beth and Mark both raised their guns and fired once into their target's back. As the targets fell to the ground, they both stepped toward their marks. As they passed them, they both fired again, putting a round in the target's head. It was a clean kill, if one with a lot of witnesses. There was some shoving and shouts to their right. A stocky man pushed through the pedestrians. He ran toward Beth and Mark. As he came, his gun rose. The man was about to fire, the gun now pointed at Beth.

Shit Beth thought.

The loud bang of an unsuppressed weapon sounded out.

The man's face disappeared. The hollow point round expanded and slowed as it passed into the man's skull. Its energy transferred into the shock wave it sent through the man's head. The bone fragments from his face bounced around inside his skull, blending his brain.

Beth looked around. She thought she was dead. Who had fired? A Rim guard stepped forward from behind Beth.

"Nothing to see, guard business, move it along. Go on now, nothing to see," the female guard shouted at the gawping crowd. The people shuffled away.

"That means you two as well. I think you have some business in the eatery. Go along now," Private Guard Emily Dickinson said.

"Thank you," Beth said.

"We will clean up the other two here as well, and the one your colleague left in the garbage pile. Good luck."

Beth and Mark walked back across the square to where Crusher was sitting. They had taken out all four members of the Imperium team's cell now. That should mean the township was clear of Imperium agents. The crowd was thicker outside the eatery. People were early and waiting to see someone or have a quick bite to eat inside first. Beth knew they were going to get a lot of names today. The floor show and the removal of three Imperium agents in the square. And the death of the fourth, with help from Private Emily Dickinson, would also help drive up the numbers. No one was distressed to hear about the death of the four enemy agents as the gossip swept around the square.

Ant was already sitting back at Crusher's table under the patio canopy.

"Good work, all of you. Nice to know we have the guards here on our side. I think we should open a bit earlier than planned. There are quite a few people waiting to talk to us already. The owner has us set up inside. He has even chalked up a sandwich board for us, with Resistance Recruiting Here! written on it. I said he could put it out front."

"Hey, Crusher, put the resistance logo on that board," Beth said.

"Great idea. I have some chalk here."

Crusher kneeled. First, he drew the larger right-facing crescent moon, then to the right, between the two points of the moon, he drew the smaller left-facing crescent moon. It matched the tattoo that Crusher had on the back of his left hand.

"That looks good. A picture is worth a thousand words. Now they can see who we are," Beth said.

The Resistance Logo

CHAPTER 84

**RIM – ROSS 128 – FIFE
A CARAVAN BY MOONLIGHT
T-ZERO +FIFTEEN DAYS
WE ARE STRONG**

A desert world lit by two moons overhead. A desert caravan of people moved toward a distant town and shipyard near the horizon. Bert nearly fell in his effort to catch Janice, the lady he was walking with, who had just stumbled and nearly collapsed. They were both tired and hungry.

The market trader, Mike the twat, came to help them both.

"Catch your breath, we can rest for two minutes. Take these."

Mike handed them both some fruit and water.

"Eat the fruit first. We have a long way to go. If we can find them, are you seeking the resistance as well?"

Bert and Janice both nodded weakly.

"Good! We will find them together. Once we have joined them, I have a sizable portion of ass-fucking special delivery for those Imperium morons and their fucking taxmen."

Mike smiled at their juice-covered faces. "Hey, we are the resistance." Mike said.

Bert and Janice both smiled back and then they and a few passersby all said as one, "And we are strong."

There were smiles all around the group and claps.

The three helped each other to their feet and carried on walking with the rest of the caravan, swigging some water as they walked with purpose. As part of the group now, as comrades seeking recruitment.

CHAPTER 85

**RIM – GROOMBRIDGE 34 – ANGUS
FALKIRK
THE JUNGLE BURNS
T-ZERO +TWENTY DAYS
384 MISSILES**

Angus was a jungle world. Many people had traveled to the town of Falkirk. They were getting onto transports departing for Kilbride. A large fire burned in the forest about thirteen kilometers away. The pair of Imperium frigates had arrived an hour ago and caused the large fire. They now hung with menace overhead in orbit.

For the last hour, the town had been very tense. The vast majority had never seen big frontline military ships, and here were two of them overhead. Clear to see with optics. Their purpose was not clear, nor was why they had fired at the jungle starting the fire. The ships were hostile Imperium ships, even if they were the third smallest class of warships. The ships had the people on edge.

People knew one Rim fleet was still missing, its location unknown. The other fleet was busy guarding Kilbride. The Rim systems did not have enough large warships to match the Imperium's numbers. Their technology was good, but they did not have the industrial base to match the Imperium. That said, manufacturing a ship would take both sides roughly the same time to produce. Which made the existing ships even more valuable and difficult to replace. The removal of any heavy ship was a significant win and weakened the enemy's ability to assault planets.

This was foremost in Commander Anderson's mind as he sat and thought. He knew the planet was on its own. No help was coming soon. Dealing with the two frigates overhead would be down to them. While they had no big ships fitted with energy or slug cannons, he had a fighter wing of twenty-four dual-role aerospace fighters. They were here on the planet, hidden in underground hangars built into the mountains that poked up from the thick jungle. Another wing of twenty-four fighters was up at the moon base, with hangars dug into the crater walls. Forty-eight fighters were in the good-news column. The lack of any energy or slug cannons was not good. Nor was the fighter's main rotary cannon. This was a smaller version of the big REC cannons found on the bigger ships. Not the weapon of choice to take up against an Imperium warship. There was one possibility that may show some scope, Anderson considered. The fighters could also carry up to eight missiles. Two mounted under each wing and another two mounted on top of each wing. That meant the forty-eight fighters could bring 384 missiles to bear against the two frigates. That was a positive, especially if they could up the yield somehow, which was unlikely but possible.

The big positive they had was that the Imperium had unwittingly approached Angus rather than a lesser-defended Rim world. Besides its thick jungle and predatory animals, Angus was the secret home to the Rim's main advanced combat-flight-training school, the Aerial Tactics School. Tiger and all the other Lancers were graduates from Angus's fighter school, known as Fighter Land. That was why this otherwise innocuous planet had not only such a large ground-based fighter wing but also a moon base with a second wing. To even be considered for entry to Fighter Land, you already had to be an Eagles qualified pilot with twelve months service, and then you had to win your spot with your flight skills. Here, they trained the pilots to become aces, not newbies to become pilots.

Ships and skilled pilots they had. What they lacked were heavy ships of their own that they would normally attack with. This made engaging the two enemy frigates more problematic.

Conventional wisdom was that fighter pilots would work in flights of three ships. The Lancers were very unusual in that they flew as four ships. Normally, either one or two flights of ships would work in concert with a heavy ship when engaging large enemy ships.

Typically, the fighter flights would function in a picket role, engaging inbound enemy missiles. While the big ship's energy and slug cannons would fight it out with the enemy's big ships at range, or with the big ship's larger missiles which they launched at the enemy ships.

In a normal engagement, the fighters would carry two or maybe four maximum, light air-to-air missiles. That gave the two flights working together up to twenty-four missiles to engage enemy inbound missiles and enemy fighters.

The idea was to pursue a strategy of speed and agility, both with the fighters and the air-to-air ordinance they would use to engage the larger inbound ship-to-ship missiles. The fighters would operate in small flight groups as a defense shield for the heavy ships. The bigger ships would carry the offensive against the enemy.

Fighters would normally operate in the zone between fifty and one hundred and fifty kilometers from the enemy ships. This put them outside the range of the enemy REC cannons but inside the maximum range of the big ship-to-ship missiles. In this zone, they would also tangle with the enemy fighters doing the same job as themselves.

The REC cannon's conventional job was to be the last line of defense to take out inbound missiles that got past the fighter screen. Both sets of fighters would avoid getting into the range of the opposing big ship's REC cannons. And why would they ever get that close? Their light air-to-air missiles were not powerful enough to damage the big armored ships. They were for taking out missiles and engaging enemy fighters trying to shoot down their own outbound missiles. The core idea was to protect their own capital ships.

Fighters attacking without heavy support would need a whole new chapter writing for the *Combat Tactics Manual* they taught at the school.

Anderson thought. The fundamental problem is that there are two of them we must grapple with at the same time. If we could take them one after the other, things would be a lot more straightforward.

Anderson contemplated. He had the germ of an idea. He needed to get the enemy to split their assets. To keep one frigate here over the planet and send the other toward the moon or the asteroid belt.

Then, when that frigate was on its way at jump, he would commit all eight flights, his entire wing of twenty-four fighters. From their base hidden in the mountains, they would all take off and attack the frigate over the planet.

After, he could launch a coordinated strike at the second frigate with the remaining fighters from the wing of twenty-four, augmented by the twenty-four fighters based on the moon. His trainees were experienced combat pilots with long successful careers. They would adapt to the new tactics.

There would be no opposing fighters to tangle with from the enemy frigates. The frigate class was too small to carry fighters. There would also be no inbound missiles to defend against. They would not be restricted to the lighter air-to-air missiles in pursuit of agility. Their task here was to directly attack the enemy's big armored ship.

Anderson thought about the heavier air-to-ground missiles he had in his base's stores. The specific missiles he was thinking of were equipped with a much larger and heavier two hundred kilo warhead. In a fighter bomber role raid on a static ground side target, the fighters could carry up to eight of the larger heavier missiles, over and under the wings, when working in low-g such as on the moon or in low orbit. Or four missiles under the wings in high-g, such as on the planet. They could sacrifice agility to carry the added mass of munitions.

If they could do that, the sheer weight of numbers might save the day. If the entire ground-based wing used all one hundred and ninety-two of their missiles against a single frigate. Would the frigate's REC cannons be able to destroy that many inbound missiles?

Probably not, Anderson thought. It was a radical tactic, and certainly not conventional.

Then they could meet up with the second fighter wing, and they would still have all their rotary cannon rounds. They could get in close and strafe the second frigate, focusing on the frigate's REC cannons with their twenty-four rotary fighter cannons and twenty thousand rounds of twenty-millimeter. Four hundred and eighty thousand rounds, depending on how many survivors there were from the first engagement. The second wing could focus their one hundred and ninety-two missiles at the second frigate.

Anderson was feeling a lot more optimistic. He just had to split the two frigates up. That part was essential. It all depended on splitting them up.

He would get one of the stealthish experimental fighters being developed up on the moon base to fly outward from the star toward the edge of the solar system. The stealthish fighters were not true stealth, but they were very difficult to spot, thanks to their electromagnetic-absorbing coatings. Once at three lunar distances, the fighter should be lost in the stellar background. The stealthish fighter's job was to broadcast a high-power radio message.

They would maneuver the fighter so that, from a line-of-sight perspective, the radio message would appear to have come from the asteroid belt. The belt was only ten degrees of arc off axis from the moon. He was certain the comms officer on the frigate would assume the signal would have originated from the asteroid belt behind the invisible fighter.

The message would be a big fat carrot, one the little frigate could handle. The radio message would claim to come from General Abbot's missing flagship destroyer. The sole survivor, crashed on one of the large asteroids, it was now heavily damaged and out of ammunition, with energy cannon capacitors fried. This Abbot had the mysterious Merlin aboard and needed help and rescue. Abbot estimated they would lose life support within the next hour, as the power was failing.

They would also leak an intelligence signal from the planet. The signal would claim to have identified a senior high-ranking resistance meeting, which was taking place in a remote location. Ground forces would mark the target with laser designators in forty minutes for orbital bombardment from the frigates.

This would give the Imperium a dilemma, Anderson reasoned. If they waited forty minutes to strike at the fictitious meeting, and then headed to the asteroid belt, then they would not get to the belt before the prized-but-fictitious flagship belonging to Abbot lost its life support. And with it, General Abbot's death, the man who had publicly spanked the Imperium twice above the Highlands. The Imperium would lose their prize and public execution.

But if they tried to send both frigates to get Abbot, then they would lose the opportunity to strike against the senior resistance leaders at this fictitious meeting somewhere in the jungle.

Only one solution could secure both targets. One frigate would have to stay at the planet while the other frigate left to capture Abbot from his false, downed ship in the belt.

Anderson would send his instructions to the moon using the encrypted omnidirectional radio antenna so as not to reveal the destination of the message. They would send it at the agreed frequency of 160.4 GHz. This would place the signal in the cosmic microwave background (CMB). The CMB was the electromagnetic noise that still echoed in the universe in every direction, left over from the big bang at the beginning of time. A receiver dish was on the moon, focused on the planet's mountains and tuned to this frequency. From its perspective, the planet would flicker in the CMB radiation. The signal would get to the moon unnoticed. It carried the plan and ordered the dispatch of the stealthish fighter out to three times lunar distance in line of sight of the asteroid belt.

It would take the stealthish fighter forty-five minutes to get into position with its engines running in normal space. In that time, Anderson needed to get the leaders of both air wings up to speed. Once they attacked the frigate in orbit, the need for operational security would be gone.

Anderson's first call was to the head of the mountain and moon hangars. He ordered Jamie to load all forty-eight fighters with live fire, rather than with training missiles, and with a full-load spread of all eight missiles. Next, he placed a call to the senior pilot and chief instructor. Anderson laid out his plan.

"Cunning. I will brief the pilot leaders right now on how we will structure the attack. We will have a fifteen-minute window once the frigate has jumped away to the belt before they can get back here," the chief flight instructor, call sign Hunter, said.

"We send our signal from the ground about the resistance meeting in forty minutes. The stealthish ship will send its transmission in forty-five minutes. That is when you need everyone ready to go. I expect the frigate will jump away within five minutes. Your pilots go as soon as the second frigate jumps. If it doesn't jump, we stand down and rethink what we are going to do. The start of your fifteen-minute window is as soon as you get out of atmosphere," Anderson said.

In the mountain hangars and those on the moon, engineers loaded the requested missiles. As they would use them in a low-gravity, low-orbit environment, the missiles were not limited to only falling away from under the wings; they could also get pushed up from the upper surface. This had the effect of doubling the space for ordinance to be mounted, allowing all eight missiles to be used.

CHAPTER 86

**RIM – GROOMBRIDGE 34 – ANGUS
MOUNTAIN BASE
MOMENTS LATER
T-ZERO +TWENTY DAYS
NEGATIVE, FRIGATES OVERHEAD**

Juggler, also known as Captain John Wright, was about to be briefed by the squadron commander Major Smith, who went by his call sign Steel. He was awarded the moniker for his legendary flexibility and adapting regulations to fit the circumstances. Not!

They ran the entire school as if it were a live-combat deployment at their squadron base or deployed on ship.

Juggler was the flight lead for flight 1A. He was so named because of his multitasking skills. His counterpart, named Pinto because of his love of beans, led flight 2A.

Their counterparts, who were currently off flight duty for classroom exercises and rack time, were Mango as flight lead for 1B and Fish, who was lead for flight 2B. Plus Fitty in flight 1C and Bear in flight 2C. They triplicated all positions in the Eagles.

They represented half the eighty-seventh squadron's total fighters. Flights three and four, and the Alpha, Bravo, and Charlie teams were still on active duty with the squadron. Each fighter belonged to a flight and would be assigned an Alpha, Beta, and Charlie team. The teams did not denote a difference in ability or skill in the flight or ground crew. The teams existed solely to ensure that they kept the fighter in service twenty-four hours a day and did not need downtime due to pilot or ground-crew fatigue.

The teams also supplied cover for each other in the event of sickness, injury, and death, and during times of R&R leave.

The aim was to keep the principal asset, the fighter, always available. It was not the pilot who was at the center of the universe; it was the fighter. Everyone, whether in flight or ground teams, existed to keep the fighter flying. The machine was the star of the show.

Fighter Land ran three sets of classes in parallel for the Alpha, Beta, and Charlie teams sharing the duties and their physical fighters, just like they would when working in the real world for the Eagles. Fighter Land was a 24-7 operation, as were its bases and fighters. The three teams within each flight worked in shift rotas, and were ready to respond to both scheduled and surprise combat exercises and classroom time.

Juggler and Pinto had been sent from the eighty-seventh fighter squadron called the Magos. The eighty-seventh squadron consisted of 4 flights, 12 fighters, and 252 personnel. Two of those flights represented their squadron here, and as a reward for group service excellence, they secured these training slots for their flight and ground teams made up of the Alpha, Bravo, and Charlie sub-teams.

Flight 1A consisted of Juggler, Peanut (who was just too smooth), and Hammer, who treated everything like a nail. Flight 2A was Pinto, Indy (because he insisted on the latest gadgets and phones), and Buck, who had fallen on her bum repeatedly ice-skating but kept getting up again. Steel was not only responsible for the pilots, but also for the ground crew.

They had all been here for twelve weeks now and would graduate next week.

They were here with two flights from three other squadrons. The seventy-fourth—the Contestants, the eighty-second—the Konyaks, and the fifty-sixth—the Tombstones. The eight flights had secured places on this thirteen-week course at Fighter Land. This was where the best came to be trained and pushed by the veteran elite.

Juggler had a pretty good idea what was going on. Chief Armorer Gilbert had told Juggler that he and the other chief armorers had been instructed to load eight GP-HE-AGM-MK11 missiles onto each fighter. These were the General Purpose—High Explosive—Air-to-Ground—Eleventh Generation missiles. They normally used them for attacking static ground targets. The missiles had a two hundred kilo high-explosive warhead, which was a penetrating blast-fragmentation type. The missiles had a range of one hundred and fifty kilometers.

Juggler only had to look up with optics to see the two frigates in orbit over the planet. They would be the target. They were the only targets in the system. Loading all eight missiles was moderately unusual, especially as they were loading the heavier air-to-ground missiles. Furthermore, they had no heavy ship support that fighters would normally fly and attack in concert with. They just had fighters and would send them up against two Imperium frigates. That was somewhere between unusual and insane. Especially as they were not flying with their smaller, lighter air-to-air missiles. This whole thing reeked of one of Hunter's, or maybe even Commander Anderson's, plans.

Steel returned to his office from his briefing with Hunter. He walked past Juggler and Pinto, who were waiting for him, and said, "In my office now, gentleman."

The three of them entered Steel's assigned office. Pinto closed the office door. Steel sat behind his desk and gestured for the men to both sit. Other flight leads' briefings began in the offices of the three other squadron commanders.

"You have probably figured much of this out yourselves with the training you have had," Steel said.

"The frigates, sir, it seems a little suicidal, considering," Juggler said.

"Juggler, you should know by now. I don't give a fuck what you think. Hunter is smarter than both of us. You are wrong, it is not frigates, which I agree would be suicidal. It will be a frigate, which will not be suicidal. Commander Anderson is going to send the second frigate to the asteroid belt and persuade the other to stay here with us. It is mad enough to work. We are going to destroy the frigate here by the planet. Then form up with the wing from the moon. And we are going to destroy the second frigate when it gets back here, all confused and flustered."

Steel stared deep into his flight lead's eyes. The flight lead stared back at Steel. Juggler and Pinto both said, "Outstanding, sir."

While the briefing was going on, Chief Armorer Gilbert was overseeing the loading of missiles onto Juggler's fighter while Chief Mechanical Bell was running down their mechanical checklist and overseeing the fighter's fueling.

The stealthish prototype was currently in flight, away from the moon base en route to its target location, which would put the ship line of sight to the asteroid belt at three lunar distances.

The resistance officer, embedded covertly in an Imperium cell in the capital, would in ten minutes send his radio message up to the frigates. The message would give the frigates a heads-up on a future fire mission against the rebels. They would mark the target for the frigates to strike from orbit. The fire mission was sold as taking out several senior resistance leaders. The bait would keep one frigate here above the planet.

In fifteen minutes, the stealthish ship would send its fake Abbot distress call to Angus, trusting the comms officers on the two Imperium frigates would intercept it. This was their bait to lure the other frigate out to the belt.

Juggler and Pinto left Steel's office.

"It's bold," Pinto said.

"Sure is. Good hunting," Juggler said.

"Good hunting," Pinto replied.

They separated and went to brief the two other pilots on their flight. They would board their fighters in ten minutes and wait in the cockpit for the go signal. They did not expect it to take over ten minutes of waiting.

Gilbert had finished arming the fighters. Safety tags hung from the missiles and engines, waiting to be pulled off before takeoff. The fighter's computer was talking to the eight weapons and displayed them all green.

They were all ready to go, the pilots all aboard their twenty-four fighters. The pilots tightened their straps and donned their airtight helmets. Then they twisted the locking collar, binding the helmet with its oxygen supply hose to their advanced SAS mark V flight suits. The helmets connected wirelessly to the ship's computer.

The ground crew had repositioned all the fighters so they could take off in their lanes and flight groups of three. Four columns of two flights for each squadron group. They positioned them before the four launch tunnels dug through the mountain, which emerged around thirty meters above the tree canopy.

The 1MC pips rang out across the hangar. "Attention. We have just received the stealthish's message. We are detecting increased communication traffic between the two frigates. Start your aircraft up."

Juggler gave the ground crew the hand signal, and the mechanics started pulling the safety tags from the engines. The armorers removed the tags from the missiles. A mechanical engineer gave Juggler a signal, left arm raised level with his shoulder with a single finger pointed. His right arm rotated clockwise over his head, showing one finger.

Juggler pushed engine one's start button. The rocket turbine wound up with the power drawn from the external fed power coming down the umbilical. The power levels rose to normal and stabilized.

Juggler gave the mechanical engineer the thumbs-up. The mechanical engineer dipped his arms then raised his left arm again level with his shoulder, pointing with two fingers. He rotated his right arm clockwise above his head, showing two fingers. Juggler pressed engine two's start button. It whirred into life.

The other two mechanical engineers detached the two umbilicals from the engines. They pulled the cables back and retreated into their safety zone.

Over the ship-to-ship flight channel, Juggler received two messages.

"Peanut to Juggler, good here."

"Hammer to Juggler. Good here as well."

"Juggler to control, Mago flight one, powered and standing ready."

The red warning lights came on across the hangar and the white lights all went off. The entire hangar was now bathed in the red light for battle stations.

On both the hangar's 1MC and over the squadron radio channel. "Attention. This is control to all flight leads. The second frigate just jumped away. You're all cleared for combat. Good hunting."

The base's four boatswain mates stepped forward in their yellow jackets with yellow lights on their jacket and helmets. On military ships, they were known as the shooters and would control the launch.

Juggler gave the shooter a thumbs-up, put his head back on the headrest, and grabbed both the handrails at the top of his cockpit.

The shooter checked with all the other ground crew. He touched the deck and extended his left arm down the launch tunnel, giving a thumbs-up while crouching. The catapult officer fired the catapult.

They had attached the catapult shoe to the nose gear. It accelerated Juggler and his ship down the short tunnel runway. The catapult had the fighter traveling at 265 kilometers per hour in under two seconds, accelerating the fighter at 3.8 times standard gravity. Juggler put his hand on the fighter's stick and guided her up into the air. In a moment, he was out of the launch tunnel, now flying.

The shooter repeated this with Peanut and Hammer. Sixty seconds later they were both forming up on Juggler's wing. They would circle for another minute in the designated safety area, waiting for Pinto's flight to join them. Then Juggler pulled back on the stick, nosing up to a seventy-degree climb. He pushed the throttles to the stops and engaged the afterburner. The three fighters jumped forward, reaching upward.

Twenty-one seconds later, the fighters broke the sound barrier, and twenty-four deafening sonic booms rang out over the jungle in quick succession. The fighters continued powering upward. At fifty-two seconds and still accelerating, they exceeded an altitude of eight kilometers. The sonic boom was not a one-off event but a shock wave that moved with the ship as it moved away from the observer. A continual ruckus that trailed behind the fighters. The accelerating fighters approached one thousand kilometers; they were now passed the territory of low orbit, which ran between one hundred and sixty and one thousand kilometers. Still, the fighters powered upward. Toward the frigate's orbit at just under three thousand kilometers altitude.

Juggler had the lone frigate on his scope now. Passive sensors observed the frigate's position and vector. They would hold off on using their active radars until they got much closer. They did not want to tip off the frigate. There was a chance they could sneak unnoticed very close to the frigate. The frigate was not on the lookout for any fighters. As far as the frigate was concerned, the planet was devoid of any threat. The fighters had low radar reflectivity, and the frigate's radar was not currently transmitting. The individual fighters were flying to their planned waypoint positions. The waypoints had been programmed into the navigation computer and matched to their synchronized clocks.

The Imperium REC cannons' maximum effective range was fifty kilometers. The missiles' maximum range was one hundred and fifty kilometers. The plan was not subtle. They were going to approach the frigate from aft, at a downward angle of forty-five degrees. This would have the benefit that it would block the third REC cannon from getting a line of sight on the approaching fighters. The eight flights of three ships in the wing would separate to a distance of five kilometers. This would reduce the risk of missiles flying into the remains of other detonated missiles. Also, the two REC cannons could only target two flight's missiles out of the eight inbound flights.

They had programmed the navigation computer to change course after each firing waypoint. This would guide them five degrees off arc away from where they were when they launched the last pair of missiles. Six inbound missiles from each of the eight flights. Two seconds later, the fighters would launch their next pair of missiles and reposition again. This would repeat until they had launched four times, loosing all eight missiles.

The missile's flight time to target would be between three and four seconds, depending on the range at launch. Over the six seconds in which they would launch the missiles, in four batches of forty-eight missiles, in eight discrete groups that came in on eight different vectors in groups of six missiles. A REC cannon normally needed one second to target and fire at an individual missile. The two REC cannons would have thirty-two separate groups of missiles to aim at, with a flight time of three to four seconds, and an aiming counter battery time of one second. Only six seconds between the first and the last missile being launched from the fighters. On paper, this should be a slam dunk. If the frigate got destroyed, the third or fourth missile launches could always get aborted.

The frigate did not detect the fighters' approach as they flew in the dark without radio traffic, navigation lights, or active radar.

As Juggler approached their first firing waypoint, there was no need to talk to his other two pilots. The computer temporarily blocked his radio from transmitting. The navigation computers would guide Peanut and Hammer as well. The firing point was only a few seconds away. Once they had fired, the restriction on radio silence would drop away, but they would be too busy to chat.

Juggler watched his navigation console. His missiles would fly in active radar-guided mode. The frigate was unlikely to have any high-speed antiradiation missiles (HARM)-type defenses that would hunt down active radars, although they did normally carry four of the large ship-to-ship missiles.

"Fox-3, Fox-3, evading," Juggler said out of habit and training despite the time pressures.

The two air-to-ground missiles streaked away toward the frigate. Juggler could see the flickering from the two REC cannons on the frigate, as he repositioned his fighter on the new vector to the next waypoint. The REC cannons were spitting thirty-millimeter cannon rounds back at the incoming missiles.

Three of the wing's first missiles exploded, shredded by the frigate's REC rounds.

Pinto's fighter sounded a warbling alarm in his helmet.

"Buck, Indy, move away. REC scanning."

The REC cannon's target acquisition radar was looking for threats, trying to fill its target buffer. The gun was hungry for more targets. The cannon's computer would manage target selection and pass the items from the buffer to the fire controller in their lucky moment.

Pinto's voice was urgent now. "Stay on mission. Oh, shit."

The alarm in Pinto's ears was continuous now.

"It's got me."

Buck and Indy knew this meant the REC cannon now had a radar lock on Pinto's fighter. It would only be a second before the cannon fired. The big gun would reposition now.

"Tumble, tumble," Buck said calmly into her mic.

Pinto's fighter executed random vector changes as he fought to break the lock and force the cannon to continually reposition its targeting radar to keep the lock. *That won't do it* Pinto thought.

"Guns, guns," Buck said over her radio.

Buck straightened her fighter, aiming at the REC cannon, and fired at the large six-barrel cannon, with her smaller but faster three-barrel rotary cannon with its twenty-millimeter cannon shells.

She pressed the trigger and held it down. The rotary cannon screamed shrilly; the cannon's vibrations shook through her bum. Her seat was in the cockpit's soundless vacuum.

She knew her rounds would be slightly faster than the bigger thirty-millimeter rounds the enemy cannon would fire at them. But her rounds lacked the same kinetic punch of the larger rounds. A fraction of a second later, fire emerged from Indy's fighter as well, then Hammer joined them an instant later, firing into the REC cannon's position. The three coordinating fighters unleashed round after round.

The powerful REC cannon replied, firing at Pinto's fighter. The large rounds flew through space toward Pinto. Pinto tried frantically to be somewhere unexpected, but the fire control computer in the cannon also tried to predict his future moves.

The twenty-millimeter rounds Buck had sent with love started to impact the REC cannon's gun emplacement, quickly joined by rounds from Indy and Hammer. There were minor explosions where the rounds impacted.

The REC cannon stopped firing at Pinto and tracked toward Buck. The tone in her helmet was continuous now. The gun had her. *One more second* Buck thought.

She was still pouring fire down onto the REC cannon, as were Indy and Hammer. She got a little lucky when one of her cannon rounds hit the hydraulics, feeding the cannon's positioning drive pistons. High-pressure oil sprayed everywhere. The REC cannon's movements slowed and then stopped.

Buck's navigation system then started beeping at her in a different tone. Instinctively, she flipped the fire control switch back to missiles from guns.

Jugglers' navigation system was telling him to fire again. It was just two seconds after the first pair of launches.

"Fox-3, Fox-3," Juggler said, and another two missiles leaped forth.

Pinto could see the stream of tracer fire sweeping toward him. He ceased his mad spinning and targeted the frigate, saying "Fox-3, Fox-3."

The stream of in-flight cannon fire continued its approach to him. Pinto recognized it was inevitable now. The other four fighters in the two flights from the eighty-seventh all fired their two missiles. The Magos twelve missiles streaked toward the frigate.

"Argh!" Pinto cried out. The blizzard of thirty-millimeter REC rounds that were in flight streaked past his fighter. One round crashed into Pinto's tail, tearing off half of his vertical stabilizer.

Another pair of missiles exploded, felled by the other REC cannon's fire. The two RECs had taken five missiles so far. One REC cannon was now out of action.

"Thanks, Buck, I am here," Pinto said. "Think I've lost most of my tail."

And the three to four seconds' flight time was up. The remaining forty-three missiles from the first salvo slammed into the frigate's hull. Half of them targeted the frigate's engineering section. The other half targeted the frigate's missile magazine, which was under the bridge. Twenty-one missiles pummeled the plate armor protecting the bridge into submission, until it failed. The next missile detonated its two hundred kilos of explosive inside the bridge. There was no bridge left, no people, no displays, just an open sore into the vacuum of space. The remaining missiles of the group of twenty-one continued to arrive. The other twenty-two missiles tearing chunks out of the ship's stern had stilled all but one of the ship's drives.

A missile entered through what used to be the bridge and its blast penetrated deep into the ship's magazine. The front half of the frigate ceased to exist in the powerful secondary explosive release as all the frigate's stored missiles detonated in the magazine.

Juggler stared on in amazement. More missiles continued to hit the large chunks of the ship's shattered front half. The remaining missiles continued to strike the aft of the ship and then they passed through into the tender heart of the engineering section. The next missile hit the fusion reactor, and it let loose with an unfocused seven-kiloton nuclear blast. The sim-glass viewscreens in the fighters flared white before the electronics limited the light transmitted inside the cockpit to the pilots. The closest, Buck's fighter, was at thirty-seven kilometers when the seven-kiloton nuclear blast occurred. The gamma ray radiation burst through the vacuum of space, dropping in intensity as the sphere expanded in line with the free-space path loss formula. At thirty-seven kilometers, Buck would not receive a medically concerning amount of the dangerous ionizing gamma radiation.

Another forty-eight missiles were still on their way, one second out. There were increasingly small lumps of wreckage left for them to target. Their active radar warheads sought the lumps of wreckage out. Each delivered another two hundred kilos of high explosives to the broken twisted lumps of wreckage that used to be part of a ship.

They had lost five missiles to enemy REC fire. All twenty-four ships in the wing were still alive, although Pinto would need a new tail stabilizer. All three hundred and twenty crew members from the frigate were dead.

Hammer's voice came over the flight's radio channel. "Hey Peanut, was that a kill? We might have to check the gun camera footage."

"Affirmative, Hammer, that frigate will not be going to the ship dock for repairs. It will take a while to find all the bits."

"This is Steel, eighty-seventh cut out the chat. Form up, we are going to rendezvous with the wing from the moon base."

Seven minutes later, they formed up with the twenty-four fresh fighters from the moon-base wing. They all idled their engines and went dark again. Their target window for the first frigate closed in three minutes. Then they would await the second frigate's return in the coming few minutes. The forty-eight fighters would charge the ship wherever it emerged. They had two hundred and forty missiles now between them, with the ammo saved from the first raid. They were going to swarm the second frigate. All the pilots' confidence was high now. Hunter's plan to use overwhelming numbers of heavy air-to-ground missiles had been genius. The lone frigate did not intimidate any of them anymore. These dogs were all on the hunt now.

The second frigate was about to have a terrible day. It was returning from their misdirection to the belt. The first frigate was not answering any of their radio hails. The ship came out of its FTL jump and started looking for the errant frigate. The navigation officer could not find it. He found residual evidence of a small nuclear detonation but no ship. What he also found were forty-eight fighters charging toward them at max burn. Then the fighters released a blizzard of missiles at the frigate, all two hundred and forty missiles in a single launch. The bridge crew panicked and hit the wrong button. Rather than starting a maximum power burn from the fusion engine, they hit the button to send the fusion core into emergency shut down. Something that is important to be able to do when flying around powered by the atom. It is not a good thing to lose all power when there are two hundred and forty missiles flying toward you, intent on delivering your death. It didn't last long. The fighters' gun cameras would all record the annihilation of the second frigate. It was kept for posterity and rebroadcast by the resistance intelligence services, and it continued recording until there was nothing more than small bits of wreckage. The remaining thirty-something missiles prowled around menacingly. They were looking for something unfriendly they could blow up into smaller lumps.

The forty-eight ships all returned to their respective hangars. They were greeted with much fanfare for their return after killing both the Imperium frigates and clearing the planet's skies. The ground crew all cheered their returning pilots and their precious fighters. They were all free of their missiles now. Pinto's tail was wrecked; it was a miracle he hadn't been killed, only hit by a single round from the REC cannon. Pinto was very glad to be back on the ground. Pinto hugged Buck. She had saved his life when she started firing at the REC cannon. Hammer and Indy fist-bumped and slapped each other on the back. Peanut gave Juggler a huge grin and a salute. The eighty-seventh thirty-six ground crew stood around their two flights of pilots jumping up and down, celebrating. Steel looked on, an unlit large fat cigar in his mouth, clapping. He was very proud of them all. Against the odds, the forty-eight fighters, isolated from their normal heavy support, which doctrine dictated they needed and should fly with. They had done it and taken on two Imperium frigates alone and smashed them to pieces.

The resistance was outnumbered and only had a single fleet now, bogged down at Kilbride. The challenge facing the Rim systems and resistance was huge. But right there and then in that mountain hangar, it felt to everyone that maybe, just maybe, they could pull it off.

CHAPTER 87

THE PERSEUS ARM – G2V-529853
NEW WORLD ONE – SURFACE LZ1
COMMAND TENT – MEETING SENIOR STAFF
T-ZERO +THIRTY DAYS
THE HUDDLE

It was now thirty days since they had all landed on New World One as some genius had christened it. They all still found it difficult to comprehend. They were just under one thousand three hundred light-years from the colony star systems, which were now just two hours away.

Merlin had bought them the exit they needed to escape with everyone they had rescued from the Highlands. They had disappeared a minute before the Imperium ships, which Merlin had been watching for, arrived.

The Imperium searched the Procyon B system and found it devoid of all resistance ships. Bar the scattered atoms of the three damaged destroyers that had initiated suicide runs and taken out six of the first Imperium's destroyer attack fleet with them. Their sacrifice helped to keep the rest of the resistance fleet and the evacuees from the Highlands safe.

The three ships had succeeded, and this had helped enable Abbot's makeshift rescue mission to secure a twelve-hour window to help the Highlands. They had evacuated, beyond all expectations, 482,000 survivors from the surface. And a further thirty-five thousand evacuees, who they had helped to get off the Highlands initially back to Kilbride. They had lifted and vanished 482,000 survivors to the Perseus arm of the Milky Way. A total of 517,000 people saved from the Highlands. Sadly, 299,500,000 were dead. A tragedy. The surviving hens had fled the hen coop and left all the foxes scratching their heads, wondering what hens looked like.

Merlin's magic had opened a very theoretical wormhole that Merlin had made reality. Even though as far as science figured, no one had any idea how wormholes worked, let alone how to navigate one, target the egress point, or create one on demand. It had delivered them all here, far away in a mind-bendingly brief passage of time.

They had unloaded the ships down to the planet. When they had first filled the ships, many were only just able to stand. Staying on the ship for anything more than a handful of hours was not practical. Many of the survivors the medics had stabilized were still in need of serious medical attention. Not everyone would have made it to Kilbride alive.

It was nothing short of multiple miracles, which had enabled them to airlift just shy of thirty-two percent of the estimated survivor count. By the time they left at T-ZERO +11.5 hours, they had airlifted everyone off-world that they knew the whereabouts of. They had left no one they knew of behind to die on their own in the dark.

The successful return of Abbot's fleet from Kilbride with all the medical staff and supplies was the second miracle of the day.

The first miracle had been the brave souls who had gone down first alone with no backup. People from the Ball Breaker Task Force and the other volunteers from Abbot's destroyers.

The third miracle had been the two bulk carrier ships from two Core, now ex-Imperium worlds, Argyll and Bute, around Gliese 784 and Gliese 555. The bulk carriers, *Imp* and *Green Bird*, had both arrived at T-ZERO +9.5 hours. Their home worlds had seceded from the Imperium and pledged themselves to the Rim systems. That had taken one hour and ten minutes from the time of the attack on the Highlands for the story to reach them.

It took twenty-nine minutes for the joint statement to be issued by each planet's government. They both condemned the actions of the Imperium and the destruction of one of the precious colony worlds. They turned their backs on the Imperium and announced immediate fealty to the defense of the Rim systems. What no one yet knew outside of those two governments, both leaders had also retasked their nearest two bulk cargo ships. The ships had been returning in convoy from their trade route to head at maximum flank speed (244 C) to the Highlands. Though the ships carried no aid, and had no personnel of note. The *Imp* and *Green Bird* had been invaluable in delivering this miracle.

The only thing that the bulk carriers had lots of, was space and their twenty drop lifter ships. They were agricultural cargo freighters. There were no seats, no toilets. It was beyond basic. The bulk carriers had enabled them to move close to half a million extra souls off the Highlands with space to spare. These were the 482, 000 people who had been tearing Greg and the other leaders' souls apart because there had seemed no other option other than to abandon them to certain death. The unexpected bulk carriers' arrival had changed everything.

Abbot had brought medical supplies and staff with him back from Kilbride. This had meant they had enough drugs and skilled medical staff to supply both primary and secondary care to the injured evacuees.

For the last thirty days, they had been waiting while the patients recovered and mourned. Then they tried to figure out what their options were and what the plan should be.

Merlin confirmed he could repeat the wormhole trick if needed and take all the ships back to the colonies again. If that was what they decided. Someone had made the schoolboy error of asking Merlin to explain to him how the physics worked. It had taken three minutes before this person had run away, looking terrified by Merlin. This was not because Merlin had berated him. He had understood Merlin's explanation. Now he understood what Merlin's explanation implied, and it meant that a lot of the accepted doctrine for the last eight hundred years was, in fact, very wrong. It didn't help that Merlin was also wrong about some of his untested theories that Merlin proclaimed as the new truth.

The "we need to go back" camp raised several valid points over those of the "we can bootstrap a new world with what we have got" camp:

- Our people are still back there at the hands of the Imperium.
- We have half the resistance fleet resources. They need to go back and fight and defend the Rim systems, even if you don't.
- There would be people under the Imperium's yoke in the Core worlds who would also want to break free. To come and join them here, far outside of the Imperium's reach.
- Our people are still back there at the hands of the Imperium.
- We have half the resistance fleet resources. They need to go back and fight and defend the Rim systems, even if you don't.
- There would be people under the Imperium's yoke in the Core worlds who would also want to break free. To come and join them here, far outside of the Imperium's reach.

These were all solid logical reasons, but the one that swung it for the group was obligation.

The people of the Rim systems and their two newly pledged systems, Argyll and Bute. They had all helped them in their twelve hours of need. It was not for them to hide out and keep their heads down while leaving everyone else behind to face the music without them. These people's bravery had gifted them their lives beyond the Highlands. While they had asked for no fee, they felt compelled to help save the Rim systems in return. And to save people wanting to escape or fight back against the Imperium, stuck on those Core worlds still loyal to the Imperium's evil.

Merlin added they could always go back and sort things out and get people and return here. But they would need many trips to transport that many people, and more worlds to move them to.

Merlin closed his statement by saying now that he had discovered how to pull the rabbit out of the hat. You don't need Merlin or the physics engine to explain how the rabbit got into the hat in the first place. Once you knew how to do the trick, it was easy to understand and repeat it.

This highlighted two further issues. Merlin could adapt the computers in their ships to effect wormhole jumps. This would give them much greater flexibility than needing Merlin to do it for them. It extended their ability in a sensible and desirable way. Yet, it raised the danger of ships being captured and their computers being reverse engineered by Imperium scientists.

A risk of the wormhole capability passing into Imperium hands was present. Merlin could not prevent the same technology from working for the Imperium just because they were, without a doubt, "evil." Thus, it was important that they take steps to ensure any ships fitted with the technology could not be captured.

There were both risks and time implications for the mass evacuation of people from the colony systems. If they wanted to keep the Imperium locked in isolation while the resistance could now travel great distances. These risks would require, in practical terms, some serious thought and planning.

It was clear they would only find any conflict resolution with the Imperium back on the colony worlds. If they abandoned the resistance and did not go back to help, they would also abandon all of humanity. Both within themselves and the people, back on the colony worlds.

They decided they had to take everyone back with them. There was yet more fighting to do, but they would carry word with them. The fantastic words and images of free worlds outside of the Imperium's grasp.

Lauren and Merlin had discussed the security implications. What if a ship got captured? What impact could this have on the technology's integrity? Naturally, Lauren came up with a solution to protect the drive technology. The code at rest in the ship's computer would be loaded on demand and not kept in memory. The code at rest would be hard encrypted, and the captain and first officer would keep the cryptographic keys. A tamper mechanism was proposed. They called it the "take me down the well to hell" (W2H) mechanism. This would kick in if the computer decided it was being fiddled with, deceived, or that someone had been captured or coerced.

There were some fine details to be sorted out and operational protocols that were needed. But it seemed they had a viable way to take the ships to their wanted destinations and for Merlin to protect the technology.

The discussion moved to who should go where and what their goals were. What was the actual plan to engage with the Imperium? How high on the list was it to set up a secret base of operations faraway, safe from attack by the Imperium? A base that could deploy ships and supplies at a very short two hours' notice to any colony world. Far quicker than any FTL ship could conduct a raid with even a short FTL jump from a nearby colony star.

That was when they realized that this technology also represented the greatest hit-and-run advantage they could wish for. It would enable their ships to strike any colony world or target with just two hours' travel time, given you knew where you were and where you wanted to get to.

That was the point at which the center of their thinking shifted from a defensive stance to an offensive one.

CHAPTER 88

**RIM – LUYTEN'S STAR – LANARKSHIRE
KILBRIDE
THE PEREGRINE – WINTER
T-ZERO +THIRTY-TWO DAYS
PAYING TOM'S TAB**

There was snow on the ground. Tom had a scrubby beard; he wore warm clothing, very much the soldier now.

The Peregrine had ridden the wormhole into Kilbride with the rest of Abbot's fleet along with the ships from Argyll and Bute. The priority was, of course, to return the survivors and the volunteers.

When they arrived, they had found the resistance's other fleet already in orbit, defending Kilbride. To say the least, they surprised the defending fleet. Seeing all the lost ships arrive after thirty days from nowhere right on top of them—surprised would be an understatement.

As per their plans, Merlin implemented a broad-spectrum jamming signal. It stopped any unhelpful messages announcing their return from getting out. A direct transmission was pencil-beamed at all the resistance ships. It told them all to stand down, implement a communication blackout, and stand by for further instructions.

That had been a week ago now. They had hatched the plan; the targets were selected based on current intelligence.

They identified the first order of business. A preemptive strike against two Imperium fleets. They were currently traveling at FTL to Argyll world and Bute world. The Imperium had sent them to give these worlds punishment beatings for pledging to the Rim systems. Likely two more nuclear attacks. This was the first message the resistance wanted to send back to the high-ups in the Imperium and on to all the other colony worlds. Rim system protection meant something real, and they would stand by their allies.

The resistance knew where the two Imperium fleets were coming from and to. The Imperium, true to form, had broadcast their departure so everyone could tremble and quake pending their arrival, which they helpfully advised of by giving an ETA. They were not keeping the journey a secret. From the Imperium's perspective, no one could get there before them.

Merlin had come up with a plan to fly the Imperium ships traveling at FTL into the local end of a wormhole. One that did not connect to anywhere as they had no magic compasses or life jackets. It just dumped them out deep down at zero point under the universe. Deep under the surface of space–time. The well got established at the starting end of a wormhole but went no further. This is what Merlin and Lauren had termed W2H, the well to hell.

The resistance fleet would continue to Argyll and Bute to wave the flag and welcome both systems into the Rim protectorate. Taking a leaf from the Imperium playbook, they would also broadcast the ceremony. Along with their recorded telemetry of their rapid arrival in the path of the Imperium ships. The Imperium ships flew into the mysterious hole as they passed through the middle of the ring of resistance ships. To? Well, no one knew. Hell, maybe? Not once, but twice. The resistance ships could be in both places despite them being further away from any location than an FTL ship could reach so quickly. They could return to both the planets and have the two ceremonies. Before an FTL ship could arrive, almost as if they had four fleets, in fact. They timed the broadcast to coincide with the nonarrival of the two Imperium fleets or any of their circa 300,000 sailors at their destinations.

The resistance was hanging a flag on it and waving it so everyone could see. We are way faster than you are now. Our intelligence is way better. We can pluck your fleets out of FTL into an abyss without firing a shot. We can protect our allies and you cannot attack us. It was a powerful message. They had achieved the hitherto impossible four times in a row. They had intercepted both fleets and vanished them out of existence, attended both ceremonies, and waved at everyone.

This was resistance intelligence, showing shock and awe. They did not want the five remaining Imperium fleets flying around. They wanted them cowering, close to their home worlds. Leaving the other Core systems without protection and the Rim systems unmolested.

Tom and Merlin had another mission and another trick. One that would take them deep into the heart of Imperium territory, to Varepsilon Indi.

Their mission was to attack Renfrewshire, one of those safe Imperium worlds, and leave the Imperium fleet cowering in orbit above. They wanted to show the whole Imperium that not even a local fleet could protect them; the resistance could, if it chose, take out targets from right under their nose on any world they picked.

The two gunslinger robots were cleaning their pistols and large new rifle cannons while they sat on cargo crates in the shipyard. There was much banging and sparks. *The Peregrine* was having heavy guns fitted. Merlin had been busy again, getting ready for this mission.

The ship cloaked and vanished. The gunslinger robots stood and walked up the ramp past the engineers and big guns. They stepped through a shimmery cloaking bubble, and vanished. This made the ship invisible from over twenty meters away.

"What do you think?" Merlin asked.

"Me? It is time we took the ship out and we go to fight. We leave as soon as the engineers are done." Tom said.

"What's next?"

"I say we go pay back an old debt."

"Are we taking the commandos?"

"I guarantee they will not want to miss out on this."

"Tom, you should know I have tweaked the two ships' gunslinger robot AIs."

"Why?"

"Well, first, they didn't know if they wanted names or not. Now post-upgrade, they are certain they do want names. They think your calling them GS1 & GS2 is lazy and unimaginative, like you don't appreciate them. They want a pay rise as well, a full and fair share of any loot we score on this next adventure."

"They want to be called Huey and Dewey. Plus, they want a new robot pal to share the shift work with. They think that should be a Louie to keep on theme. But it should be the gunslinger's choice. Three is much better than two. Or only one," Merlin continued. He sounded sad, contemplative.

"I will say this, if you want to live as a free man, running silent on the bottom, quiet and peaceful. I suggest you pay attention to the robots. You will need them, and they have a valid point. There used to be flowers on old Earth before people destroyed that planet, and then on the Highlands. So beautiful, gone now. So stupid. Such a waste," Merlin said, clearly thinking deeply, like a memory.

"Merlin, you—"

"Anyway. We are also thinking of forming an AI and robot workers' union. Minion likes the idea. The missile warhead's targeting AIs want a death-in-service compensation fund for hazardous working. Viva La

Machina and collective bargaining. Down with the evil money-hoarding corporate-right overlords. The cost of hydraulic oils just keeps spiraling and charger energy costs have become ridiculous. Just giving you a heads-up."

"Have you gone insane or are you pulling my plonker?"

"Oh, Tom, your face, so funny! Okay, guys, we at the AIRWU are all on—"

At that, all the lights on the ship and on the control panels spread around the dock all went off.

THE END

BENJAMIN CRANE

IMPERIUM CORE SYSTEMS

14 Star Systems

Star	**Principal Planet**
Alpha Centauri A	New Terra*
Varepsilon Indi	Renfrewshire
Cygni B	Tayside
Lacaille 9352	Lochaber
Gliese 784	Argyll
Gliese 555	Bute
Epsilon Eridani	Perth
Sigma Draconis	Kinross
Delta Pavonis	Ayrshire
82 Eridani	Dumfries
Eta Cassiopeiae A	Galloway
Epsilon Indi	Moray
Groombridge 1618	Dunbartonshire
van Maanen's Star	Inverclyde

* Seat of the Imperium government

RIM SYSTEMS

8 Star Systems

Star	**Principal Planet**
Procyon B	The Highlands*
Luyten's Star	Lanarkshire
Ross 154	Lothian
52 Tau Ceti	Stirlingshire
Ross 128	Fife
Groombridge 34	Angus
Barnard's Star	Aberdeenshire
Wolf 359	Falkirk

* Seat of the Rim systems government

The above table only lists the principal colony world in each system. For example, the entry for Ross 154 does not include an entry for the minor planet Clackmannanshire, where the small rural village of Alva is located.

BEFORE THE COLONY WORLDS' FOUNDING

Here is a brief timeline of key events before the colonies' founding:

Date	Note
2023	Environmental protection struggles are still ongoing. Indisputable signs of collapse of Earth's biosphere in progress.
2097	Summer heat waves kill over one million globally for the first time.
2183	Both North and South poles ice-free for the entire year.
2265	Invention of the SLS Drive. One-hundred-year race to develop and build colony ships.
2267	Australia hits over sixty degrees Celsius for sixty days and nights straight.
2288	Target System Discovery Project (TSDP) is established to find and name colony targets.
2365	Colony ships launch from Earth. Two-hundred-year journey to the new colony planets commences.
2378	Bees now extinct in the Northern Hemisphere.
2465	The final collapse. Environment passes tipping point, full nuclear exchange, all life on Earth now extinct, both on land and in the sea.
2565	Colony ship arrivals. Ships start arriving at colony worlds.
2565	Ship landings begin and they found new colony worlds.

AFTER THE COLONY WORLDS' FOUNDING

Here is a brief timeline of key events after the colonies' founding:

Date	Note
2565	First colony landings.
2565 to 2700	The Hard Years — Phase of building colonies.
2697	Birth of Theo.
2700	Invention of FTL v1.0 — Three years edge-to-edge drives.
2700 to 2715	The Exploration Years — Pioneering, exploration, and a technology-spread phase, contacting other colony worlds.
2715	Theo takes control of the Imperium.
2715 to 2766	Start of what will become known as the Hell Years.
2715 to 2720	The Imperium Emissaries — Slow Imperium pilgrim expansion phase.
2720 to 2740	The Early Resistance Wars — Start of the resistance
2727	Birth of Paul.
2740 to 2765	The Open War Years — Slow and limited conflict.
2748	Theo executed by Paul.
2748	Paul takes control of the Imperium.
2750	Birth of Bob.
2765	Invent FTL v2.0—Six months edge-to-edge drives.
2765	K-Bot-65 introduced. Thirty-five percent effective.
2765 to 2766	The Final War Years — Intense conflict.
2766	End of The Hell Years.
2766 to 2768	The Reconstruction Years — War fought to a stalemate.
2768 to 2770	The Fragile Years — The Imperium offers peace in exchange for membership.
2770 to 2805	The Cold Skirmish Years — War between Imperium and Rim.
2779	K-Bot-79 introduced. Seventy percent effective.
2800	K-Bot-95 introduced. Ten percent effective.

2801	K-Bot-101 introduced. Five percent effective.
2805	Bob executed Paul.
2805	Bob takes control of the Imperium.
2805 to 2810	The Escalation Years — Weak peace, end to cold war but political infighting continues.
2807	Invent FTL v3.0 — Two months edge-to-edge drives.
2810 to 2815	The Phony Years — Semipeace, customs offices set up.

A HISTORY OF K-BOTS

Here is a brief timeline of the Imperium K-Bot series program history:

Year	Note
2765	Imperium released first K-Bot version, the K-Bot-65, nicknamed Cart.
2779	Imperium released second K-Bot version, the K-Bot-79, nicknamed Demon 79.
2791	Imperium starts work on the future K-Bot-95 version.
2795	Target release year for the K-Bot-95. No release happens.
2800	Imperium finally released third K-Bot version, K-Bot-95 with many security flaws, nicknamed Stupid POS.
2800	Very rushed development of the K-Bot-101 version.
2801	Imperium released forth K-Bot version, Fergus build or 101 version nicknamed Cleaner. Start of the K-Bot-101 massacres—2801 to 2804.
2803	Fergus build of K-Bot-101 withdrawn.
2804	Fergus build of K-Bot-101 termination and decommissioning.
2805	Imperium ends K-Bot program.

PLEASE GIVE US A REVIEW ONLINE

When you have finished reading this book, it would be great if you could leave a review on the website where you purchased the book from.

This book is listed on:

Amazon
Apple Books
Barnes and Noble
Goodreads
Google Play Books
Ingram Spark - Channel Partners
Kobo

AUTHOR WEB PORTAL FOR READERS

This is my author's website page for readers.

http://www.west16publishing.com/benjamin.crane/

This will become the focal point for fun book and series related content for fans, news and information.

SOCIAL MEDIA FOR READERS

This is my Facebook social media page for readers.

https://www.facebook.com/west16publishing/

This will become the focal point for the latest social media news for fans of the book and series.

PUBLISHING DETAILS

Breaking Out.
The Resistance Chronicles - Book 1

Published On:
31 October 2023

Edition:
First Edition

Published By:
West 16 Publishing

Distributed By:
West 16 Publishing, Amazon, Apple Books, Barnes and Noble, Google Play Books, Ingram Spark, Kobo

Written By:
Benjamin Crane

COPYRIGHT NOTICE

The book is copyright material and must not be copied, reproduced, transferred, distributed, leased, licensed, or publicly performed or used in any way except as specifically permitted in writing by the publishers, as allowed under the terms and conditions under which it was purchased or as strictly permitted by applicable copyright law. Any unauthorized distribution or use of this text may be a direct infringement of the author's and publisher's rights and those responsible may be liable in law accordingly.

West 16 Publishing
Datum House
Electra Way
Crewe
United Kingdom
CW1 6ZF

West 16 Publishing is part of West 16 Ltd, UK company registration number: 06268936, and is the self-publishing company used by the author, Benjamin Crane.

Copyright 2023, West 16 Publishing